DON'T B

'I don't think it ... said. 'Please! It ... was afraid to say more.

'Is there something you can tell us, Miss O'Brien?' the detective asked. 'Something you know that we don't?'

Then she was seized by fear, a panic so acute it suppressed all other feelings – grief, loneliness, all others. This detective was part of the force aligned – no, not the force aligned, the *plot* – against her father. It was she this detective was investigating, not her father's murderers. The purpose of his questioning had nothing to do with finding the killers.

'No,' she hissed at the detective . . . She hung up the phone and fell forward on her bed. She pushed her head into the pillow and began to sob.

By the same author
THE MASDA PLAN

DON'T BE
NO HERO

Leonard Harris

Hamlyn Books

DON'T BE NO HERO
ISBN 0 600 34615 3

First published in Great Britain 1979
by Hamlyn Books
Hamlyn Paperbacks edition 1981
Originally published in USA by Crown Publishers
Copyright © 1978 by Leonard Harris

Hamlyn Paperbacks are published by
The Hamlyn Publishing Group Ltd,
Astronaut House,
Feltham,
Middlesex, England

(Paperback Division: Hamlyn Paperbacks,
Banda House, Cambridge Grove,
Hammersmith, London W6 0LE)

Made and printed in Great Britain by
Cox & Wyman Ltd, Reading

To S.P.H.

Chapter

1

FOR NEARLY AN HOUR, O'BRIEN'S BODY LAY WEDGED BE-
tween two parked cars, right arm dangling almost to the ground,
head on a rear bumper, ear down as if listening, left knee on the
bumper, left arm flung across the trunk, before the police car,
cruising slowly through the downtown streets, spotted it. The
length of time was not a surprise, nor was it a reflection on the
police, because no one lived on this street, and almost no one
had worked on it as late as O'Brien had on this balmy Thursday
evening in late June.

First the cops saw his shoes, the left, coming from the leg on
the bumper, about two feet off the ground, the right, on the
ground, at an incongruous angle to the left.

"Hey, hold it, John," said the cop in the passenger seat to his
buddy, who was driving. "I see a pair of feet. And they're not

moving. Someone's either fallin' down drunk. Or just fallin' down.''

As it turned out, O'Brien had had a couple of drinks; the cops would find that out later. But he hadn't fallen down drunk. The cop in the passenger seat saw that as soon as he leaned over the body. He saw the blood, and almost at once figured he was looking at a corpse. He checked for a pulse at the wrist, at the neck—his hand came away from the neck sticky—but that was to make sure. No one whose head looked like this one, whose neck was bent the way this one was, could be alive.

They followed procedure and did not move the body. They called for an ambulance; they called the station. The ambulance got there in six minutes, three minutes ahead of the team of homicide detectives.

"He must have bounced like a goddamn billiard ball," said one of the detectives, thinking that the row of parked cars had acted as the side wall, and the hit-and-run vehicle as the cue stick.

"Yeah, well, drivers really shoot through these streets. Fast. Too fast," said the cop who'd first spotted the body. "Especially at night, when they don't expect anybody to be around. And the street lights are lousy."

That was the easy diagnosis—hit-and-run, caused by some or all of the usual elements: excessive speed, bad lighting, victim possibly walking in street or stepping out from between two parked cars. Victim possibly intoxicated. A little later they were to change that to: victim with alcohol in bloodstream, just below the legal intoxication reading.

Hit-and-run, and an accident. That didn't change even when they found out the body was Henry J. O'Brien's. The detectives came across the ID cards in his shabby brown wallet. He was *the* Henry O'Brien, the special prosecutor. "Harebrained Hank."

The sobriquet had been pinned on O'Brien by a newspaper columnist and had been picked up by politicians, particularly those who had been the subjects of his investigations. An editorialist had written: "Henry O'Brien makes New York's Maurice Nadjari look like Tom Dewey and Oliver Wendell Holmes rolled into one." Like Nadjari, O'Brien had been appointed by a governor to investigate official corruption in his state's largest city. Like Nadjari, he was a zealot. Like Nadjari's, his methods were questioned and his indictments thrown out. Unlike Nadjari, he had no public relations sense. Shy, distrustful of the press, he grew paranoid about publicity, which isolated him from any public constituency.

More and more, O'Brien became an embarrassment and an object of ridicule, and at the same time, ironically, grew more and more untouchable. The governor, elected as a repository of the state's small-town New England virtues, had felt it a political necessity, rather than a cause, to appoint a prosecutor to check big-city corruption, and now couldn't fire O'Brien without looking stupid and without arousing the few who always side with a zealot. Moreover, O'Brien was noticeably Irish, and the governor was an old-line New England Wasp and didn't want to arouse any religious or ethnic antagonisms.

The corrupters and the corrupted, who had most to fear from a rackets buster, most wanted O'Brien to stay on. They felt comfortable with him; he was precious to them. They lined up to be investigated by him, calculating, and correctly, that a botched prosecution was protection, for a while at least, against an effective one. Besides, he was giving reform a bad name. When the term of his appointment expired he would surely not be replaced. Meanwhile, he was most useful as a scapegoat.

Even the detectives who identified him, faced with a battered corpse, found it hard to be respectful. "If this is murder, then definitely, the do-gooders did it," said the detective holding the wallet. That got a few smiles, cut short when the cops and the morgue attendants realized they were making fun of a dead man. But the macabre joke was as close as anyone came to suggesting it might be murder.

The reasoning was twofold: he hadn't threatened anybody, and it was generally believed he was a drinker, a belief strengthened when the blood samples showed alcohol.

Even press coverage was subdued. It was typical of O'Brien that he couldn't even exit with any impact. His body was found after midnight, timed badly to catch the late news on TV or the Friday morning papers.

There would be an investigation—that was reported perfunctorily. Much more attention was given to the alcohol. One radio station went so far as to say he was "drunk," which was unkind and erroneous. But he couldn't complain, and there was no one to complain for him—no supporters, friends, admirers. In the

3

minds of virtually everyone, he had no good name to protect. Besides, it was hard to libel a public figure, and impossible to libel a dead one.

Actually, he had one defender. She was his one survivor, a twenty-three-year-old daughter. This fifty-six-year-old widower had left no wife, no glory, virtually no estate—nothing but a mediocre law practice and a daughter, his only child, Felicia.

Felicia was a second-year law student who'd gotten good enough grades to make law review, but was even shyer and more reclusive than her father. The public ridicule which had made him seem paranoid turned her almost catatonic, quiet, expressionless, apparently in a trance. She worked for him as a clerk, and was his closest and most trusted—his *only* trusted—assistant. He had six lawyers and four investigators on his staff, but he and they exchanged only suspicion and hostility. To avoid charges of nepotism—they were made anyway—he paid her the lowest-grade clerk's salary.

But he confided only in her. In court, at hearings, press conferences, it was always Felicia he turned to, for long, fierce, whispered conversations. If he did first whisper to someone else, he'd almost always then turn to her, as if to check on what he'd just heard. And his eyes were different when he spoke to her—they were like hers, conspiratorial, embattled. One of the court reporters called it their "two-against-the-world" look.

With one of those two gone, it was simple for the detective to know whom to notify, for Felicia had been mentioned often enough in the stories about "Harebrained Hank." And it was simple for him to get her unlisted number. But contacting her was another matter. Starting at 12:30 on Friday morning, he dialed her number, again and again, and listened to it ring. But no one picked it up.

Chapter

"SON OF A BITCH. YOU ROTTEN SON OF A BITCH!"

Schroeder wondered if she meant that as a compliment. No, he decided. Nor was it much of a way to start a weekend, especially not this long weekend.

By ten o'clock on this Thursday morning in June he'd picked up a rented car and his mother and was standing in the elevator with his son and daughter, waiting for the doors to close on his ex-wife's parting blessing. They'd been separated for two years, divorced for one, and still she clawed at him. Had he been such a devastating loss to her? Or was he really just a son of a bitch?

The elevator doors closed with a thud and he was on his way down, with two kids, one huge suitcase, and a tightening, twisting knot in his stomach. He reached an arm around each child, trying to counterfeit a message of serenity and confidence.

Bobby, seven, was red-eyed; Patty, nine, held back the tears, barely.

He squeezed hard. "We're going to have a terrific time. Grandma can't wait to see you."

Were they? Couldn't she? We'll see. He smiled to himself, imagining his mother's nervous determination to make a hit with the children. Even before the separation she hadn't seen much of them, and afterward, a lot less.

Maybe this weekend would build a few bridges. Planning it, he'd hoped so; beginning it, he worried. Five hours in the car, three on a ferry, three and a half days in a Nantucket house with the kids sullen and grandma stuck once she got beyond her three openers: I'm glad to see you. How are you? How is school?

He hoped to hell it wouldn't rain.

Once he'd actually looked forward to this long weekend. Now he was drastically reducing its possibilities. He'd settle, he decided, for a couple of long walks on the moors, a couple of evenings soothed by the Beaujolais he'd stashed in the trunk, a couple of drinks with the Cobbs—if they were on the island this early in the season.

Again, he squeezed the children's shoulders, not sure if he wanted to transmit comfort or receive it. "Give grandma a big hug and a kiss, will you, kids? It means a lot to her. All right?"

In reply Bobby grew more sullen, Patty tearier. Please, let's get through it, he begged silently.

The elevator opened; with his arms still around them, Schroeder walked through the gloomy marble lobby out into the gusty June brightness. He looked at his watch: five hours and ten minutes to make the ferry. No problem, beyond how to use up the five hours.

"Don't forget, kids," he reminded them softly. He opened the car's rear door, and as the two children climbed in, his mother turned around in the front passenger seat, putting an arm on the back of the seat. He was startled. Such a frail arm, soft skin and bone, the arm of an old woman. He stood at the door, anxious to see and hear their first exchange. Then dismayed, when to get through it, his mother used up two of her three conversational openers.

"Oh, I'm so glad to see you!" she said. "How are you, Patty? How are *you*, Bobby?"

"Hi, grandma," said the girl. "Hi, grandma," said the boy,

not close enough to be in unison, too close to be an echo.

Then, absolutely together: "Fine." Routinely, they leaned forward to be pecked.

Well, he thought, she could have used up, how's school? too, in that first burst.

He closed the door on the children, walked around to the trunk, opened it, put in their suitcase, taking care not to harm the wine, slammed the lid shut, and climbed into the car.

They'd made it up to Ninety-sixth Street and the East River Drive—five minutes of the five hours—when the fight started over who'd read the new comic book first.

"Whose is it?" he asked.

"Mine, daddy," the girl said.

"But she told me I could read it first! She's in the middle of something else!" Bobby shouted it.

"Let her read her book, Bob," he said. "Then you. Meanwhile, you read something else. And don't shout."

"Mommy shouted at you."

"That doesn't make it right." He felt sanctimonious as he said it.

"Mommy called you a son of a bitch."

"She shouldn't have, Bobby, and I don't want to hear you say it. Understand?" He felt worse, evasive. He got no answer.

He made a point of not looking over at his mother, who he knew was embarrassed by this, but didn't know what to say. After a twenty-seconds' silence she spoke.

"How's school, you two?"

"Fine, grandma," said Patty.

"OK, grandma," said the boy.

On the front seat next to him he saw the small, veined hand of his mother. She was sixty-eight years old. An old woman. Oh, stop it, he told himself. Don't get maudlin, because it's not your mother you're feeling sorry for. Stop it. Next to her hand, a folded road map. Which gave him an idea.

"All right, here's a quiz. Which states do we go through to get to Nantucket? We'll let Bobby go first."

The boy hesitated a moment, then said, "Connecticut."

"Massachusetts," his daughter added quickly, and waited.

Bobby seemed puzzled. "The one we started in," Schroeder offered.

"New York," he popped back.

"No fair," said the girl. "You helped him."

"Well, there's one more. If you need help, I'll help you, too, honey."

Silence. She didn't know it, yet didn't want to ask.

"It's between Connecticut and Massachusetts."

He looked at her in the rearview mirror, her face was a study in concentration.

He tried again. "You should get it, with the help of Providence."

This time she looked puzzled. Bobby's face was relaxed. He'd done his job and was content to let her sweat out the tough one.

"I don't get it, daddy," she said.

"It's a pun, sweetheart, because Providence is the name of the biggest city in the state."

"Rhode Island," she yelled.

"Right, good. Two each. Terrific!" And I'm pretty terrific, too, he thought, master of the minor pun, thrilling to old and young, mostly young. Well, he told himself, it's what they pay me for at *Scope*.

The quiz over, the children resumed their battle over *Batman*, grandma continued her silence, and Schroeder turned down the volume in his head, and let the cries of war go on. Let the problem solve itself. He tried that on all his problems.

It worked, sort of. After all, he was functional if not happy, solvent if not successful, alive if not well. His career up to now amounted to eleven years at *Scope*, the magazine that proclaimed it covered "All the News Weekly," which Schroeder suggested should be changed to, "Some of the News, Weakly." Eleven years, he'd been there—at least it would be eleven in the late fall, when he turned forty-one. He was in a rut, and the travelin' was easy. If not easy, at least habitual.

A road sign said Larchmont. Next to him his mother had put her head back and fallen asleep.

In the back the war had ended, the children reading *Batman* together, Patty holding it, Bobby occasionally telling her not to turn the pages so fast.

His kids. He kept staring at them in the rearview mirror, and had to remind himself to watch the road. He loved those two kids so, and yet he could never get close enough to them for long enough. And they were growing up. Patty was nine. *Scope* minus two. Children, he and his wife Marty had decided, couldn't come until he was making a decent living. And that came with *Scope*. *Scope*, and one year to make sure the job and he could get along—which they could, back then. Then a month or two to conceive. Then Patty, born at nine o'clock on a Monday morning, the pinkest baby in the nursery. And the prettiest, of course.

And all made possible by *Scope*, and a starting salary of sixteen thousand a year. Marty, who'd yelled "rotten son of a bitch" at him a few minutes ago, had shouted "my hero" back then—she'd actually shout things like that. *Scope!* At sixteen thousand dollars a year! To a newspaperman making eighty-five hundred it seemed enough for quintuplets.

After three years, they'd made Bobby, he'd made associate editor at twenty-two thousand five-hundred dollars, writing the Faces and Places section. His salary was now up to thirty-four thousand dollars a year, barely enough to get by, and representing advancement at a pace he'd hesitate to call more than a leisurely walk. Eight years at Faces and Places! Perhaps five hundred words a week, twenty-five thousand a year, adding up to an epic novel. Only he'd never written more than seventy-five on one subject at one time. When he was asked to describe the cute, cutting cameos—his phrase—that were his life's work, Schroeder responded with the story about the mother and children at a cheap summer resort, who sent a postcard home to daddy: "The food is poison. And such small portions!"

Sam Schroeder, king of the mini-zingers. Calling John Warner Taylor-made. Quipping about Nixon's protean secretary of state, "I wonder who's Kissinger now." He'd invented that one; at least he thought he had.

Did he hate himself? Sometimes. On the one hand he was sensitive, clever. A fair man, repelled by cruelty. Wanting to help people. Didn't often, but wanted to. He paid his bills and tried to maintain a fairly healthy mind in a healthy body.

On the other hand, he was unambitious, uncommitted, and, most of all, a man of questionable bravery. Which was not to say he had conclusive proof of his cowardice. No, nothing that clear, that certain. Just suspicions. He'd never been tested, he told himself. Then he'd answer, sure, because you keep avoiding the tests. Well, where in hell am I going to find tests? (These debates would go on, these "I" and "you" parries and thrusts, complaints and denials and countercomplaints.) Where? Well, you spent eleven years at *Scope*, writing one-liners, all right, *two*-liners. Hating it most of the time, *all* the time lately. What do you call that, if not a test? And you've flunked it. I've only flunked it, so far. All right, *so far* you've flunked it. What are you looking for, a chance to parachute behind enemy lines?

Physically, Sam Schroeder was well cast to be a hero. He was six-feet-one, weighed 177, a little flabby around the midsection, but generally in good shape. He had all his hair, which, once blonde enough to get him the nickname "Whitey," was now a faded, sandy brown, lightened by gray at the sides. His eyes were blue, not bright blue like his kids', but a little dulled by age—by the dullness of life. The only time he was displeased with the regularity of his features was when he was told he looked like the typical FBI man. He'd pretend to laugh at it, but he actually let his hair grow a little longer to avoid it.

Maybe if he looked the part less, he'd not be so worried about his heroism quotient, or cowardice quotient. He thought about it a lot. So much, in fact, that he'd begun thinking of them as HQ and CQ, and applying them to hypothetical situations he encountered or invented all the time, lying in bed at night, jogging in the park, swimming at the Y, reading crime and violence stories. Seeing a physical confrontation—that most of all. That he could never resist, on the street, on a bus, in the park. He always stopped, always watched, sized up the adversaries, saw who was bluffing and who wasn't, who stood and who backed off. Invariably he identified with the one who backed off. Invariably, he ended up sweating, sometimes walking away as filled with tension and adrenaline as if he'd been in it himself.

He spent many a lap of the pool, mile of the track, hour of the night, inventing tests, telling himself that by playing them through in his mind, he was preparing his responses for the real ones, should they occur. Knowing that when the real thing happened, all the preparation in the world wouldn't help, that his juices would take over and—what? Betray him? Probably.

He passed a sign that said Bridgeport. They'd been on the road more than an hour. The kids were silent, Patty, having proved the point, now no longer contesting the comic book, but deep in a *Nancy Drew* mystery.

"Is everything all right at the magazine, Sam?" His mother wanted to talk, and, as usual, began with an anxiety question. He wondered why, decided that his so-called career inspired anxiety, even in himself, so why the hell not in his mother?

"Yeah, everything's just fine."

"What's your next step there?"

"Oh, senior editor, mom, then editor-in-chief, publisher. Then president. Of the United States, that is. And that's just *this* week."

"Don't be funny, Sam. Can't I be interested in your future without being subjected to that kind of sarcasm?"

"Sorry, mom. Can't help being funny, bright, acerbic, cutting. They pay me for it. Weekly. Very weakly. Did you see the current issue? Cher signing to do a series for MGM? And I called it the lion's Cher?"

He glanced over at his mother. Her face was a blank. He couldn't tell if she resented his bright, acerbic, cutting wit.

She deserved better. And he wanted to start the weekend right, giving her better. "It's a good job, mother. I may not want to do it the rest of my life, but it's secure and it pays pretty well, and it's not hard, and I'm good at it, and I've got mouths to feed. Four, including my own." He ended it with a smile, and as he looked quickly over at her, her face softened.

"And what do you want to do for the rest of your life, Sam?"

"God knows, mom. I don't." God knows, that's the truth, he said to himself. If there was one subject that took up as much of his ruminating and daydreaming as his HQ or lack of it, it was his future or lack of it. Should he look for another steady, workaday job, or try to free-lance? Should he move into legitimate journalism? Or legitimate fiction? Instead of the bastard art he was now practicing.

"Why don't you try for something else at *Scope?*" his mother asked.

"Uh huh." He tried to make it an all-purpose grunt, suitable for meaning: I already have, or: It's a good idea, or: I'll think about it. Actually, he had tried, several times, most recently just two weeks ago, when he and the managing editor had been discussing a replacement during Schroeder's three-week August vacation.

Sitting in Ben Daniels' office, he'd said: "Ben, we've spoken before about my taking on another assignment at the magazine . . ." And he waited.

The editor said only, "Oh?" which kind of chilled Schroeder's blood, but then his blood chilled easily. He'd hoped for another kind of response, something more like: What did you have in mind? Or: Let's see what the possibilities are. Something that would open a door. That's what he'd hoped for, without expecting it. Chilled blood and all, he moved ahead, cautiously.

"I mean, I like to think I've kept Faces and Places pretty fresh for eight years . . ." Again, he paused, this time waiting for a compliment.

"You have, Sam. Surprisingly fresh." Ben was a kind, gentle, generous man. Schroeder managed to find a worry even in the praise. Why surprisingly? Was Ben expecting staleness just around the corner? Were Schroeder's days on the section about up?

He'd wanted to duck for cover. But he mustn't, he told himself. He must go on.

"But there are other spots I'd like a crack at—maybe just as a sideline." The last was hedging.

"Such as what?" Ben was not making it easy.

"Well, other back-of-the-book stuff. Reviews, of books, movies, theatre. Show biz stories. I could do that. The Media Report. We might even consider a move up to the front, to politics. Maybe I could give it a fresh, witty approach."

"You know as well as I we've got new kids moved in to all those spots, Sam. I hadn't realized you were unhappy where you are."

For a kind man, Schroeder told himself, Ben had managed to pack a lot of menace into those two sentences. The age: All those new kids were in their late twenties, the oldest perhaps thirty. Sam was forty going on forty-one, a few months older than Ben. The discontent: It stood to reason that someone unhappy where he was had to be watched.

Schroeder fought the impulse to run and hide. "I'm not unhappy, Ben. I just think I might contribute more to this magazine than I am doing now. You know my writing is right for *Scope*, and you know no new kid is going to handle an entire section all by himself, or herself. I could have a try at something else, while I keep on doing Faces and Places. I realize how irreplaceable I am there." The ending was both a try at jocularity and another casting for a compliment.

Ben smiled, and Schroeder didn't even like the smile. "Let's talk about it after vacations. Meanwhile, we can see how the new people are doing and how well Faces and Places goes while you're away."

Oh, Christ, more to be afraid of, Schroeder thought, a pang of worry shooting through him, tempting him to cave in, to say, forget it, I'm happy, *don't* see how my substitute does. Suddenly, achingly, he found himself Willy Loman in *Death of a Salesman*, beginning by asking for a better job and ending up pleading to keep the one he has—and losing it.

But goddammit, he told himself, it was too late for retreat. And he hated himself for wanting to. He'd planted the seed of an idea for a replacement, and he couldn't dig it up even if he wanted to. And he didn't want to. And he didn't want to sound as scared as he felt.

"Yeah, Ben, I'd appreciate it, if you *would* keep it in mind while I'm gone. And I'll be thinking of what assignments I might have a go on—on the side, while I keep on Facing and Placing."

He was neither displeased with himself nor too proud as he left Ben's office. On his HQ scale, he'd give himself a C plus, maybe a B minus. On the one hand he could have avoided the subject. On the other, he could have said something like: I've had it with Faces and Places, so move me if you don't want to lose me; and you know I'm too good to lose. An ultimatum, polite, but an ultimatum.

He hadn't done that. Nor had he caved in, though he'd come close twice. Once when Ben brought up the age thing. Goddammit, he asked himself, am I an old man at forty? I can run six miles in forty-two minutes. Am I an old man? Yes, was the answer, at *Scope*, at the associate editor level, he was an old man.

The second crisis had come when Ben announced that his vacation replacement would be the twenty-six-year-old woman who worked as Sam's assistant. Her title was researcher-writer, and she made only fifteen or sixteen thousand dollars a year—about what he'd made when he started. She was smart, witty, a phrase maker, everything you needed for Faces and Places. And think of the money they'd save. And Schroeder had just handed Ben a perfect way to move him out.

Oh shit, that's paranoid, he'd reminded himself on his way back to his own desk, trying to swallow the taste of Willy Loman. I'm forty. Willy Loman was—how old?—fifty-five? Sixty? In this business, he'd told himself, forty is sixty.

Lost in his anxiety, he had to remind himself to focus on the

Connecticut Turnpike. He'd been in a trance, helped by the silence of his passengers. His kids had curled up and gone to sleep. His mother, cut off from his conversation by the anxious reminiscence she'd triggered, was looking out the window. She'd like him to be more successful. And more respectable. And more respectful. And pay more attention. And not be divorced. And live in a big substantial house, not a cramped, semi-shabby, two-bedroom apartment on the West Side.

They sped by a sign saying Mystic. He looked at his watch. He was OK for a 3:15 ferry. He'd make it.

Would he make it? *Scope* didn't fire people, but it could make them want to quit. If he came back from vacation and the girl had the job, and they left him floating around with no special department, just back-of-the-book odds and ends, he'd have to quit. Jesus, he scolded himself, you've got a way of snatching defeat from the jaws of victory. Getting out of Faces and Places is what you've been wanting; now you're interpreting it as defeat. Quitting is something you might need; it might be the best thing for you.

Yeah, quitting to do what? I'm forty, he reminded himself. No, *only* forty. And clever and talented, and I can run six miles in forty-two minutes. Peggy, the researcher, is only twenty-six and clever and talented, and works cheaper. Yeah, but can she run six miles in forty-two minutes? Well, she's got terrific legs, maybe she can. Besides they're not paying off on the six-mile run this year. Not at *Scope*.

When he was married he always blamed his cautiousness on Marty, for whom the world was filled with wicked witches and yawning chasms. Now that he no longer had her to blame, why was he still scared?

A shout from the rear shook him out of his reverie. "Daddy, Bobby is just *pretending* to read the new *Batman* so I can't have it. He's just being *mean!*"

"I'll tell you what," he said, trying to sound authoritative. "Bobby, that's Patty's book. You let her finish it now and you each get a new one on Nantucket. How's that?"

A shameless bribe, and he hoped it would work.

"OK, Daddy. Here, Patricia, take it."

The girl, a little angry at her brother's being rewarded for what she considered his intransigence, snatched the book.

"She grabbed it out of my hand, daddy!"

"I did not," the girl said, and punctuated the answer with a jab of her elbow to the boy's shoulder.

Bobby punched back and snarled, "Cut it out, Pat!"

"He hit me, daddy!" she shouted. "I didn't hit *him!*"

"Stop it, the two of you." This time he said it with genuine force and anger. "One more push, or punch, or anything, and I take that comic away, and you get none on Nantucket. Understand?"

Silence.

"Understand?"

"Yes, daddy." They said it almost together.

"We're coming to Providençe, ladies and gentleman," he announced a few moments later. "That means we're about seventy-five miles from the ferry."

"How long will it take?" the girl asked.

"An hour and a half," he said. "Maybe a little longer. We'll make it with about a half hour to spare."

"Where are we staying?" she asked. She was getting at something.

"In a lovely house on North Liberty Street, which is just a couple of blocks from the center of town, the movie, the bookstore, everything. It's been rented for the season by a friend of mine, who is letting us use it for the weekend." He'd done it carefully, not identifying the friend; even structuring the sentence to avoid a pronoun that would give away gender. Now he waited for them to sniff it out.

Patty went right to it. "I suppose the friend is Jane Brewster."

In the two years of his separation, Schroeder had gone out with many women, but only three with some frequency. Jane, the third of them, he'd been seeing for about six months, plenty of time for her to be posted on the enemies list.

"Yes, Pat, the friend is Jane Brewster. And it was awfully nice of her to lend it, because to be perfectly honest, it's expensive, and I don't know I could afford it."

Now, he knew, the hairs on the backs of their little necks were standing on end. Bobby asked: "Will she be there?"

"Why? What would be wrong with that?"

"Oh no, daddy, I don't want to stay there with *her.*" He was amazed at the steel in his daughter's voice.

"How many times have you met her, Patty? Once? Was she so bad?"

"I don't like her."

"I don't like her, either," Bobby offered, suddenly a solid front with the sister he'd been battling a few minutes earlier.

"No, kids, she is not going to be there. But someday you'll get to know her, and you'll like her, and you'll be sorry you were so silly about the whole thing."

Well, ha ha, he'd said *that* before, about the other two women, and the kids hadn't gotten to know *them,* and their animosity had outlasted his friendship, and each time he'd broken off with the women, Schroeder had thought, well, they've won another.

"We'll be the judge of that." Patty had inherited her father's flair for the quip, for better or worse. The better was, he was proud of her quickness. The worse was, she could end up writing two-liners for a news magazine.

"Fair enough," he said, smiling into the rearview mirror. "I'll let you be the judge of that. Only keep an open mind. Don't let it be poisoned by . . ." he almost said, your mother, . . . "prejudice."

"Anyway," he went on, "Mrs. Brewster will *not* be there. We'll have the house all to ourselves for the entire weekend."

Please, make it a *sunny* weekend, he said in a silent invocation. A peaceful weekend. With happy thoughts. Close to his kids. More than anything else, he missed the closeness, the long leisurely times with them. Kissing them good-night. Seeing them first thing in the morning. Going into their rooms at night, and watching them sleep. Bending over to smell their separate, distinctive smells. Where that had been, he felt a huge cavity, and hoped he could fill a bit of it this weekend.

As he neared the Cape he began watching the road signs more carefully, and again they lapsed into a stretch of silence. He realized he and his mother had spoken little on the whole trip, not at all for a couple of hours. He had three and a half days to make up for that. But were three and a half days enough for a major overhaul, which he needed, vis à vis his mother, his kids, his job, himself?

He kept watching the road.

And then they were at Woods Hole, on the pier. Slowly, stiffly, he got out of the car and looked around. No ferry was at the dock or in sight. The day was warm for June, the wind blowing from the southwest. For the moment the sun was out, although moving clouds presaged an overcast by the time the ferry ride was ended. Gulls stood on the pilings; at a corner of the pier, four or five boys threw bread on the water and watched the gulls swoop down after the pieces.

Patty and Bobby got out of the car and walked over to watch.

"Be careful. Don't go near the edge!" his mother shouted after them.

Always on the lookout for a culprit, he said to himself, *that's* why I'm always tiptoeing around. Tell a kid often enough to be careful, and he'll be careful for life. And no one, sure as hell, has ever accused me of recklessness. God, how I wish someone had. How I wish I deserved it—being called a mad, impetuous fool, back when I was twenty, or thirty. When I was single and supposed to be out taking chances.

Well, it's too late for that, he reminded himself. You'll never be under forty again. So the only time left for the headlong dash is now, and hereafter.

With some of the volume and vehemence aimed at himself, he lifted his voice. "Go on, you two! Don't worry about it! Have a good time!" He tried to tone down before he turned to his mother, but managed only halfway. "It's bad to keep telling them to be careful, mom. It makes them afraid to move."

"Sam, I don't *keep* telling them to do anything. I don't talk to them that often. I just don't want to see them getting hurt."

Touché. She was hurt. And showed it. And is right. Don't lay it off on her. It's you, your problem. He smiled at her. "C'mon, get out of the car. Have a peanut butter and jelly sandwich— they're in that bag on the seat. Let's go near the edge. Live dangerously." He smiled again.

Impulsively, he reached out and seized and squeezed her hand, to help her out of the car, but more as a clutch of affection. Gratefully, she smiled back, handed him the bag with the sandwiches as she got out of the car. "Here," she said. "Take them, I don't want one now. Give them to the children. Have one yourself. I don't believe you New York playboys eat properly anyway."

He grinned and leaned over and kissed her on top of the head. "Us New York playboys have to watch our weight. You give them to the children, and tell them to throw some of the bread to the gulls. *Don't* tell them to be careful." She's never asked for much, he thought. And by God, I've never offered much.

She looked up at him earnestly. "The children should eat."

"We'll buy some crap on the ferry."

The hooting of a ship's horn made him look up; the ferry was approaching, it had gotten close while he was talking, it was about to pull into the slip. He and his mother walked toward it; he saw his son and daughter watching, timorously, while off to the side bolder youngsters climbed down onto the pilings.

Well, my kids are city kids, he told himself. *My* kids. He said it lovingly, possessively. Also he said it to mean, if they're timid, I know where they get it.

He kept looking at them. Such handsome children, so bright, so sensitive. Oh, come on, he told himself, don't be one of those parents. But they are. Objectively. They are. Besides, what's wrong with being one of those parents?

He stared. Patty had lustrous dirty-blonde hair; Bobby's was darker, finer, silky, so shiny you felt you could see your face in it. Both of them had light blue eyes, like his, like his mother's, only not faded.

Reluctantly, he said: "OK, they're going to start loading cars onto the ferry. We'd better go back." Then trying to build on the moment, added: "There are lots of docks and boats on the island; we can spend as much time around them as you want."

Patty looked blank; Bobby shrugged. He got the point. Don't get too enthusiastic about anything daddy says, or you're not being loyal to your mommy. Two years of conditioning, full time, all their waking hours; and he had them a day at a time, or, rarely, a week at a time, to fight it off. No, he couldn't do it. Whenever he saw that solid front of theirs, he wanted to take a swing at his ex-wife. Metaphorically, of course. And sometimes he let that hostility show through to them. He didn't want to, but he did.

"OK, come on, we'd better get in the car." This time he heard the anger in his voice, and in the car, waiting to drive aboard, he tried to soften it.

"All right, peanut butter and jelly sandwiches for sale, cheap. And special reductions today on Granny Smith apples, Anjou pears and . . . let's see . . . one banana. And dry roasted peanuts, the kind you don't have to shell. What do I hear?"

"Can I get a hot dog on the boat, daddy?" Bobby asked. "Me, too, daddy?" Patty followed.

Schroeder smiled, looked at his mother. "Yes, by God. Hot dogs for all hands. Even grandma!" He was on the defensive, and giving favors away, and knew it, and didn't care.

They rolled onto the ferry and when the car was in place went out on deck. For a while Schroeder stood there and let the wind cleanse him, aerate him as he watched gulls gliding easily in the ferry's slipstream. He stared up at the sky, pivoting to see as much as he could; a wide-angle 180-degree sky was something you didn't get to see in the city. Ahead of them clouds were piling up, but he ignored them, preferred to look toward the stern, where the shoreline of the mainland was receding and the sky was still blue.

A half hour later, he took a piece of leftover bun from the hot dog splurge and held it aloft with two fingers. And waited. The big gulls began to swoop and float closer; one by one making a pass at the bread. The third one plucked it from his fingers. Patty and Bobby stared, enthralled, not holding back this time. They wanted to try yet were afraid, he could see it.

"Go ahead," he urged. "Take some of the bread from the peanut butter sandwiches."

They ran and got the sandwiches, snatched pieces of bread, each holding one in the air. But when a gull got close they either flinched or tossed the piece into the air.

Schroeder reached down to the deck for a stray piece, held it between his index finger and his third finger, lifted his hand and held it steady. A diving gull snatched the bread.

"This way, you can't possibly get a finger hurt," he said. And, with more bread, held his hand up till a gull came and snatched it away clean.

Both children tried it again. Bobby got it first, then Patty. Soon several other children were following their example and they took on the proud look of pioneers.

Well, that's a tiny building block, one small step for fatherhood. Little blocks, small steps like that one, might grow into an OK weekend. They were suddenly so happy, so clearly pleased with themselves as they held the bread up, then scurried around looking for more pieces. Accomplishment is an exhilarating feeling, he thought; at seven, nine, or forty.

Clouds were now making a serious attack on the sun, and he glanced at his mother, who seemed uncomfortable.

"OK, mom, let's hit the great indoors," he said, and led her into one of the big lounges, where they sat down. She fished a paperback from her purse. He stared out through dirty, scratched plastic at the sky, then picked up a Boston paper lying on a banquette nearby.

Schroeder had worked for two newspapers, but he could not bring himself to the state of adoration for journalism his years of travail should have inspired. Every time he looked through a newspaper, he realized how much shit it was filled with, even the bigger ones like this one. Sometimes it bucked him up to know that journalists all over the country were wallowing in the same trivia he had to wipe from his shoes every work day. Maybe worse. Smaller and smellier, and not even amusing.

Then he'd stop himself. Most of those, he'd remind himself, were twenty-four, and school lunch menus, 4-H club meetings, obits, church suppers, would be behind them by the time they were forty. At forty, you're in it hip deep, he told himself. And even if it is amusing, and sprinkled with big names, it's still shit.

He scanned the first page of the Boston paper. A Middle East story. An African story. A state budget story. A local graft story: City Corruption Probe Reported at Standstill. Perversely, because it was the page-one story that interested him least, he looked through that one first. The investigator was crying feet-dragging, cover-up, and whitewash. The investigatees were crying politics, fishing expedition, and constitutional rights.

The real winners were the clichés, so many, so rampant, they were funny. Probe, and standstill, and cover-up. They spread all over the headlines and the body of the story itself, like a blight, wiping out language and thinking. He especially got a kick out of the headlines, which were written by desk men in the shorthand that was the cover-up for all ailments—lack of space, lack of energy, lack of brains and wit.

Once, at a suburban paper, he'd been through that. I was a newspaperman myself once, he said, almost aloud. He'd been on the copy desk, and written heads. Those one-column heads were a bitch, no space for anything. And he'd found the magic word as others had before him, and, he was sure, others after. The word was Fête. It was useful for a coronation or a Little League parade. Not to mention anniversaries, birthdays, religious ceremonies, holidays, Kiwanis luncheons, and the Fourth of July. For a one-column head that dandy *little* word, fête, fit all. And in the face of a slot man who actually thought you were supposed to be *awake* to write headlines, Schroeder would try to slip as many through each day as he could. And the slot man would catch one in the first edition, and ask the desk, "How did that one get through?" and Schroeder would call it a "fête accompli." Jolly days on the copy desk.

He slammed the paper down with a slap that made his mother look up. "I get *tired* of reading newspapers and magazines," he told her. "There are too many *of* them and too little *in* them. I'm going out on deck and let that sea breeze air out my brain. Why don't you come out, too?" Schroeder looked at his watch; he'd spent more time with the newspaper and accompanying reveries than he'd thought. "We should be sighting Nantucket before too long."

"It's too windy." His mother said it, and paused. "Why should your brain need airing out?"

Oh, God, not now. "No more than anyone else's." He tried to be jocular. "Maybe even yours does. Come on."

She didn't want to be jocular. "I'll just have to make do with the same stale old air I've been getting by on all along. It's too chilly out there for me."

Oh, Christ, no, her feelings weren't hurt! They couldn't be! Well, he was not going to deal with that now. He was going to stay light. "All right, I'll go alone. But be ready for some breezy conversation when I come back!" And he threw a big smile and headed aft, where the kids were still feeding gulls.

"Let's go up front," he said to them, "so we can start looking for Nantucket."

"It's not called front, daddy," said Bobby, reprimandingly. "It's called bow."

"Don't mind if I do," said Schroeder and bent over in a deep bow.

"Oh, daddy, don't be so silly," said Patty, looking amused in spite of herself.

"I don't get it," Bobby said simply.

"Bow, Bobby booby," said the girl derisively. "Bow, front. Bow, bend over. Booby!"

The boy pushed her hard. "Don't call me booby, dunce."

As Patty charged back at her brother, Schroeder stepped between them.

"We're not going to have three and a half days of this!"

"He pushed me, daddy, and you won't let me touch him," Patty said angrily. "How come you always favor him?"

"I don't favor him," Schroeder retorted, and then swivelled

toward the boy. "And you, don't hit her or push her. No violence. Get it?"

"She always bugs me!" the boy yelled. "She calls me booby 'cause she knows I hate it. I'm really gonna punch her."

"You do, and I'll . . ."

"Stop!" he shouted. "Nobody is going to punch anybody." Schroeder reached into his pocket, pulled out a couple of dollar bills and handed them to the boy. "You run and ask grandma if she wants ice cream and then go buy some for us all. Meet us at the bow."

Bobby paused, looked at his father and went into a deep bow. Schroeder bowed back, grinning at his son, and while bent over, kissed the top of his head.

"Now get moving."

The boy ran off and Schroeder put his arm around his daughter's shoulders. "You're the big sister. Be kind. And grown up. You know you're my firstborn, and I love you. And we're going to have a terrific weekend."

They met forward, and, buffeted by wind, ate their ice cream and watched for the island. "You'll see the highest piece of land first. Or the tallest spires," Schroeder said, "just as out at sea, you'd spot the top of a ship's mast before you could see its hull. Why is that, do you suppose?"

Patty answered patiently, "Because of the curvature of the earth, daddy."

"Wow, you kids are smart!"

"We learn a lot at school," said the boy. "Only you don't know about it, 'cause you're not around."

Schroeder was about to come back with his standard reply—come live with me anytime you want—when Patty announced: "There it is!"

And there it was, the low land mass of Nantucket, a dull gray on this cloudy afternoon. For a few moments they just stared. Then the children lost interest, went back into the lounge to recontest *Batman*. Well, he'd wait and let grandma handle that one.

He felt elated as the land grew close. Journeys always excited Schroeder, often more in the anticipation than the act. Departure promised newness, however false the promise might be; always he wanted changes he hadn't wrought, excitement he hadn't earned. Years ago, he'd always liked blind dates, however often he got "stuck." Unearned excitement. Invariably, he didn't get it.

Still, the shiver came over him as they got closer, close enough so that he could make out the Brant Point light clearly. Then the mouth of the harbor. Beyond that, soon, he'd be able to see the dock. And the people waving.

Without seeing them, he knew what they looked like. On Thursday, mostly women and children, mostly blondish, a lot of sun-streaked hair, freckles, early season tans, for these were not your frantic two-weekers, with kids just out of public schools. These all had houses on Nantucket—none of which would sell for less than a hundred thousand dollars. These all had kids in private and prep schools, which had been out for two weeks. These wore Lacoste shirts, tennis shorts, or cut-off jeans, maybe the women had wraparound skirts. All shod in topsiders, no socks, of course, with the space between shoe top and short- or skirt-bottom occupied by tanned shapely legs, particularly noted for their curve of calf. The calf was an absolute must for meeting the Nantucket ferry. He wondered if the Nantucket cops had an unwritten rule about putting the dock off limits to stringy calves at ferry times. So as not to spoil the ambiance.

No one would be waving for him, but he didn't mind, he rather preferred the serendipity of it. Friends have got to be earned, strangers came around by luck. Like blind dates. About thirty, tall, beautiful in a rangy way, slim ankles, terrific calves, of course; and big tits wouldn't be half bad, although he never rated them top priority.

His friend Jane Brewster met those requirements pretty well, and, had he asked, would have been waiting, waving on the dock. But he hadn't asked. Not that he wouldn't have liked her there, but he was damned if he was going to fight with his kids over her presence. One more battle he'd stepped away from.

And if the Cobbs were on the island, and if he had phoned, they'd have been waving from the dock. And their calves were exemplary. Four of the best you'd ever see.

Stoney—Walter Stonington Cobb—and Schroeder had met through a mutual friend when both had come to New York to go to Columbia, Stoney to the law school, Schroeder to get his M.A. in journalism, and they'd shared an apartment for a year, and stayed close friends, even though, first, Schroeder had left New York for a newspaper job, and then Stoney had left it, for good and for Boston, to practice law. Since then, they'd never lost contact, vacationing together in the summers, skiing together, visiting each other on weekends, fixing each other up with dates in New York or Boston.

Stoney hadn't married until five years ago, when he was thirty-five, to a tall, majestic woman ten years younger. Her name was Rochelle, and while Schroeder didn't know exactly how the Rochelle became Rocky, to go with Stoney, it happened quickly and it stuck. Schroeder of course capitalized on it at their wedding reception, offering a toast replete with bon mots like "rocky road" and "stoney stares," and people with their names not living in glass houses.

It was not Schroeder's best work, but it was his most prophetic, because their marriage was rocky right from the start. Several times they'd almost separated; once they had, and came back together, they announced, for the sake of their daughter, Pamela, who was born somewhat too immediately after their marriage. Pam held their marriage together without helping it.

The ferry gave two long hoots preparatory to docking; Schroeder turned and walked into the lounge, where his mother and his kids were reading.

"Do you think we'll have sun tomorrow?" his mother asked.

"The Boston paper says no, but I don't care. I brought my own son with me. Not to mention my own beautiful daughter. So we'll have a great time, anyway." He wanted them to believe that; he wanted to believe it too. Dammit, he'd just have to *make* it happen.

"OK now, everybody get your things together and let's get back to the car. We're close to docking."

When the car pulled off the ferry, Schroeder asked: "Well, what shall we have for our first dinner on Nantucket?"

"Pizza," answered Bobby.

"Or heroes," his daughter added.

"Look," he said, "This is a famous seafood place. Save the pizza and heroes for First Avenue. How about you, grandma?"

"Oh, I don't care. Whatever you all would like."

Oh, care, grandma, for Chrissake, care. He said it to himself.

"All right, we'll see," he said aloud, and asked himself, why the hell don't you make some forceful choice instead of putting the others down? Take charge of this weekend. Make it work. "First let's do some grocery shopping," he announced. He drove to the A&P, where they bought fifty-four dollars' worth of food. Then to North Liberty, where he showed them the charming house Jane had rented, waiting for a touch of enthusiasm. His mother's was pro forma; the kids were indifferent. Schroeder felt his lips tighten. Saying little, he unloaded the car; then they chose bedrooms. Each kid would get a sleeping loft. He and grandma would get the downstairs bedrooms.

Summoning up some enthusiasm, he announced: "No cooking tonight. No pizza, no heroes. We dine out, in style!" With apathy all around him, he led them to a seafood restaurant just off Straight Wharf, where his mother found everything overpriced and the kids found everything distasteful, and he found a vodka martini and some white wine a passable shield against their indifference.

By the time they got back to the house it was nine thirty and the children went to bed without argument. He and his mother sat down in the living room.

"What do you think of this place, mom?"

"It must be terribly expensive."

He fought off the aphorism about knowing the price of everything and the value of nothing. "Yes, but how do you like it?"

"It looks very nice."

Very nice. OK.

"What are you reading there, mom?"

She held up the book, the paperback version of last year's best seller, an "honest, revealing" memoir about life among the rich and powerful, written by the daughter of a famous man.

"The language is terrible," she said. "Just terrible."

He smiled. Judging by her bookmark, she'd been eating it up.

"I think I'll phone the Cobbs," he said, getting up. "See if they're here yet."

What am I doing? he asked himself as he thumbed through the phone directory. It's Thursday. Stoney won't be here. If anyone is, it'll be Rocky alone. No, little Pam, too. Yeah, but she'll be asleep. It'll be Rocky alone. I'm just looking for one kind of trouble or another.

He snapped the directory shut.

Then he picked up the phone and dialed.

Chapter

THURSDAY EVENING CAME UPON FELICIA O'BRIEN WITH SUCH softness, such clarity, such temptation, she left her desk at 8:15, walked to her father's cubicle, and said: "I'm going to leave, father. I'll be at Maury's place . . . for dinner." Although they were the only two left in the office, she called him father, as she did always. Never dad, or daddy, or pop.

She leaned over and kissed the crown of his head; there were fewer hairs than ever, almost none, between her lips and his scalp. And they were a drab gray; once they'd been a pale reddish blond, as hers were now. He looked up; the tired, faded eyes acknowledging he'd heard her, and asking her, why? Why she was going to Maury's apartment? Why was she going out with a Jew? Not that he expected any answers; he'd grown used to not getting answers, from her, from the rest of the world.

Henry O'Brien was not an anti-Semite. Two of his six staff lawyers were Jews, and he liked them as well as he liked the others, as well as he liked anyone. But not for his daughter. Nor was Maury's, or any man's, apartment for his daughter. O'Brien was a good Catholic and a sexual puritan. He hoped his daughter would be a virgin when she married; suspected it was already too late, but refused to confront the suspicion or learn anything that would confirm it.

He'd been against her going to Boston University instead of a Catholic college, and, given his hopes, he'd been right, for she first slept with a man when she was a junior, and had she been cloistered on a Catholic girl's school campus, she might not have. She'd slept with several since then, none frivolously, but several. She realized she was something of a disappointment to her father; she also realized that what he really wanted was for her to be a nun, untouched.

She'd been sleeping with Maury Janowitz for more than a year. Once he'd wanted her to move in with him; she'd refused, out of deference to her father. Lately, she noticed he had not renewed the offer; not that she'd changed her mind, but she wondered why he no longer asked. (From her father she'd inherited a certain expectation of rejection.) Though she often spent the night at Maury's, she always went back to her apartment in the morning before going off to law school or the office.

"Don't work too late, father, do you hear?"

O'Brien looked up, smiled and shook his head no.

The smile didn't stay long. It didn't look comfortable there, she thought. His was not a face built for smiling, but then he hadn't had much to smile about. He'd scratched out a mediocre law career, known as someone who did good solid work, but was unfriendly, undiplomatic, a religious zealot—in short, not the kind who'd bring in business. He'd married late, had one child, and then his wife had died early, when Felicia was fifteen and he was forty-eight. Since her mother's death, Felicia had never known her father to have "a lady friend," as he called them. The few times he'd taken a woman out to dinner, Felicia could tell, it had gone badly.

He was not social, not successful, not "fun to be with," not particularly attractive; at fifty-six, he looked sixty. Even the minor cachet of his prosecutor's job had been dispelled by the broadcast word that he was making a fiasco of it. He didn't have much to smile about; nor did she. Until now. Now, she thought, maybe we both have something to smile about. The thought made her grin at him, and his face softened in return.

"Good night, father. See you tomorrow."

She took the elevator down and stepped out into the spectacularly clear June evening. Maury's apartment was about a mile away and she wanted to walk.

Maury Janowitz was a tall, broad-shouldered, good-looking lawyer who, at twenty-eight, was on his way to success and on his way to looking it, in dress, apartment, and style. He was a partner in a middle-sized and growing firm, a good lawyer and a great entrepreneur, a budding millionaire.

She couldn't understand why he was interested in her, and in her serious self-deprecating way, said so. "As far as I can see," she'd told him, "it's the one false step in an otherwise superbly planned life."

"Don't you know," he'd replied, "it's every Jewish boy's ambition to go out with a beautiful shikse?"

"I may be a shikse," she'd said, "but I'm not beautiful."
"I'm not blond," she'd said. "I can't get you into the country club, because they wouldn't have me, either, I can't help you professionally and I don't have a big bosom. I'm not even fun to be with."

He'd laughed again. "That red hair of yours is nicer than blond, and genuine; I don't want to get into the country club, I don't want your help in business, and I love your tits, the way they stand up. What did Spencer Tracy once say about Katharine Hepburn in a movie? 'There ain't much, but what there is, is cherce.'

"Your ass is perfect. And you're fun to be with in bed."

She'd slapped him when he'd said that, and her pale skin reddened, from the effort of the slap and from embarrassment at his explicitness.

That only made him go further. "Do you want to know what I like about you most?"

"No!" She already knew what he'd say.

"Yes. It's those rosy nipples. They have no pigmentation in them! I've never seen anything like it!"

"Stop it!" This time she turned an even deeper pink, but she didn't at all mind the attention; she'd had so little of it. And he was right about the pigmentation; she had so little of it anywhere. Her hair was soft and pale, so were her eyes. Her skin was almost perfect, almost transparent; when he first saw her naked he had the feeling he could see right through to the blood vessels, the nerve endings, the bones, the organs within. More than anything else, the pale purity of that skin turned him on.

She was attractive, despite the mousiness of her self-image. The skin, the silken hair, small, delicate features, a body that was petite, small boned, and soft, that might perhaps later turn pudgy, but was now well-formed and, Maury thought, sexy.

And because of him, Felicia began to enjoy lovemaking, to concentrate on it, to respond to his compliments, to experiment with and enjoy "perversions" she'd never before dreamed of.

In bed together, they improved; out of it, things got worse, largely because of her father and his job.

It was about two months after they'd met that her father was appointed by the governor. Janowitz was astounded; he began asking around: Why Henry O'Brien? He was an undistinguished lawyer from a middling suburban firm, who'd years before been an equally undistinguished assistant D.A. in the city, but had had no prosecutorial experience since. That there was corruption, links among mobsters, judges, prosecutors, cops, Maury didn't doubt. That anyone could put together a case that would stand up in court, he did doubt. Even more, he doubted that O'Brien was the one to do it.

What he found out was that the governor, who'd started with the purest of reformist intentions, saw his entire legislative program endangered by the new prosecutor's office he'd established, and at the last minute, had bailed out of it by accepting the recommendation of O'Brien by a state legislator. The crusade was going to be dumped, O'Brien was to be the patsy, and everyone around the appointment knew it but O'Brien. Everybody was to go through the motions but O'Brien, and he was picked because of the prevailing opinion he could not get the job done. And for the legislator who'd suggested O'Brien, there was an extra bonus: O'Brien resigned from the legislator's brother-in-law's firm, where he was dead weight.

At first, Maury was going to tell Felicia what was going on; then he realized it would have devastated her and her father. Both of them believed in their mission; they needed a mission, they needed something to believe in, they had nothing else. So he contented himself with pessimistic remarks about how difficult the job was, about how she must not expect too much, about how deeply entrenched the corruption was. Even so, he had to be careful, for she grew fierce if he suggested too bluntly that her father was accomplishing nothing.

"The only times you get really excited," he'd once said to her, "are fucking and defending your father." He thought he'd said it affectionately; she got angry. It didn't help their relationship, which was getting more and more troubled. Since her father was appointed she'd wanted to go fewer and fewer places. Everywhere she saw enemies, people ridiculing her father, laughing at him. So either she wouldn't go, or would stay so tight and quiet, Maury took to treating her at parties and dinners as if she were a social cripple.

"Christ, why must you act just like your father?" he'd once shouted. And she'd shouted, or come as close to shouting as her personality allowed, "I'm proud of my father!"

"Don't you see your father is a joke in the legal profession?"

"Why is it," she'd answered, "that a profession should laugh at an honest man? Is he the only one?"

"How dare you!" was all Maury said.

"How dare *you* call my father a joke!"

"All right, all right, let's both stop," he'd said. He was getting a little edgy about her, she knew it.

And now, as he opened his apartment door, she saw the reserve even before she said anything. The eyes were wary, the smile a bit forced, and therefore a bit the broader for it.

"Hi!" he said, and kissed her on the lips, lightly.

"Hi," she responded, looking at him, wondering how he felt about her at that instant. And she about him.

She sat on his black leather sofa, very new, very expensive, bought without even telling her about it.

"A glass of wine?" he asked.

"White would be lovely," she said.

He poured two glasses, handed her one, sat next to her.

"How's it going?" His question was reluctant. In ten months now, he'd heard a string of stories, dismissed indictments, uncooperative officials, recalcitrant staff people, plots, ridicule—a litany that was part defensive, part paranoid, part pitiful. And never had he been able to talk to her about the realities of the situation; he'd been stopped cold the first few times he'd tried. No longer did he try. She was off floating on her own magic carpet; it had no room for two, nor did he want to get on.

She didn't want him on. "Oh, let's not talk shop," she said. She took a sip of the wine. "Let's say something personal to each other."

"That's a good idea," he replied, so eagerly, she grew frightened of what he would say, and stopped him.

"But I go first," she commanded. She held up her glass. "Here's to having a wonderful dinner. And to the handsome cook. Here's to a sweet, lovely evening." They both sipped, Maury never taking his eyes off her.

"Felicia, I . . ." he began, but she cut him short.

"I'm not finished. Here's to not talking seriously. To putting aside all the worries that lie in the world outside this apartment. Just for tonight. Please! Tomorrow we'll talk seriously. OK? Please!"

Six months ago, he'd have asked what was troubling her. By now he'd heard the litany so often that he didn't want to hear it again. Besides, there was something bothering him, about "tomorrow."

"Well, uh, not . . . not tomorrow, Felicia. I'm going to have to leave for the weekend. Next week, first thing, OK?"

Her stomach seemed to sink; more than anything she did not want to be alone. Her fear of total isolation took first place over everything else, over her misgivings about their relationship, over her distaste for the way he treated her father, over everything. Felicia didn't have anyone but her father and Maury. And like her father, she couldn't express the waves of feeling, the need, the fright, the despair, the anger, the hopelessness. While they bounced around inside her, outside she seemed stolid, unresponsive; "lethargic" and "stoic" were two of the words Maury had taken to using—but not aloud, not to her.

All that could surface was a kind of resignation. "Well, Maury, that really says it, doesn't it? You don't have to wait until next week to say it, do you?"

"No, Felicia, it doesn't. It doesn't say what . . ."

Again she stopped him. "No, please. I meant what I said, not tonight. I'm sorry for driving you to it. But please, tonight, let's concentrate on dinner, and the evening. Please!" This time her tone moved from command to a kind of pleading.

He nodded, moved by the plea. "All right." He smiled and lifted his glass. "Here's to dinner. And the evening."

He'd cooked a paella, which she thought marvelous. The conversation moved like a high-wire act, taut and tense with the job of keeping balance. At a few moments during the meal she felt like leaping to her feet and shouting, it's all over, let's not stretch it, let's not go through this. But of course she didn't feel like it enough; she never did. Besides, she desperately didn't want to go back to her apartment, where no one ever phoned except her father and Maury, and no one ever visited except her father and Maury.

The rest of the evening was better, more palliative anyway. She went after his body fiercely, grabbing, clutching at the hairy slimness of it, pressing her fingers, her breasts, her belly, her thighs into it, kissing, licking, sucking, as if to weld him to her and to unfasten from his mind the announcement he would make to her "next week, first thing," but had really already made.

After the lovemaking she slept fitfully, awakening at 6:30 to get up and dress, kissing Maury as she left, and barely getting a stirring of his body in return. By eight o'clock, when her phone rang, she'd been home for a half hour. She hoped it was Maury, not her father.

It was neither. It was a homicide detective. There'd been an accident. He was terribly sorry. Her father had been killed by a hit-and-run driver, right in front of his office. Last night, probably just before midnight, and he'd been trying to reach her. When they couldn't get her, a member of her father's staff had been brought to the morgue to confirm the identification of the . . . of her father. But of course she was welcome to view the body, too. The detective was sorry. He offered condolences.

The shock rolled over her, and she was almost too weak to open her mouth. "And what are you doing about it?" she managed to whisper.

"We're investigating it, of course," he said. "At this point it looks like we've got a case of vehicular homicide."

"Vehicular homicide?" she whispered. "How about first degree murder? You don't think it was an accident, do you?"

He tried to be delicate. First of all, those streets were narrow, dark, and empty at night; second, her father had been drinking. What he wouldn't say was that in his opinion no one took O'Brien seriously enough to bother to knock him off. Cops, judges, honest and corrupt, laughed at him. What he did say was, of course, no possibilities were being disregarded in the investigation.

Suddenly she felt alone, devastated, wiped out, a robot created by Vonnegut in a scene created by Antonioni. Abandoned, in one evening, by the last two people in the world left to abandon her. Abandoned, too alone even to cry. No one would hear her, so what was the point?

But more than that, she had an answer, and couldn't give it. She wanted to say: Now, for the first time, we've uncovered something. Now, for the first time, there are some who are no longer laughing at us. There are some who, for the first time, have a good reason to kill my father. But she could not say it to this detective, because among the things she and her father now knew, was that the police, a lot of them, anyway, were involved, too. Maybe this detective was. And if he wasn't, he could still, innocently, pass along the information until it was seen or heard by a cop who wasn't innocent.

"I don't think it was an accident," she said. "Please! It was no accident." She was afraid to say more.

"Is there something you can tell us, Miss O'Brien?" the detective asked. "Something you know that we don't?"

Then she was seized by fear, a panic so acute it suppressed all other feelings—grief, loneliness, all others. This detective was part of the force aligned—no, not the force aligned, the *plot*—against her father. It was she this detective was investigating, not her father's murderers. The purpose of his questioning had nothing to do with finding the killers.

"No," she hissed at the detective. She wanted to shout, but her shock was such she couldn't manage it. "No, there's nothing I know that you don't! Just that he was a prosecutor, which you know, too. Isn't that enough?"

"Well, of course, Miss O'Brien, we are investigating this, we always do investigate hit-and-runs. And I think you and I should have a talk. My name is Detective Mulcahy, Ray Mulcahy. Would you like to drop by the station house—it's only five minutes away from you—or would you like me to come to see you?"

The fear became almost a paralysis; she tried to calm it. Am I being paranoid? she asked herself. What makes me think this isn't an honest cop, who means to investigate, as he says? Because of what we know, she answered herself. What we *knew*. Now only *I* know it. Because if they killed my father—and she was getting surer each second that they had—they'll be out to get me now. Maybe this detective is after me. If he *is* a detective! How do I know?

"No, no, Detective Mulcahy," she said, trying not to sound panicked.

"No, to which one?" he asked, patiently.

"Don't come here. I'll come to you. Only I need a little time to pull myself together; you understand. Perhaps noon. Or 12:30. Is that all right?"

"All right, Miss O'Brien. Let's say 12:30. And I hope I can count on you. Please don't disappoint me. Detective Mulcahy. Just ask for me at the desk. And I'm sorry about your father, miss."

She hung up the phone and fell forward on her bed. She pushed her head into her pillow and began to sob.

After ten minutes she forced herself to get up, changed into a T-shirt, painter's pants, sneakers. If they killed him—and they *did* kill him—it was because they knew what he had. If they knew that, they'd be after her now. She walked to her closet, fished in the pockets of an old coat, and came up with two objects: a small pearl-handled pistol, and a black leather loose-leaf book, pocket-sized and an inch thick with pages.

First she looked to see if there was a magazine in the gun, and gave the heel of it a push to make sure it was seated properly; she checked to make sure the safety was on. She just held the notebook in her hand and looked at it. For that notebook, they had killed her father. Now she had it. And if they could, they'd kill her for it, too. She put it and the pistol into her leather purse.

Then, quickly, she walked out of the apartment and double-locked the door behind her. She was running away. But where was she running *to*? For the moment, away was good enough. She spotted a cab and waved at it, jumped in and closed the door, said nothing. The driver hesitated for a moment, then, hearing nothing, asked, "Where to, miss?"

Her answer almost surprised her: "574 Commonwealth, please." Her father's address. Stupid, but she had to, and she wasn't sure why. Part of it, she thought, was just to see, to touch what belonged to him. What *had* belonged to him. Part of it was to see if anyone had been there. If her father had been murdered, they'd go after the book. They'd go to his apartment; in fact they'd have been there by now, and she'd be able to tell.

It was more than stupid, she said to herself, it was crazy. Yet she could not tell the driver to change direction. She didn't know where to tell him to change direction *to*. She had to go. When the cab pulled up in front of her father's building, she first looked around. A police car on the street, a big man—she thought of *them* as big, big men—loitering, almost anything, anybody, would have scared her off. But seeing nothing, she paid the driver, got out, went quickly to his apartment and let herself in.

Everything seemed in order. If *they'd* searched here, *they'd* been extraordinarily neat. Maybe *they* hadn't. Maybe it had been an accident. Maybe *they* hadn't come yet, and would, at any moment. The prospect sent a bolt of panic through her, and she told herself to calm down, to look around, to see what, if anything, was changed.

Had that little ashtray stood just that way, on the corner of the lace doily on the little round table? Probably.

Had the liquor bottles stood in two neat rows? Probably.

And the records, had they always stood so straight, so lined up? Probably.

With three or four records in a pile in front, unjacketed? Probably.

Her father always had records out, he was always listening to music. "My only friends," he'd say of those records. Those dear friends, she said to herself as she picked them up and looked at them.

Tchaikowsky's Pathetique . . . No.

The Mendelsohn Violin Concerto . . . No.

Rachmaninoff. Another Tchaikowsky . . . No, No!

Her father never listened to nineteenth-century music. When these had arrived, one of the rare presents a client had ever sent him, Felicia had had to restrain her father from smashing them. She'd never seen him so vehement. "Goddamn romantic, ego-maniacal crap!" he'd shouted. "It's what's wrong with the human species, music like this!" And he'd pulled out some Telemann, some Bach, and put them on, to show her what real music was.

No. It was wrong. Someone had probably been through every jacket, searching, and forgotten which records had been out.

Could he have changed? Was it she and not the records that were disordered? How could she know for sure?

Then, all at once, she knew. For sure.

On the corner of her father's desk, staring across the room from within a leather frame, stood her mother's picture. Even in a picture, Felicia thought, her mother could not look happy. Felicia stared back.

She knew for sure.

For her mother's portrait had not stood upright in eight years, not since the day of the funeral, when her father, in grief, had turned the picture face down on his desk. He had not intended to have it stay that way permanently, he told his daughter years later. But as the weeks, months, years, went by, the down-turned picture created its own tradition, affixed itself to the desk top, and more and more the idea of standing it upright again became unthinkable. Then, when he'd moved out of their house into the city apartment, and had a chance to break the pattern, he chose not to take it. When they unpacked, the picture went face down on the desk, as if the woman, after a tough, drab life, had lain down for a rest, and didn't want to get up again.

And now, there was her mother staring at her.

No.

She ran out of the apartment. It had been searched, with more care than the police would take. But *they* had not found what they wanted; that she knew, because *she* had what they wanted. Which meant they would go to her apartment next; indeed might be there right now. Then, having failed again, they'd go looking for her.

Felicia hurried along the street, still not knowing where to go, but knowing she had to go somewhere. When at last she spotted another cab, she flagged it, again with no destination in mind.

"Just keep going this way, while I look for the address," she told the driver, and pretended to search in her purse. In it, she saw the notebook, the pistol. She looked up and said, "I guess you'd better take me to Harvard Law School, in Cambridge." Though she was not a student there, Felicia often used the law library; she always felt safe and warm there, and it seemed as good a place to go as any other, better than any other, in fact the only one she could think of.

The school year being over, the place was virtually empty. She found herself an alcove, sat down, then walked to a shelf and grabbed at a nearby textbook to make it look proper. She sat again, took a piece of paper and a ballpoint pen from her purse. On the paper she wrote, in capital letters, FRIENDS.

And left a space about two inches deep. Then, again in caps, wrote OFFICIALS. And left another space, and wrote PLACES TO GO.

Making lists had always helped her organize things, but she found she didn't have much to organize; these lists would not be long. First she contemplated FRIENDS, and then wrote the name Maury. She paused, thought, and under OFFICIALS, started to write La . . . , stopped, then went on to finish it. Larry Friendly. One of her father's staff lawyers, a stocky, round-faced, jovial man, the only one on the staff who seemed at all willing to help or even to support her father. She didn't spend long on OFFICIALS. Her relations with most of them, on her father's staff, elsewhere in the city government, had been hostile.

PLACES TO GO. First she wrote Seattle. Her father had spoken occasionally about his first cousin, Patsy, there. But Patsy was married and Felicia didn't even know her married name. Seattle was just a name to put on a list. So was the second: Nantucket. Though it was not far from Boston, she'd never been there. She'd never been anywhere. New York a couple of times, the White Mountains a couple of times, and one or two beaches south of Boston for a few weeks. They'd never had much money; her father had never seemed to enjoy vacations. Once, Felicia had told one of her law school classmates she'd never been to Cape Cod, Nantucket, or Martha's Vineyard. The classmate was incredulous.

Nantucket made the list through Maury. He, too, hadn't believed she'd never been there, and had suggested the two of them go, telling her about the island's charm, its long stretches of lonely beaches, its eighteenth-century houses, its freedom from the garishness of most resorts. She'd almost felt this was a vacation she'd like. Now she'd never get there, not with Maury, anyway. But in her fear, her paralysis, she thought she must have a *list* somewhere, not just three categories with one name each. And Seattle was not even a legitimate name. So Nantucket made the list through Maury. And through desperation, which also made her add, to PLACES TO GO, South Station, Greyhound, Hertz, Avis, Logan.

Logan, yes Logan. To fly away. She looked at her watch, a couple of minutes after nine. Quickly she stuffed the pen and paper into her purse and got up and left. Again she walked until she found a cab, and in ten minutes was waiting in a doorway across the street from her father's office. She saw several staff people arrive and she stood farther and farther back in the doorway to make sure she wasn't noticed. How she hated those people, those sneering, cynical antagonists who, she was sure, were there only to spy and report their findings to political friends. How she hated the icy way they'd treated her father, the snickering behind his back, the lethargic response to his directions.

How she hated them! How alone she felt. I am probably paranoid, she told herself. But this time I am not wrong. This time, there is the notebook. Then she spotted Larry Friendly, walking along in the snappy muscular stride so many stocky people have; he was perspiring, red-faced, his seersucker gray and white suit properly baggy. She raced across the street.

"Larry!"

He looked around, saw her; his bright button eyes widened; she saw in his face guilt, embarrassment, sympathy. He reached out both hands. "Oh, Felicia. I heard about your father on the radio this morning. I am *so* sorry! God, how awful!"

"Larry, can you take a couple of minutes to have a cup of coffee with me? I need some advice."

He didn't want to. It flitted across his face and then was gone. Another time she would have withdrawn, now she wouldn't.

"Please."

"Yes, of course." He started toward the coffee shop in their office building.

"No, not there. Let's go around the corner." She didn't want to be seen by anyone else from her father's office. If they weren't *for* him—and they weren't—they might be *against* him. If they were against him, they might be hooked up with whoever had killed her father, whoever had searched his apartment, whoever would be looking for her now. There was no possibility she was willing to dismiss right now. She grabbed at the lawyer's arm, and gently but insistently led him around the corner, where she walked to the rearmost booth of the luncheonette.

"Larry, the police think it was an accident. What do you think?"

"Why should one think anything else?"

The waitress walked up. "Two cups of coffee," he said to her. "And I'll have one of those French crullers. Would you like anything?'' He asked the last of Felicia, who just shook her head. The waitress walked away.

"Do you think it could have been deliberate?"

"Why do you think it might be deliberate?" he replied.

"You keep answering me by *asking* me," she said, exasperated. "Please, Larry, I'm asking *you!*"

"Why would . . ." he began, and stopped himself. "I can't see any reason anyone would want to kill him. Pardon me for another question, but can you?"

"Because of his *investigations*, Larry." She looked at him as if he was not serious, and could see he was looking at her the same way. The waitress walked up; they became silent.

Then he spoke, trying to be careful. "Felicia, I don't want to hurt you. This is the wrong time to be saying this, but . . ."

"Wrong time? Now is the time you *must* say it." She burst in on him.

"All right. We don't have a single conviction, or the prospect of one. Several of our indictments have already been dismissed—and those were the cases your father considered the strongest. In others, five, I think, we couldn't even *get* an indictment. Your father was simply no threat to anybody."

"Maybe someone thinks we're on the verge of something." She watched him carefully. All she saw was a touch of exasperation, followed by a determined look of patience.

"Felicia, I don't know of anything. Do you?"

She was afraid to answer. Finally she said: "Possibly."

He had a tough job staying patient. "What do you mean, possibly? Do you know something the rest of us don't?"

Yes, welled up in her throat, but she swallowed it. Maybe she was thoroughly paranoid, but she couldn't. What came out was: "No."

He was patient again, and sympathetic. A nice man, she thought, but she couldn't count on him, and failing that, must tell him nothing. "Look, Felicia," he said, "I understand how upset you are, and I know that you and your father looked at the rest of us with a . . . certain caution. I'm not trying to talk you into anything. What have the police said?"

"They think it's an accident. Hit-and-run, of course, but not deliberate."

"OK. On the basis of what we know at the moment, so do I. At least we know of no reason it should be anything else."

"Well, you see, Larry, if it was deliberate, maybe they'll be after me. I'm so frightened."

With the sympathy and the patience, there came the kind of look an adult takes on when trying to calm a child. "Why you, Felicia? First, there's no reason to think it's deliberate. But if it is, it's not a blood feud, is it? So they'd go after the staff lawyers, the investigators, next. I'd be in more danger than you. And you don't see *me* worried." Then he paused.

"Unless there's something only you and your father know. Something you're not telling. Is there?"

Again, it came up. For just an instant she didn't want to be the only one carrying the weight of that damned notebook. It was too heavy. She wanted to turn it over, to tell someone. It had been a danger and a burden ever since it arrived.

And it had arrived in the mail, literally in a plain brown wrapper, just two days ago. From Florida. An old loose-leaf binder, but expensive, made of leather, in it the name of a now retired lawyer, famous for being a power broker and a bagman. Then lists of initials, and, next to them, money sums. It didn't take much, using rosters of judges, legislators, cops, to establish the identity of the owners of the initials.

They didn't know who had sent it, or why. The lawyer himself, or a member of his family? Someone who'd gotten hold of it? An enemy?

It didn't matter. They'd been handed dynamite in a plain brown wrapper. And someone wanted to take it away from them, and had not wasted much time, had found out very quickly who had gotten the book, and had acted very quickly. And would act quickly again. Against her, for it was only logical that if they hadn't gotten the book from her father, she'd be next, despite what Larry said. She, not the lawyers, not the investigators. But then again Larry had no idea how much her father had distrusted his staff. Including Larry.

If this is paranoia, I'll make the most of it, she said to herself. She swallowed the impulse to talk about the book, and the moment was gone. All she said to Larry was, "You think I'm being silly, frightened for no reason, don't you?"

"Let me speak to you honestly," he began. "I think you're very upset, because of your father, and you have every right to be. I also think you've swallowed your father's conspiracy theory of the city: that *everybody* is paying off or being paid off.

Felicia, that's nonsense. Did it ever occur to you to wonder why, in ten months, now, your father has not been able to make one single case stick? Not one! Have you ever asked yourself why, Felicia?"

Yes, she wanted to scream, I've asked why! And I've answered: Because his own yellow, rotten, corrupt staff doesn't believe in him! Laughs at him! Probably spies and leaks information!

All she said was: "So you think I'm paranoid."

He shook his head. "No, just upset. As you have every right to be."

He's humoring me, she thought. "What do you advise me to do?"

"Take it easy. Stay home for a while. Call the police, call me, if you come across anything tangible. I'm sure the police are investigating the hit-and-run. And if I can be of any help . . ."

"Yes, Larry, thank you." She started to get up, then went for her purse to pay for the coffee, but remembered what was in it, and stopped. "And thank you for the coffee, too. I'm sorry to have taken so much of your time."

"Don't be silly. Do you want to come up to the office? I'm sure the staff would want to see you . . ."

"Oh no," she replied, already out of the booth. "I guess I'll . . . do what you said. Go home. Lie down. I suddenly feel so tired. Then, there are the funeral arrangements . . ."

"And, please, if I can help . . ."

"Thanks, Larry, I appreciate it. You have already helped." She turned and walked out. Yes, he had helped, for now she knew what to expect in the way of help from others. Nothing. What her father got. Clutching her leather purse frantically, she walked, but not home. She just walked, for block after block after block, her hand clamped on the purse till it ached and she had to switch hands. Then she opened the purse and groped for her list, pulled it out and looked at it. Not much to see. But she knew she must not go home. She must go away from home. Far away, and as quickly as possible.

She began looking for a cab, and when she found one, she jumped in and said, "Logan, please."

When they got near the airport, the driver asked: "Which airline, miss?"

"Which airline?"

She looked out the window, saw a sign that said, "United."
"United, please."

She paid him, got out, walked through the United Airlines ticket area, through the corridors of the terminal, with fear, isolation, sorrow, clogging her breathing. She was so alone. There had been only her father and Maury. Now her father was gone, killed while she and Maury were in bed together—as if she needed any extra guilt. And Maury was going too, bailing out, and to ask his help now would seem so pitiful. But who else was there? Maury was the only one around, and might not be around much longer.

Through her despairing reverie broke the professionally bored voice of a flight announcer. "Air New England announces first call for the boarding of Flight 355, to Nantucket and Martha's Vineyard, at Gate 9. Flight 355, to Nantucket and Martha's Vineyard, now boarding at Gate 9."

Nantucket, calm little Nantucket. Where she'd never been, but which was in her mind a corner of safety and serenity, where no one was corrupt, or cruel, where the lump of fear and despair in her stomach might melt away.

In front of her and off to the left, perhaps fifty yards off, she could see the Air New England ticket counter. She ran to it. "Can I get one seat on the Nantucket flight?"

Without uncreasing her smile, the ticket clerk punched the keyboard in front of her, and waited while it clacked an answer. Smiling even more broadly, she looked up. "We do have a single seat."

"That's fine," Felicia almost shouted, "I'll take it." It seemed the first thing that had gone right for her all day.

"How will you be paying for it?"

"Will Master Charge be all right?"

"Fine," said the clerk and began writing out the ticket.

The momentary triumph of finding a seat faded; Felicia felt the panic growing again.

"Gate 9," said the clerk, still smiling.

"What?" asked Felicia, and something in her face made the clerk stop smiling.

"Gate 9," she repeated.

"Where is that?" The clerk now looked startled, and pointed behind Felicia.

"How much time do I have?" Felicia asked.

"Fifteen minutes."

42

"Yes. Good. Thank you." Felicia turned and walked away. She found the boarding gate, and as she walked toward it, she felt the fear and loneliness building, building, building, until they were more than she could handle. She stopped at a pay phone, called Maury's office. It was 4:45, maybe he'd still be there.

"Jesus," he said as soon as he heard her voice. "I've been trying to get you all day. I didn't hear about your father till I got to the office. It's just awful. I'm so sorry. How are you doing?"

She tried to take hold of her voice and make it behave. "Pretty well. Not badly. But I must go away for a few days. Remember how we used to talk about Nantucket, Maury? Well, I'm about to get on a plane to Nantucket. Maury, it would be so nice, it would mean so much to me, if you would come with me. You could catch a later plane. I could either go on this one and meet you there, or wait at the airport for you. It would mean *so* much to me." She tried to stop short of pleading, but didn't really care if she went over.

"Felicia, I wish I could, but it is impossible."

She caved in. "Oh, please! Please!"

"I really am going away for the weekend, honey, to New Hampshire. It's clients. There's nothing I can do; I wish I could."

"Maury, I need you. So desperately. Could you get me invited? Take me with you? Please!"

His voice took an edge of firmness. "Felicia, it's just out of the question. I know how you must feel about your father, and it's just dreadful. My heart goes out to you. Let's see each other right after work on Monday, and I'll hold your hand."

For a moment she said nothing. Then: "Maury, forgive me for begging."

"Don't be silly, honey. I wish I could do more."

So do I, so do I, she repeated to herself as she walked away from the phone. She boarded the plane with a bunch of chattering children, one or two upper-middle-class mothers, and a line of tanned businessmen carrying expensive attaché cases. She so much wanted to belong to someone on that line, to be someone's wife, or mother, or . . . more than anything, someone's child.

But she was alone, and for all she knew one of those big men might be after her. No, she thought, they all look too respectable, too successful, for that kind of work. They might be paying for it, but they wouldn't be doing it themselves. Well, at least being alone meant no one knew where she was going. But, yes, someone now knew. Maury knew. She should have warned him not to say anything. But it was too late; she was aboard now. Besides, he wouldn't. Maury was all she had now; not much, but all she had.

She sat herself next to the most fatherly looking man she could find, but was just as glad when he buried his face in his open attaché case and his papers for the flight. When the stewardess came around selling drinks, she took a vodka martini. She hated the taste, but she thought it might calm the shakes coursing through her. It didn't. They flew south through intermittent clouds, and she could see little of the island as they landed, had no idea where to go or what to do, feeling so lonely, so envious of the businessmen, all of them getting into parked cars, or being met by tanned wives in station wagons.

She walked to a taxi and got in. "Goin' in to town?" the driver asked.

"Uh, yes," she said. "Could you suggest a decent place to stay, not too expensive?"

"Would you like a hotel or a roomin' house, miss? The roomin' houses are cheaper."

"A rooming house will be fine."

"Well, a good friend of ours, Mrs. Metcalfe, has a real nice place at 17 Hulbert Avenue. Only lets out two rooms, so that's all shares the bath. Big rooms, clean, quiet. Hulbert Avenue sound all right?"

"Yes, it sounds fine." She had no idea where Hulbert Avenue was.

In ten minutes they pulled up to the house. It was not one of the sober whaling captains' houses for which Nantucket was renowned. Mrs. Metcalfe presided over a turn-of-the-century Victorian house, yellow with white trim, a porticoed porch on the front and the right side, a spotless walk leading through a carefully tended lawn to the front steps.

"You tell Mrs. Metcalfe, Hawkie said to take good care of you," the driver told her jovially as she paid him. She tried to return his smile, but felt her lips trembling. She managed a "thank you" and walked up and rang the bell.

Mrs. Metcalfe, a carefully dressed, white-haired woman, said yes, she did have a room. The other room was rented, but the people would not arrive until tomorrow, so for tonight she'd have the upstairs bath all to herself. Would she sign the guest register, please?

Something made Felicia hesitate, and when she signed, she wrote Mary Jane, and then, thinking of her best friend at Saint Mary's High School, wrote Bresnahan.

The older woman showed her to her room, which was indeed large, light, and cool, and waited for her to pay it a compliment. When she didn't, Mrs. Metcalfe asked: "Do you like it?"

"Oh, yes, yes, it's lovely," said Felicia.

The landlady's face wrinkled into a smile. "Good. Make yourself at home. Go downstairs, if you wish, and use the sitting room. I'm just on my way into town to visit friends. Another ten minutes and you'd have missed me. You'll have the house all to yourself."

Felicia went back into her room and sat on the bed. Being alone on a gray evening in a big old house on a strange island was the last thing she wanted. She tried to calm herself, couldn't. After three or four minutes, she ran downstairs and found the old woman, who had her purse in hand and was ready to leave.

"Mrs. Metcalfe, could I ride into town with you?"

"Of course, dear. Where do you want to go?"

"I don't really know. Where the restaurants are, where the movies are. Where the people are."

"Well, dear, the old movie house has *King Kong*, the original one, that much I do know."

"Good," said Felicia. "Would you drop me there?"

"But it doesn't start until seven and it's just six now. Why don't you go and have something to eat first? If you're hungry."

"Yes," Felicia replied. "Where do you suggest I go?"

"Why don't I drop you at the Sandpiper? It's a cute little place, and not really expensive, like some of the restaurants." Mrs. Metcalfe shook her head.

"Good, that sounds perfect."

The Sandpiper turned out to be small and bare, more a lunch counter with tables than a restaurant. She ordered coffee, then a grilled cheese sandwich, then more coffee. At 6:45, she paid her check and asked the cashier, "how do I get to the movie theatre that's playing *King Kong?*"

"Just go right over to Main Street, then down Main toward the docks, till you see Washington Street on your right. Go down Washington and you'll see it."

Along the cobblestone streets of one of America's most famous resort towns she walked, past art galleries, bookstores, gift shops, without seeing anything but the projection of her own fear. Main Street had some people, but Washington was dark and empty. Felicia was afraid to walk it. She lingered at the corner, pretending to look into windows, waiting for someone else to start down the street.

In a few minutes a buzzing group of teen-agers came by and turned onto Washington. Felicia hurried after them, following so closely one of the girls turned around to look, then said something to her friend. The two of them turned, and both snickered. But Felicia stayed close, followed them into the theatre.

She settled down to watch the movie; though she'd seen it before, she was eager to trade, for a while, her own private nightmare for the remote histrionic menace of *King Kong*.

IN AN OLD CUTOFF PAIR OF JEANS AND A WORN DENIM WORK shirt, Rocky was sitting on her deck, sipping brandy from a snifter, looking up at the stars, when the phone rang. The first three rings she didn't hear. The next three she ignored, because she was sure it was Stoney calling to tell her why he couldn't get there tomorrow night. On ring seven she went for it, hoping he'd hang up. Just after nine, she picked it up, and said, "Hello."

"I was going to give it one more and then hang up," said the voice. It was not Stoney.

"Who is this?"

"Your old friend Sam. Sam Schroeder."

"Why, Sam, what a delightful surprise!" The sound of any human who was civilized and friendly would have been a delightful surprise. "Where are you?"

"Cozy and entrenched, with my mother and my kids by my side, in a house on North Liberty, island of Nantucket."

"How wonderful! Why didn't you let us know you were coming?"

"Oh, it was a last-minute thing. Jane took the house and asked me to break it in for her, so I rented a car, threw some things and some people into it, and here we are."

She knew damned well it was no last-minute thing; it was that fight on the ski trip, when he'd been caught between the warring Cobbs and gotten ripped up for it. She'd written him a letter of apology, and he'd answered it, politely, but then Sam always stepped away from a fight, she knew that, too.

"How's it going, so far?" she asked.

His voice dropped to a whisper. "Well, aside from the fact that my kids have nothing to do, my mother has nothing to say, and I have neither, it's just great. And helped a lot by this bottle of Beaujolais, which is fast approaching the halfway mark."

"You and grandma tippling, eh?"

"No," he answered, his voice still low, "I'm doing a solo. Grandma doesn't tipple; she doesn't even sip."

He wanted to have a drink with her, she knew it, yet he didn't want to ask. He wanted to know if Stoney was here, she knew that, too, yet he didn't want to ask. Well, hell, let him pussy-foot, she'd answer both his questions at once.

"Why, Samuel, solitary drinking is so unsatisfactory. Why don't we eliminate two solitary drinkers simultaneously by having you come over here and share my brandy?"

A hesitation at the other end of the phone, then Sam speaking, trying a little too hard to sound noncommittal. "Oh, Stoney not down yet?"

"No, he's still in town, doing whatever it is successful lawyers do—robbing widows and orphans, I suppose. He'll get here tomorrow evening, or Saturday morning, or evening; or Sunday. Or not at all." She hoped she wasn't sounding too angry, or too drunk, but feared the worst on both.

"Why don't I wait and see both of you?" he offered.

"Why then, SamSam, you wouldn't be solving the dilemma of the solitary drinker. And besides, he may never get here at all, and then I'd be denied your company for God knows how long. Oh, come on. Pam's asleep, the TV set is still in Boston, the night is dark and long and the lady is desperate for company.

We can get drunk and be ruthlessly honest with each other, have a fight and then not talk again for another four or five months."

"First of all," he said, "No SamSam. Second, no ruthless honesty, maybe no honesty at all; third, no four-month freezes. Fourth, let's meet somewhere and I'll buy you a drink. While I'm here, I may as well sop up a little local color."

He wanted to meet on neutral territory, to protect himself, she thought. "Oh hell, why not here, what do you think the Cobb house is, if not local color? Come on over."

Again, a hesitation. "Let's have a drink at that waterfront bar. What's the name of it? The one where the whaling captains all hang out?"

She laughed. "The whaling captains all hang out at the old cemetery. That bar is called The Crow's Nest, and I'm not going to turn down a drink even though you prefer a dingy joint like that to our place. But first I'll have to pick up my babysitter down the road and get her back here. Give me, let's say, twenty minutes. OK? I won't even change."

"Twenty minutes. Terrific. I'm sure you look sensational unchanged."

She laughed. "Well, you'll soon see." She put down the phone, stood up, and walked into her bedroom and looked in her full-length mirror.

Sensational? No, just not bad. If you liked big women: five feet ten, a hundred fifty pounds. Why should she look bad? She was only thirty, and used to being called the best-looking girl in the room. Not a big room, but what the hell. Why should she look bad? She answered herself: Because you're fifteen pounds overweight, and you've started drinking too much, which makes your eyes look bloodshot a lot of the time, including right now, and you have no makeup on whatever, and your hair needs—something—and you're not wearing a bra—which at your age and weight you're beginning not to be able to get away with; and the shirt is too worn, and the shorts too short, and too much of you is showing, principally because there's too much of you to show.

To remedy all that in time to have a drink with Sam would be impossible. To remedy some would leave her with the problem of which, so she left it all alone, except for a few brushstrokes and then a rubberband for her long brown hair, and got in the car, fetched the teen-age babysitter—she'd never bothered to consider the possibility the girl might be at the movies, but God looks after drunkards, she decided—and was at the little waterfront bar in twenty minutes.

Sam had just walked in and was looking for a booth. She walked up to him and grabbed his arm; he turned quickly, and then smiled. She leaned into him and kissed him on the lips, lightly but with juice. With her clogs on she was about six feet tall, almost as big as he.

"Handsome as ever," she said to him. "Why, thank you," he replied, "And you're more beautiful and sexier than ever."

More filled out than ever, was what he thought. More matronly. Older. Yes, sexier, too. Less like the prototypical Junior Leaguer.

"From one solitary drinker to another, welcome," she said.

"Thank you. I've always said, if you've got to be a solitary drinker, it helps to have company."

For an instant her dark brown eyes looked startled, then she broke into a grin, her teeth gleaming against the tan of her skin. Rocky was smart and well-educated, working on her doctoral thesis on Henry James, which was an apt choice: she had almost no sense of whimsy. Only lately had she begun to spot wisecracks in others. She had a touch of lyricism to her, a lot of theatre, and increasingly a cutting sarcasm, but little lightness.

"Let's sit right here," he said. "OK?"

"Fine with me. And I'll have a brandy, Sam, but you'll have to get them from the bar."

"All right." He stood and walked to the bar. She watched him. A damned handsome man, she thought, bright, sensitive. But missing something—a kind of weight, a gravity, an assertiveness, she wasn't sure what to call it, but something that would make others feel his touch, his will, more than they did.

Sam came back with two old-fashioned glasses, each half-filled. "They don't have snifters, and rather than take two of those little thimbles they wanted to give me, I asked for these."

"Terrific. Good move." Why did he have to ask approval? she wondered.

She lifted her glass. "Here's to your not being pissed off at me anymore. You're not, are you?"

Sarcasm and vulgarity she'd learned in the course of her marriage—they served the dual purpose of armor and offensive weaponry.

"Angry, you mean?" he said, feeling stuffy as he said it.

"Oh, you prig!" She hit the last word hard.

"How do you spell that?" He asked with a smile, deciding righteousness was useless, and a little boring.

"P-R-I-G." And she raised her glass.

"*That* pisses me off, dammit." He felt tight saying it. "It's not a question of morality, it's a question of esthetics. Faces like yours, with mouths like yours, are simply not suited to expressions like pissed off."

"And what *is* my mouth suited for, SamSam?"

"Cut it out! The SamSam, the profanity, the provocation, all of it. You're one of my best friends. What I just said had a lot of compliment to it, because I don't *care* what comes out of most people's mouths. It also had some advice to it. I was *not* out to pick a fight. Is that what you want? I'll oblige if it is, but please know, in that case, it will only be a game—for me, anyway."

"I'm sorry. No more SamSam. And an attempt will be made to cut down on the profanity and provocation—my, how I wish I could play with words the way you do, Sam—but those two have become a way of life for me. I'll try my best."

"Your trouble is," he told her, "that you're trying to live down being a Henry James scholar. Just because he was effete doesn't make your blood any thinner than if you were specializing in Joyce, or Hemingway. Or Henry Miller."

"Oooh, a literary conversation," she said. "Well, I must tell you that Henry James was not effete. He may have been a homosexual, but not effete. Prissy, yes. He was a *prig*."

"Like me, huh?" Schroeder said. "I'm flattered."

"He was a prig of genius," she said. "You are merely a clever, *minor* prig." Immediately, she regretted saying it. And added: "OK, please, truce—love, not war. I'm so glad to see you; so glad to be able to talk to you." Sam was not a heavyweight. But he *was* easy to talk to, quick, responsive, and, most of all, *not* her husband. That seemed to be the *sine qua non* lately: not her husband.

"I'm glad to see *you*, Rocky. Love, not war, is OK with me." She reminded him of the heroine in O'Neill's *Moon for the Misbegotten*, powerful, oversized, yet beautifully formed and feminine. Perfect calves for the Nantucket dock. When he'd first met her six years ago, she'd seemed a girl, twenty-four going on nineteen. Now she was thirty going on forty. Bigger, older, angrier, tougher, sexier. Much sexier.

Just then, from the bar of the small, shabby, darkened saloon, they heard an increase in conversational volume and they stopped to listen.

The first words they could make out, because they were suddenly at full voice, were: "Cheap, goddamned New York Jew faggots."

"Oh, come on, John," the bartender said. "Keep it down."

Instead, the man swiveled around and addressed the eight or so tables in the room. "Anyone going to tell me New York is not full of cheap Jews and queers come here to louse up this island?"

The man looked like a fisherman, not particularly big or young, but with the rugged look of an outdoor worker. He looked around for crowd reaction. All he got was "John, will you keep quiet?" from the bartender.

"Now wait a minute, Tom" he shouted, clearly drunk. "I just wanna see who's gonna tell me different. Who?" He glared around the small room. Schroeder looked straight at Rocky, shook his head.

"Any New York faggots goin' to disagree?"

"Oh, for Chrissakes, what a noisy bore," said Rocky in a stage whisper.

"What was that, lady?" The drunk was trying to focus on an antagonist.

"Rocky, just ignore him!" Schroeder whispered, urgently.

But she had caught the man's attention, and for lack of a more suitable adversary he walked toward their booth. "You talkin' to me, lady?"

"He doesn't know what he's doing, Rocky," said Schroeder. The man heard him.

"What are you doin', stickin' up for the New York faggots?"

"I didn't say anything" said Schroeder. Rocky heard him try to be tough, without reaching the point of provocation.

"Anybody got anythin' to say?" he shouted, now taking on the whole room. The bartender had put down his cloth and was moving out from behind the bar. But Rocky was exasperated.

She stood up, about three feet from her antagonist. She was a couple of inches taller than he was. "Yes, I've got something to say. You're a stupid, loud-mouthed xenophobe, and I'm tired of listening to you. You're so dumb you don't know what a xenophobe is, do you?" Her eyes were lit up, her tanned face red, and she'd shoved it to within a foot of his. "DO YOU?"

It changed the battleground at once, and put the drunk on the defensive. "No, I don't know what it is, what the hell does . . ." But he had been thrown off balance, and Rocky kept him that way by jumping in on him. "I happen to be a New Yorker, and I'm not a Jew and I'm not a faggot. And *I'm* not a *xenophobe*. And you are, and you're drunk, and you should not be *served!*"

By this time the bartender was there and anxious to avoid trouble. He took the man by the arm and led him to the door. "John, you better go home and have some coffee." The man was drunk, and the outburst had been his last gasp, and he went unsteadily but quietly out the door.

Rocky came back and sat down. They both knew she had stood up to the drunk and Schroeder hadn't. Neither said anything, then Rocky finally said, "Why is it the Know-Nothings always have the loudest voices? Oh, how I hate loud, ignorant *bullies!*"

"I do, too," Schroeder said. "I also hate confrontations."

"I suppose I should shut up, but I can't sit there and listen to it. Something in me rises." She felt she should be comforting him. "It takes a certain personality to respond to people like that, and I'm stuck with it. You're probably right—they should be ignored." Neither of them was satisfied with that, neither wanted to pursue it.

"Shall we have another?" he said, "and resume our own head-to-head bullying contest, which was so rudely interrupted by an outside bully, who was entirely uninvited?" Schroeder could not make his feeling of cowardice go away. He really wanted another drink.

"Yes, let's," Rocky said, "but . . ." and she looked at her watch. "I must get my babysitter home by eleven, she's only thirteen, so if you want another—and I certainly do—you'll be reduced to drinking my brandy at my house. Let's go."

He had paid for the brandies when he'd picked them up at the bar, so they just got up and walked out, the timid little man exiting with the big strong woman.

"Why don't you just follow me?" she said, as they got into their cars. They headed out to the Cobb house off Cliff Road.

He remembered the house well as they pulled up in front of it, the long unpaved driveway, the boardwalk leading to their door, the simplicity, austerity of their modern house of weathered pine and glass. He had to laugh at that; Stoney and Rocky and they *did* live in a glass house. At least partially glass. It stood in landscape that was almost moors—heather, plus some beach roses and low brush. The house was fairly new, yet typically Nantucket and typically Cobb, expensive and at the same time defiantly plain.

"Suited to us New England puritans," Stoney had said years before when he'd first introduced Schroeder to the island and the house. "None of the lushness, the blatant colors, the abundance of Hawaii or Florida or the Caribbean. If you want tropical splendor, Nantucket's not your place. It's a place where a Yankee can relax without the discomfort of opulence."

Schroeder, being from West Hartford, Connecticut, was a Yankee too, but not a Bostonian, and more of German than of English stock, so he never challenged the primacy of Stoney's Yankeeism, for the tall lawyer was almost a professional New England Puritan. Stoney became so aroused on the subject of New England's contributions to thrift, industry, and simplicity in America, Schroeder once called him a "work ethnic."

But he was a dry New England wit, too, and all the more effective for his straight-faced delivery. Physically, he was like his house and his island, handsome in a bleak way, tall, almost gaunt, very strong, once the number five oar on an outstanding Harvard crew. His accent was Ivy League rather than Boston, until he needed to sound like a New Englander—and then suddenly he was more lobsterman than Brahmin.

When they pulled up in front of the house, Rocky jumped out of the station wagon, ran over to his car, and said, "I've got to run and take the babysitter home; you just go in and make yourself at home."

By the time he reached the wooden walkway, Rocky and a blond teen-aged tennis type were on their way out. "Be right back," she said in passing. Schroeder walked in and looked around. Too austere for him, he thought, too many grays, blacks, tans; but, he thought, very elegantly done. The look Stoney wanted.

Rocky was the look Stoney wanted, too: from Maryland, the hunt country around Frederick, but appropriate wherever handsome, aristocratic women were needed. Schroeder, when he first met her, had called her the all-purpose WASP; she'd blend in perfectly at a tennis court in California, a ski lodge in Aspen, a Lightning on Long Island Sound, or a Buckley School parents' meeting in Manhattan.

Schroeder found himself a snifter and poured an inch of Remy Martin into it. He strode around the room, looking at photos: there was one of Stoney and the Harvard crew the year they won the Easterns; there, Stoney and Rocky on a sailboat, looking like Cary Grant and Katharine Hepburn in *The Philadelphia Story*—only better; there, one of Rocky with her arm around Schroeder, on the beach. He remembered when that had been taken, here on Nantucket, by Stoney, five years ago just before they got married. He was looking at it when she returned.

Rocky walked into the big living room, saw Schroeder gazing at the photo, saw him look up at her, saw the startled look in his eyes. She smiled.

"Let's see," she began. "There's five more years; there's fifteen more pounds—no, twenty; the stretch marks of one child, the lines on the face—but no one's counting those. There are the streaks in the hair; *they* are *not* an act of God."

Schroeder smiled back at her. She'd gotten it just about right. He said, "Nor are they an act of the sun. They are man- or woman-made, and they look terrific. In fact, whatever changes have happened have been for the better, the more beautiful, the sexier." For the first time he was looking at her in a good light, and she *had* grown heavier and older. But he meant what he'd said. Maybe she should take off weight, and wear a bra, and shorts that were a bit longer, but she looked terrific.

"Thanks for thinking so, or saying so, anyway. Thirty is a dangerous age for a woman, my dear."

"Only dangerous to the men around her, my dear. You never looked so good. And the best is yet to come. At thirty-five you won't be safe to be on the same island with, let alone in the same room."

"Sam, you speak such welcome and such desperately needed bullshit. Let me get you a brandy. Ah, but I see you already have one. So I'll get myself one. Go and sit down on our sofa."

She half filled a snifter for herself, walked over and sat heavily on the other end of the sofa, sloshing a bit of brandy on her bare thigh as she did.

Instinctively, he reached for a paper napkin on the long low table in front of them, to blot the spilled brandy, then aborted the gesture almost at once, converting it into a meaningless fidget with the napkin. Then as casually as he could, he moved to the far edge of the sofa.

She smiled at him, and used her fingers to wipe the brandy on her thigh, licking it off after each wipe. His eyes followed her hand down to her leg, and he had to command them up again to her face. Despite the extra weight her thighs did not seem fat; they were big, solid, tanned to a golden brown.

"You are a sweet man, Samuel, one of our dearest friends, one of the people I enjoy being with most."

"Well, it beats being called a clever, minor prig. Not even a *major* prig."

"You're not still on that?" she asked.

He took a drink of the brandy, more than he'd wanted to. "Still?" He laughed aloud. "I'm just getting started! You don't know what it's like to be called that. You make me sound so admirable. Can you see John Wayne playing the title role in *The Sam Schroeder Story*, subtitled *The Clever Minor Prig?*"

"Oh God, why would a grown man want to see himself as John Wayne?"

"No, no, this grown man wants to see John Wayne as himself. But he'll not object to Cary Grant, Paul Newman, or Robert Redford."

"Whom do you see playing you, really, Sam?"

"After clever, minor, prig? I'm ready to settle for Clifton Webb."

"Come, come, SamSweetheart . . ." She'd caught herself before finishing SamSam . . . "Don't manipulate my sympathies; you're too good at it, and I'm too on to it. I, for example, can see Leslie Howard. Or Joseph Cotten. Even Rex Harrison."

"I must say that's an improvement, but I doubt they'd be right. Clever, yes, but hardly minor, or prigs. Not if their agents could help it."

Rocky finished wiping the brandy with her open palm, which she rubbed on her blue shirt. Then she moved the hand to her neck, and half scratched, half stroked it, then to her clavicle, then to her breastbone. The movement caused her shirt to gap, and he noticed for the first time that the top three snaps of the shirt were undone. Again, he forced his eyes up to her face.

"Well, Samuel," she said. "For Christ's sake, you're forty years old, the ending hasn't been written yet!"

"No," he answered, "But you don't really expect any surprises, do you?"

"Do *I* expect? Sam, the question is what do *you* expect?"

"You mean, will I stand up in the waterfront bar and thrash the bully who disparages my hometown? Instead of letting a mere slip of a girl do it?"

"No, I don't mean that. I mean will you take the time and the pain and the juice to make your life more than just a clever one-liner?"

"You mean a clever, *minor* one-liner."

"Why, Sam, is there any such thing as a *major* one-liner? And is your glass empty? Mine is."

He was astounded at the speed with which she'd finished hers. He looked down at his; he'd done almost as well. He was beginning to feel the glow of it. He looked over at her. She had the creamiest skin, especially at the neck where the shirt was open; it was soft, unblemished, clear. It seemed to be lit from within, and from the way she was downing the brandy, it probably *was* lit from within.

If he could see the alcohol at work on her, she could see it on him. She looked at the lean face, with its square jaw; Sam had complained that he looked like an FBI man, and so he did. Except for something in the eyes. Something that at the best of times was deep and kind and questioning, that seemed to see both sides of an issue or a fight. That at the worst of times looked weak, indecisive, with no inner direction, but a vacillating, a what-do-you-expect-of-me expression. She'd seen that look in the bar; he hadn't known what to do. His own instincts had told him nothing.

"Another," she said, impatiently. "Or do I have one alone?"

"Yes, another. But just a little." He handed her the glass, and as she was taking it, added: "I don't want to write my own ending. That's the problem. I want someone else to do it for me. I like to be surprised."

She snorted, and walked away. He let himself stare, at the worn, high-cut-off jeans, the full buttocks, the solid thighs, the big calves, the strong back, the broad shoulders. She poured the brandy, letting it plop into the snifters, more than she'd had last time. She turned back.

"You mean there's a divinity that shapes our ends."

Schroeder took the glass, laughed, and stared at her. "I was almost going to say, there sure was a divinity that shaped *your* end. But I decided against it."

She threw herself onto the sofa, this time right near him,

though this time, miraculously, the brandy stayed in the snifter. She tucked both legs up, took a gulp from her drink and fixed him with a look of friendly contempt.

"Clever, minor, prig? That didn't quite get to it, Sam dear. There's something else has to go in there. Maybe not quite coward, but cautious, equivocating, tiptoeing. Something a hell of a lot *like* coward." And she raised her glass, not sure if in tribute to her perception or to seal the putdown of Schroeder.

He held his up, too. "Why, thank you, Madame. Stoney always said you admired me, and I didn't believe him. I wonder where I could have gotten that idea?" He threw Stoney out as a red herring, to get her off the scent, but she wasn't having it. She took another drink.

"You want to pay me a lecherous compliment, do it!" she announced. "I won't tell Stoney on you. In fact I like it. You want to be strong and silent, OK, keep your mouth shut. But don't try to have it both ways, by telling me you like my ass, and then saying you're *not* going to tell me! Goddammit, Sam, that's the way you do everything!"

She didn't know why in hell she was attacking this man this way. She *liked* him. She needed his company. Why? Maybe to keep him there, to keep him attached. In pain, but attached. Maybe, thanks to her dear husband, she'd lost the ability to talk to a man without a machete in hand. Maybe she was just enjoying it. She took another drink, too much, too fast, and coughed. She was surging with anger, more directed at herself than at him. Inside she felt a little like a fishwife, yet something wouldn't let her stop.

"My, this is flattering," he answered. "I'm not used to getting to people this way. I really must have hit something."

Maybe if he had simply said, cut it out, she would have stopped. His answer only made her angrier. "Oh, boo! Boo!" she yelled. "From freshman logic to sophomore psychoanalysis. More evasiveness. More games-playing bullshit. No wonder you don't get to people! I can't get a simple yes or no on my ass, right? Want to venture an opinion on my tits? Oh, beg pardon, bosom. I saw you looking, Sam, and making yourself look away! How about it?"

Unsteadily, she put her snifter down, and stared down at her chest. Then with a movement so quick and decisive that Schroeder couldn't do a thing about it, she ripped all the snaps open, pulled the shirt apart and out of her shorts, revealing her bare breasts. This time he was too startled to command himself not to look. Her breasts were as tanned as the rest of her, nipples surprisingly big and dark; the full, slightly pendulous breasts of a thirty-year-old mother.

"Do you like them, Sam? Say something nice. Something straight."

He stood up quickly. "I think I'd better go, Rocky." Without waiting for an answer, he turned and headed for the door. He'd reached it and begun to turn the knob when she spoke.

"Please, Sam, don't! Please!" The panic in her voice made him look back. She'd jammed her shirt together and was tucking it into her shorts, as she ran toward him. She grabbed his arm. She could not be alone; she'd just spent a week in this house, alone with a five-year-old daughter who was too young to talk with and a bottle of brandy that never said anything but yes. She'd wanted to shock Schroeder; he was, or pretended to be, so straight-laced. But she didn't want him to go. She wouldn't release his arm.

"I'll tell you what I like about you. I'll tell you what I don't like about your friend and my husband, Stoney. I'll tell you what I *hate* about myself. I'll never unbutton again. But please, I'm not sleepy and I can't handle another evening by myself. Please, I need you to stay."

His hand still on the door, Schroeder looked at her uncertainly.

"Please!"

He let the pressure of her grip on his arm pull his hand from the door. She grabbed the hand and tugged at it, leading him back toward the sofa. He let himself be led. They sat down again, Rocky at once starting to refasten the snaps on her shirt, Schroeder unwillingly watching her as she did. The rich tan of those breasts stayed in his mind, with it the even richer image of her lying in the sun, naked, to get the tan. He thought of the chocolate brown—bittersweet—of the nipples, the slight, sexy sag. He remembered it well.

"There," she said, finishing and looking up. "Now, let's talk about anything you want."

"OK, but starting here, the only thing you are to bare is your soul. Making a clean breast of it is to remain a figure of speech."

Ah, but he was interested, she saw it in his face, she heard it in his wordplay. Always wordplay, the all-purpose cover for Sam Schroeder.

"Can't control the jokes, can you?" she asked, because she didn't want to deal with the sexual part of it any more than he did. Just know it was there, as he did.

"Why should I?" he replied. "Haven't you ever heard the expression, ah, but that a man's speech should exceed his grasp, or what's a metaphor? Get it?"

"I get the childishness of a forty-year-old who keeps playing word games, personally and professionally, because he doesn't have the balls to put away childish things. And that is, I'm sure, a mixed metaphor, for which I apologize." She waited for an answer. Nothing. She took another swig of brandy, and added: "Want more?"

"Of what?" he asked. "The brandy or the beating? Either way my glass runneth over."

She'd pushed him again, she didn't know why, whether it was she or he. But she knew she dreaded his leaving. "OK, OK," she said quickly. "We'll talk about anything you want and won't talk about anything you don't want."

But she'd angered him, and he, buoyed by the brandy, was not to be so easily pacified. "Hell, I'm egocentric enough not to mind being the subject, but since you've already called me a coward six different ways, is there any point to going on? Except for you to show off your repertoire? Which is not all that interesting, by the way. For someone immersed in the fine sensibility of Henry James, you can be awfully crude. And dull! You show me either your fangs or your tits. Don't I have any other choice?"

Her face flushed as if he'd slapped it.

"Hurts, huh? At least I didn't call you cautious, tiptoeing, a prig, a coward, with no balls. Maybe you're lucky. Just think what I might have said if I *had* balls." He paused, softened. "You see, I get hurt, too. And I swing back. And now that we've both proved we can draw blood and shed it, let's stop. Let's say something nice to each other—if we can come up with anything."

Her face was still flushed behind its tan, so he went on. "I'll go first. You've got lovely tits and a marvelous ass. As the song from *The Mikado* goes, 'Were you not to Ko-Ko plighted . . .' and so on. There, a straightforward compliment, no backhands, no metaphors. Now you."

She smiled, her face relaxed. "Oh, it's easy, Sam. You're gentle, and God, how wonderful that is. You're smart, and funny, and great company. And damned attractive, although your decorous attire keeps me from matching your compliment for specifics." And then quickly added, "And of course we're going to keep it that way."

"My God, what a terrific list!" he said.

"Shut up," she replied with mock ferocity. "There's more."

"Go on," he said. "I've got all the time in the world."

"All right, here's the best thing about you: You listen to a woman. You take her seriously. Not only me. I've seen you do it with your wife, even when you weren't getting along. With Jane. You know, Sam, not many men do that. Stoney doesn't. Not in all six years we've known each other. Not once in all that time has he ever really listened to a single opinion of mine on an abstract or, quote, 'serious,' subject. Not once. He doesn't care what I, or any other woman, thinks about politics, life, death, busing, morality, the Middle East, finance—especially not finance—and on and on. He'll never ask. And if a woman volunteers an opinion, he doesn't listen. *Unless,* unless, he's trying to make her."

She'd been working at the brandy; her snifter was almost empty. "You know, I'm smart, Sam, and well educated, in many ways better than Stoney. Coming from a family of lawyers, he knew what he was going to do before he started college, and in some ways he treated it as a kind of pre-law vocational school. You know, he stressed political science, economics, the things he figured a lawyer would need. But in literature, or music, or art, or philosophy, he's virtually illiterate. I, on the other hand, was graduated *magna cum laude,* I have a master's in American literature and damned near all my doctoral credits. I was well into my dissertation when I met him. And I got knocked up, and got married—I wanted to, I wanted to have the baby, I'm not blaming him for that. Of course, I stopped studying and started being nursemaid and housewife. Which I mildly resented, since it was not a financial necessity—he just felt a woman should rear her own child, tend to her own house. But what I resented a lot more was that it never even occurred to Stoney that I might mind! He never once asked! Never once suggested ways I might continue to take courses. For him, it was just natural and inevitable for the woman to drop everything to take over the house. Küchen und Kinder."

She took a pause to catch her breath and stared at him. To herself she was beginning to sound like a fishwife. She should stop. With long fingers, she reached for her snifter again. Schroeder looked at the fingers, with their nails cut square and unpolished. No garbage on them. Elegant, beautifully formed. Caressing the glass. Sexy.

Before putting the glass to her lips, she said: "Do I sound like I'm overreacting? Believe me, I'm not." Then she tilted it to her mouth, but there was no more brandy in it.

"I'm going for more," she said, and ran to the bar; she was in a fever to say more, hungry to be listened to. She returned quickly, the snifter almost full, and sloshed some of the liquid from her glass into his.

"Have it, please," she begged. "I'm trying to keep this spell going, to keep you listening. I'm not used to having a man pay attention to my, quote, 'serious' thoughts. It's intoxicating."

"That, and the brandy," said Schroeder with a smile. He took a tiny sip, enough to show he was with her, not enough to add much to his own haziness. How in hell did she do it? he wondered. She'd had twice as much as he since he'd been there, and God knows how much before.

She'd guessed what he was thinking. "Brandy's become my modus vivendi. I have a couple everyday, and I consume three or four bottles sub rosa for every official bottle."

"What is an official bottle?" he asked.

"Official ones are those Stoney gets as part of his monthly booze order. The others are the ones Rocky buys, for cash, at liquor stores where the estimable Mr. Cobb isn't known. But let me finish. Don't get me off on shopping lists, because after that, the next tangent is recipes. And how to get your husband's white shirts clean—no ring around the collar."

Her face glowed from the brandy and the suntan, but her eyes were focused and intense. She was right, he thought, the intoxication *was* from the talk. Hers was, anyway. "Go on," he said. "I'm not leaving. I'm listening."

Abruptly, she leaned forward and kissed him, half on the cheek, half on the mouth. "A sisterly kiss," she said, looking happy. "No, I take that back. From one human to a fellow human."

Then, "See that? A *fellow* human. *Man*kind. All those masculine terms to refer to the entire species. No, Sam, no, it's not just a way of speaking; it's a way of thinking. *We* are people. *You* are something else. Now I'm not for a moment suggesting my dear husband singles out women to look down on. His xenophobia has a whole hierarchy to it. Whites are better than other colors; Americans better than other whites, New Englanders better than other Americans. Real New Englanders of course, WASPs, not Portugees or Canucks or Dagoes. Jews, he has a certain reluctant admiration for, I've got to grant him that. But, and here's the shittiest part—and the part that'll sound like more overkill—women are on the bottom rung, when it comes to, quote, 'serious' matters. Even the lowliest, most despised on the male pecking order—and there I leave the pun to you—rates higher than the most highborn Boston WASP, if she's a she."

She took another swallow of her drink. "It's carefully cloaked, mind you," she continued. "The man is terribly clever and sophisticated about it. But it's there. And I live with it. And with *this*." She held up the glass. "This is the liquid with which I down my bitter pills."

Rocky took a deep breath, told herself she was going too far, that even if this was truth, Sam was learning more about it than he cared to know, that she was coming off witchy, shrewish. Told herself, and then kept talking.

"OK, now the peroration. Stoney detests women. When I told him that, he got furious; he thought I was accusing him of being gay. He told me how he loved women, the little darlings. And oh, yes, I believe that. He does love them—every chance he gets. I may get to that. I may get to everything tonight, Sammy. He loves the little darlings as China dolls, accessories, child-bearers, housekeepers, cooks, dancing partners, secretaries. Most of all as receptacles, holes. I know it'll shock you, Sam, but I want to. As cunts. That awful, demeaning term, when it's used to describe an entire woman."

She saw the repugnance on his face. "Sorry about that, Sam. But you must understand, must feel the anger, the humiliation, I feel."

He was embarrassed to hear the word. He was also saddened to see this "perfect" marriage crumble into such hatred. He just shook his head. If those two couldn't make it, who in hell could? No, he didn't believe all the things she said about Stoney. But he believed *she* believed them; he believed she hated him enough to say them and mean them. And loved him enough, too.

Much as that sounded like soap opera. For he knew that when he stopped really caring for his wife, he stopped hating her so hard, too. And Rocky still hated Stoney pretty hard. To her, he said nothing.

"That's right, baby," she said. "Be cool. Be noncommittal. Don't take risks. Don't take sides. Don't sweat, it might crease your suit." She'd just seen him the way, in his worst moments, he saw himself, and it infuriated him.

He took a sip of his drink and then punched back. "First of all, I'm not wearing a suit. Maybe I always look as if I am, to you and a lot of other people. Well, all I can say is I'm god-damned tired of apologizing. You can all fuck off. What would please you, anyway? Want me to say you're a wonderful, long-suffering, unappreciated woman and he's a male chauvinist shit? OK, it's said. Want me to say you're a spoiled, overprotected brat, sitting home lapping up brandy and knocking a superhubby because some blueplate special you ordered from the world hasn't been served to you? OK to that, too. Want me to say marriages can't work? Can work? That you should split? Not split? OK to all of it, because I don't know the right answers. I don't know for me, or for you, or for anyone.

"You want some simple rules, some—what did you call it, dime-store analysis—? There's a bookstore on Main Street where you can find it. They have The Joy of . . . Everything. Living, Dying, Cooking, Fasting, Running, Walking, Fucking, Aging. Pick your Joy. You want a better audience for your maudlin, brandy-soaked monologue? Get one. I'm Cool Sam, the linear lout, unfit for group therapy, group sex, consciousness expanding, mind boggling, blood letting, ego rinsing and all the other current hots. And I apologize for it. For everything. Said and unsaid, express and implied. And I rise to tell you: Fuck off and good-night."

He almost made it to his feet, wobbling, pushing up with his hands, flexing his thigh muscles to do the job, but not quite, for Rocky, who'd been sitting on her haunches, moved faster, leaned over him, put both hands on the sides of his face and kissed him on the mouth. Her mouth was open, her saliva eighty proof, warm and tasty. He couldn't move, and began not to want to. She took her mouth away.

"Why, Sam," she said. "Did anyone ever tell you you're beautiful when you're angry?"

"Uh uh," was all he could manage. "Uh uh."

"It's true, Sam, it's true."

That was not what he'd said uh uh to. "Get away," he told her, remembering what he was so angry at. "You might wrinkle the suit."

She remained kneeling over him, and put her hands on his chest. "May I, Sam? May I wrinkle it?"

"Get your hands off me, or big as you are, I'll knock you on your ass."

"OK, OK!" She jumped back to her old position on the sofa, making a show of obedience. He could not leave, he must not. There was more she had to say, and she was getting to it, getting close. He must not leave now. "Talk," she said. "*Only* talk. Please stay. OK?"

"OK," he repeated, wondering if he sounded as fuzzy as he felt, wondering how in hell she stayed so frisky, resolving that one of those moments, he'd have to get organized. And leave.

"We'll *talk* about sex," she said. "But that's all. You want to go first, or shall I?" Before he could answer, she said "I'll go first."

Briskly, she reached for her snifter and took another drink, then pointed to his glass, which was empty. "God no," he said. "How do you do it?"

"Practice," she answered. "Practice makes perfect—except in the area we are about to discuss—and I go first. Sex. Stoney cannot fuck worth a damn." Why am I saying this, and in this way? she asked herself as soon as she'd said it.

Schroeder wondered about it, too, and didn't want to hear it—not the profanity, which upset him coming from someone like Rocky, not the intimate details of his friends' lives in bed, together or separately. Yet he couldn't stop her anymore than she could stop herself, partly because he was as fascinated as he was repelled, partly because he was reaching the point where he found it tough to say no—or yes, or anything else. He was close to being smashed, stoned, crocked, ossified, blotto, petrified, tipsy, bombed. By any name, drunk.

And, his equivocal reluctance to hear was no match for her determination to tell.

"To Stoney, a woman's clitoris is excess baggage, a vestigial organ, like an appendix. He doesn't know what it's there for."

He didn't know he was ossified, petrified, crocked, bombed,

or whatever enough for this. "Why, Rocky? Must you do this? Isn't there a goddamned Supreme Court decision against invasion of your own privacy? I mean, I'm no prude . . ."

"No," she interrupted, looking angry and offended. "You're not afraid of dirty words and dirty thoughts. You're afraid of *intimate* words and thoughts. Don't anybody open up to Sam Schroeder because he won't, can't, open up to you, and it might make him feel deficient. I don't care about the Supreme Court. I *want* invasion of my privacy. I'm begging for it. My privacy is so uninvaded, I can't stand it. You know how lonely it can be in your private garden? Yes you do, Sam, I know you do. And you don't like it, you can't. Don't hold it against me that you can't throw open the gates. Don't keep me from trying it, please!"

Drunk and miserable, he knew she'd had enough strength to knock the breath out of him. As soon as he got it back, he hit back. "What have we been calling it, dime-store analysis? And so fucking facile we can even sling it on half a bottle of brandy? And what's the conclusion? That anyone who doesn't want to hear us spill our pickled guts about our unhappy sex life has got to be sick. What bullshit!" Without thinking, Schroeder took the last sip of his brandy, and felt, as it went down, he'd gone way beyond his capacity; he tilted his head back on the sofa.

Rocky's eyes filled with tears. "I'm sitting here begging you to listen to me. And you just won't, will you? All right, get the hell out! I guess the Schroeder fortress is just too threatened. What the hell have you got in there, anyway, Sam? No, never mind, I don't want to know. Go on, escape. Run. Get out!"

Dizzy, Schroeder pitched his body forward to get his dead weight off the sofa, and as he was about to fall, with a hand on the coffee table, he managed to get his legs under him and stagger toward the door. He groped his way along the boardwalk toward his car.

Rocky watched from the sofa. Neither had said a word since she'd shouted, "Get out!" Both knew that had she said, instead, "Stay and make love to me!" he'd have done that.

Chapter

5

EVERYONE CALLED HIM MR. B., BUT ALMOST NO ONE WAS sure what the B stood for. Some thought it was for Mr. Boston, some for Mr. Big, in both instances because of his prominence. In fact, B was the first letter of his second name, but no one used that except the newspapers, and they used it so rarely and for such august reasons, that very few connected the name with Mr. B. Actually, when the name did appear in print, in connection with a charity ball, or some arts committee, or for other civic reasons, it has a "Mrs." in front of it, for his wife involved herself in things like that. She was *never* called Mrs. B. And she never lent her name to any cause without her husband's approval. In his sphere, no one did *anything* without Mr. B.'s approval.

Except, as Mr. B. put it himself, angrily, "that idiot, Henry O'Brien," and "that bastard, that traitor, down in Florida," who sent O'Brien the notebook.

Mr. B. knew O'Brien was dead, of course, and knew it was no accident. Not that he had ordered it, not exactly. He didn't order things like that. He didn't even suggest them. His tactic was to let others suggest them, and then not to say no to the suggestion.

So O'Brien was taken care of; the traitor down in Florida was as good as taken care of. But the notebook was not. By Friday afternoon, hardly more than twelve hours after O'Brien's death, Mr. B. knew the notebook was *not* in the special prosecutor's office; that was easy. Nor in his apartment; almost as easy. On the other hand, they didn't know where it *was*, and that wouldn't do.

Guccis up on his ivory-inlaid teak desk, Mr. B. was telling the man with the hoarse voice it wouldn't do, and letting him work his slow way around to the conclusion that Mr. B. had reached hours earlier.

"Think out loud," he told the hoarse voice. "Let me hear your thinking on this."

"Well, if the guy had no friends," said the voice, "that would narrow it down to the people on his staff . . ." he hesitated, waiting for a reaction.

All he got was, "Yes, go on."

"And since we got a pipeline to his staff, we know there's no one there to worry about, except . . ." He barely paused this time, when Mr. B. jumped in impatiently with, "Go on, go on."

"For his daughter. We figure if we find her, we find the notebook."

"I like your thinking," said Mr. B., which encouraged the man with the hoarse voice.

"When we find the notebook, what do we do with it? You want it?"

This annoyed Mr. B. "Don't be ridiculous. That is a book *nobody* wants, nobody needs, nobody should have. That book should not *exist*. Do I have to spell everything out?"

"No, no, I got ya." The hoarse voice said this quickly; he did not want to ruffle Mr. B. No one did. "The book will disappear."

"And?" said Mr. B.

The hoarse voice pondered for a moment; he hated to have to ask, "And what?"

"Supposing the book doesn't only exist on paper?"

Again he thought, again he came up with nothing; reluctantly, he asked again: "What do you mean?"

"Supposing the book also exists, in whole or in part, in the memory of the person who possesses it?"

"Oh, you mean the daughter!" The hoarse voice jumped at it. Silence.

"Then she's gotta disappear, too."

"Leave me out of that kind of thinking," said Mr. B. And he hung up the phone gently, shaking his head at how long it took those people to understand anything, at how much time he had to waste on trivia, when he had so many important matters to deal with.

At the other end of the phone, the man with the hoarse voice felt a little nervous and put down, as he usually did after a conversation with Mr. B. The son of a bitch never says good-bye, he thought. Just hangs up. His nervousness turned to anger.

He got up, stuck his head out of his cubbyhole of an office, and yelled: "Hey, Red, get the fuck in here!"

With insolent slowness, Red looked up, then put down the wrench he was using, then wiped his hands, then turned and sauntered toward the office. He was huge and beefy, his short-sleeved shirt showing off a pair of oversized, tattooed arms. Red was neither classy, nor charming, but he did the job. You did not use him for anything delicate. If you wanted a politician's wife seduced to get information, you didn't use Red. If you wanted her teeth knocked out to get information, you used Red. He was cunning, fairly bright—he'd actually been to college for a term or two. He was mean. He was loyal only out of fear, and the hoarse-voiced man was sure Red was after his job. But Red got things done; he'd taken care of the O'Brien matter. Hoarse voice did not like Red, but used him.

"Where's O'Brien's daughter?"

"How the fuck should I know?" Red answered. Red reminded himself how little he thought of this dumb prick.

"What I mean is, you gotta find out. Right away. You can do that, can't you? What I mean is, you got enough friends who can find out, don't you?"

"Yeah, yeah," Red answered. "I did all right with O'Brien,

didn't I? Anybody got any complaints?"

Hoarse voice hated the way Red could put him on the defensive. "No, no complaints. Just find out where she is, right away."

"OK," said Red, and turned to leave.

"And the notebook, the black one you couldn't find at O'Brien's apartment."

Red didn't like that. "The goddamned thing wasn't there, or else we would have found it. How many times have I got to tell you that?"

The hoarse voice was pleased; now Red was defending himself, instead of attacking.

"Just go find the girl. And the notebook."

Red walked out without saying another word. He used the phone out in the big room of the shop. He resented having to spend time working in the shop. He resented not having an office. He resented hoarse voice having the job that should be his, that *would* be his, someday, if he could help it.

Red took the direct route; he plugged into the police investigation, which was easy. He had a lot of friends in the department. He had to make four or five calls to find out which of his friends was closest to the O'Brien investigation. And he was lucky; one was *very* close. The problem was, the police didn't yet know where she was either.

They did know where she wasn't, though. She wasn't at her father's office; she wasn't at home, although she'd told one of her father's lawyers she was going home. From him, the police got a description of the girl and what she was wearing: T-shirt, light tan painter's pants, blue sneakers, large brown shabby purse. She wasn't at her father's apartment, or at her boyfriend's. She hadn't shown up for her scheduled interview with the homicide detective. The police asked the staff lawyer, Friendly, and the boyfriend, Janowitz, to call as soon as they heard from her. But the police weren't actually looking for her. They had no reason to.

Red's friend assured him he'd hear as soon as the police did. And they had some photos of her. Red drove right over to get them. Then he walked back into the office of the hoarse-voiced man. He didn't knock because he did not want to show any respect for his superior, whom he considered superior only in rank, not in brains or toughness.

All he said was, "We're working on it; we'll having something real soon." Then he got out of sight, so hoarse voice wouldn't ask why he wasn't out "busting his ass," which was one of the man's favorite expressions. All Red actually did was wait for the phone to ring. After an hour, just when he was starting to get fidgety, the phone did ring, and he got the word.

Janowitz, the boyfriend, had called, as the police had told him to do. Felicia O'Brien had phoned him from the airport; she was headed for Nantucket, in fact the flight she was on would be landing just about now.

Smugly, Red reported the information to his boss. He'd delivered again, he told himself. "You want me to get her?"

"Yeah, her and the notebook."

"Bring them back?"

"Just the notebook."

"I'll take Mike with me."

"OK. What are you gonna need?"

"We've got to charter a plane, to get there fast. And a car, maybe one that can go on beaches, too, like a Jeep or a Land-Rover. And a power boat to get off the island, and take care of the girl."

"Jesus," said the hoarse voiced man, "that sounds like a lotta dough. You need a plane? You need a boat?"

"What the hell is this?" answered Red, disgustedly, "Filene's basement? I need the plane to get there in a hurry. She's already on her way there, understand? I need the boat because it's the best way to dispose of her. If they don't find a body, they'll think she's gone off somewhere, for a vacation, for a retreat, to get away from it all, to recover from her father's horrible accident, see? They can think anything. If they *find* her body, two O'Brien bodies in two days, they're going to start some heavy sniffing around, even if we do have a lot of friends. Understand? That's why we need a boat. We need the Jeep or Land-Rover because we may have to go off roads, onto the beach, or somewhere. Besides, I like to drive them; I like the four-wheel drive. I tell you what, I'll pay the difference between a Land-Rover and an Aspen out of my own pocket. OK?"

"Just do the job, and save the wise-ass cracks, OK?" Hoarse voice growled it, even deeper than usual. "Just get goin'."

Red gave him a contemptuous look, turned, and started walking away.

"Wait a minute, Red," came a shout from hoarse voice. "Take the Pussycat with you, too."

"Oh, no," said Red. "Not that fat old fart! What the hell are we going to do with him? He's fucking useless!"

"I don't care what you do with him. Let him polish the brass on that boat you're gonna rent for a goddamned fortune! *Take* him."

"Oh, shit."

"I said take him."

Without another word, Red turned and stomped out. Hoarse voice smiled. There was only one reason the Pussycat was going. And it was not that they needed him. Not that he had any special ability, or could be useful. In fact, Pussycat wasn't useful for much anymore, just an old guy, fat, not too smart, who'd done some decent work years ago that hadn't taken much brains. The one reason was that Red didn't like him. And that was reason enough.

In his mind, Red gave his boss the finger, but he didn't really have much time to bother with that; he had to move fast. First he got hold of Mike and told him to get ready. Then he worked on the rentals. Red had this down to a science. Always rent from a legitimate source, but using phony identification. Red was ready with a beautiful-looking driver's license and credit cards, all bearing a fictitious name. Then you never had the complication of a stolen car, or boat, or plane.

Red called someone he knew who chartered small planes. He had to have one ready to fly to Nantucket in less than an hour. It could be done. The boat charter, he had to work through two people, but he found one. He'd take a twenty-eight-footer, single screw, but the bill would be made out for a thirty-two-footer with twin props. The vehicle, which turned out to be a Land-Rover, took a couple of extra calls. Red would get his customary kickbacks. Maybe as much as five hundred dollars on the three. Not bad.

And how bad could this job be? Red asked himself. A frightened girl, who had no friends—her boyfriend had told the cops that—alone on an island, where she knew no one, where she'd never been. Never been! Why even Red had been there a couple of times. How many places could she go? To the town itself? Tiny place. Where would she stay? Hotel or rooming house? They'd look for the cabbie who drove her. She'd have to go out to eat. They'd look for her. They'd find her. Chances for getting off the island were limited to ferry or plane. The stupid kid had made it easy for them, he thought. She'd trapped herself. If she'd gone to New York, they'd never have found her. But she was a frightened amateur. And he was a pro.

And Mike was passable. But Pussycat was a stupid asshole who should have been put out of his misery a long time ago. He was too old, too dumb, too fat, too squeamish. He had the build of a Sumo wrestler and the brains of a gorilla. No, Red thought, Pussycat didn't like the work—if he ever had.

Mike showed up in a few more minutes. They called him Black Mike because he was so swarthy. Red had once accused him of being "half nigger and half spic." It was one of several reasons Mike didn't like him. He did respect him, and was a little afraid of him—not so much physically, although Red was two inches taller and about twenty pounds heavier. Mike was careful because he was pushing forty, knew that Red might be his boss someday, and didn't want to antagonize him. One thing Mike hated was the way Red put down Pussycat, but he never challenged Red on it.

"Hey, go get the fat old fart, " Red ordered Mike, pointing to the garage next door, where Pussycat hung around and helped out. In a couple of minutes Mike returned with the old man, Pussycat wheezing with the effort of squeezing his bulk through the small, low connecting door.

Red loathed the old man, but restrained himself from showing it to the man's face because Pussycat had a reputation for toughness, his age notwithstanding. Even though his five-foot-eight-inch, 225-pound frame now had a lot of flab on it, he was built like a bulldozer, and it would take a bulldozer to budge him if he didn't want to be budged.

"The boss wants you to go to Nantucket with us," Red said. "Any reason you can't?" He hoped there might be.

"You want me to go, I go." The Pussycat's voice strained through a deviated septum. Actually, he was anxious to be asked, pleased to be given something to do, to feel useful, both for the sake of his pride and because his line of work was not noted for its pension plans. "You don't want me to go, I don't go."

"All right," said Red. "We fly there. We put you on a boat. You just sit there and hold the fort."

"Waddya mean, hold the fort?"

"The *boss* wants you to go," said Red, ignoring the question.

"And we're leaving right away. Get ready. And don't slow us down."

"Yeah, yeah." The Pussycat hurried off to get his satchel and some stuff. He was a good soldier. When he returned, Red made a show of sitting around for a few minutes, just to humiliate him. Then the three men drove to the airport.

Chapter

SCHROEDER AWOKE A LITTLE AFTER TEN AND WAITED A couple of minutes, checking out the state of his mind and body before trying to get up. Not so bad, he told himself, better than he expected, better than he deserved. He stood up. Not so good, either. Dizzy in the head, queasy in the stomach. He tried to ignore it, put on a robe, looked at himself in the mirror over his dresser.

He decided he looked no better than he felt. He saw a middle-aged man, who looked not only forty, but older, baggy-eyed, slack skin beginning under the chin and jaw, a touch of jowls, more gray hair then ever.

Trying to think brisk, he strode into the living room and said, "Good morning" as vigorously as he could manage.

His mother returned a bright, "Good morning!"

Bobby and Patty, bent over a Monopoly set in the middle of the floor, offered something like "Uh."

He looked at them for a moment. "After that," he said, "I go directly back to bed. I do not pass Go, I do not collect a hundred dollars."

"It's two hundred dollars, daddy," said Bobby.

"Well, if you don't collect it, it hardly matters, does it? But I'm glad to hear you can talk, Bobby. And how about you, sweetheart?"

"I said good morning, daddy," his daughter replied.

"Oh, it sounded like 'uh,' but my ears don't work too well in the morning."

He gave up on that and turned to his mother. "How did you sleep?"

"All right." Schroeder had a feeling that his mother was afraid to let on that anything went well, lest she jinx herself. The "all right" he knew meant things could have been better but why complain. But he was damned if he'd invite her to complain. He saw in her hand the same "revealing" paperback she'd been reading last night. Evidently she'd gone a long way through it.

"How's the book?" he asked

"Oh, just awful. I don't see how anybody can say those things." A smile escaped from her moral sternness.

He hadn't read it, but from what he'd read about it, it was the lurid memoir of the daughter of famous Hollywood people, who by the time she was fifteen had been a bed wetter, boozer, hooker, junkie, home wrecker, and who now considered herself a social philosopher. She was getting high marks and a couple of hundred thousand dollars for telling all, explicitly, but in a tone of modestly lowered eyelids. On talk shows the author discussed her accomplishment as if it were comparable to discovering radium or saving France, and she couldn't decide if Madame Curie or Joan of Arc were more her style.

"You look like you're moving through it pretty fast, mom."

"It's such trash. Anybody could write something like this, as long as she has a dirty enough mind."

"I wish I could; she's going to make a quarter of a million out of it—maybe more."

"Well, why don't you?"

"I guess I don't have a dirty enough mind. Anyone want

breakfast?" He looked toward his children.

"We ate, daddy," Patty said. "An hour ago."

She made it sound like a reproach, Schroeder thought. "What did you eat?" he asked.

"Grandma made us fried eggs and bacon," said his son.

"Sunny side up?" he asked. "With buttered toast? And marmalade?"

"Yup," said Bobby.

"I hope you had your juice and milk."

"Yes, daddy." They said it together, in the put-upon intonation they'd come to use so often since the divorce.

Schroeder was used to it. Even more used to the fried eggs, sunny side up, with bacon, toast, marmalade. And juice and milk. Later, the milk gave way to coffee. His mother's class-A breakfast, for Sundays, holidays, visitors, vacations and other state occasions. The eggs never scrambled, poached, boiled, omeleted, or even over. The toast always white, always buttered, always with marmalade. Never brown, or pumpernickel, or rolls, or croissants, or corn bread, never grape jelly, or strawberry jam, or currant, or beach plum, or guava. Always three strips of bacon, never two or four, and never sausage. And he'd never discussed it with her, never asked why she thought her menu the best of all possible breakfasts. He'd never once, as man or boy, asked, mom, why not something different? Just for the hell of it.

He'd ruminated on all this while standing and staring at his mother, a look of amusement on his face. Finally she asked, "Why are you looking at me that way?"

The question startled him; then, to his surprise he noticed pleasure on her face. She was delighted with the attention from him; she didn't get much of it.

His smile widened. "Oh, the breakfast," he said.

"It's the same breakfast I always make," she said.

He wanted to laugh but didn't. Just said: "Yes, I know." Didn't add: That's the point. He'd said so little to her in the last few years—perhaps in the last many years—he didn't want this small intimacy to turn into a put-down. He added, instead: "It was always my favorite."

"Good," she said, putting down the book. "I'll make the entire menu for you." She started to rise from the rocker.

"No, mom. Thanks," he said. "I've gotten out of the habit of big breakfasts. All I want is some coffee, which I'll make my-self." He turned toward the kitchen; she kept rising, and fol-lowed him into the kitchen.

"Why just coffee?" she asked.

"Because I'm not hungry. It's all I want."

"That's no way to start the day. Let me make you a decent breakfast."

"Today I'll have an indecent breakfast," he answered firmly. "Coffee is all I want, mother, and I can make it myself. Go on, you sit down and take it easy. Go ahead and read your book. I'll bet there are still perversions to come."

His mother shook her head and walked away. The intimacy he'd felt about the breakfast had dissipated itself into the kind of mild intolerance with which he usually fended her off.

Waiting for the water to boil, he pushed aside the striped cur-tains on the kitchen window and stared out. The day was mild, but dark, gray, windy, a light rain sprinkling.

Three beach days a year suited Schroeder. After that, lying in the sun and turning, like a pig on a spit, to get roasted evenly, bored him. A day like this was a good reason for staying away from the beach, for going on a long, exhausting hike. Which was what he'd do. He measured some instant coffee into a cup, poured hot water on it, and added a little milk.

"Who wants to go on a thrilling hike through the wind and the rain? Down dirt roads, over moors, along beaches!" He turned on a mechanical enthusiasm, designed to dissuade rather than entice. Not that real enthusiasm would have changed the result.

"Are you kidding?" said Bobby.

"Yech!" said Patty.

He just nodded. Looked at his mother, who obviously hadn't thought the question was even aimed at her. "I wish I could," she said.

"Why can't you?" he asked.

"Because I'm too old." Her tone seemed combative, as if his question had been an accusation. And in a sense it had.

"Mom, did you used to take long hikes when you were younger?" He tried to make it sound friendly, but they both knew it was smart-ass. He wasn't sure why he'd asked it, why he was so unwilling to let her get away with a small thing like that.

He supposed it was something he'd done often. Usually she

let it go. This time she struck back; she put the paper back down and clasped her thin, veined hands. "Sam, tell me why it is that when you talk at all, you're critical? Do you think you're so much better than other people? Ever since you were in college you've had a way of letting people know they weren't as clever as you." She was angry, angry enough to say this in front of his children; he couldn't remember ever having seen her do something like this before. Not since he'd been an adult, anyway. He had no answer at hand, and while he was groping, she went on.

"Why are you running off? Do you see so much of the children? Of me? You don't really want us to go with you, do you? I can hear it in your voice. Why aren't you spending this time with us?"

He tried to make his answer sound sincere, but he was slanting off on an angle and he knew it. "I *do* want you to go."

She knew it, too. "Why don't you stay *here,* and chat with us?"

"Kids," he announced, "Why don't you stop the game now and let's talk about things?"

"We can't, daddy," answered Patty, sounding annoyed.

"We're right in the middle," said Bobby, picking up his tone from his sister.

He looked at his mother and shrugged. "There's a groundswell for me to hike."

She was not going to let him off. "We haven't had a talk for a long time." Maybe never, mom, maybe never, he said to himself. "Let's do it tonight," he said to her. "It'll give me a chance to hike and you a chance to finish up the life of Joan of Arc."

"Who?" she said.

"Just a bad joke, mom." He leaned over, patted her book, and kissed her on the top of the head.

"All right, let's try tonight," she answered.

"It's going to take me ten minutes to get ready," he announced, as if to make one last try at a heartfelt offer. "Anyone who wants to change his or her mind still has time."

The kids didn't even look up from the Monopoly board. An "uh-uh" came from one of the bent heads. Schroeder walked into his bedroom, put on a cotton shirt, chino shorts, high woolen socks, hiking boots, and a nylon shell parka. Then he walked into the kitchen and stuffed into the parka pockets an apple, an orange, a bag of peanuts, and a small box of raisins.

He paused dramatically at the kitchen door. "OK, last call." Then, waiting a decent interval, he said, "See you later, in a few hours." He opened the door, walked out, closed the door behind him.

Outside, a misty rain sprinkling him, he thought for a moment. Should he head west, toward Madaket? No. The Cobb house was in that direction; he wanted to stay as far away as he could. He'd go east, toward 'Sconset, Quidnet, Wauwinet. He started through Nantucket town, the only walker on this dark June day.

The absence of walkers on the island had always astounded him, for Nantucket was scaled to human size. The length of the island was only about fourteen miles, and when you started from the town, which was pretty much in the center, you'd be hard put to find a coastal point more than nine or ten miles away. There were few cars, lots of dirt roads, pleasant but not difficult rolling terrain. Yet almost no one walked, and even the bicycling once so popular on the island seemed to have diminished.

Schroeder felt a contempt for the sedentary; it was one of the few realms in which he could feel pure and superior. At the same time, other people's laziness left the roads to him, and he was grateful for that. He set out along North Liberty, then Gardner, Main, Pleasant, and the 'Sconset Road. At the fork, about a mile and a half out, he decided to go the longest route, the Polpis Road, then way up to Wauwinet. Coming back, he'd go along the beach to Quidnet before heading inland, then cut over along dirt roads through Sauls Hills, perhaps along the cranberry bog, then over to the 'Sconset Road and back to town. About twenty-one or twenty-two miles, he figured, and if he could keep up a fifteen-minute-per-mile pace it would take nearly six hours, allowing for a couple of short breaks to eat the food he'd jammed into his pockets.

He walked. He could feel the rhythmic swinging of his arms and legs, the stretching of muscles, the first beading of sweat, begin to loosen his mind. He liked the feeling. He looked down at his legs striding out, saw the fine rain in drops, rivulets, on his lower thighs, saw the right knee with the arching scar along its inside. Six years ago, a surgeon at Lenox Hill Hospital had cut in to try to repair the tendons, ligaments, cartilage, he'd torn up in a skiing accident. The operation had helped; he could move on the knee, walk hard and long, even run. But he couldn't turn easily, or pivot, or stop short, which meant no tennis, or basketball, or downhill skiing, although he could jog, swim, cross-country ski. And he'd been left with a resident ache in the knee, which asserted itself most mornings and on every walk, jog, dance, swim, until he loosened it up. He felt the tightness even now, and reveled in the anticipation of the relaxation, the warming, in his knee and his head.

Six years ago, he remembered, when he'd injured the knee, he'd also had his last stab at free-lance writing. He'd done what he thought was a tight, informative piece, combining his crash on the slopes, his feeling about being babied down the hill by the ski patrol, and a clear explanation of the fragile mechanism of the knee. He was pleased with it, so pleased he sent it to *The New Yorker*, which had not been as pleased as he, and returned it with a polite, pro forma rejection. Rejection slips also came from *Sports Illustrated*, *Playboy*, and *Reader's Digest*.

"Four weeks of hard work," he'd said to his wife. "And nobody wants it. Why the hell did I bother?" What he wanted was for her to disagree, to tell him how good the piece was.

"You should have queried them first," she replied. "The best writers in the world submit to those magazines. Whatever made you think you could break in, first try?"

"But you liked it," he said.

"Oh, it was all right. I didn't want to discourage you."

"What do you think you're doing now?"

"Be realistic," she replied.

He'd told her the story of the man who said to his wife, "I'm my own severest critic." And she answered, "Not while I'm around."

And he blamed Marty, or used her as an excuse, for never trying a free-lance piece again. In the past couple of years, in fact, he hadn't even formulated any ideas for them. Yet he knew his years, if not his days, at *Scope* were numbered. He looked around for writers over forty and saw only four, including himself. Over fifty, there was only one. Traditionally, a writer at *Scope* had only two honorable choices when he hit forty: become an editor or leave. Schroeder would not become an editor. First, he didn't want to; he'd seen those harried men haggling over facts, rewrites, cuts, shoehorning copy into spaces too small for it; as one of the editors had said, "trying to fit ten pounds of shit into a five-pound bag." Second, he had no prospect of becoming one. The favorites of the gods had already received clear signs from Olympus. Schroeder had heard nothing.

Schroeder's buddy Fred Kingsley was forty-five and still just a writer. The title shared by him and Schroeder and fourteen others, associate editor, impressed outsiders. But they were only writers. Fred had decided to hang on until he was fifty, and had put in twenty-five years, which would guarantee him a good pension when he reached sixty-five. Fred called it "running out the string."

"Jesus, Freddie," Schroeder had said to him dismayed. "You're forty-five years old, and you're talking about running out the string? What are you going to do till you're sixty-five, a time step?"

Fred, a tired, dried-up man with a bitter sense of humor, shrugged and answered, "I'll try the Great American Novel and PR, and see which I click with first."

The Great American Novel or public relations. Both knew which it would be, for Fred and for Schroeder. Schroeder had a feeling that anyone who was going to write a good novel, let alone a great one, would have announced himself by the time he was thirty, would have demonstrated the talent, and, more than that, the guts.

Schroeder had once interviewed Maureen Stapleton, and that tough-fragile lady had, in talking about actresses, given him sound, if depressing, advice about writers. "When a girl asks me if she should be an actress," she said, "I tell her, anyone who has to *ask* will never be one." As she said it, her tired face, with its little girl's eyes, took on a stony strength that said Maureen Stapleton would have made it onto the stage if she'd had to break through the side wall of the theatre to do it.

The rain was coming down harder, which pleased him. It rattled on his parka, washed and tickled his face and his bare legs. He lengthened his strides, and, reaching a fork, took the left tine, Polpis Road, leading him toward Quidnet and Wauwinet.

Public relations. Is that where he'd play out his string? For a foundation, or a ballet company—if he was lucky. For an insurance company or a bank, if he wasn't. Retired at sixty-five, if he was lucky. To do what? To remember and relive what? The possibilities, even the lucky ones—*especially* the lucky ones, made him shiver. He pulled up the hood of his parka and tightened the drawstring; then, angry with himself, loosened it and flung back the hood.

As Schroeder reached the first of the low Polpis hills, a pickup truck came shooting around a bend, startling him with a splattering of water. He reached a wet hand up to wipe his eyes; he was soaked, chilly, yet invigorated, the rain cold on his bare legs, his hands, his neck, reminding him his core was warm and dry. Safe. Just like his spirit; whatever daring he feigned on the outside, he felt like an old maid on the inside. Playing it safe at *Scope*, when he should quit and . . . do what? Using what for money to support his kids and his ex-wife, and himself? His bank account had six thousand dollars in it; he had another ten thousand in stock of the Seligsohn Communications Corporation, the parent company of *Scope*. How far would that go? Six months? Enough to start off in a new direction? And which direction? Another magazine job? Nothing new about that, and he'd be no younger there than at *Scope*. A newspaper? Again, too old to start, and the pay too low, except for a handful of papers, and for those he had no specialty they'd want. Why not a gossip column, or a People column?

The thought angered him, because he'd just confessed his specialty. People. Gossip. Great minds dealt with ideas, he told himself. Ordinary minds with events. Small minds, *his* mind, with people. What a specialty! He supposed the culmination of his current career would be getting his own column. And what would he call it? Sam Spies? Schroeder at the Keyhole? Sam the Snoop?

Suddenly he saw himself at sixty, with white hair, a natty sports jacket on, maybe a bow tie, reporter's pad in his outside pocket, table hopping, swapping chitchat and then, dramatically, whipping out the book and pen, and asking, "How do you spell that, dearie?"

Exciting. But at least steady work.

Then there was television. But he heard they were no longer in the market for Cronkites. Just boys and girls, all of them twenty-seven, all of them with hair covering their ears, even the boys, all of them with deep voices, even the girls. He didn't have a deep voice, his hair didn't cover his ears. And he wasn't twenty-seven. And he'd had his brief try at TV.

Last year, when he was thirty-nine, going on forty, he'd auditioned for *Scope*'s syndicated TV feature service. They'd wanted to do his section, Faces and Places, on TV, and asked him if he wanted to try it on camera. He said he would, but regretted it almost as soon as he began the audition. As he was made up, sweat started beading on his upper lip; he felt like Nixon. His hands were shaking, and his eyes stared at the camera lens as if he were a zombie.

Then someone waved a hand at him, he began reading, and the prompter rolled to follow him.

"When the room clerk at the Hamptons' posh Ocean Dune Inn heard the name, he reacted as if it were Greek to him. So with a smile the striking brunette spelled it for him: O-n-a-s-s-i-s. Blushing, the clerk realized his gaffe and apologized for not understanding the name. 'It's all right,' Lady O responded graciously, 'It's not as if it were Smith.' No indeed. Especially not at the bank."

When he'd written the copy, Schroeder had thought it clever enough. Hearing himself say it, it sounded trivial, arch, crappy. He stopped reading.

"Shit," he said aloud. "I can't read this. I feel like an ass. It's bad enough I've got to write it. Get somebody else to read it." The syndication producer and the director had protested—all too briefly, Schroeder thought—and then thanked him.

"Could you play it back for me?" he asked.

The director put on the face of a man trying to be patient, and then looked at his watch. But he agreed. Schroeder sat and watched the stiff, staring man with the gray sideburns and the lines in his face. He was embarrassed, not for his performance, although he realized it was about as amateurish as one could be, but for his copy, the junk he'd written, which, he realized, was as good as most of the work he turned out for *Scope*. And he was embarrassed to see that face, *his* face, approaching middle age, perhaps already there, that face of a man who'd been Phi Beta Kappa, with an M.A. in journalism, defacing the dignity of his years by reading such crap. And obviously not liking it.

Schroeder said no to television, knowing well enough, after having seen the tape, that he'd just managed it before TV could say no to him. Still, he put it down in his ledger of acts of courage, a ledger hardly overflowing with entries. Underflowing, he thought, would be more like it.

Then the syndication people had tried out the young researcher who worked for him, and, yes, she was the right age, and her hair covered her ears, and though her voice was not yet deep enough, it would in time, no doubt, add sonority and sound like every other woman broadcaster's, and most men's. Not like Rona Barrett's, which, Schroeder felt, should go down in Rona's ledger. Actually, he thought, Rona Barrett's voice was a perfect match for Schroeder's copy. Maybe he should apply for a job as her writer.

But now he had more important business, he had to decide between heading out the north fork of the road, toward Wauwinet, or the south, toward Quidnet. North was longer, and he wanted to prolong this walk. Alone, walking, everything seemed clear to him. Fifteen miles, maybe a little more, to go. He'd finish at about five o'clock, depending on how long he stopped. And the last five miles he could really move, clock himself on the big milestones on the 'Sconset Road, get down to fourteen, thirteen, maybe even twelve minutes per mile. Finish exhausted, after twenty-one or twenty-two miles, not the forty-yard dashes he reeled off at work. A long, satisfying job, well done merely for having been sustained. Anticipating those last five miles, he picked up his pace, feeling his knee loosening, warming, for the first time almost pain-free. He looked down at his legs, saw the quadriceps muscles over the knees tensing with each step. Firm quadriceps for a man of forty. Damned firm. He looked good. Handsome, good body, good athlete, and he knew it. Had known it and ridden on it all his life. He wasn't defensive about his abilities as a hiker. As a journalist, that was another matter, which is why he liked hiking better than working. Felt stronger, calmer, more serene at it. Felt better, looked better.

Schroeder's friend and lawyer, Milt Raymond, had once called his looks The Schroeder Curse. One evening they'd bumped into each other on West Forty-fourth Street, each going to different plays, Raymond with his wife, Schroeder with a blond, twenty-five-year-old graduate student. The following day, the two men had had lunch in one of those East Side places which affected the simplicity of an Irish family bar without trying to affect the modesty of its prices.

Sipping a glass of red wine, Milt had said: "Aren't you something? A man on the threshold of middle age, using co-eds to stay young! And pretty ones at that. Do you like her, at least?"

Schroeder was having a Bloody Mary. Two drinks of it on an

empty stomach had already given him a jolt of alcohol, and he felt warm and loose. Later it would make him drowsy. (My writing, he always told people, I can do in my sleep. In fact, *better* in my sleep.) At the moment he felt good. "Whatever threshold I'm ready to cross, I cross willingly, Milty. And you're reading the whole situation wrong. She was just a would-be journalist, doing a graduate paper on news weeklies. *Scope* turned her over to me; they figured I wouldn't be too busy to look after her."

Schroeder took another sip at his drink, and added in a mocking voice: "They don't realize how much painstaking craftsmanship stands behind the breathtaking artistry that is the Schroeder oeuvre."

"What exactly are you saying?" his friend had answered. "You're making it sound like a put-down, right, but you're not fooling me. What you're really doing is showing off, saying how weak you are in the stick-to-it-iveness department, but just loaded with natural talent. A regular diamond in the rough, but can't be bothered to do any buffing, right? Blond young students, you want to adore you, right? But forty-year-old editors, who might give you assignments, them you're not interested in, right?"

"For Christ's sake," Schroeder replied. "You graduated from some first-rate Midwestern college—what was it, Wisconsin?—you were law review at NYU. Why on earth do you always make it sound like you just got off the boat, and Yiddish is your mother tongue?"

"Anti-Semite!" Raymond pronounced it the Yiddish way, *ahn*-tee seh-*mitt,* and he smiled a smile Schroeder wasn't quite sure he meant. When he continued, he put on a pompous Yiddish accent, in the style of Mel Brooks. "I retain a slight accent because I wish to remind those who are not cognizant of my baronial estate in Great Neck, and my thirtieth-floor corner office in the Seagram's Building, not to mention the eighteen-thousand-dollar Mercedes, not only how high I have risen, but how humble were my beginnings. And, by the way, it was Michigan, not Wisconsin."

"Well then," said Schroeder. "You're pulling the same shit as I am, so why be so tough on me? It's cant, pretense, illusion. And indispensable, ask Eugene O'Neill. You must love O'Neill, Milt. He wrote such *long* plays, not one-liners like me."

"Let's not call it cant, or pretense," Raymond answered.

"And even more important, let's *not* call it the same bullshit. We both tend to, let's say, dramatize our positions. But what a difference! What is the nature of my dramatization? That I have taken the meager gifts conferred upon me by mother nature, and I have done, let's say, all right with them. No looks, no money, no social position, no contacts, no nepotism, didn't know a finger bowl from a cup of clear consommé. OK on the brains. Fairly able, but *very* ready and willing. And I've come a fair way. At thirty-nine a partner in a major firm. Pretty well set for life, not to put any false modesty on it.

"So I pretend a little to emphasize the distance I've come. Because I'm proud of it. And I have every right to be. Sam Schroeder, on the other hand, having been born into upper-middle-class WASP respectability, and been handed all sorts of blessings of face and form, not to mention an IQ easily equal to mine, not to mention automatic entree through many, many closely guarded doors, chooses to dramatize how *little* he has done with his gifts. How short the distance traveled, how little polishing the diamond in the rough has been given.

"If your dramatization is the same as mine, kiddo, then I'm George Plimpton."

Now Schroeder was at the end of the road. The sight of Wauwinet shook him out of his daydreaming. He strode out onto the beach, walked close to the edge of the water before sitting down to remove his boots and socks. He tied the bootlaces together so he could carry them over his shoulder when he walked along the beach. But he didn't start immediately.

As far as he could see, there was no other person on the beach, the weather had taken care of that: the wind continued to gust, driving a light rain. Clouds glowered, but not with the flat gray threat of a New York sky. They had the depth, interest, and variety of clouds over the British Isles. And the ocean! As a boy, going to Cape Cod in summers, he felt the ocean, especially, belonged to him. He'd listen to it, as he was doing now, and it came to epitomize for him what was best about his work, or his pretended work, and indeed all art: the comfort of discipline broken by the delight of surprise. Regularity alone was monotonous; surprise alone was chaotic. The ocean meant to him comfort without boredom, quite the opposite of his own life. To him it also meant a serene self-confidence, the ease of a great soprano who didn't have to go after a high F to show you who she was, the security of a strong man who didn't have to take on any man in the house to show his muscles. Quite the opposite of his life.

The surf was easy, the water just beyond it choppy, and as always the sea took its color from the sky, today a deep gray, somber but not angry; assertive, but not sullen.

He reached into his pocket for the apple, and took a bite; it was a Granny Smith, juicy, green, tart, crisp. Clean, like the beach and the ocean and his rain-washed legs. And like his spirit as he sat alone there. If only, he said to himself. If only what? If only you could make a living watching waves or counting grains of sand? Beachcomber? Lifeguard? Don't kid yourself, Schroeder, he warned, this is not discovery, this is not revelation, this is escapism, and every rat-race type has his moments like this, of feeling pure and simple and exalted, on the shores of Nantucket, or the Vineyard, or the Cape, or Boothbay Harbor, or the lighthouse at Montauk. You're no different, Schroeder, you buy yourself a few days or weeks of escape, but you don't belong here anymore than you belong alongside Pavarotti in Verdi, Olivier in Shakespeare, or Nureyev in tights. Or Updike, or Pynchon, or Mailer, or Bellow, or Vonnegut, or Heller in the public library. You're just another escapist, except maybe you can afford less escape than most of the others. Which says you're not even a first-class rat-racer. You've offered your soul for sale, and can't even get a decent price.

Or, as my disturbing friend Milt Raymond keeps asking, what the hell am I going to do with the rest of my life?

I'm going to enjoy this apple, he said to himself, as he bit another chunk out of the Granny Smith. Each bite of it. Oh, soulful, soulful, he chided himself. Now let's come down from the ethereal and talk about your next job, after you leave *Scope*. Because you're going to have to, soon. No, he countered, let's not talk about it. Let's get up and walk. He jumped to his feet, slung his boots over his shoulder and started along the beach, his only company a couple of sandpipers pecking their finicky way ahead of him.

He took each step hitting on his heel, feeling the hard, wet sand give way slightly, then rolling on his foot, the center taking up his weight, then the ball, finally the toes, giving him a push off to the next step. On each step the slight slippage, the wasted thrust, gave him a sensation of luxury. He was not walking because he had to be somewhere; the action itself was important; he could afford to expend effort pushing a couple of cubic inches of sand backward, rather than propelling his body forward. Besides, the yielding of the sand made him feel effectual; he was moving something. That was a feeling to enjoy. So was the flex of his calf muscles. Walking on sand worked them harder than any other exercise, including running. His muscles were working, they could be doing no more at the moment; he need not worry about wasting his time, or what he might better be doing. For hiking, for ocean and beach watching, for calf flexing, this was the best you could do.

For writing, he could be doing a lot better. If he dare dignify his quips with that job description. OK, call it journalism. He didn't come out of it well, no matter what the name. And suddenly he was hit by a gut-twisting fear: it would be worse in the fall. He'd take a three-week vacation in August—didn't even know yet where he'd go, but assumed it would be here, with Jane—and spend it all worrying about how well the young researcher would be doing as his replacement, at half the salary. The same young researcher who'd stepped smartly into the TV audition he'd stepped away from, and who was now, he heard, doing beautifully as the syndicated electronic image of Faces and Places. Her name was Doris Kirkwood, and immediately after he'd turned down a chance at the TV job, she'd walked over to his desk and asked if she could buy him a drink. At that point, a year ago, she'd only been a researcher-writer for three months and he barely knew her. Sure, he'd said, a little computer in his head clicking off the sexual possibilities—what and where the drink might lead to.

He'd had a vodka on the rocks, she a white wine, and the drink led to nothing good. Doris was a compact blond, full-bosomed and attractive, but, he guessed, only a few years away from being square and stocky. Her outstanding feature was a pair of brilliantly determined brown eyes. Her eyes, and her manner—she treated him as if he were a cross between an elder statesman and a senile old fool—fed a quick "no-go" into his sexual computer.

Apparently she'd watched his abortive on-camera attempt, because she patronizingly explained to him the stylistic differences between magazine copy and TV copy, and even more patronizingly consoled him about his weak audition, telling him she understood why after all these years, he felt uncomfortable in front of a camera. Finally, fortified by a second vodka, he told her she was very kind and quite right. In fact, he said, he hadn't really come to terms with radio yet, let alone television. It was a weak quip, and he could see by her expression she spotted the defensiveness and the maudlin self-pity in it; he saw his weakness in her eyes. Then she made some perfunctory "Oh, no, you're not old" noises, before going on to ask about auditioning, no, more to announce she was *going* to, and didn't want to do it behind his back.

"Why, my child," he'd said, "Go, audition, and my blessings with thee." The phony avuncular tone was to recoup his moment of fear and weakness by showing largesse and strength, and to elicit some more of the oh-you're-not-old noises, with perhaps a sexual come-on to follow. It did none of the above. The sex part of it was pro forma, the fear was real, and it hadn't gone away. Whether or not she was actually *after* his job, and she probably was, she was on her way to getting it, if not now, when he was forty and she twenty-six, then next year, when he was forty-one and she twenty-seven, or the year after, or the year after that.

Then, quixotically, Schroeder went on to say, "And success there is just the starting point. After learning to *read* the Faces and Places column magnificently, there's no reason you can't learn to write it that way, too." He tried to make it daring, a challenge, as if to say: Let's see you handle that one, kid. Perhaps he wanted to embarrass her, to assume the upper hand.

He couldn't; she handled it with a straightforward ease that made him feel simultaneously like a naughty boy and a dirty old man. "Oh, you write the column so adroitly. I couldn't learn to write it that way, not for a long time." Then she made the first uncalculated statement in their conversation, and it hurt the most. "Besides, I don't really think I'd be interested in staying on Faces and Places too long."

Without wanting to prick his finger, she'd stabbed him to the heart. He smiled, but imagined he'd made it too broad; she realized almost at once, she'd hurt him. Without even having the good grace to blush, she tried to fix it. "I don't mean there's anything wrong with Faces and Places," she said. "My God, you turn it into an art form. It suits your style, it doesn't suit mine. I'm after more probing stuff; I'm more interested in understanding Watergates than in quipping about them.''

The twenty-six-year-old slip of a girl was explaining serious-ness to the forty-year-old man. The girl was wiping up the floor with the man. Ahead on drinks, by three to one, but way behind on points, feeling childish, he made a childish try for a knock-out. "Not only ambitious and sexy," he said to her, "but ideal-istic. And she even buys the *drinks*. The least I can do is to reciprocate by buying dinner." Once more, she handled him as easily as if he were a child.

"Why, thank you for the offer. It's most attractive, but I'm meeting my fiancé for dinner. In fact, I've got to be going soon." She looked at her watch to confirm the necessity, but Schroeder doubted she'd even seen what time it was. "Perhaps some other time, " he said, to which she just nodded, mechani-cally. And walking along the beach, a year after his drink with Doris Kirkwood, the recollection hit him physically. Which made him think of Rocky Cobb and last night. Another con-tender for the lousiest night of the year. How was he going to face her again? Or Stoney? He should phone today. What would he say?

His eyes searching, he spotted the low cluster of houses that was Quidnet, and wondered if there was a public phone, so he could call her. And say what? I'm sorry we got so close? I'm sorry we got so close without getting there? I won't tell Stoney how we lusted in our hearts, if you won't? I won't tell Stoney if you won't tell Jane?

He reached into his pocket. The problem was solved, tempo-rarily, at least. He had no change. As he thought, argued, ques-tioned, regretted, he kept moving. By this time, he figured, he'd covered at least ten miles, nearly half the walk, and he felt stronger than when he started. No fatigue, no aches, his right knee warmed up and pain-free. He left the beach, feeling good despite the unsettling thoughts; he sat down at the edge of the road to put on his socks and boots. Then he strode along the macadam, grateful for the change to firm footing and good trac-tion.

The rain had stopped, the weather brightened; the remaining clouds were higher, more broken, blue peeking through. In a couple of miles he'd start looking for the dirt road through the hills, then cut south, maybe through the cranberry bog until he hit the 'Sconset Road and milestones, and his speed walk home.

He looked up at the sky: actual chunks of blue. Tomorrow might be a beach day.

To his left he saw an inviting dirt road, and he turned onto it; he was headed southwest, toward the sunken forest, and somewhere after that, the island's highest point, and then the cranberry bog. He couldn't be sure, he had a small map, but the roads weren't marked too accurately. Well, on this island it would be hard to get lost; Nantucket was only fourteen miles long by six wide, and he was in a small V, headed for the point formed by the road he'd just left and the one he was cutting across to reach.

No wilderness exploration needed here, which suited him. He looked at his watch, 2:30; in the sky, islands of blue in a sea of gray. Tomorrow might *not* be better, he reminded himself, just in case he'd been using that as a metaphor.

He wondered how his mother and his kids were getting on. Should he whip himself for bugging out? Hell, no, he answered, with extra vehemence to make up for his uncertainty. This walk was important. He was entitled to it. Marty would have accused him of selfishness, of immaturity, of refusing to grow up, like Peter Pan. Well, shit, he told himself, I *asked* them to go. Stop feeling guilty. Marty had done a great job on that. There was always something to feel guilty about, if you looked for it. No day need be empty of it—like the pain in his knee.

The road climbed slightly; here, moors were all around him and there were no trees. Striding uphill this way strained his lower thigh muscles, set a small twinge going in that knee; yet it felt good, reminded him he was alive and feeling. Like the guilt? No, not like the guilt.

Here, a modest vista; the modest splendor of the gentle moors. Austere, prototypically New England, like Stoney. Schroeder never really thought of himself as a New Englander. Being the son of a second-generation German father, who'd been an engineer at Pratt and Whitney, being a resident of West Hartford—he was just too peripheral a New Englander to be mentioned in the same breath with his buddy Stoney.

His buddy, whose wife he'd almost fucked last night. But only in your mind, he told himself. Then he had to add: The bodies weren't too far from it, either. Ten years ago that could not have happened; neither he nor Rocky could have come close. He supposed the opportunism, the selfishness, the weakness, came with age. It's called maturity, he said to himself. Ha ha. No, it isn't, either, he answered. It's called reaching forty.

To his left he saw a small hill covered with heather, and he walked off the road to climb it. At the top he sat and pulled from his parka the small box of raisins. Around him he could see knobby hills covered with heather, occasional scrubby pines; in front of him lay the brown band of the road, stretching to both sides for only a little way before disappearing in the roll of the terrain.

Here, he told himself, I could build a house and spend the rest of my life.

Oh yeah?

With whom?

Doing what?

And what'll you need here? A TV set for your occasional football game? Enough wine to make the evenings glow? Parties, with beautiful people, to liven up your occasional weekend? Just another clichéd dream, brought to you straight from the Rat Race.

He finished the raisins, tucked the empty box into his pocket, stood, walked down to the road, and walked on, angry with himself for bringing a mess of problems to the island and not attacking any of them. There was last night's confrontation, his job, his mother, his kids. And he'd gotten nowhere. Well, not exactly; he had found a location for his dream house! On land that was not for sale, and too expensive had it been, and too far from any real life he had a chance of carving for himself. Yeah, and next time he was on vacation, hiking in the White Mountains, skiing in Vermont, drinking in the Hamptons, he'd find another escapist site for his hideaway. Mr. Bland Builds His Dream House.

In a half hour he reached the 'Sconset road; he walked onto the bicycle path and headed toward town, looking for the five-mile marker. He checked his watch and picked up his pace and sped the next four miles, to the outskirts of town, in fifty-three minutes, a little more than thirteen minutes per mile, not bad for a forty-year-old in crisis. For the final mile, through town, he slowed, reaching the house on North Liberty warm and loose and relaxed. For the past five miles he hadn't solved any problems, but at least he'd outwalked them.

He strode into the house. "Boy, you three really missed a

walk!'' he announced. From his mother he got a smile which completely dismissed what he'd just said. From Patty came, "Oh, daddy!'' from Bobby, "Boo!''

He looked down at the children, still hunched over the Monopoly board. "Don't tell me you've been at that all day,'' he said.

"No, daddy,'' said his daughter. "Grandma took us to town, and we had lunch, we went to the sweet shop, and we bought books.''

"And daddy,'' Bobby shouted. "You know what's playing at the movies tonight? *King Kong!* Can we go?''

"Can we?'' Patty added.

"What time does it go on?''

"Seven and nine,'' said Patty.

"Yeah, seven and nine,'' Bobby repeated.

He thought for a moment. "OK,'' he said. "I'll tell you what. It's now ten to five. Let's eat at six and all go to the movie at seven.''

"Yay!'' they both shouted.

"How does that sound to you, grandma?''

"It sounds fine,'' his mother replied. "But I don't think I'll go. I'd rather stay here and read. I've seen *King Kong* twice.''

Schroeder nodded toward the book and smiled. It was still the one about the movie mogul's daughter. "More interested in the apes who *make* the movies than the ones *in* them, eh?''

His mother smiled back. "It's just a horrid book. But I can't put it down.''

"All right,'' he said. "You have time to change your mind. Meanwhile I'll go see what there is to eat.''

His mother got to her feet. "There's striped bass, and corn, and salad, and I'll fix dinner. After walking for six hours, you should rest for a while. You're forty years old, you know. Almost forty-one.''

He nodded. "Oh yes, mom. I know. I certainly do know that.''

He walked into his bedroom, closed the door, lay down, and fell asleep.

Chapter

7

AT A QUARTER TO SEVEN, ON SCHEDULE, SCHROEDER, HIS mother, and his children finished dinner. "It's off to *King Kong*," he announced. "Grandma, why don't you come with us? It's a classic, you know."

"Twice is enough, even for a classic," she answered. "I'll stay here and finish the book."

The theatre was a meeting hall, with hard folding chairs on an unbanked floor, and they couldn't find three seats together with good sight lines, so he sat near them, slightly behind and off to one side. He spent the beginning of the movie looking at their intent profiles, thinking how, when he spent every day with them, he took them for granted, never really examined them the way he was now. At the first appearance of the mighty Kong, his son turned and beckoned to him in the darkened hall, then ran over.

"We decided to sit together on one chair, so you can be next to us, daddy."

Schroeder grinned. They were scared, and the little devil didn't want to admit it. "That's all right," he answered with a straight face. "You don't have to."

"*Please*, daddy!" said Bobby. He grinned again and went over next to them, stretching an arm around the two of them. He watched the movie in tired contentment, hardly paying any attention to the screen, involved in absorbing the smell and feel of the two young bodies next to him.

The picture over, the three of them filed out into the mild June evening, around them the fifty or so others who had filled a third of the hall. Bobby and Patty still reverberated with the fright and stimulation of *King Kong;* he was still heady with the nearness of his children. He walked with an arm around each, unwilling to let the glue of the movie come apart. He steered them onto quiet Washington Street, headed toward Main.

They'd gone no more than ten steps when he heard the voice.

"Do you mind if I walk with you?"

A woman's voice, no, more like a girl's, soft, scared, pleading. With no alarm, he and the children turned. She was of average height, perhaps a little shorter, pale, her hair a pale golden red, her eyes a pale blue. She was small boned, but seemed almost plump, although he could see that the baggy T-shirt and the lumpy, shapeless painter's pants made her look rounder than she was. She was in her early twenties, and everything about her seemed subdued, not the kind of young woman he'd look at twice. In fact, not even once. His instant response was one of sympathy; no attraction at all.

"No, we don't mind at all," he said. "But why do you want to walk with us?"

She stared at him, looked away, and said only: "The street is dark. And empty." Schroeder thought she wanted to say more, but she stopped at the six words.

The prospect of a mugging on Nantucket seemed to him remote, almost amusing. And, he thought, she seemed the kind of girl who'd always be safe, who faded into the background. How unkind, he said to himself. But true. To atone for the cruelty, he smiled at her. "You must be from New York," he said. He smiled again, so as not to sound derisive.

If she had discerned anything in his face or voice—derision, condescension, kindliness—she didn't acknowledge it.

"No, I'm . . . not." Her voice faded, but he somehow thought she'd been going to say where she was from, and then decided against it. After that first glimpse of her eyes, he never met them again; they remained downcast.

"I assure you," he said, "you have nothing to worry about. Although you are most welcome to walk with us."

"Thank you," was all she said.

The block was long, and they had about forty yards to go before reaching Main Street. Obviously she was not going to reward her escort with conversation. He looked down at his kids for their reaction. Their faces asked, what's going on? His daughter looked a little apprehensive. He just shrugged at the two of them and winked, as if to say, I don't know either, but it's nothing to worry about. As they walked in silence, he wondered if he should introduce himself and his kids. He settled for: "Are you here alone?"

Her look turned frightened. "Yes," she replied.

He almost said, I'm not prying, just making conversation till we get to the end of this endless block.

He tried again. "For the weekend?"

That seemed to scare her, too. "Yes," she said, and hesitated, then: "I'm not sure."

"What did you all think of the movie?" He tried that briskly, and opened it to the three of them. It had to work better than the abortive duet, he figured.

"Terrific!" said Patty.

"Great!" said Bobby.

The young woman said nothing.

Then they walked out of the lonely street. Thank God, he said to himself. Main Street was better lighted, and fairly well populated with strollers—middle-aged couples, overdressed, looking in shop windows; teen-agers in clusters, eating ice cream cones, puffing on cigarettes, looking one another over.

Schroeder turned to the girl, with a smile. "Well, we made it. That wasn't too bad, was it?" Again, he tried to sound sympathetic.

Her only answer was, "Thank you." As she said it, she looked straight at him, and he was struck by the beautiful clarity of her skin and the delicacy of her features. Even more by the strange look in her eyes, which said that she did not want to continue talking and yet did not want to go off alone.

Then, as if afraid to give in to the desire to talk, she turned and walked off. For a few moments he watched her, short and baggy looking in that T-shirt, those clumsy pants, and the old blue sneakers. She's really quite attractive, he thought, and delicate. Why does she wear those clothes? Surely, she can't think they enhance her appearance. But he knew the answer even as he asked. There was one forlorn girl, he told himself, one girl who did not have her appearance on her mind. He wondered what she *was* thinking about, hoped it didn't bother her, make her look that way, all the time. A lousy way to be on Nantucket, he thought. Alone, afraid, dressed like a sack. And she's probably here to have fun, he thought.

He found himself feeling sorry for her, and a lot better about himself by contrast. If his kids hadn't been there he'd be tempted to run after her, and say, for Christ's sake, be happy! Smile! Let me buy you a drink and tell you some funny stories.

No, not that. She'd probably think him a dirty old man. Besides, it wasn't his style. Impetuous, impulsive acts were beyond him. He had to brace himself, consider the possibility of rejection—even by a humble little creature like that one. Being with the kids had nothing to do with it. He had already died too many deaths trying and failing to leap before he looked. No, leave the kids out of it.

He turned to them. "Well, how about that?"

"Was she scared, daddy?" Patty asked.

"What of?" asked Bobby.

"I don't know, but she looked so sad, and frightened, I felt sorry for her, didn't you?"

They didn't reply, for they'd just spotted the ice cream parlor.

"Daddy, can we have ice cream cones?"

"Can we?"

Bobby had a lime sherbet; he always did. Patty and Schroeder both tried the malachite, which looked and tasted like a livelier version of pistachio.

The ice cream, the walk back to the house, the talk about *King Kong* and its technical marvels, the kids' baths, the goodnight kisses, all took him farther and farther from the frightened young woman with the pale skin.

It was after ten when Schroeder sat down in an old rocker and tried to begin a conversation with his mother. "What do you think of this house, and this island?"

"I think they're nice."

Nice. Terrific. Well, what did he expect? His mother had

never in her life—that he had heard, anyway—said something like: It stinks. Or: It excites me. Or: On the whole I'd rather be in Philadelphia, or Cape Cod, for that matter, or the mountains, or Hawaii, or Miami, or anywhere. She had, in short, never let loose with a screaming enthusiasm, or criticism. That he had heard, anyway.

Schroeder wanted to put more time in on this. "If you could pick a vacation house, anyplace in the world you wanted to, where would it be?"

"I've never really thought about it," she answered, putting the dirty Hollywood book in her lap.

"Well, think about it." Then to help prompt her, he added: "Would it be at the seashore, or on a mountain lake? Would it be in New England or down in the warmer climes?"

"Well, gosh," she answered, "I like all of them. I don't know which I'd pick."

"What about dad? Which did he like?"

Sam Schroeder's father had been named John Otto, and so had his eldest son. Sam, on the other hand, had never been given a middle name at all, which he took as a deprivation and a sign of his father's stinginess, an unwillingness even to give away an extra name. The senior Schroeder, who'd died five years ago, was a cool, efficient technocrat, to whom his son never felt very close. But at least *he'd* have had an opinion on the mountains versus the shore. Well, then, Schroeder asked himself, how come I didn't know it?

"Your father always preferred the ocean," answered his mother, relieved and proud to be able to come up with something definite, as if that gave her a stronger identity.

"Then how come you never bought a summer place?"

Schroeder knew the answer to that, or at least had an impression of what had happened. He wanted to hear his mother's version.

"Oh, we looked at so many places, but I don't know, we never did buy one." A non-answer if he ever heard one.

"It's not that you couldn't afford one, right, mom?"

"Well, I don't know, Sam, don't say that as if we had a lot of money. You know your father never made more than thirty thousand a year at Pratt and Whitney. So we might have scraped up the money, but it wouldn't have been easy, what with putting you and Jack through college."

"Are you sorry now you didn't buy a place at the beach?"

"Oh, I suppose. But the house in West Hartford is enough. Two places, on your father's pension, might have been too hard for me."

Equivocate, equivocate. If she had ever said: yes, I'm damned sorry, he would have keeled over. But he knew why they didn't have a summer place. At least he had his recollections. He remembered, for example, about thirty years back, overhearing his parents talk about houses they'd seen along the Connecticut shore. Each one, his father seemed to have liked. Each one, his mother found something wrong with. One was too far from shopping, another too far from the beach, a third on too rundown a street, a fourth not large enough. He remembered his father's litany, "Well, dear, if you're not sold on it, we're certainly not going to get it." Each house put on the table, each put down by his mother, each crossed off by his father. He remembered that; he also remembered the prices. Less than twenty-five thousand for the most expensive, about eighteen five for the cheapest. How much would they be selling for now? Probably seventy or seventy-five thousand dollars, he figured. Well, shit, he thought, suddenly angry. Pussyfooting! If they had just taken the step, we'd all have a beach house now.

Immediately he was ashamed. He was no better than they. What decisive moves had he ever made? What trophies had he to show for his timing, his astuteness? Well, wait a minute, he thought. Two kids in private school, a New York apartment, fighting to keep afloat. At least I haven't sunk, he reminded himself. The excuses are superior, he answered. First class. As always. The results are mediocre. As always.

Anyway, one interesting thing had come out of this little chat. Sam, at thirty-four thousand per annum, was making more than his father ever did. But let's see now, his father had retired eight years ago, when salaries were a damned sight lower, and he'd been working in the Hartford market, which was not the Big Apple, and he had a rock of Gibraltar pension. And young Sam would never stay at *Scope* to see his pension, he knew that. He needed nine more years to qualify, so he could start collecting at sixty-five. Nine more years? Never.

"The West Hartford neighborhood is still like the country, anyway."

He snapped to attention. His mother, expecting a reply and not getting one, had added a defensive line. Chastened by the thoughts that had distracted him, Schroeder replied quickly, "Oh, absolutely. And having two houses would be nothing but a big headache. You're much better off the way you are. Especially when you have a rich son to take you to Nantucket."

Schroeder's last sentence was meant to be ironic, and he knew it would prompt his mother to ask a worried question. Sure enough.

"Sam, where do you go from here? What lies ahead for you?"

"The future, mom, the future."

"Don't be funny. The question is, what kind of future is it going to be?"

He got up from the rocker, found his wine glass, filled it from an open bottle of Beaujolais in the kitchen, and started back toward the rocker. "The answer is, I don't know. It's obviously not going to be in the field of brain surgery—not as a surgeon, anyway. As a patient, maybe. I hope it will have something to do with writing or journalism. Let's face it, it's got to, that's the only thing I know. But where, how, what, how much—I don't know."

He sat in the rocker, started it moving, sipped from the glass. "I'll tell you something, though, mom: I'm smart, good at what I do, handsome, charming, and loved by all. I've got a great future. Can't miss. So don't worry about a thing."

The wine made him feel good, strong, expansive. He almost believed all that himself. His mother, not having the benefit of the alcohol, was not so sure.

"I hope so, Sam, I certainly hope so." She looked worried. His mother had come down from West Hartford on Tuesday, stayed with him in his apartment, which meant Jane had to stay at her place for that time, not so much for considerations of propriety as of space. His mother had seen the cramped apartment, the unpaid bills, the casual bits of food in the refrigerator. It all smacked of transience, disorganization and limited money; it had none of the anchored solidity of his brother Jack's suburban West Hartford house, where everything was in its place, the quarts of milk in the fridge, the children in their upstairs bedrooms and the wife in the double bed. Not a girl friend who moved out when mom came to visit.

"What about *Scope?*"

"I don't know, what *about Scope*, mother?"

"Where can you go there?"

A wisecrack came up in his throat, like a badly digested lunch, but he swallowed it. "Well, I can stay where I am, which I would not be crazy about. Or I could be a senior editor, or an executive, but my chances aren't too good for that, and, besides, I wouldn't really want it, because I wouldn't get to write. Or I could write for another section. I've asked to do that, but . . ."

He shrugged. "You see, they're all set in those sections. They tend to put you into a groove and keep you there, and put new people into other openings as they occur. So, at forty, I'm in the Faces and Places groove."

"You're just a young man, Sam."

"Listen, mom, don't worry about a thing. I'm gonna do just fine." He took another sip of wine and threw a big smile at his mother. "Did anyone ever tell you you're lookin' good for an old lady?"

She thrust that aside by ignoring it. "You and I hardly ever talk to each other. I mean, really talk."

"Now don't make me self-conscious, mother; I have enough trouble pronouncing words when I'm relaxed."

"That's more like what I get from you most of the time," she said. "Wise remarks so you don't have to face your problems."

"Why, mother, you could be getting fifty dollars an hour for insights like that."

"See what I mean?"

Suddenly he stopped. "Yes, you're right. I use that to fend people off. Not only you, others, too."

"Yes, but I'm your mother, I'm not others." And then, after an attempt to stifle it, she succumbed to a profound yawn, some of which she covered with her hand. Schroeder laughed.

"You see, Mom, that's why I never want to go into a long discussion of my problems. It puts people to sleep."

She shook her head, but had to smile, as another huge yawn burst out of her.

"Go on," he said, "go to bed. Read yourself to sleep with that dirty book."

Her yawn was contagious, and then his yawn reinfected her. After her third, she stood.

"I guess I will," she said, looking at her wristwatch. "Eleven is *past* my bedtime." She walked over to him, put a hand on his cheek and stretched up to kiss him. "If you ever need anything, Sam, you know I have some money . . ."

He kissed her back on the cheek. "I don't need a thing, mom, I'm in fine shape. I really am."

"If I can help, don't be ashamed to ask."

"Don't be silly, mother, I won't be ashamed. But I don't need anything. Now go to bed. You won't mind if I go out for a while, will you?"

Immediately a wary look crossed her face. "Where are you going?"

"Just for a walk, mom." He tried to answer her unspoken question with his tone.

"Where to?"

"To one of those places around Straight Wharf, for a brandy, maybe." He hoped to use her temperance campaign as a red herring, but she wasn't having it.

"Don't look for trouble." She hesitated, not sure if she should finish. Then she did. "With a married woman."

"No, mom, you're absolutely right, I'm not. I won't. You don't mind if I go out for a walk then? If you're frightened, wake the kids, they'll look after you. OK?"

"OK," she answered. "Just don't look for trouble."

"I'll run the other way, mom, as always."

"All right, good-night. And get a good night's sleep."

"I will, don't worry. You too, mother. See you in the morning."

She smiled at him, and once again it was thrust upon him. There stood an old woman. Then she closed the bedroom door.

What Schroeder hadn't told her was that his walk was designed expressly to keep him from calling Rocky, which would lead to her inviting him out there again, which would lead to his going, which would lead to . . . No, that would not happen. He would walk; he would not pick up the phone. He jumped to his feet and headed out the door.

The night was warm, the sky clear, the light of a half-moon did not dim the stars. Schroeder paused for a moment on the quiet street and looked up. He didn't know Cassiopeia from Virgo, had no idea which star was how many light years away. Suddenly he thought of Whitman's poem, "When I Heard the Learn'd Astronomer." That's the idea, he thought, screw the science, just bathe in the poetry. I'd rather be Shakespeare than Galileo, rather be able to write something like "this brave o'erhanging firmament" than be able to identify every goddamned one of them by name.

But then, you can't do *either*, Samuel, he reminded himself. So maybe you ought to concentrate on grabbing whatever comes your way. He readjusted his sights to ground level and went down India Street toward Center. The street was empty, with few of the cars which, in July and August, would clutter the town's narrow lanes and destroy the intimate scale and the eighteenth-century textures that made Nantucket town so serene.

Things should be no bigger than this, he thought as he walked. Houses no bigger than these, hotels no bigger than India House here on his left. These were the sizes a man could cope with. But these would just not do for the world, he said to himself. Well, hell, he didn't care about the world. For him, this was the right size. Maybe he should get a job here. Or open a bookstore. Yeah, and starve to death on an intimate scale.

Schroeder turned right on Center, paused briefly at an art gallery, looked through the window at what he figured must be the fourteen thousandth batch of watercolor seascapes he'd seen on this island. There, a sailboat pulled onto a beach, there a gull on a piling, there a boat and a gull *and* a piling. He walked by, to the storefront window of a tiny restaurant called the Sandpiper, where the view promised to be better, or at least livelier. There, two posters: for the movie house, and for a church supper. There, a tanned girl, bleached hair drooping out of a bun, working the cash register.

And there *she* was. The frightened girl. Waiting to pay her bill, handing it to the cashier. The pale girl. And she was still alone. She took her change, walked back to the counter to leave a tip. Poor girl, Schroeder thought. Not only alone, but eating at a counter.

Now she was headed for the door. Schroeder's first impulse was to walk away. He didn't know, would never know, why he didn't follow it. But he stayed. And when she came out, said: "Pardon me, this is such a quiet street. Mind if I walk with you?"

No, not flirting, he was to decide much later. A desire to cheer her up. But the reason didn't matter. What mattered was he didn't pass by. He stayed and spoke.

If he expected her to be pleased at the turnabout, he was wrong, and startled at how wrong. Her first reaction was fright. Schroeder thought she hadn't recognized him, so, somewhat embarrassed, he added: "I'm the one you walked with after the movie. Remember?"

"Yes, I do," she answered, with no change of expression. Then added, "thank you," as if she felt it were required. She stood forlornly in front of the restaurant. Schroeder was puzzled; he didn't know what to do next, or say, so he settled for "Just had dinner?" which he thought inane, because it was obvious she just had.

"Yes," she answered.

"How was it?"

"All right."

Christ, he thought. This is excruciating. Had he been able to think of a way to back off, he'd have used it. Marking time, he said, "I'm out having an after-dinner walk, which I might follow with an after-dinner drink. Would you like to join me?"

Acceptance, he was used to. A "no" he disliked, but could handle. This absence of response threw him, and he found himself going on like a flustered teen-ager.

"I'll bet you don't drink," he said, and then turning his uneasiness into a quip, "Do you walk?"

For the first time, and so faintly he thought he might be imagining it, a smile thawed her face. "I don't drink very much," she replied. "I do walk."

"Well, would you like to do one or the other or both?"

If a smile had indeed surfaced, it was there no more. The scared, resigned look returned.

"I'll walk with you, anyway," she said. Not: "I'd like to," he thought. Not: "that would be nice," or "thanks." She made it sound as if she was doing him a favor. Had he been more assertive, he would have shooed her away, either saying "Don't do me no favors, kiddo," or suggesting it. But she was too diffident, too mousy, too timorous. Like Robert Burns's field mouse: "Wee, sleekit, cowrin, tim'rous beastie, O' what a panic's in thy breastie!" It sure was in her breastie. He wondered why.

So he said, "That would be nice," and they started across the street when, quickly, he grabbed her arm. A Land-Rover was coming along, two big men in it, both wearing hats and dark glasses. Schroeder smiled and made a sweeping gesture, to tell them to go ahead. They seemed not to see him. The vehicle drove by. Two charmers, he thought. He let go of her arm. They crossed.

"Did you say you were here for the weekend?"

"I'm not sure," she answered. "I guess the weekend."

"By the way," he said, "my name is Sam Schroeder."

He waited, she said nothing. Schroeder had to smile at that. "Aren't you going to tell me yours?" he asked.

After a moment's hesitation, she answered, "Mary."

Then, "Mary Jane Brosnan."

He was no detective, but he didn't believe that. Her pause, the way she said Mary, like an imposter on "To Tell the Truth." Mostly, the way she completed the name. Nobody named Mary Jane would first call herself Mary, it would always be Mary Jane together.

"Do people call you Mary or Mary Jane?" he asked.

"Oh, either one," she said. "I guess mostly Mary Jane."

Now he knew he was right.

"Tell me, Mary . . . Jane, do you like spending the weekend, or vacation, or however long, alone this way?"

"It's all right."

He laughed aloud. "Mary . . . Jane, I think it's safe to say I have not sparked you conversationally. Am I bothering you? Why are you walking with me?" Schroeder knew the answer to his last question before she gave it.

"I guess I'd rather not be alone."

"You'd better stop the string of compliments," he said mockingly, "or you'll turn a man's head."

"Oh, I guess you're used to flattery," she said, shocking him. Either her perception was quick, or his ego apparent. "You're a tall, handsome man, and you look very trim, which is rare for a man in his forties. My father had a pot belly when he was in his forties."

Schroeder's middle-aged sensitivities caught the kicker in the praise. "I'm only forty," he said. Then he was ashamed of himself. "How old is your father?" It would turn out, he feared, this girl's father was hardly older than he.

"He was fifty-six. He's dead."

Christ, Schroeder thought, that's what this soggy conversation needs, another dampener. "I'm sorry," he said.

She did not answer. They had been walking along Center, then down Main. They found themselves at the end of the street, down at the docks.

"Would you like to walk along and look at the boats?" he asked. "There are some mighty grand yachts here."

He stared at her, and she stared back. She was frightened

again. Her eyes held that combination of fear, wariness, and submissiveness he'd first seen just after the movies.

"No," she said. "I'd just as soon not see the boats. Boats don't interest me."

At least, he thought, she's finally spoken out on something. Score one for me. But on what scoreboard? Why am I in this . . . contest . . . or whatever it is? Is winning so important? And winning what?

Is it possible he was just being a nice guy? "A giving person"? Marty loved that expression: a giving person. She used it all the time, most often to tell him he was *not* one. Probably she was right; he didn't for an instant suppose he rated high grades on generosity. With material things, he was OK, he figured. But not on generosity of spirit—another of his ex-wife's favorites. No, he was not much on "giving of himself." On the other hand, he didn't think that even there his marks fell much below the class average.

But what about . . . Mary Jane, or whatever her name was? Why was he putting in this time and effort? He tried a couple of tests.

If sexual conquest was not his aim, would he have befriended a man in the same way? No. So his generosity failed that one. Not a conclusive test, he decided.

If he merely wanted to get laid, why was he pushing this arid, strained conversation with this unresponsive creature, when he could be with Rocky, who was beautiful and eager and supplied her own bed and brandy? Did that make his motives pure? Maybe. Maybe it just meant he was after sex, but not with his best friend's wife. Inconclusive, again.

As if it might serve to make something—just what, he wasn't sure—more conclusive, Schroeder asked: "Well, if no boats, why don't we have a drink, then, even though you don't drink much." Then, suddenly, there welled up in him, again, the feeling, why am I bothering, and he added: "Unless you'd just like me to walk you to wherever you're staying."

"I think I'd like a drink," she said slowly.

Well, what do you know? Schroeder said to himself. To her, a little more enthusiastically than he meant to, he said: "Good! We can go to Cap'n Tobey's right over there and have a drink. A nautical milieu, no boats!"

Another kind of test, but this time for her. He didn't know

anything about her—was she a secretary for an insurance company, a philosophy instructor at Boston University, a clerk at Filene's? Would "nautical milieu" puzzle her? Or would she think him pretentious?

She didn't bat an eye; she seemed to take it so easily she never bothered to comment on it. "That sounds fine" was all she said.

So they headed for Cap'n Tobey's, got a small table, and for the first time, he was able to look at her, closely and at length. Full face, close up, she was far more attractive than she'd seemed at the oblique angles at which he'd watched her before. Her eyes were large and set far apart, pale blue, quick and alert. Her jaw and mouth were both wide, a cross between Jacqueline Onassis' and Valerie Perrine's. Her reddish blond hair was shoulder length and silky; it moved whenever her head did, like the shampoo commercials. Her skin was pale, pink, almost transparent; he bet she had a hell of a sunburn problem. And she did not tweeze her eyebrows; Schroeder liked that.

"All right, then," he said, smiling, "what does someone who doesn't drink much, like to drink?"

She looked at him, tried another pale smile, and asked: "Why? Am I the first person you've ever known who doesn't drink?"

Ah ha, he thought, knows how to sting, and probably is *not* a clerk at Filene's. He tested her some more. "Touché," he said. She didn't blink, so he put a little more to it. "If the number of my drinking friends is legion, the nondrinkers I know add up to at least a cohort. You must understand my generation relies more on alcohol and less on other pain killers than yours."

The "touché," the "legion," the "cohort," all left her unstartled. "I've tried pot," she responded simply, "and haven't liked it." And then she added: "I suppose I should apologize for making you older than you are. Forty is really not old."

Oh, the pain of faint praise, he thought. And it hurt even more because she was trying to be kind. "Don't be silly," he answered, trying to sound grand. "To someone who's—how old? Twenty-four?—forty and fifty-six are pretty much the same."

"I'm twenty-three," she replied, looking sad again, at the reference to the age of her father. "Sixteen years is a lot," she continued, "and he looked more than sixteen years older than you. He had less hair, and it was grayer, and he'd gotten fat."

All at once he felt tender toward her. "Believe it or not, the point to this was to make you forget, not to remind you." Was that the point? he wondered. "I guess I've done badly. Let's change that; let's make this drink some fun. Does that sound too flippant?"

Her answer was a shrug. "By the way, what would you like to drink?"

"What are you going to have?" she asked.

"Cognac. Remy Martin, if they have it. If not, Hennessey."

"I'll have it, too."

He waved to the waitress, in a few minutes she arrived, a squarely built co-ed type, big thighs, wide hips bulging under a short black dress. "Two Remy Martins, please."

"I'm sorry, I didn't get that."

Schroeder repeated it, this time anglicizing the pronunciation. Still, the waitress looked blank.

"It's a kind of cognac. If they don't have it, we'll take Hennessey."

She walked off, came back with two full liqueur glasses. "This is Hennessey," she said, looking at Schroeder uncertainly.

"That'll be just fine." She walked away, pleased. He figured she'd given up on the Remy Martin and just asked for the one she could pronounce. What the hell, it didn't make much difference. He looked at the liqueur glasses; they were thick, flared at the top, having neither the charm of antiquity nor the chic of newness. He'd bet they hadn't been used in a long time.

"Obviously," he said to Mary Jane, "they're no more used to serving brandy here than you are to drinking it."

She looked at him as if he'd just interrupted something. "What do you mean?" she asked. Schroeder felt he'd taken two backward steps.

"Well, usually brandy is served in a snifter, one of those big balloon glasses on a short stem, so its fumes can rise up and attack your nose before the liquid attacks your liver."

It wasn't all that funny, he knew, but, damn, she might have made some recognition of the attempt. All she said was "Oh." The less she responded, the more determined he became to cheer her up.

He lifted his glass. "Here's to having a good weekend."

Reluctantly, she raised hers, and managed, "Yes," before sipping the brandy and making a face.

"Like it?"

An expression somewhere between smile and grimace came over her. "I'm not sure. I guess I don't like the taste, but it does feel warm going down." She took another sip.

"Careful," he said. "If you're not used to it, you'll feel it very quickly."

"I don't care," she replied. It was the closest she had come to letting go.

"What are you going to do to have a good time this weekend?" he asked.

"A good time?" She looked at him, almost startled. "I haven't thought about it. I don't know."

"Then I'll make some suggestions. You can swim. The beaches on the south side, on the ocean, have surf, if you like that; the ones near town, the Jetties Beach and Dionis, are calmer. And you can walk to the Jetties Beach, if you don't have a car. You can fish, in a pond, in the surf, off a boat; you can bicycle, the island's terrific for that; you can walk; I spent the whole day doing that; you can look through the Whaling Museum or browse in the shops, you can visit the old houses in town, you can go to see *King Kong*—again. Or you can sit and drink brandy. How's that?"

She smiled, and he was astonished, because her smile was dazzling, her teeth white and flawless.

"Anyone ever tell you you have a beautiful smile?"

"Yes," she said. "Sometimes." She actually seemed pleased. For an instant he thought he had charmed her, then saw that more likely it was the brandy. She had finished her glass; her face was flushed. The smile receded but the face remained more open and enthusiastic than it had been.

"I like the brandy, it makes me feel better."

"Then I'll get you another." He paused; he didn't want to appear—to her or to himself—to be forcing alcohol on her, to seem a semi-dirty, semi-old man. He added: "If you'd like it."

"Yes, please."

He signaled to the waitress, gesturing toward their glasses. Usually that was enough, but not this time. She came over, smiling, and asked: "May I help you?"

"Yes, two more, please."

"That was?"

"Hennessey . . . brandy."

"Oh, yes," she said, and walked off. Schroeder wondered

what she was majoring in, and hoped it didn't take too much mental acuity. The waitress returned, still smiling, placed the glasses on the table, and left.

"Would you like to tell me what you do in Boston, or shall I guess?"

She shrugged.

She is so dispirited, Schroeder thought, so pliable. He wondered how she *did* have fun.

"All right, I'll guess." His first impulse was to say, librarian, but he decided she'd be hurt by that. So he said: "You're either a teacher, or getting a master's to become a teacher."

"Which grade?" she asked.

"Nursery school, or kindergarten."

She stared at him, as if hesitating. Then: "No, I'm not a teacher at all."

Her response seemed fishy, as it had when she gave her name. If she wasn't a teacher, why had she first asked which grade? "I give up," he said. "Tell me."

"No, first you tell me what *you* do," she said. Schroeder was willing to bet she was stalling so she could fabricate an answer. But he wouldn't press her.

"Don't you want to guess?" he asked.

"No." She took a sip of brandy, then corrected herself. "Yes." She stared at him for a couple of seconds. "You're a stockbroker," she said.

"Ouch. Christ, I guess that hurts worse than hearing I look like I'm in my forties. I'm a writer for a news magazine."

"Why should that hurt?" she asked.

"I guess what I'd like is to have the look of a writer and the money of a stockbroker. Instead, I'm stuck with just the opposite, at least in your eyes. It's not the way I see myself. How would you like it if I said you looked like a librarian? You're not, are you?"

"A librarian? No."

"All right then, what?"

Another hesitation. "I work for a lawyer."

What was she hiding? "What do you do for the lawyer?"

"I'm a legal secretary."

My God, he thought, that's as bad as a librarian. He hoped she didn't think so. But she did.

"I suppose that's as prosaic as being a librarian, isn't it?"

"Hell, no, sounds a lot more exciting," he replied, gallantly. "Anyway, don't pay any attention to my judgments. Besides, I'd rather talk about the weekend. Why did you come here alone? What would you like to do, if you had your choice of anything, anywhere, with anyone?"

"Oh, my," she said, and took another drink of brandy. And smiled again. Only bigger. Radiant. Stretching wide the Jackie-Valerie mouth with its gleaming, regular, white teeth. It was her one outstanding physical asset, he decided. "That's a difficult question."

"Maybe I can help," he said. "I know what you *don't* like."

"What?" she asked.

"Walking alone down dark, empty streets."

The smile started to go, but the brandy held it.

"That's something new. I never used to be afraid. I used to *love* dark places, like the beach at night—hearing the surf, watching the stars. I loved swimming. I guess I still do. And I guess I don't half mind the warm feeling of brandy going down my throat."

"Why, you're becoming positively voluble!" Another small vocabulary test, and again she went by it easily. "I guess I have been kind of quiet," she said, with the smile that now came a little more easily.

She had too much education for a legal secretary, he thought, and decided to ask about it. "What made you become a legal secretary? Did you take special courses to learn?"

"I graduated from Boston University," she said, turning wary. "Then I didn't know quite what to do, so I went to Katharine Gibbs, to learn some skills I could pay my way with. And got a job as a secretary in a law office."

"How long have you been doing it?"

"Let's see," she said. "I graduated two years ago, and I started work just before Christmas of that year, so it's been a year and a half."

That time reconstruction, he thought, was more for her benefit than his, to let her figure out what would make sense. No, he didn't believe her.

"Like it?" he asked.

"The law part of it's fine; I hate being a secretary, though."

"Funny, isn't it," he said, "how so many people spend so much time doing things they enjoy so little. I'm doing it myself. Did you ever wonder why?"

"I suppose they have no choice; they have to take what they can get."

"If you could do whatever you want—anything," he asked, "what would it be?"

"You mean right now?"

"No, no, I didn't . . . but, OK, right now."

She hesitated. "I think I'd like to be sitting and listening to the surf."

"Look," he said, "now that we've established that I'm old enough to be your father . . ."

"I didn't say that," she interrupted.

"All right, *almost* old enough to be your father. I have a car and wouldn't at all mind driving you to a beach where you could hear the surf."

"Oh, I don't know . . ." Her voice trailed off. Her diffidence had returned, and with it the alert wariness of an animal being tracked.

He smiled. "You'd be safe. And I think I'd kind of like it myself."

Her face eased. "Could I have one more brandy first?"

Schroeder glanced at her glass. Empty, again. This would be the third, a lot of brandy for a non-drinker. "Do you think you should?"

"Don't act old enough to be my . . . father." She'd started the sentence lightly, but had to tiptoe over the word father.

"All right, one more. We'll each have one." He finished his glass and signaled the waitress. This time she understood the gesture, and brought the drinks at once.

He raised his glass. "I hope you get to do what you want."

"I do, too." Then, abruptly remembering to return the wish, she said: "Same for you."

"Are you getting drunk?" he asked.

"I'm feeling very warm," she answered. "I don't have enough experience at getting drunk to know if that's it."

Schroeder had to laugh. "Sounds like it's it. Or on the way, at any rate. No more."

They finished their drinks, speaking no more, and she stayed silent as he paid the check.

Out on Main Street, they walked slowly up toward Center and back to Schroeder's rented house, where his car stood. Behind them, a vehicle moved slowly; he could hear its engine, and once he turned. It was a Land-Rover. He thought it might be the same tan vehicle that had gone by them in front of the Sand-piper, but Jeeps and Land-Rovers abounded on this island, like gulls and watercolors. When he turned, the tan vehicle stopped, the two men in it, busy in conversation. He was catching her apprehensiveness, he thought, and turned back and kept walk-ing, saying nothing to the young woman. But it *was* the same vehicle; those *were* the two in the wide-brimmed hats and the dark glasses.

After they turned the corner, she said to him: "Will your wife like your being out this late?"

"She *likes* me to spend my time drinking, womanizing, and gambling. She says it keeps me out of trouble." When she gave him a blank look, he explained, "That's an old Joe E. Lewis joke." Then, seeing no change on her face, added: "You don't know who Joe E. Lewis is—was, do you?"

She shook her head. He grinned at her. "Forget it. I don't have a wife, not anymore. I'm staying at this house with my two children, and an older woman. My mother."

"Who is Joe E. Lewis?"

"Oh, he was a comedian, who used a lot of material about what a roué he was. And I guess he was; at least he looked it."

"Oh."

Bringing this bit of trivia to the quiet streets of Nantucket made Schroeder suddenly feel old and banal, as if he should be on Seventh Avenue, in front of the Stage Delicatessen, instead of on India Street, walking by the two-hundred-year-old home of some whaling captain.

He got away from Joe E. Lewis as quickly as he could. "You said you liked to look at the stars. Can you tell one from the other?"

"No," she replied. "Not a one."

"I can't either," said Schroeder. "Well, with some luck, I might find the Big Dipper, and I think it's supposed to lead you to the North Star, but I can't remember whether you're sup-posed to follow the curve of the handle or of the mouth of the dipper."

"I think I could find the Big Dipper too," she said, and he heard, or thought he heard, a small laugh from her as she spoke.

Another surge of sympathy swept over him as he heard it. No one should have to go away alone this way, not for a good time. Go to the movies alone, eat alone, walk dark streets alone. Well, maybe some people, those with strength and purpose, with thoughts to sort out. Not a timid little girl like this one. He wanted to cheer her up.

"Someone once tried to teach me all about the stars," he said. "Do you know why I couldn't learn?"

"No, why?"

"Because standing there, looking up, gave me a stiff neck. It was an awful thing to have to admit when you were trying to be a good learner, and soulful, to boot. To say, I have a stiff neck, no more for today. But that's the way it was."

She didn't laugh; instead, she said, seriously, "One could lie on one's back, couldn't one, to prevent that?"

"One could indeed. In fact I have an old blanket in the trunk of the car, for the express purpose of saving one's neck." They were almost at the house; Schroeder looked ahead, he could see no lights inside. Just as well. The car was on the street, not in the driveway, not directly in front of the house. Just as well, too. He'd rather not wake anybody, rather not have his mother peeking out the window, seeing him climb into the car at—he looked at his watch—ten minutes after midnight, with a twenty-three-year-old girl.

Edith Schroeder already viewed with alarm the romantic and sexual habits of her own son. And Schroeder had the feeling her objections were less moralistic than pragmatic. If she could write a scenario, he figured, its theme would be security, not purity. If he were riding off to the beach with a woman, his mother, he'd bet, would like it to be the daughter of the president of Connecticut General, or Aetna Life, or Hartford Fire and Casualty, object: matrimony, and a job for Sam Schroeder as the insurance company's vice-president in charge of public relations. His mother wouldn't really care what happened on the beach, he'd bet, as long as it furthered the scenario.

He got in the driver's side, leaned over and opened the front passenger door, motioning for her to climb in and keep quiet. She clicked the door shut gently, and he started the engine and drove off.

"Is this your first time on the island?" he asked her.

"Yes, it is."

"Well, what do you think?"

"I haven't been here long enough to tell, I haven't seen much."

"What made you choose it? I mean, alone, not knowing it?"

Watching the road, as he made a left onto Main and then almost at once a right onto Pleasant, he couldn't see her face, but thought he heard in her voice a return to the old wariness. "I just wanted to get out of town, and I was able to get a seat on the plane. I thought I'd try it."

"I certainly hope it gets better for you." He turned onto Surfside Road.

"The brandy helps," she replied.

"You really feel it, don't you?"

"Yes, it makes me warm and sleepy, and not as scared as I was before. I can see why people use alcohol, it's good, it's comfortable to feel this way." She put her head back on the seat. "I have wine sometimes, but it doesn't do *this*."

"I'm surprised," he said, "you haven't used pot to get that same good feeling."

He looked over toward her; she smiled. "I've tried it, but it never did a thing. Maybe it's because I don't think I ever really learned to inhale properly; maybe it's because I'm so close to the law all day that I get worried because it's illegal. So I can't relax and enjoy it."

"That's funny," he replied, "because your name is a slang term for marijuana." She gave him a blank look.

"Mary Jane, you know?" he said.

"Mary Jane means marijuana? No, I didn't know that."

More proof, he said to himself, that she is no Mary Jane. Anyone with that name would have known long ago. "Now you know," he said.

"Thank you," she replied. "And thank you for being so kind to me. And for the brandy."

Schroeder pulled the car to a stop at the beach and turned off the lights and the engine. One other parked car stood there, a small MG, and in it a boy and a girl were necking. Funny, he said to himself, a forty-year-old parking at the beach at night. It's for teen-agers like those. Or a twenty-three-year-old like her. But not with me.

"Do you want to try the beach?" he asked. "Or sit here in the car?"

"Oh, no! The beach!" She answered with real enthusiasm. "I want to hear the surf, and lie on the blanket and see the stars. Without getting a stiff neck." She looked at him and grinned.

No question, he thought, her Jackie-Valerie smile *was* her best feature. "I want to feel the sand between my toes." And she leaned forward and began taking off her sneakers; she wore no socks. He took off his sneakers too. Then he went around to the trunk, opened it and got the blanket. He walked to the right side of the car and opened the door for her.

"Come on," he said, "we should walk down the beach a bit, to get away from this street light; it'll help our star-gazing."

Schroeder was palpably aware that in a few moments, they'd be on a blanket, on a warm June night, on a darkened beach. He looked at her quickly. He could see the couple in the car had made her think of it, too. Just as quickly he looked away.

They started toward the beach, the girl clutching the leather purse she had been carrying all evening. She swayed slightly, bumping him. "I'm sorry," she said. "I can't see too well."

"Do you suppose the brandy might have something to do with that slight collision?" he asked.

"I suppose," she answered, almost with a giggle. "But it feels so good, I'd like another one."

"Another one and I'd have to carry you," he said, as she stumbled again. "Here, take my hand." He reached out and she seized his hand, squeezing it. He led her to the right, in the direction of Miacomet Pond; the night was surprisingly warm for June, for their proximity to the ocean. As they walked, and the dunes began to block the light on the road, they were in darkness except for the half-moon and the stars, which were brilliant, crisply defined, and countless on this cloudless night.

After a hundred yards of trudging through the sand, he turned and looked, and was satisfied they were away from the road light. "Near the water, or the dunes?" he asked.

"The water," she said. As they headed for it, he said: "Sorry I can't produce any thunderous surf for you. It's just too calm. You'll have to settle for some steady, gentle, lapping sounds."

"They suit me just fine," she said. She had not let go of his hand, and when he disengaged it so he could spread the blanket, she loosened her grip reluctantly. It's fear, and it's brandy, he reminded himself; he sat next to her on the blanket, keeping an unthreatening distance.

"The waves seem to glow in the dark as they break," she said.

"Yes," he answered, "There's supposed to be something,

maybe algae, that's phosphorescent in them. I'm not sure what, I guess I'm as weak a naturalist as I am an astronomer."

"You know more than I do, anyway," she said. As she did, she leaned forward, watching the gentle surf, lifting her knees close to her chest and clutching them with her arms. "I think they could use ocean waves to hypnotize people, they could me, anyway. My problem is, I don't know whether to concentrate on the water or the sky."

He laughed. "Take them one at a time. That, as they say, should be your biggest problem."

She looked at him. "Are you Jewish?" she asked suddenly.

"No." He was amused. "Why?"

"Because of the way you said, 'that should be your biggest problem,' which sounded like the kind of thing some Jewish people would say. And your name, Schroeder, I thought it could be Jewish."

"No, it's German. But in New York, everyone takes on a Jewish intonation here and there. It's part of the city's flavor."

He stared at her. "Do you dislike Jews, or something?"

"Oh no," she answered quickly. "Some of our best lawyers are Jewish. I mean, in the firm."

He grinned. "How about some of your best friends?"

"I know how it sounded, but I didn't mean that," she replied. "Yes, a few of my best friends are Jewish. My school, BU, had a lot of Jews." She hesitated. "My . . . ex-boyfriend is."

"OK," he said, "you're clean on that, no bigotry charges. Go ahead and make up your mind on the stars versus the ocean." He'd heard the "ex-boyfriend," and felt more sympathy for her.

She let go of her knees and fell back. "My first vote goes to the stars," she said. As she stretched out, her T-shirt rode up to uncover a couple of inches of flesh at her waist. Beneath the folds of the baggy clothing, she was thinner than he had thought.

The girl put her hand to her forehead and said, "Oh, my. Oh, my!"

"What's the matter?"

"I got dizzy. I guess it's the brandy."

"It's probably because you lay back. If you sit up again, it might help. Here." He held out his hand. She took it and used it to sit up. "I guess it's the ocean again, for me." Without loosening her grip on his hand, she sat there, looking tentative, waiting to see if the dizziness would go away.

"OK?" he asked.

"A little better."

"Maybe if you doused a little water on your head . . ."

"Yes, of course," she said. Then, "No, I've got a better idea." She turned and looked at him. "I want to go into the water. If I go, will you go with me? I'll only do it if you do, too."

"The water's kind of cold, it's only June."

"Oh, come on!"

Of course, he'd have to go. Because he was supposed to be cheering her up. Because he was forty. Because he didn't do things like that. Because he began to sense what it would lead to.

"OK."

"Then help me up."

Schroeder got to his feet and held out a hand, pulled her up, too. Without pausing, she slipped her T-shirt over her head, revealing a plain flesh-colored bra, through which he could make out the nipples of her smallish breasts. Around her neck, on a thin golden chain, hung a small crucifix. She was soft, pale-skinned, tending toward pudginess, but as the strip of skin around her waist had presaged, not as stocky as she'd appeared in her baggy outfit. She unzipped her painter's pants, dropped them, stepped out of them and stood facing him. Her underpants, of white nylon, were bikini cut. Below them, her thighs and calves were heavy and well formed; above them, her abdomen was rounded, but not flabby, and the width of her hips tapered gracefully to a small waist.

Even in the semidarkness, he thought he could see her face flushed, and was not sure if it was the brandy, the effort of bending over to remove her pants, or modesty.

"Well, I'm going to go in this way," she said, as if to warn him there'd be no further undressing from her. When he didn't move, she said, as she had before, "Come on!"

With his eyes on her face, Schroeder began unbuttoning his shirt, and then took it off. Then he unbuckled his belt and opened his jeans, looking down as he slipped them off, knowing he was beginning to get hard, wanting to see if it showed. It did; he didn't care.

"All right, come on," he said. She reached out and took his hand again, and they walked down to the edge of the water.

When the first wave hit their feet, she let out a little scream, and he gasped. It was damned cold.

"I think I'll just dab some on my head," she said.

"Oh no, you won't!" he answered, clutching her hand. "Not now that you've gotten us down here. Now we go all the way!" He walked forward, pulling her with him. Damn, the water was cold!

"No! No! I can't! It's too cold! Please!" But she was happy and titillated as she shouted it.

"Oh yes, you can!" He dragged her forward; they were in water up to their knees.

"I can't swim, please!" She was gasping and laughing.

"Don't worry, you won't go in that deep. Just enough to wet you."

She dug her heels in and threw her weight back toward the shore, trying to free her hand. Schroeder pulled her toward him, and as she turned away from him, trying to walk toward shore, put his arm around her waist, and hugged her to him, his semi-erect penis pressing against the softness of her buttocks.

Did she feel it? he wondered. How could she not? Yet she made no attempt to get away. In fact she virtually stopped struggling, and he, being eight or nine inches taller, lifted her off her feet easily and carried her out so the water was just below his waist. Without letting go, he dunked her so that her entire body, except for her head was submerged.

"Oh, no! Please, no! It's too cold!" And the water was cold; he had trouble catching his breath. But he knew she was enjoying herself for the first time since he had met her.

Schroeder let go of her, and used both hands to splash water on her face and hair, to complete the dousing. She gave one splash in return, and then raced for shore, her plump rear jouncing as she ran. Schroeder loped after her, gaining easily, but letting her stay ahead of him, until she reached the blanket and threw herself down on her stomach. She lay there, breathing deeply, gasping. Schroeder stood above her looking down on her. He found her body sensuous. Her shoulders were soft, up-holstered; so were her back and her arms. Her waist was narrow, and it widened to a substantial rear end and hips. Her flimsy underpants, soaked and pasted against her, were almost invisible. Her buttocks seemed bare. Her upper thighs were chubby, and he could see the beginning ripples of cellulite, which boded no good for the Mary Jane—or whoever—of ten years hence.

For a moment she lay gasping, he stood looking. Then he lay down on his stomach next to her, his face turned toward hers. First she said, "Oh, it does feel good now!" She fell silent, and the two of them stared at each other, saying nothing, for perhaps five seconds. Then, in a quick motion, she reached her left hand to the back of her neck to scratch herself. "The drops of water make me tickly," she said, sounding for the moment like a carefree young child.

He lifted up on his elbows and turned toward her. "Let me do that for you." He didn't wait for her to reply, but reached with his left hand and gently began scratching her neck and between her shoulder blades, slipping his hand under the golden chain when it got in his way.

"Do you like hard scratches, or soft?" he asked.

"Soft," she said, softly. "Like you're doing, only softer. Almost a tickle, but not quite."

For a few moments Schroeder ran his nails as lightly as he could over the skin of her neck and back, within the area marked off by the straps of her brassiere. Then he said, "This thing is interfering with the flow of my scratching," and again without waiting for an answer, unhooked the bra. "Now that I've got a bigger stretch to work on," he told her, "I'd better use two hands." Schroeder got on his haunches, and devoted himself to the artistry of his scratch-tickling, using both sets of nails, with vertical strokes, then horizontal, then diagonal, then circular, descending slowly as he did from her neck and upper back to her ribs, to her waist, to the flare of her hips and the tops of her buttocks and her bikini underpants.

He let his scratching, tickling, stroking fingers slide under the slippery nylon pants, then paused and said, "This thing is interfering with the flow of my scratching." And once again without asking, he slid the pants down. Until then her only response to his hands had been to close her eyes and to breathe deeply; when he started to remove her underpants, she lifted her hips slightly to make it easier.

This time Schroeder began from her ankles and worked up, but as he did, the scratching was more and more replaced by a gentle rubbing. When he reached her upper thighs and buttocks, he was stroking and kneading her skin, running his fingers deeply into the creases where her buttocks met her legs, prob-ing between her legs, briefly, teasingly, then withdrawing his hand.

"OK, that side's done, now turn over."

Obediently, she did.

Schroeder began again, at her neck, with the delicate scratch-ing, but now did not linger at it quite so long; he moved his hands to her breasts, which were small and soft and, surpris-ingly, outthrust, considering she was lying on her back, pressing them, teasing the nipples, then worked down her waist, to the soft round abdomen. He slid one hand between her legs and as he did she opened them slightly.

Schroeder leaned forward and kissed her mouth. Then her left nipple. Then her mouth again. The two fingers of his left hand, between her legs, slid into her vagina easily; it was moist and slippery.

"Do you like that?" he asked, and then thought, what a stu-pid question, what a goddamned stupid question.

"Yes. Oh, yes."

He moved his fingers in and out of her, running them to her clitoris at the top of each stroke; she began thrusting with her hips. Quickly, he took both hands away from her and slipped off his shorts. Then he stretched his body full length on top of hers. She put her hands on his back, and rubbed it fervently. Before he went into her, he asked: "Is it all right if I have an orgasm inside you?" Schroeder always asked, and was never satisfied with the wording, but at the moment he was not disposed to rewrites.

"Yes," she answered in a soft, thick voice. "Yes, it's all right. Yes. But don't hurry. Go slowly."

He laughed to himself as he answered, "Don't worry. I'll go slowly." He almost added: At my age, speed is not such a prob-lem. But didn't. His penis slipped into her as easily as his fingers had, and she wrapped her legs around him. As he thrust in and out, she kept repeating, "Yes, it's all right. Yes. Yes," the sounds moving from words, to sighs, to gasps.

Faster and faster they moved, harder and harder she clutched at his back, closer and closer he came to an orgasm, more and more he had to hold back, trying to wait for her, higher and higher he soared. And then, unable, unwilling, to control the eruption, he came off in a burst of sensation and delight.

She kept thrusting at him, and he back at her, but when they both felt him grow soft she settled back and he let his body sag onto hers. He kissed her mouth.

"I couldn't wait any longer. You didn't come, did you?"

"It's all right," she said. "It feels so good, so good. Don't worry." As she spoke her body gently undulated against his. After a few more moments, he rolled off her and lay on his back.

"That was so delightful, Mary Jane"—and for the first time he used her name flowingly, as if he believed it was really hers—"so marvelous, I wish you had had one, too."

"Oh, stop worrying. It felt lovely."

But Schroeder was determined. After thirty seconds of lying still, he said: "Come on, let's go in the water again, it's better with no clothes on."

"It's so cold," she said, but not decisively, so he stood, seized her hand and hoisted her to her feet.

"Come on; it'll make a new man of me."

"The old one does pretty well."

"Not well enough." He half led her, half dragged her to the water, carried her in, and dropped her with a splash. Again she ran out, but happily. Again he caught her; this time she stood on the sand near the blanket, shivering, jumping up and down to keep warm.

"Let me pound the blood into all those capillaries" he said. "That'll warm you." He began kneading and slapping her skin, gently, as she stood there. His hands ran over her breasts, her belly, he kneeled to work on her hips and thighs, then her buttocks, kissing each buttock lightly as he did. She grew quieter, more intense, expecting more. But he stopped, and stood up.

"OK, now you work on my capillaries."

Enthusiastically, she began rubbing and pounding his chest and shoulders, and worked down to his midsection.

"Hey! That's not much fat . . . for a man of forty!"

"At least you didn't say 'in his forties.' Thanks!"

Then, more carefully, she moved below his waist, kneeling to reach his hips and thighs, but avoiding his penis, which was now fully erect again, until she kissed it—first one side, then the other, then the tip. Then she took it into her mouth.

"Wait," he said, putting his hands on the sides of her head. "Let's do it together."

They lay down on the blanket, with her head toward the dunes and his toward the ocean. He tasted the saltiness, hers and the ocean's, both delicious.

Schroeder was sure that this time he wouldn't have to worry about coming before she did. And he was not surprised when she had an orgasm first, writhing, feverish, exultant, astoundingly energetic for so docile a girl. What did surprise him was that his came so effortlessly—a second orgasm in a night was no longer anything he took for granted.

His contentment was so deep, he just lay there with her in that reversed position, both of them chilled, yet glowing, for a few minutes that seemed an hour before they roused themselves, dressed, and walked back to the car.

Chapter

A FEW MINUTES AFTER EIGHT, THE THREE MEN LANDED ON Nantucket, Red and Mike both wearing light-colored windbreakers, chino trousers, big hats, and dark glasses, the Pussycat, a fedora, sports coat, and trousers so faded their colors were hard to determine. All three carried satchels, of the kind athletes use to carry their equipment.

Red looked around until he saw the Land-Rover, approached the man standing alongside, and showed one of the fake driver's licenses he always carried. The man looked at it, nodded, and Red then paid him in cash.

"You want a receipt?" the man asked. "I trust you," Red replied. "You trust me?"

"Of course," the man said. "Thanks, then. And I'll pick it up at Straight Wharf, right?"

"Right," said Red, "Tomorrow. Sunday at the latest."

"OK," said the man, and started to turn away.

"Hold it," said Red. "You got a ride to wherever you're going?"

"Yeah," answered the man. "My wife's right there in the Chevvy."

"Good," said Red. "See you." He watched the man walk away; he was pleased, he didn't want the man to take any of the cabs; Red had to talk to the drivers.

Red had told the other two to wait alongside the terminal while he found the vehicle. Now he waited till the Chevvy drove off before walking back to them.

"Do me a favor, Pussycat," he said. "Go sit in that Land-Rover. It's in a no-parking zone, and we don't want to get in trouble."

Obediently, the old man waddled off. There was no point in attracting a cop's attention for a stupid little thing like a parking violation. At the same time, Red never missed a chance to humiliate someone he didn't like. And he didn't like the Pussycat at all.

Mike he was not crazy about either, but Mike was no lead anchor, like Pussycat. Mike could do the job, and at the same time was no threat. "I'm going to talk to the cabbies, Mike. Why don't you go inside the terminal, look at the schedules or something. When you see me walk toward the Rover, you walk out, head out the road away from the terminal, we'll pick you up." Red knew they might have been seen leaving the chartered plane together, if anyone was looking, but he thought the sooner they stopped marching around as a highly noticeable trio, the better. He was methodical with details like that. Not imaginative, but careful; he wanted to take no unnecessary chances.

Red walked toward the line of waiting taxis and approached a cluster of three drivers standing together. "Listen," he said, "My niece, my sister's girl, left home, and I'm trying to locate her." Without using Felicia O'Brien's name, he described her and showed the snapshot he'd gotten from the police. Each man looked at it and shook his head.

"There's ten bucks in it if you can help."

Again they shook their heads. "Nope," said one. "Sorry," said another.

Red walked to a driver standing alone, repeated the request, showed the picture. "The only people from that flight I drove," said the driver, "I took to the White Elephant." He, too, shook his head. Then, as Red was about to move on, he added: "Why don't you try Hawkie over there?" He nodded toward a hatchet-faced man sitting in a nearby cab. "He got a fare off that flight."

Yes, Hawkins did recognize the girl, and knew exactly where he'd driven her, because she'd asked his recommendation, and he'd taken her to Mrs. Metcalfe's. She was one of his and his wife's best friends, and her house was clean and neat, and had a lot of . . .

Red interrupted him with the promised ten-dollar bill, and said, "There's another ten if you draw me a little map to show me how to get there. I've only been on the island once before and I don't know it too well."

Hawkins did, and watched him walk off. Then the driver walked over to the others. "Well, I just made a quick twenty bucks," he said with a cackle.

As arranged, Red, with Pussycat in the back seat, picked up Mike on the road and they headed for the town. Following the driver's instructions, they found the house at 17 Hulbert Avenue and stopped on the street just beyond it.

"So far, so good. In fact, couldn't be better," said Red. "With any luck we could have her on the boat in a half hour."

"And then we take right off." There was as much question in Mike's voice as there was statement.

"Maybe," Red said, "Maybe not." He hated anybody to try to take the lead from him. "I've only handled a twenty-eight-footer a couple of times, and I don't know I'm ready to go out of the harbor after dark. You ready to do it, Mike?"

"Naw," Mike said, "I ain't even skippered as much as you."

Red looked around at the old man. "Then how about you, Pussy, you going to be captain?"

"I can't steer no boat," said the old man.

"So I guess it's gotta be up to me." It was not a question, it was another putdown. "Once we get hold of her, what's the hurry, anyway? No one's going to be looking for us. I'd rather wait and go out first thing in the morning. Play the percentages. We'll see."

"Yeah," said Mike. Pussycat said nothing.

"OK, then," said Red. "Next step, I go in. Mike, you keep an eye on that side door, I'll call you if I need you. Pussycat, sit in the car so we don't get a ticket. You know how to drive, don't you Pussy?"

"Yeah," said the old man. The repeated putdowns were beginning to get through even his thick skin.

From force of habit, Red patted his left hip, where he wore a small snub-nosed .44. The two men got out of the vehicle, leaving Pussycat sitting there. Red watched Mike walk to the side door and station himself there, then, tipping his hat down, he went up to the front door. Instead of ringing, he tried the door. It was open; he walked in, quietly, and listened. He could hear nothing. He looked in at a small living room crammed with overstuffed furniture and the bric-a-brac accumulated by someone who has lived in a house for many years; but Red was not interested in decor. At once, he dismissed the room, walked through to the dining room and into the kitchen. Then, delicately for a man of Red's bulk, he tiptoed up the back stairs. For an instant he stood, frozen, listening. When he heard nothing he tried the bedrooms, two of which Mrs. Metcalfe rented, one of which she used herself. All were empty. So were the two baths. He spotted the door leading to the attic. He went up. Empty. Softly, he said, "Shit." Then went downstairs quickly. In the kitchen he found the cellar stairs, and went down, silently. There was no one in the basement. Through the window of the kitchen door he could see Mike standing, staring vacantly off into the distance. Red opened the door and said, "Boo!"

Mike jumped and whirled around. Red laughed at him. Red had a touch of sadism that went beyond the call of duty.

"Just wanted to see if you were on your toes. There's no one around. Looks like we don't get away with any fucking half-hour job." He walked back to the Land-Rover, Mike following, and climbed in, indicating with a jab of his thumb he wanted the old man to resume his place in the back. Again, saying nothing he pointed to Mike and the driver's seat. The swarthy man got behind the wheel.

"We gonna sit here and wait for her to come back?" he asked.

Red thought for a moment. "No," he answered. The three of us sitting here, it might scare her away if she spotted us. Especially you two guys. Me, I could pass for her religion teacher. Isn't that right, Pussycat?"

"Her name O'Brien?" the old man said. "That's Irish, right?

That makes her a Catholic, right?" He pronounced the *th* in Catholic as if it were a *t*.

"So what?" Red asked sharply. He hadn't meant to start a conversation with the old man.

"So if she's a Catholic," answered the Pussycat, "her religion teacher would be a priest or a nun, and you don't look like no priest or no nun."

Red grew more annoyed; he felt that contending with the old man was beneath him. "What the fuck are you, old man, a religion expert? When's the last time you went to Mass?"

"Sunday," replied the old man. "When's the last time you went?"

"What the fuck is this, confession?" said Red, and seeing he wasn't humiliating the Pussycat this time, changed the subject. "Let's drive into town, Mike. We've got to find that boat we've chartered. You drive down Main Street to the docks."

With some directions from Red, the swarthy driver found Straight Wharf. From a public phone, Red called the yacht's owner, who met them at the dock in five minutes. He walked the three to a dinghy powered by an outboard. On its bow was the name "Sloppy Joe." The four men got in, the owner looking like a reed next to the bulk of the others. He started the engine and they headed for the yacht, the *Sloppy Joe*, a twenty-eight-footer tied to a buoy perhaps a hundred yards out. "Let's see now, Mr. Redding, is it?" the owner began.

"Yes, Mr. Redding." It was one of the names for which Red had fake identification.

"Mr. Redding, you say you know how to handle a boat this size?"

"Oh, yeah," said Red. "Done it many times. Just give me a little run-through and I'll be OK."

They pulled alongside and climbed aboard, and the owner showed Red around the boat, while Mike and Pussycat stayed aboard the dinghy. In a few minutes Red and the owner got back into the dinghy, and Red jabbed a thumb at Pussycat.

"OK, old man, climb aboard and stay there so we don't get any parking tickets." Red gave a short laugh, at which the owner smiled, to be polite. Pussycat stood up and laboriously lifted his bulk aboard the *Sloppy Joe*.

"Hey, Pussycat," yelled Red, "Don't try to work anything except the head, understand? Or, better still, pee over the side."

Satisfied that he had finished ahead of the old man this time, Red told the owner to get started back to the dock. When the two men were back in the Land-Rover, Red showed Mike the snapshot of Felicia O'Brien, and gave him the description the police had given. "Very ordinary," he told Mike, "except for the skin and hair. Which are pale; they say you can almost see through 'em. And she's got on a light blue T-shirt, blue sneakers and painter's pants, you know, the ones like jeans, except they're light-colored, almost white, and baggy. But I don't think we'll have too much trouble. It's a small town on a small island, and the tourists haven't packed the place, yet. Another couple of weeks, it'd be like a needle in a haystack. And it'll be a lot easier now that we're rid of the old fart. That fat old fart sure is dumb. It must have taken him a lot of years to get so stupid; no one could do it quickly—not *that* dumb."

Mike smiled unenthusiastically; he didn't like the way Red was on the old man all the time, but he didn't want to start anything. This time he did venture to say, "Y'know, we could all be like him when we get old."

"Are you kidding?" said Red. "Not *me*."

"Where you gonna be?"

"I'm going to work my way up, so I don't have to do crummy little jobs like this one anymore. I'm going for a better spot, a chance to get a bigger hunk of the pie."

Almost at once, Red was sorry he'd announced his ambition; quickly he changed the subject.

"All right, Mikey, how about moving out of here?" The dark man started the engine, and they drove off. The men cruised the streets for an hour, looking, saying little, before Mike went back to the subject of Red's ambition.

"How high you wanna go, Red? You after Mr. B.'s job?" Mike thought it funny, and was amazed when Red answered: "Why not?"

"You're kiddin'!" Mike looked at the hefty redheaded man next to him.

"No, I'm not kidding. You think I want to be some broken-down has-been, like the old fart, hanging around all day, waiting for somebody to throw me a bone?"

"Mr. B.'s a *lawyer!*"

"So what's the big deal about that? I already got some college credits. Hell, I'd go to undertaker's school if it would help!"

"You been to college, no shit?"

"Yeah, no shit. And some day you're going to be calling me Mister, just like everyone calls the Big Man." He wondered if he should be saying this; he decided to stop. "Hey, come on, keep your eyes open for that dame."

He'd already decided to give it ten more minutes, then go back to the house on Hulbert Avenue and wait her out; it was getting close to 10:30. Three minutes later, Red spotted the girl, coming out of the Sandpiper. "I think that's her, goddammit," he announced exultantly.

They were only fifty yards from her, when they saw the tall man with the graying hair and the athletic build approach her. They watched the two talk and then walk off together.

"Slow down," said Red. "And just keep following them. Always some fucking complication. Maybe we ought to run them both down." Mike gave him a dubious look, and Red added: "No, I'm just kidding. We got time; let's wait 'em out."

The couple started to cross the street; Mike at once slowed down to let them, but the man turned and saw the Land-Rover moving toward them. He grabbed the girl's arm to hold her back and let them go by. Seeing this, Mike accelerated slightly and went by them, then driving much faster, went around the block and picked them up again.

"He looks like an FBI man," said Mike.

"Yeah, but would an FBI man wear jeans? Naw, I say he's a married stockbroker, or a lawyer, looking to get laid. Why else would he bother with a nothing of a broad like that? Just follow 'em."

Slowly, skillfully, Mike stayed behind them, watched them go into Cap'n Tobey's. Then the two men sat in the vehicle for more than an hour, until the girl and man came out. Again Mike followed as they walked to a house and quietly climbed into a car.

"See?" said Red. "What did I tell you? They can't go into the house because probably his wife and kids are there. So here they go. Off to the beach, for a quickie."

"Hope she don't get sand in it," said Mike, laughing.

They followed the man's car as it headed out toward Surfside beach. As they approached the road's end, Mike slowed down.

"Just give them a chance to get out of the car and go onto the beach," Red told the other man. "Then we can go right to the end of the road, like we're here to look at the ocean and the stars. All those fucking high-class types come here to do that.

To watch the ocean and the stars and get away from it all. That's why the assholes pay so much dough to sit on this boring island."

Slowly Mike pulled up to the end of the road and stopped the vehicle. For less than ten seconds their headlights picked up the forms of their quarry and her friend, then the two were out of sight, gone into the darkness.

"Turn off your lights," Red ordered. Mike did, and they sat in a darkness which, as their eyes grew used to it, turned into the dim light of a half-moon. Three cars were parked near them, two of them occupied by couples.

Red looked around. "You see," he told Mike. "Star gazers, ocean watchers. Kids necking. Queers. Very sensitive. We could sit here as long as we wanted, as long as we looked sensitive. But you'd have to hold my hand, Mike."

The dark man looked startled, and Red laughed at him. "What's the matter, don't you have any fucking sense of humor?"

"What do we do now?" Mike asked, forgetting the subject of humor.

"We could go out on the beach and find them. Maybe catch them in the act. Make them put on a show for us. That'd be fun, huh? Think they could fuck with a gun in their ass, Mike?"

The other man didn't know if this was more humor or not. Red was such a mean son of a bitch he might do it. Red laughed at him again.

"Well, now that we know she's using that guy for a quick fuck, not a getaway—unless she's a helluva swimmer, that is . . ." Red laughed again. "I guess the smartest thing to do is go back to her rooming house and sit and wait for her gray-haired lover boy to drop her fucked-out form at the house. Although I wouldn't half mind going out on that beach and maybe joining in. Huh, Mike?"

Mike just started the engine. He didn't know about Red's jokes any more. And didn't want to guess, just get out of there. Red was sick, college or no college. Mike had killed people, but that was work. Red was so gung-ho, so vicious, and Mike couldn't understand that, any more than the Pussycat could. Red knew, as Mike did, you shouldn't involve an outsider, like the gray-haired guy on the beach, if you could help it. The difference was, Red could string out all those sick thoughts about it. Mike just wanted to do what he had to, the safest, quickest way possible.

Mike found the way back to 17 Hulbert, and was ready to stop there when Red motioned him forward until they were three houses beyond. "Now make a U-turn," Red instructed. When they did, he had Mike stop at once so they were facing the Metcalfe house, but across the street from it and still three houses away. The two settled down to wait.

After ten minutes Mike reached into his satchel and pulled out a quart bottle of gin, a cheap house brand. With his big thumb and forefinger he untwisted the cap, and held the bottle to his mouth. He took a short drink first, paused to wrinkle his face at the taste, then a long swig. "Yeah," he said, as a kind of long sigh. Then he offered the bottle to Red. "Want some?"

Red grabbed the bottle. "What else have I got to do?"

Red took a long drink, held the bottle, took a second, then handed it back.

Greedy bastard, Mike said to himself.

For a while the two sat silently, passing the bottle back and forth, the level in it dropping quickly. When Red spoke, his words sounded slightly slurred. "Christ, Mike, did you see the son of a bitch *bounce?*"

"Who?" asked Mike.

"*Who?* Who the fuck do you think? O'Brien! That's who." Red laughed and had another drink. "First he bounced off our car. Then off the parked car, then off the ground. Like a fucking carom shot!"

Mike's monitor was let down and he ventured to ask: "You get a kick out of that, Red?"

Red glowered. "No, you fucking meatball. Just talking. You been sitting there like a fucking zombie. Give me the bottle." He grabbed it and took another long swallow, then put his head back on the headrest.

Mike looked at his watch: 3:30 in the morning. Then looked at the burly man next to him. Red was falling asleep. Red *was* asleep. Yeah, hotshot, Mike thought, fine, asleep on the job. Mike would let him sleep, and when the girl showed up, he'd wake Red, and the hotshot would be embarrassed, because he'd have fucked up, and Mike had saved him. Mike smiled to himself, took another drink of the gin, which was now almost gone.

Those two must really be going at it on the beach, he thought. About ten minutes later he put his head back. Just resting; he'd remember to keep his eyes open.

A little after four, he fell asleep.

The day was already bright when Mike was awakened by a powerful elbow in the ribs. "What?" he muttered. "What?"

"Shit! Goddammit!" Red growled. "You know what time it is?"

Mike looked at his watch. "Twenty-five to nine."

"Yeah, that's right. Why didn't you wake me?" Red was furious.

"I guess 'cause I was asleep, too," Mike replied.

"Did you see the girl, or anyone go into the house, or come out?"

"I told ya, I been asleep!"

"Oh, shit." Angry as he was, Red was hardly in a position to berate Mike. "Come on," he ordered, "pull up to the house, we've got to go in."

No sooner had Mike stopped across from the house, than Red jumped out of the car and headed for the front door. Mike had to race to catch him.

"Keep your hat on and your glasses, and don't say a word. I'll do the talking." Red hated to have to present himself to an outsider this way. It made him more vulnerable. He'd hate to get screwed up because some old lady on Nantucket might recognize him or a picture of him. But now he couldn't help it. He rang the doorbell and stood there muttering, "Shit, shit, shit," to himself as he waited.

It took the old lady five minutes to come to the door, but finally she was there, in a flowered dressing gown.

"Yes, gentlemen?"

"You Mrs. Metcalfe, ma'am?" Red's voice, which had been a growling baritone, was suddenly a light, pleasant tenor. It surprised Mike.

"Yes, I am. May I help you?"

"Well, Mrs. Metcalfe, we, my brother here and me, are looking for our niece, who . . . ran away. We're her uncles, you see, her mother is our sister, and she's very upset, and asked us to help find her daughter, who's a good kid, but kind of mixed up, you know how kids are. We know the girl came to Nantucket, and a cab driver who says he's a friend of yours, a Mr. Hawkins, says he drove a girl who looks just like her to your house. She's in her early twenties, medium height, pale skin, light reddish blond hair, wearing a blue T-shirt, painter's pants, and blue sneakers."

"What's her name?"

Red hesitated. There was a slight chance, only slight, he figured, this old lady would have read the story about O'Brien's death and spotted the name of his daughter. No reason to take the chance.

"Well, she's always using fake names, you see, she's tried this before, nice kid but mixed up. Her real name is Mary Maloncy, but I doubt she used it."

"The girl who took the room last night registered as Mary Jane Bresnahan, or Brannahan, it's hard to read. But her description fits your niece."

"Oh, good, ma'am." Red tried a winning smile, which came from under the hat and glasses like the mouth of a shark. "We'd like to see her, right now."

His eagerness startled her. "I'm afraid you can't"—Red took a step forward, frightening the old woman—"because she's not here."

Red's smile was gone. "What do you mean, she's not here?"

"She went out last night." Mrs. Metcalfe spoke quickly, trying to keep the threatening size of these men away from her. "Just as soon as she arrived. In fact I drove her to town. And she has not come back."

"But she probably got in real late, or real early this morning. Mind if we look?" As Red asked, he moved forward, his bulk so formidable, the old woman gave ground. "But that's not possible," she said, "because . . ." Red wasn't listening. He'd turned to Mike and motioned him around to the side door. And he kept moving into the foyer. "Which did you say her room was?"

"Upstairs, second door on the right," said Mrs. Metcalfe, by this time thoroughly cowed. Red was on his way upstairs two steps at a time, and she followed him, more slowly. "You see," she said, "I lock the front door at eleven every evening, and after that a guest must ring the bell to be admitted. So I'd know. She didn't come in."

Red was in her room, looking around. The bed had not been slept in. He left, slammed the door, once again examined the other rooms, went up to the attic, then down to the main level, Mrs. Metcalfe trailing helplessly. He ran through every room on the ground floor. No sign of her.

"Where's her suitcase?" he asked roughly.

"She didn't have any, only a big brown leather purse." The old woman was wide-eyed with fear.

"Shit," said Red, under his breath. He headed for the front door.

"Who's going to pay for her room?" the old woman asked.

Red remembered where he was. He didn't want her calling the police. He reached into his pocket, pulled out his wallet, found a twenty-dollar bill and handed it to her. "Hope this will cover it, ma'am. Sorry to trouble you." He wheeled and walked out the front door.

He yelled to Mike, and walked quickly to the Land-Rover. When the other man climbed in, Red shouted, "Goddammit, we blew it. We had her, easy, and we let her slip. Get going. Move!"

Mike started the engine. "Where we goin'?"

"To find the guy who fucked her. And *fucked us*. Remember the house they walked to last night? Where they picked up the car? Find it."

"You remember what street it was on?" Mike asked.

"Don't you?"

"No."

"Well, keep driving. It's a small town. The house had brown shingles, right? And red shutters and a red roof, right?"

"I don't remember, Red."

"Well, shit, it was only six or seven blocks from the bar they were in. It can't be too hard to find."

But it took them an hour of driving and cursing and fuming to find it. Red raced to the front door, Mike hurrying behind. He rang the bell. Again, an old woman came to the door.

"Yes?"

Red sized her up quickly. "We're looking for your son," he said."

"Sam?"

"Yes, Sam. We're . . . business associates of his."

"At the magazine?"

"Yes, right, at the magazine."

"Well, Sam's not here. He took the children to the beach."

Red took a stab. "And the young lady?"

"What young lady?" asked the woman.

Red backed off. He didn't want to raise any alarm; he figured that he and Mike, in their hats and dark glasses, were questionable enough business associates. He didn't want this old lady calling the police, either. But then it occurrred he might have the wrong Sam.

"Listen, I just want to make sure your son Sam is the Sam I work with. Is he about my height but thinner? Blondish hair, getting gray at the sides?"

"Yes, that sounds like my son."

"Can you tell us what beach he went to?"

"All he told me was he'd be going to an ocean beach."

Not comprehending the difference between a beach on the open ocean and one on the protected Sound, Red shook his head impatiently, as if that were no help.

"Thanks," he said and started for the door, Mike following.

"I'll tell him you were here," the woman offered. "Where can he get in touch with you?"

"Never mind," Red answered over his shoulder. "I'm sure we'll find him. Thanks." And the two men closed the door and raced for the Land-Rover.

"Head for the nearest beach," Red ordered.

"I don't know where it is," Mike answered. And then remembering their last exchange on directions, added: "Do you?"

Again, Red refused to admit ignorance, just said: "Well, ask the first person you see."

Mike spotted a teen-ager on a bicycle and pulled up to him. "Hey, where's the easiest beach to get to from here?"

"Jetties," said the boy. "It's that way." And he pointed. Mike gunned the motor and sped off, drowning out the second part of the boy's answer . . . "But there's no surf there!"

Within a few minutes, they were driving through the town, lost. But this time they had a beach to ask for. They stopped a woman with two toddlers. "Which way to Jetties Beach?"

"Right out that road," and she pointed as she spoke.

They had to ask twice more until they found it, and Mike drove the Land-Rover out onto the sand. Now Red was glad he had such a car. He was also glad he had the binoculars in his bag. He pulled them out and began scanning the beach. At eleven o'clock the day was gusty and increasingly cloudy; the beach was almost empty. Looking to his right, Red saw no Sam. He could also see that the beach ended. Turning his glasses to the left, he saw the beach stretch out endlessly.

"That way," he told Mike, and they headed left, to the west. As they drove, they saw few people, no Sam. They went by Cliff Beach, Dionis, all the way out to Eel Point, around it and south, until they ran out of beach.

"Goddammit, we either missed him, or we're on the wrong beach. Go back the way you came," Red muttered. By the time they got back to Jetties Beach it was nearly noon, and they saw one person who hadn't been there before, a woman with a miniature poodle nearby.

"Drive up to her," Red ordered.

When she heard the car getting close, the woman sat up, startled. She was heavily tanned, a sun worshipper, big bosomed, wearing a skimpy bikini. Her halter straps had been untied, and she held the top in front of her with one hand, while trying to find the strap ends with the other; she was not managing well. One breast slipped free of the covering of the halter and her arm.

Red forced himself to concentrate on business.

"Pardon me, is this the nearest ocean beach to town?"

She hastily picked up a towel and held it in front of her, but not before the two men got another look at her bare breast. "This is not an ocean beach," she said. "The ocean beach closest to town is Surfside."

"How do you get there?"

"You have to go back into town and then out Surfside Road."

Red looked over at Mike, whose attention was fastened on those breasts. "Get going," he hissed, and waved at the woman in a halfhearted gesture of thanks.

"I sure would've liked to help her with them straps," said Mike. "Didja get a look at them tits?"

"Let me tell you something," Red replied. "If we screw up, they'll have our tits—in a wringer. I kid you not. Let's find that Surfside beach."

Again, they had to ask directions several times before they found themselves on the Surfside road.

"Recognize this?" Red asked.

"No, why should I?"

"Because it's the same road to the beach we took last night when we followed them."

"Too bad we didn't think of that sooner," said Mike, again countering Red's putdown. "But at least we got to see that dame. She had a terrific pair!"

"When we catch this O'Brien dame, Mike, you can do whatever you want with her, tits or anything else. But we got to get her."

Mike didn't answer. He'd been in this business all his adult life, not as long as the Pussycat, but a long time. And he agreed with Pussycat that Red was the meanest son of a bitch he'd ever come across. Just a cruel Mick. No heart. Not like an Italian. And not a pro. A pro wasn't supposed to enjoy it the way he did.

They were fifty yards from the beach when Red shouted, "Hey, there's his goddamned car! OK! OK!" They drove onto the beach, and Mike asked, "Which way you wanna go?"

"I don't know. Try the left," Red answered.

They drove half a mile, passing almost no one, when Red ordered Mike to go back. Then they tried the right, Red straining through the binoculars. After they'd gone only twenty-five yards in that direction, he said, "Hold it!" Mike stopped. Red looked carefully.

"Yeah," he said. "Son of a bitch! That's him. And those must be his kids down the beach. But no girl."

"No porn show to watch, eh?" Mike said.

"Oh, fuck off, will you?"

"Yeah, well, what do we do now?"

"We wait right here, and watch. Maybe she's collecting shells down the beach. Maybe she's sunbathing in the dunes."

"You wanna go look?"

"Just keep it in your pants. We wait right here."

For twenty minutes they waited. Red, staring through the glasses, saw the children playing near the water, moving farther down the beach, saw the man sitting and reading. But no girl. He grew impatient and angry and his anger focused on the man in shorts. He reached into his bag, found a pencil and a piece of paper. He started writing.

"Waddya doin'?" Mike asked.

"We can't sit here all fucking day. God knows where that dame is. She could be getting ready to get off this island. God knows; I don't know. But I'll tell you who *does* know." He stopped writing, folded the paper in half, and then in half again. He gestured with the binoculars. "I'll tell you who knows where she is. *He* knows. And he's going to deliver her to us."

Red put the binoculars into his bag, then unzipped his windbreaker almost to his waist. "OK, get going," he ordered.

"Get going where?" Mike asked.

"Go by the guy. Go right for those kids."

The Land-Rover moved forward.

Chapter

SCHROEDER STARTED HIS CAR AND PULLED AWAY FROM THE beach. For the first hundred yards, both of them looked straight ahead, neither said a word.

Then she spoke. "Would it be possible for me to spend the night with you?" It was not a romantic request, he could hear that; gone from her voice was the enthusiasm of her lovemaking, mild as that had been. He heard again the forlorn, passive creature he'd met at the movie theatre.

Schroeder felt guilty. Since their orgasm together, he'd said only: "Shall we go back now?" and that was after what he thought a suitable pause, so he couldn't be charged with fucking and running. He never knew what to say after a one-night stand. "Dear" or "darling" would be insincere. "That was lovely" would be self-serving. "See you soon" would be a lie. So he just kept quiet. He felt guilty of exploiting her helplessness, her vulnerability.

"I wish you could," he lied. "But it would be impossible; my mother and my kids are there. You can understand."

He felt guilty for lying. He didn't want her to spend the night, and didn't give a damn whether she understood. He didn't want her next to him all night—not that there was much left of it, his watch said 3:20—he didn't want her around for morning coffee and conversation.

He felt guilty for not saying, straight out, something like: Look, that was an OK fuck, now let's us both go about our business. No, he could never say that. He still hadn't tried to look at her; yet he knew he should offer something. "That was simply marvelous . . . on the beach. Marvelous. I hope it was for you, too." Actually, he told himself, it was not at all bad, and why not tell her so? But he was amused that he'd start by offering a compliment and end by fishing for one.

She didn't have much to give. "Yes," she said, and then, as if the two thoughts belonged together, added: "I wish I didn't have to spend the night alone."

It's fear you're listening to, not longing, he told himself. To her he said: "Impossible. I think you can see that. Tell me where you're staying and I'll drop you." He felt cruel and tried to soften the brush-off. "I'll phone you tomorrow—later today, I guess it'll be—and see what you're doing."

"Uh huh," she said.

"Where are you staying? What's the phone number?"

"Oh, I have a room in a house at 17 Hulbert Avenue, out near Brant Point. But I don't know the phone number." She hesitated. "Besides, I don't know how much longer I'm going to stay." The tone of fatalistic lethargy had returned.

Schroeder started to ask why, where was she going, then caught himself. Several times, the hero's question, How can I help you? came up in his throat; each time he swallowed it, tasting sour in the mouth as he did. He settled for: "Well, maybe I'll stop by and see how you're doing. If you're still there."

To which she said nothing.

As they reached the town, he said aloud, as if to cement his intentions, "Let's see, we've got to get into the center of town; then if we go out Easton, I think we can get onto Hulbert."

"No, please," she said, coming as close to assertiveness as he had ever heard her. "I'll ride with you to your house. And walk from there."

"Walk?" he asked, astounded. "At three in the morning? Through those dark, lonely streets? Why, you were afraid to walk one street alone at nine! Uh uh, I'll drive you." Curiouser and curiouser, he thought. Something sounded fishy. She'd heard it, too, and tried to reconcile the contradiction.

"I mustn't be afraid. I must try not to. That's why I must walk. Please." She sounded more scared than ever.

Well, hell, he thought, he wasn't going to fight it. She was giving him the out; he'd take it.

"You sure?"

"Yes."

"You going to be able to find the way from my house on North Liberty, to Hulbert?"

"Yes, I'll find it."

He considered insisting. He wanted to insist. He didn't insist. In fact, he'd already made the left turn toward his house.

"OK," he said. He was on Main Street, about to turn onto Center. "You don't seem happy. Is there . . . something I can do?" "Something" sounded less committing than "anything." "To help," he deleted.

"Nothing. Except let me spend the night with you."

You made a non-offer, you shit, he told himself, to do what she *doesn't* need, not what she does.

"I can't do that. I told you. I'm sorry." Quickly, he looked to his right; her face showed no surprise—it was resigned, downcast. But resigned to what? Downcast about what? It made him feel all the worse. He should insist on driving her to her rooming house. The urge rose, and again he stuffed it back down.

And then they were on North Liberty Street. Schroeder pulled the car up near the house, but not in front of it. He glanced at his watch: 3:30. Again, he turned to her.

"Then, Mary Jane, let me walk you part way."

"No, I don't want you to." Her voice was soft, firm, grim.

"Are you sure?" He felt so damned irresolute asking.

"Yes, I'm sure." Even she heard the weakness of his questions, he told himself.

All right, he'd done enough. He leaned across and kissed her. She neither resisted nor kissed back, and her lips were dry, cold, lifeless, like the girl herself—except for the brief excitation on the beach.

"I'll come by and look for you tomorrow, at . . . 17 Hulbert, isn't it?" He wouldn't.

She knew it.

"And I am sorry about your not being able to stay with me tonight. Really."

He wasn't. She knew it.

So when she didn't answer him either time, he wasn't surprised. She opened the passenger door and got out, without looking at him. She said nothing, closed the door softly and walked off.

"Good-night." He half mumbled it, another of his pro forma acts of the evening, and watched her walk off, forlorn and baggy again in her T-shirt and painter's pants, still clutching the leather purse she'd carried with her all evening, at the movie house, in the restaurant, on the beach, letting go only for swimming and sex.

Don't let her walk off, he told himself as he got out of the car. She needs help, find out why and help her. He opened the car door and moved out quickly, but in mid-move switched purposes and destinations, and without looking in the direction she'd taken, he walked toward the house.

Oh, come on, he said to himself. After all, I did befriend her. What, befriend? he rebutted. You happened to see her coming out of the restaurant, and you lazily cast your line, and she swallowed the hook, and you reeled the line in, thinking it might end in a quick fuck on the beach. And it did. Give yourself credit.

Oh, wait a minute. If it was a quick fuck I was after, she certainly wasn't a prime specimen! Very true, he shot back. But she was the most available, with the least effort. Going out looking to get laid would have cost you your righteousness.

His maunderings and mutterings had walked him into the house and into bed, where he lay awake till five. And so was exhausted and dazed when his kids shook him awake.

Patty first. "It's a beach day, daddy," she said, trying to be gentle but urgent.

"Can we go right away, daddy?" Bobby asked.

"Huh? What time is it?" He tried to focus on his watch. Five after ten. Oh, Christ, well, he'd nap on the beach. "Kids, give me a couple of minutes to wake up. Go on, have breakfast, clean your teeth, do a few push-ups, get me some coffee."

"We had breakfast," said Bobby.

"How about teeth, push-ups, and coffee?" he asked, head clearing.

"Get up, daddy," they both said.

"All right, here I go." He sat up. "Now you scram. Clean your teeth. Get me coffee. We'll skip the push-ups—for now."

"Hurry, daddy," Patty enjoined, and they both left.

Schroeder stood and walked to the window. He could see the wind was gusting on a fresh, open-and-shut day, brilliant blue sky with heavy cloud patches. The beach might be windy, but he was not about to say no, not for their sake or for his own. Again he felt the need for cleansing, a need all the stronger because of the vagueness of the impurities.

Let's see now, what was he feeling guilty about? Yesterday morning he'd regretted the previous night's adventure with the wife of his best friend. Of course they hadn't—as teen-agers said twenty-five years ago—gone all the way. Did teen-agers still say that? he wondered. Or did they just go all the way these days, and not talk about it? Last night, they had, and that was his burden for this morning. Why? She'd certainly been willing, not seduced, drugged, tricked, overpowered, not anything. Still he felt he'd taken advantage of her. He should have offered her more in return, but what? Walked her home? Would that have made any difference? Besides, she'd asked him not to. Let her stay with him for the night? Impossible.

Well, shit, he'd gone to bed feeling guilty, and awakened the same way. He wanted to get away from it. Quickly, he put on a T-shirt and a pair of shorts, stepped into his sneakers and walked into the living room.

"OK, let's get the show on the road. Let's see the coffee, let's see the clean teeth, let's . . . oh, good morning, grandma, how are you?"

His mother was sitting and crocheting. "I'm fine. Goodness, you must have been out late last night." She tried to make it sound nonchalant. "I had trouble falling asleep, I was awake till late, and I never heard you come in."

Must he go through this? he wondered. "How late were you up, mom?"

"Till one."

"What a coincidence, Mother! I got back at exactly one minute after one. Imagine that!"

"Isn't that a funny coincidence." She got the message, and with a look of reproach ended the subject.

He walked into the kitchen and poured a cup of coffee, black. "We're going to the beach this morning, mother. I'm going to sit and read and think about conquering the world. The kids will play, and swim if they want to, although the water may be too cold for them. How'd you like to come, too?"

"It's windy, isn't it?"

"Yes, it is."

"Very?"

"Fairly."

"It will be worse at the beach, won't it?"

"Might be."

"Will the sun stay out?"

"In and out, I'd say. Want to go?" He was getting a little annoyed at the questioning, as if he were responsible for the beach package, weather and all. And he didn't want her to get out there and ask to come back at once. "Or would you rather stay here?"

The woman looked at him, twisted her face as if to express her dilemma visually, and finally said: "I think I'll stay, and finish this"—she held up the crocheting—"and go for a walk to look at the shops, and perhaps buy something scrumptious for dinner. Would you like lobster?"

"Sounds almost good enough to eat." His mother looked at him as if he hadn't understood her, and he grinned to show he was kidding, and because he was relieved she wasn't going to the beach. He felt he'd been touting the idea, and would be held responsible if it didn't work.

"OK, then, we won't be back late." Now he was anxious to get going, so she wouldn't change her mind. And then another surge of guilt swept through him. His mother, for God's sake! How often did he see her, maybe three times a year? And he was trying to duck out. He pulled another of his half-assed reversals, just as he had with Mary Jane—or whoever—last night. "Are you sure you don't want to go?"

"I'll stay here," she said. "Keep an eye on the children."

"Thanks for reminding me. I'd forgotten all about that." He smiled as he said it.

"Don't be funny," she said. "Which beach are you going to?"

"An ocean beach, I think."

"Well, now, you're used to swimming in the Sound, and you've got to remember those breakers, and the undertow."

"Yes, mom." He said it with mock obedience, then turned to the children. "You've got windbreakers; I've got towels and a blanket." Yes, indeed I've got a blanket, he said to himself. "And I've got a book. You take along anything you might want to play with, or read."

"We've got it all, daddy. We've got it. Come on!"

As they started out the door, clouds momentarily covered the sun. Schroeder pretended not to notice. He wanted this excursion to begin wholeheartedly, unreservedly.

"The beach is going to be sensational on a day like today." Neither child answered, but he wasn't expecting an answer. That bit of pep talk he had addressed to himself.

They headed out toward the beach, using the same route he had driven with Mary Jane last night. Bobby and Patty sat in the front seat alongside him, the boy in a pair of tight blue bathing trunks, with a light blue jacket that said Mets on the back in orange; his daughter in a red- and yellow-patterned bikini and a red cotton parka. Bobby's body had lengthened and lost some of its baby fat, he noticed; Patty's had taken on a slight fullness across the hips and thighs. It had been a year since he'd seen them in bathing suits, seen those bare limbs he'd touched and held every day from their infancy until his separation two years ago. He missed that; it took a moment like this one to make him realize how much; he had to force himself to look ahead at the road rather than down at them. With his right hand he reached over and first squeezed Bobby's thigh and then Patty's.

"I'm happy to have you next to me, do you know that?"

"Yes, daddy," Bobby answered dutifully.

"Yes, daddy," echoed Patty, even more perfunctorily.

He pulled into the same spot in which he had parked last night. There were few other cars. Blanket, towels, and book under his arm, Schroeder led the march onto the beach, Patty and Bobby following, carrying a Frisbee and a tennis ball. He walked toward the right, west, the same way he'd walked last night, past the place where the blanket had lain—he thought he could see the spot—perhaps two hundred yards down the beach from the parking area, leaving far behind the dozen or so people clustered near the road.

The wind seemed strong, but for the moment the sun was out and the day was glorious. Schroeder spread his blanket and sat upon it. "Can we go in the water?" asked Patty.

"Yup, if you want to. Try it and see. Let's try it together." Schroeder stood and headed for the water. He reminded himself that while he was with his kids, he should spend time doing things with them, not just having them in his presence, not just watching them. The waves hit their feet.

"Yow!" Bobby yelled.

"Oh! It's *freezing!*" And Patty went "Brrr!" to underline her point.

And by God, it was cold; Schroeder didn't know how in hell he had ever gotten into it last night. Brandy and sex sure can turn a man into a hero, he said to himself. Or almost a hero.

"Want to go in?" he asked them.

"Not on your life!" said Patty.

"No way!" said Bobby. "Let's throw the Frisbee!"

Schroeder hated Frisbees; they bored him, he could never get them to curve the way he wanted, and he wasn't interested in learning. But he was determined to be a good sport, and so for a chaotic half hour, they threw the Frisbee in a three-cornered catch. A three-cornered miss, would be more like it, Schroeder thought, because eight out of ten tosses never made connection. Favoring his knee when he had to pursue the disc, which was often, he persisted. He would not be the one to stop, much as he wanted to. Finally, Patty dropped out, but when Schroeder prepared to sit, his son said, "Let's us keep on!"

To which Schroeder responded, with forced enthusiasm, "You bet!" And they kept throwing for ten minutes more, until Bobby noticed that another seventy-five yards down the beach, where a depression in the sand had been turned into a lagoon by the receding tide, Patty had begun work on a sand fortress.

"OK, dad," Bobby said. "Let's stop now. I think I'll help Patty with the fort."

"If you insist." He threw those ironical curves even at his kids, Schroeder thought. At least he was better at it than at the Frisbee. But then he practiced a hell of a lot more. Too much.

He walked slowly to the blanket, the uneven sand always a problem for his knee, and sat down. He looked down at the novel he'd brought with him. The title, *Round Peg*, was emblazoned in red on a white background, with the name of the author below it in black. Schroeder opened the cover. On the flyleaf was written in blue ink, by an old-fashioned fountain pen: "To Sam Schroeder, Thanks for a delightful interview and an even more delightful lunch."

The interview, the lunch, and the inscription had all happened last month on the terrace of the writer's apartment on Fifth Avenue. Christina Samuels was forty and had been married three times, each husband richer than the last. Samuels was the name of the most recent, a film producer, from whom she was separated. As Chris—which is what she insisted Schroeder call her—saw it, her curse was that she got along too easily socially, her conquests came too effortlessly, and she had therefore never bothered to develop her other talents—the nature of which she never defined. That social ease was the subject of her novel, a barely fictionalized account of her own life.

He'd already written an idea for the lead line of his article on Chris: something about the *roman à clef* going from bare-faced lies to bare-assed truths, but they'd never allow it. He had sat back and listened.

"For me," she'd told him, flashing a dazzling, capped smile, "things have always fit together too easily. That's why I called the book *Round Peg*. As in: A round peg in a round hole, you see." And she'd sat back, waiting for him to gasp at her verbal felicity.

What he'd wanted to respond was, And why not 'Square Hole'? Instead he settled for a less daring rejoinder. "And why did you choose the peg and not the hole?"

"Why, dear boy!" she answered. He could see she was sure she was manipulating him. "I thought of it! It could have been! On the social level, the peg would be applicable. On the sexual, the . . . other. That is precisely the *double entendre*, the tease, the naughtiness of it—the reason, I hope, those dear readers out there will choose to buy my little opus!"

And for shit like that, he thought, she's called a great wit in the society columns.

To his surprise, "Round Peg" got some strong reviews, and he'd decided to take it to Nantucket with him. Now, on the beach, flipping a couple of pages, he spotted the title of the first chapter. Presiding Over a President. Oh no, this couldn't be. He flipped ahead to the second. Governing the Governor. My God, he thought, what next in this tawdry parade of alliteration? Making the Mayor? Sinning with the Senate? Conquering Congress? Actually, he thought, Sexual Congress would be better. Why didn't she ask me?

He slammed the book shut. No. Not with that surf to read, and that sky. And those two beautiful children, flesh of his flesh. And they were beautiful, not because they were his, just because they . . . well, because they were beautiful. And young, that always helped. There may be lots to say for aging, he thought, but it hardly ever improves your looks. From even seventy-five yards away, he could see the effortless plasticity, the exuberant grace of his kids' limbs, as they knelt, twisted, jumped, splashed.

And I, Schroeder thought, if I wanted to jump up quickly, I'd have to favor that bad knee. Just lying there, his lower back was a bit stiff, and his using his left arm to prop up his head caused an ache in that elbow. Stiff, getting stiffer. Forty, getting older.

Saggy—just slightly, but getting saggier. And it wouldn't reverse. Especially not, he reminded himself, drinking and staying up most of the night as he had the last two nights.

Even with Spartan resolve, it's downhill, he told himself. The best trained man of fifty doesn't have the velvety sleekness of limb of an ordinary teen-ager. And that's what I'm headed for, he said to himself. "Fifty." He shouted it. "Sixty." "Seventy!"

Hell, smoothness of limb isn't all there is, he thought. Yeah, but when you watch the beauty of your children, it's a lot.

The sight of teen-age girls walking with their mothers often saddened Schroeder. In pairs, they looked so alike, yet so different, a disheartening time exposure of the decay of the aging process. It was like watching one of those *Life* magazine time-lapse photos come to life.

The mothers all seemed to be a few years on either side of forty, and they would come in two types: the ones who took care of themselves and the ones who didn't.

The latter were the huge majority. The supermarket was a great place to see them. Hair too red or too blond or too black, trapped in huge curlers, often pink, partly covered by kerchiefs. Bottoms crammed into stretch pants as if the elasticity of the fabric could suppress the explosive hips, baggy bottoms, and cellulitic thighs. Jowls pouchy, bosoms flabby, upper arms as thick as thighs, legs varicosed, they were invariably trailed by daughters who dressed no better than they. But oh, the difference! Even the most mediocre of the girls seemed a princess by comparison, face unlined beneath the curlers and kerchief, thighs bulging but smooth, breasts and buttocks springy. So different. Would she come to look like her mother? Of course. Every time. Almost every time.

And the slim mothers? The careful ones? Better, much better. Still, lines replaced the pouches; stringiness and folds the sags, billows, and cellulite. A closer contest, but the daughters won again.

Men held up better, he told himself. And what made him think so? Because you're a man, he answered, and have to think so. Maybe lines, sags, droops were measured less carefully on men, but they were there, sagging, drooping, creasing.

How would he look next to his son, using the Schroeder Test? Not too good. Facial skin beginning to go flaccid, some flab at the gut—he slapped his belly—and no bleach or curlers for the hair, but the kid once called Whitey now had fading sandy brown hair, salted with gray, receding in front, thinning at the crown. Not much, but he now combed it with guile. When Mies van der Rohe said "Less is more," he sure wasn't talking about hair. Schroeder told himself to make a note of that observation for Faces and Places.

Didn't *anyone* improve with age? he asked himself. No. Some people just held up better, fell apart more slowly, and, compared with the disintegration around them, *seemed* to improve.

He watched his children building their fort against the rhythmic onslaught of the waves. They were far enough so that the cloud between him and the sun didn't affect them; their young bodies shone and gleamed in the sunlight.

So beautiful. Patty, with her ash blond hair, light blue eyes, and pale skin; Bobby, with darker skin that took a nut-brown tan, darker blue eyes, yet blond hair. Yeah, fitting that they be in sun and he in shade, as if that were a barrier, to keep him from reaching them and grabbing hold. One barrier or another, it seemed, had been up ever since he and his wife had separated two years ago. He kept reaching out, without ever being able to hold on.

This weekend, this long weekend on Nantucket in late June, was supposed to do that: join him to his children again. That was why he was here. Not for his escapades last night with that girl, and the night before with Rocky Cobb. Those were fringe

. . . fringe what? God knows, not benefits. The opposite, what was the opposite of benefit? Fringe detriment? Hell, never mind. If he were at his little desk, in his little cubbyhole befitting his little title at *Scope,* he'd come up with something. Clever, contrived, little.

But here on this long stretch of empty ocean beach, the sand, the sky, the water all wiped clean by a brisk wind, he was supposed to be forgetting all that, the diminutiveness of it all, his job, his desk, his mind, his future, his spirit. He was supposed to be cleansing, opening, freeing his insides by letting the sun warm them, the wind sweep them, the expanse soothe them. He was supposed to end this weekend a new man; that was why he was here with his kids. And his mother. His mother—that wasn't working out too well, either. All these years she'd been tucking away money, a few dollars here, a few there—she was now thoroughly self-sufficient, which was fine, because God knows, he couldn't help her—she'd also been squirreling away resentments against him, a grievance here, a snub there. And now she was drawing on her principal—not to mention her principles, heh, heh—and laying a little on him, and he didn't mean money.

Amid the motherly love, the little old lady had it in for him. But then so did his ex-wife and his current woman friend, Jane. And his children. And Rocky, and her husband, Stoney, his best friend. Nobody loved him; not that many even *liked* him, and he returned those feelings, or lack of them. No, wrong, he reminded himself. More likely it was the others returning *his* feelings, or lack of them, not his returning theirs.

So far the weekend had been some rotten weather, some resentment from his mother, some remoteness from his kids. And two, what should he call them? Adventures? Not what he'd hoped. But at last some decent weather, some sun, which wouldn't last, because from the west he could see a weather front coming. At least they had the beach to themselves. That wouldn't last either, for from the east he heard the grinding of an engine. He turned and saw a Land-Rover coming toward him. Those vehicles defiled the beach, Schroeder thought. He didn't know why they were allowed on it. Maybe they weren't, but there it came, moving quickly along the sand, its balloon tires slipping from side to side. He hoped they saw his kids. How could they miss those two small, sunlit forms on the sand?

The car was close to him now, grinding along; it would pass ten yards from him. He watched them, resenting men and machine as a unit. The men were bulky, both wore sunglasses, both wore wide-brimmed hats. As they went by, he got a look at them, the driver Schroeder's age, swarthy, broad-faced, ham fists clutching the wheel, the passenger younger, bigger, florid, beefy.

Neither looked at him, yet he felt both knew he was there. Then Schroeder remembered. He'd seen that Land-Rover, and those men. Last night. Twice.

He got to his feet, watched the vehicle getting closer to his children and their fort. They would pass very near the children. He wondered if he should shout a warning; surely the driver couldn't help but see them.

The vehicle was near Bobby and Patty, and slowing. It stopped. Schroeder started forward.

The beefy man got out. He was talking to the children.

Schroeder broke into a run, forgetting his stiff knee.

Then the man had each child by an arm. He was half helping, half shoving them into the vehicle.

"No! Stop!" Schroeder's words came out more as gasps than as shouts, for he was now sprinting along the sand. But he still had fifty yards to cover, and the big man was in the Land-Rover, and it was moving.

Bobby and Patty turned back, threw him looks of terror and desperation, then turned to the front again, to the beefy man, who had swiveled toward the children.

And Schroeder could see why Bobby and Patty were sitting so still. The man had a gun in his hand; momentarily, its barrel glinted in the sun as he pointed it at Bobby and Patty. A gun, pointed at a nine-year-old and a seven-year-old! *His* nine-year-old and seven-year-old!

"Stop! Help!"

Schroeder knew they wouldn't stop, and there was no one even to hear him, let alone help. He drove his legs through the soft sand, heart thudding wildly, not, he knew, from fatigue, but from fear and anguish.

This was a game! Rocky! Yes, she was fooling around! He knew it wasn't. Then, God, what was it? Why? Where were they going? Why his kids? The Land-Rover was pulling away from him now, perhaps a hundred yards ahead, but Schroeder kept on, hoping to see where it went. Not knowing what else to do, sprinting, approaching exhaustion.

As if cued, clouds covered the sun, the wind picked up, setting the scene for a nightmare. What the hell else could it be? It couldn't be real. The visibility was down now, the vehicle fading. At a turn in the beach it disappeared.

Schroeder moved up onto the softer sand, toward the dunes, to try to spot it, but atop the low dunes he could see nothing. He was about a mile down the beach from his car, panicked, enraged, uncomprehending, breathing like a steam engine. But he came off the dune, broke into a jog, to get back to Surfside Road and his car.

Why? What in hell could he do? Police. But first get there. As fast as he could. But get there. Don't collapse.

Bathed in sweat, trying, failing, to catch his breath, he'd gone about a hundred yards when he heard the Land-Rover again. Schroeder turned, and there it was, only fifty yards back—the roaring of his own breathing had kept him from hearing it sooner—and gaining on him.

Gaining, and headed straight toward him. Its goal seemed clear—to run him down. His knee was throbbing; his breath scraped in his chest like sandpaper. He cut down toward the water, why, he wasn't sure. He ran a few Z-patterns, thinking he could avoid being hit—by the Land-Rover, or by a bullet. What made him think the men would shoot? Why wouldn't they?

Schroeder could hear it getting close. Turning his head, he glimpsed it only twenty-five yards away; the turn threw him off balance, he staggered, lunged ahead, managed to get his feet under him and keep going. He changed direction again, toward the dunes, digging his feet into the yielding sand, dragging each breath through his mouth into his lungs, headed toward a dune, where the Land-Rover couldn't follow.

Now he was at the foot of it, but if it was too steep for his pursuers, it was also too steep for the exhausted forty-year-old Schroeder. He was trying to climb it, but he wasn't. His feet were ploughing through the sand, which was sliding down. He turned to look; the damned thing was less than ten yards away, and coming at him. Desperately, he drove his bare feet into the side of the dune.

No, no good. He slid back. He had nothing left; his bad knee gave way and he fell, face down, on the side of the dune, heart racing, soaked in sweat, breath short and searing, knee shrieking in pain. They couldn't get up the dune to his head, but they sure as hell could run over his legs. Or just shoot.

And now the Land-Rover was there.

But no wheels rolled over him, no shot sounded.

He turned and looked. Saw the driver's thick, muscular left arm raised in the air, saw the hand flip something, a folded piece of paper, that fluttered to the sand a few yards in front of him.

And at the same instant heard the voice of his son, shouting one word, the voice imploring.

"Daddy!"

Then the vehicle was speeding away, shooting along the beach until it was out of sight, never giving him a glimpse, even of the backs of his kids' heads.

Schroeder got to his feet, exhausted, agonized, frightened, angry, impotent. Impotent. He knew they could have gotten him, any way they wanted to. Like they'd gotten his kids. But why? What had he done? Who were they? What did they want of him? Of his children?

He started toward the paper, running along the side of the dune, his knee torturing him. The paper was folded in quarters, cheap typing paper or stationery, the kind you buy on a pad in a five-and-dime. He opened it and read a message, written in pencil, all in capital letters.

IF YOU WANT YOUR KIDS, GIVE US THE GIRL. AT THE EDGE OF STRAIGHT WHARF. RIGHT AWAY. YOU WERE DUMB TO HELP HER. DON'T BE DUMBER AND GO TO THE PO- LICE. WE'RE WATCHING YOU!
DON'T BE NO HERO.

The last four words underlined. No "Dear Sir." No signature. No . . . what did they call it in school? . . . complimentary close. What did you want them to put down, schmuck? Menacingly yours?

No, what he wanted them to put down was: It's only a joke, ha ha. Just a game. Your kids will be back at the house, with a brand new Monopoly set, a year's supply of bubble gum, and full college scholarships for their troubles. And you'll all be chuckling over this in a little while.

But it was no game, he told himself as he ran, limping, in pain, toward his car. Either they'd followed him from the house, or they'd searched the beach. Whichever, they'd done it neatly. And they could have done more to him, if they'd wanted.

Over and over, he kept hearing that anguished call from his son. "Daddy!" Bobby had expected his daddy to be his champion. To stand and fight. To save him and his sister. And his daddy, his champion, had turned and run.

Chapter

10

LAND-ROVER, MEN, AND HIS KIDS OUT OF SIGHT, HIS KNEE A throbbing agony, his heart racing, Schroeder forced himself along the beach, stride by stride through the soft sand, until dripping, sandy, frightened to the brink of his control, he reached Surfside Road and his car. Luckily he'd left the car keys on the floor of the driver's seat; luckily because he'd left behind him on the beach a windbreaker, his novel, and the blanket, the one on which he'd made love last night with Mary Jane Brosnan, or whatever her real name was.

Mary Jane Brosnan! Of course, she was "the girl" of the note, the girl they wanted. Oh, Christ, why hadn't he left her alone? The smell of trouble was all around her, she stank of it. And he'd held his nose and gone ahead.

Schroeder started the car and headed toward town. What

should he do? What could he do? What were the choices? Dammit, he was no good at this kind of thing. He had no experience, no training. No courage. All he knew was, he had to get Patty and Bobby.

If those kids are harmed, he said to himself, angrily. And then added, if those kids are harmed, what? What are you going to do? You're helpless, he told himself, go to the police.

But the note said not to.

You can't handle this alone.

They've got your kids, you must do what they want.

How can you find the girl, and, if you do, how can you force her into their hands?

You've got to do what they want.

What makes you think they'll give her back?

What choice do you have?

Go to the police; they'll stake out the place; they'll do whatever it is you read about in kidnappings. Kidnapping—the word frightened him. Will the police know what to do? The police here in Nantucket? How much experience had they had in kidnappings? Would they call in outside assistance? There wasn't much time, the note said so. Would they try it themselves? If they messed up, it would teach them a lesson for next time. But that wouldn't do his kids much good.

Then he remembered a line in the note, which decided his course of action. WE'RE WATCHING YOU. One of them would be, of course. And if he tried going, they could do something to the kids, as a warning.

Yes, that's it, they *were* watching him, he decided. No police. Not yet. First go for the girl. At 17 Hulbert Avenue. He found the street and drove along it slowly, looking for 17. There it was. He stopped, walked up the front steps of the yellow and white Victorian house. There, in modest lettering a sign on the porch mailbox: Mrs. Clyde Metcalfe. He pushed the bell and waited. An elderly woman, handsome, with white hair, clear skin, big eyes, opened the door. She smiled at him.

"Yes, may I help you?"

"Do you take in guests, Mrs. Metcalfe?"

The smile widened. "Yes, I do."

"I am looking for a young woman who told me she was staying here . . ." Her smile tightened, her face grew guarded, but Schroeder went on. "She's twenty-three, of medium height and build, with pale skin and light reddish blond hair. She was wearing a baggy blue T-shirt, painter's pants, and blue sneakers, and using the name Mary Jane Brosnan, although that may not be her real name." He got it all out; determined not to let her stop him.

"Now, listen, young man," she said, her tone histrionically cold and offended. "This is getting to be quite an annoyance. I don't sleep at all well. Last night I stayed awake till three, and this morning I was awakened at 8:30 by two men, who asked me questions about a young woman they described the same way you just have, although they called her by another name, Irish, like the name you gave, only it was Malone or Maloney or something like that. I just will not *have* this kind of bother, young man!"

"Ma'am," he said, trying to make it official, authoritative, although he knew he didn't look very official, covered with sand and sweat. "If you'll just tell me what you told them, I won't bother you any further." He stood firm at the door.

"Well, all right, but this is the last of it!"

"Yes, of course, Mrs. Metcalfe."

"Yesterday, about six in the evening, a young woman came in and asked for a room. She looked like the person you and those other two men described. I gave her the blue bedroom with the flowered wallpaper. She liked it, and she signed the guest book. When she heard I was leaving for the evening to visit friends, she asked for a ride to town, which I gave her. She said something about going to a movie."

"And what time did she leave this morning?" Schroeder asked. "It must have been pretty early, if she was gone by 8:30 when those men came."

She looked at Schroeder as if he'd just accused her of lying. "I told them, and I'm telling you. She didn't leave at *any* time this morning, because she did not return last night!"

"You mean," he said, "that she didn't come back after leaving at six? Right after she got here?"

"Yes, that is exactly what I mean."

Schroeder didn't want to antagonize her any further, but he had to ask. "Is it possible that she returned real late, say three or four in the morning, after you were asleep, and then left again, very early? And that you didn't hear her?"

Again, she took on the look of one being unjustly accused.

"No, that is impossible." She said it pugnaciously. "*They* asked the same question. It is impossible because I lock my front door at eleven. All my guests are told that. After eleven, no one can enter without ringing. And I am the one, the only one, who answers it and lets them in. She did not ring. She did not come back."

"No maid, no other guests, to open the door?"

"No. No maid. No other guests last night, although I do have a lovely couple just checked in. I hope they are not frightened away by all the goings on."

"What happened to her luggage, ma'am?"

"She didn't have any. Just a big leather handbag which she carried with her. Now, you'll have to leave me, I . . . ."

Schroeder knew he could not settle for deference, for politeness, now. "I'm going, ma'am. The only thing left is the men. Did you answer all their questions?"

"Yes, I did." She seemed suddenly to grow unsure, almost frightened. "They said they were her uncles. That she had run away." She hesitated. "They were very mean-looking men; like they were ready to beat you up if you argued with them. They sort of . . . frightened me. The bigger one just walked right in and searched the house. I couldn't do a thing to stop him."

"Were they by any chance wearing big hats, with wide brims? And dark glasses? Was one of them kind of reddish skinned, and the other much darker?"

"Why, yes! Do you know them?"

"Only by sight," he replied. "How big were they? As big as I am?" He felt ashamed asking, but fear was building in him and he couldn't resist.

She looked him up and down. "Oh, bigger. One was about your height, perhaps a little taller; the other I think was a little shorter than you. But both were much heavier and wider. They must have weighed over two hundred pounds, each. And they looked tough. Like the kind of men who'd have tattoos on their arms."

Why are you telling me this, lady? Schroeder thought. To scare me? Well, you're doing it. Then another question he was ashamed of. "Did they . . . have tattoos?"

"I didn't see. They both had windbreakers on. But they just looked like the type with big muscles and tattoos. Mean, tough men."

"They said they were her uncles, did they?"

"Yes."

"Do you think they were?"

"I don't know. They *did* pay for her room. They gave me a twenty-dollar bill and didn't wait for change. The room is only twelve dollars. If you're going to be in touch with them . . ."

"No, Mrs. Metcalfe, I'm not." He said it brusquely, annoyed with her and himself, angry, frustrated, fearful for his kids. He almost added, and you know damn well, Mrs. Metcalfe, they were not her uncles. Then he asked himself, what am I doing, censuring this seventy-year-old woman, who must be all of five feet two and one hundred fifteen pounds, for being scared?

He softened. "I'm sure you're entitled to keep it for all the additional trouble the young woman has caused." He smiled his most charming smile. "I'm going to trouble you just once more, ma'am. Could I look at your guest book to see how she signed it?"

She looked at him dubiously, and he realized she was worried more about letting him in the house than about looking at the book. And she didn't want to say so.

"If you'd like," he said, "I'll stand out here, let you close the door, get the book, and bring it out here." Good tactic, he thought. It worked.

She smiled a pure Norman Rockwell smile. "That's all right. You look trustworthy." Trustworthy. He laughed to himself. When had he last heard anyone actually *speak* that word?

She opened the door and he stepped into the foyer, which was dark, musty, full of antiques, a jardiniere, an umbrella stand, a coat rack, a wall mirror, all old, none plucked from shops on Third Avenue, he knew. Mrs. Metcalfe had her guest book open and was pointing to a signature. Mary. Then a J. Then a name that could have been Brosnan, but looked more like Bresnahan, and was definitely not Malone or Maloney. The writing was stilted, not the spontaneous flow of a genuine signature. No, she was no more Mary J. Bresnahan than she was Mary Jane Brosnan, or Mary Malone, or Maloney.

He walked to the door. "Thank you, Mrs. Metcalfe. I'm sorry you've been put to so much trouble."

"If they were uncles," the old lady said as she took hold of the door, "Who are you?"

"Oh, just a friend."

"Are you sure you wouldn't like to take the eight dollars change so you can return it to her or her uncles?"

"I may not see them," he said. "You keep it."

"Is that young lady in trouble?" Mrs. Metcalfe asked as he was turning to leave.

He nodded. "Yes, I guess she is." And he wheeled about and walked away. The question and the answer brought a sudden panicky tightness to his chest. He was in trouble, too. And he didn't know what in hell to do about it. He got into his car and started it, not knowing where to go.

What were the options?

Find the girl. But he'd tried the one place he knew. He had no idea where she could be; the two men had already tried, and couldn't find her, which is why they thought Schroeder was hiding her.

Go to the police. But the chances are he'd be spotted. Smarter to phone them and ask to have a plainclothesman come to see him. Did Nantucket have plainclothesmen?

Go down to the dock and convince them he couldn't deliver the girl, didn't know where she was, had no connection with her except a casual sexual one. An accursed, casual sexual one. Persuade them to let Patty and Bobby go.

All right then, think. The first, find the girl, was too vague. That left the second and third. Call the police or go to the dock. He needed time to think. Well, he'd start by going back to the house. He could phone from there, or go down to the dock from there.

He drove to the house, got out, headed for the front door, wondered what he should tell his mother about the children. The Cobbs.

"Where are the children?" were her first words.

"At the Cobbs', mom. The weather began to blow up so I took them over there for a change of scene. They have a five-year-old daughter. How's everything been here?" He could see from the upset look on her face, everything had not been calm.

"It's been rather busy," she said sternly. "First, two men came; they wanted to see you on business."

"Just what did they say?"

"They asked if my son was here."

Don't exactly sound like close colleagues, he said to himself. To her, he said: "Did they use my name?"

"They called you Sam," she said, then hesitated. "But I don't know if they used it first, or I did. I think I may have said, Do you mean my son *Sam*?"

"Oh, I see, yeah, maybe they did get it from you." Strangely, he felt a little better. Whatever the force against him, it was not the result of a long, carefully planned conspiracy.

"What did you tell them?"

"That you'd gone to the beach. You didn't say which one, so I just said to an ocean beach. I remember your telling me that. Did they find you?"

"Did they both have big hats on, and dark glasses? Strong, tough looking guys? One swarthy, the other sort of reddish faced?"

"Yes. I see they did find you."

"Yup. They found us."

"Is everything all right?"

"Yes, mom. Everything is just fine." Oh, God, how he wished it was!

She put on her naughty-boy look and said, "Then, a half hour or so later, came your other visitor, the young lady, only she called you Sam." His mother was prepared to disapprove of her forty-year-old divorced son having lady friends in their early twenties. But he didn't give her the chance.

He took a step forward, not sure where he was going. "Where did she go?"

"She went into your bedroom to wait; I told her she'd do better to wait out here, but . . ." His mother stopped because Schroeder was racing past her. He shoved the bedroom door open.

The girl was stretched out on the bed, motionless, eyes closed, wearing the same clothing she'd had on last night, obviously the only things she had with her. In her right hand she clutched her purse, its leather thong wrapped around her wrist.

My God, he thought, suppose she's dead?

He ran to her, felt her face. Warm. And at his touch, she jumped awake. For the first instant she looked dazed, then fearful; then when she saw him, she showed the tiny relaxation of recognition.

"Where did you spend the night?" He didn't know why that burst out first, but it did.

"Here," she replied.

"What do you mean, here?"

"Do you know you have a small room in back, a kind of maid's room, on the basement level, that you can go into from the outside?"

"No, and that's just the start of what I don't know. Who are you?"

"Felicia O'Brien." She paused.

"Is that supposed to mean something to me?"

"Are you from Boston?"

"No. Don't play games with me. Just tell me who you are."

"My father, Henry J. O'Brien, was the special prosecutor." Again, she waited, as if that should be enough.

"What has that got to do with why you're hiding in my room, and my—" he stopped himself short. He would not say anything about his children yet. "Explain it."

"My father was killed Thursday night by a hit-and-run driver." This time he waited for more.

"I don't get the connection."

For the first time outside of sex, he saw her energy level rise. "It was no ordinary hit-and-run. It was deliberate. They ran him down on purpose. They murdered him."

"Who's *they?*"

"Organized crime, the Mob, the syndicate, whatever you want to call it. We've been investigating connections between them and judges and prosecutors and police. And we've found something, really found something. Evidence you wouldn't believe."

"Who's *we?*" Schroeder's questions were beginning to make him feel like his namesake, Sam Spade. Ah, but what a difference. He suddenly thought of the note, and its warning, "DON'T BE NO HERO," with the mocking paradox of that double negative.

"My father and I," she answered. "I'm not a legal secretary, I'm a second-year law student, and I am . . . I was . . . the only one he really trusted. My father was a difficult man, but honest, totally honest. No one liked him; he didn't like anyone and he didn't trust anyone besides me. He had a staff—lawyers, investigators, but I was the only one he confided in. He was suspicious of all the others, almost paranoid. That's why he made me keep *this*."

She reached into the leather purse she never seemed to let go of and pulled out of it, but only partially, a small pigskin-bound loose-leaf notebook. Schroeder thought she'd offer it for his inspection. Instead she just shoved it back into the handbag.

Maybe she was a little paranoid, too, he thought. He waited for her to say something more about it. When she didn't he asked, "What is it?"

"Evidence," she answered guardedly. "Pure evidence."

"And now you think *they* are after you?" So far he hadn't mentioned his children.

"I'm sure of it. That's why I left Boston. That's why I was afraid of the dark street. That's why I wanted to spend the night with you."

He was furious at her, at himself, at the two beefy men, at the lousy coincidence. What do you suppose they'll do to you if they get hold of you? he started to ask. But he swallowed it. He didn't want to know.

Almost as if she'd read his question, she said: "They want to kill me, you know. They will, if they get their hands on me."

Schroeder let his anger go. "Goddammit, why didn't you go to the police?" he shouted. "Why didn't you go to the mayor? To the papers? To your father's staff? To an honest judge, or an honest cop? Why did you turn and run like a scared child?"

What he wanted to shout was: Why didn't you go to Martha's Vineyard, or Provincetown, or the Maine coast? Anywhere but the one fucking little island, and the one movie house on that island where you'd run into me—and get my kids snatched? It's not fair! I been robbed! he wanted to scream.

"I tried one of the lawyers on my father's staff," she answered. "The only one I thought at all sympathetic. The day after my father was killed, I went right over to see him. And he told me how it was an accident! How I was imagining things! How the police would know if it was a murder! But you see, he was polite, not really interested. Indifferent, and a little bit afraid to get involved. And he didn't know about the notebook, and I wasn't about to tell him."

"All right!" he said fiercely. "So one guy may have been a little afraid and a little indifferent! Don't tell me you don't know a single honest cop, or honest judge, or city councilman, or whatever you call them! You leave the protection of a place where you're known and know people, and run to a little island, where you can be spotted easily, where no one knows you, and you know no one. And they've got my kids because of you!" The last sentence came from between clenched teeth.

"Your kids?" She sounded dumbfounded, not yet grasping what it meant for her. He told her, in a lowered voice. He didn't want his mother to hear this.

"Yes. Two men grabbed them on the beach this morning. With a gun. They threw me a note which said they'd give them back when I turned you over to them." He saw the terror come over her face. He saw her begin to come forward from her sitting position on the edge of the bed, her feet reaching for the floor. All she said was:

"No. Please, no."

He'd been sitting next to her, and he stood to block her. "What else can I do?" He said it as if he wanted her approval.

"They'll kill me."

"They have my kids."

"I'd be willing to go to the police."

"Not now, goddammit. It's too late. You should have gone right away. Besides, the note said they were watching me. No, it's too late. I'm not risking my kids."

"They'll kill me. Please."

"You don't know that. Anyway, I have no choice. I'm sorry." Sam Spade wouldn't be handling it this way, he thought. Or Clint Eastwood or Charles Bronson or James Bond. He thought of that line in the note. All in caps, underlined. DON'T BE NO HERO.

"What choice do I have? Maybe they just want that book; maybe they'll just scare you and let you go."

His question about choice was rhetorical; he wasn't expecting her to suggest one.

"Would you offer them *this* for your children, then?" She opened her purse wide, groped in it for the notebook. As she did, Schroeder could see in it a small pistol. He grabbed at her purse; she tried to get a stronger grip, to hold on, but he got it from her. He removed the gun, saw it had a clip in it. Her shoulders drooped, she did not even seem indignant. She was, he thought, someone used to being defeated. Schroeder held the gun in his hand, not pointing it at her, but trying to suggest he was ready to use it if she disobeyed.

"What's in the notebook?" he asked.

"Initials—I know whose, important people's—amounts of

money, dates." Her voice, her face, the set of her body were so subdued, so abject, he felt a surge of pity for her. This is a girl who can't win, he thought. Poor girl. It had taken real incompetence, and bad luck, to let a weapon he didn't even know about, fall into his hands so easily. With the gun in her hand right now, everything would be different. And she'd just thrown her chance away. He had to force himself to think of his children, to stanch the flow of pity.

"We got it in the mail, literally in a plain brown wrapper, and we know it's authentic, and very important. When my father realized it, he said, 'We've got our Nixon tapes!' I had never seen him so enthusiastic." For only an instant, her face brightened. "Two days, less than two days, after the book arrived, my father was run down on the street. It's very important. They might take it in return for your children."

She looked up at him, her translucent skin pale except where it was blotchy from sleep. Here he was, standing over her, twice her size, holding a gun, about to throw her to the wolves. Again, he felt the need to justify himself, to remind her, and himself, about the children.

"Look, Mary Jane, Felicia, I wish I could help you. Two things make it impossible. The first, by itself, would be enough: my children. The second, by itself, would be enough, more than enough: I'm not the type who can play cops and robbers. I'm no good at it. I know for sure I don't have what you'd like me to have for this situation. What you'd *need* me to have. I'm sorry for it, you have no idea how sorry, for your sake, for mine. There's just no way I can help you."

He paused and tightened his grip on the pistol. "Now, let's get up and go. And . . ." he hesitated, having trouble uttering the cliche, don't try anything. He varied it. "Don't try to get away, or anything."

She stood. Like a lamb to slaughter, he thought. "Won't you even try with the notebook?" she asked. She's not really pleading, he thought. She expects to lose.

"Look, I am not going to mess with those guys. I haven't the training, the talent, or the guts. I am an amateur; they are professionals." He'd almost said professional killers, but cut it short. "Now we have to get going." He waved the gun toward the door. She started forward; Schroeder followed. As they were about to enter the living room, he remembered his mother and jammed the gun into his pocket. "Don't say anything except good-bye." He almost snarled it at her.

He'd forgotten his mother. Probably she'd been sitting there thinking a romantic contretemps was going on behind the closed bedroom door; that was OK with him. He would prefer not to deal with her fear about the children. Dealing with his own was tough enough. Now she was waiting for some kind of explanation. She was not to get any.

"Mother," he announced, "I've got to . . ." he caught himself about to say, take this young lady for a ride, but made it "drop this young lady somewhere." He realized that wasn't much better, but didn't care. "Then I'm going to pick up the kids." Amen, he added, but not aloud.

"All right, then." Magically, his mother managed to combine in those three words offended righteousness and frustrated curiosity. "See you later." Then, directed at the girl: "Good-bye."

"Good-bye." The reply was barely audible.

Trying to be gentle, yet commanding, he took her right arm at the elbow with his left hand and walked her out of the house toward the car. He reminded himself of the 1930s prison movies, especially the scene where the condemned prisoner is walked toward execution. Should he be whispering a prayer? Let's see, where did they usually bring the sound up? "I am the resurrection and the life . . ."

He reminded himself that this was a terrified girl he was handing over to be killed. Twenty-three, pink and white, docile. A girl he'd made love to on the beach last night, and now was doing nothing to save. Nothing at all, not one move.

Well, hold it, he rebutted. Postulate yourself as a real, genuine, certified hero. What would such a person do? One thing, and one thing only, he answered. Get his kids back. Period. That's the only option. So don't whip yourself on this one. There'll be other chances, lots, don't worry about it. Whip yourself over your job, you can wear out a lot of rawhide on that one. Other women, lots of material there. But not this woman, right? Right. This woman is not the issue. Your kids are.

Schroeder put her into the car, gentleman to the end, walking her to the passenger door, closing the door behind her, before climbing into the driver's seat. Somehow he had no fear she'd break away; she didn't look as if it had occurred to her. Felicia O'Brien was not a fighter. Lamb seemed a good description.

He drove toward Main Street, the girl silent alongside him. What the hell do you say to her? he asked himself.

"I'm sorry," he said softly as they neared Straight Wharf. I wish I could help you. After I get my kids back, I can call the police." Out of the corner of her eye, he saw her, white with fear, give a resigned shrug. "Those men work fast," was all she said.

"The weather's turning rotten. It's getting dark early; they may not try to leave the harbor tonight." He said it just to say something.

"Wouldn't you *try* to offer them the book?" she asked softly.

He said nothing; then they were at the foot of the dock. He parked the car, got out and walked around to the passenger side of the car, again reminding himself of the minister walking the condemned prisoner to the chair. Or was he the executioner? How was she holding up? If it were he, he decided, he'd collapse, have to be carried. The question came up again: What else could he do? He opened her door and said, "Come on."

Listlessly, almost catatonically, she swung her legs to the side and got out of the car. Standing next to him, she looked up into his face, and asked again, "Wouldn't you try to offer them the notebook?"

His answer was to take her arm just above the elbow and walk her to the foot of the wharf. They stood and waited; the note had said he was being watched, and he was sure something would happen soon. For some reason, although he didn't know why, he was sure they were aboard a boat somewhere, one of the scores in this busy harbor. He kept watching the wharf; so far, all he could see was the dozens of tourists who'd been deprived of the beach by the weather and were wandering along, gawking at the yachts and the sport fishermen tied up at their berths.

He kept watching, pressing his fingers into the girl's arm until she whispered, "You're hurting me." "Sorry," he answered. He eased off. Three or four minutes later, among the tourists on the dock, he spotted the figure of his daughter, hurrying toward him. He stared anxiously, she was alone, pale, walking as fast as she could, but not running. He'd bet she'd been told not to run. In her hand, a folded piece of paper.

The last few steps she did run, and he grabbed her and squeezed; he was having trouble catching his breath. "Are you all right, sweetheart?''

"I'm OK, daddy."

"Is Bobby?"

"He's OK, too, but they're holding him to make sure I go back. Here." She held out the piece of paper. He grabbed it and unfolded it. The same kind as on the beach. Same printing, in pencil, in capital letters.

> SEND THE GIRL, WITH THE BOOK. SHE WON'T GET HURT. WHEN SHE STARTS WALKING TO US, YOUR KIDS START WALK- ING TO YOU. THEN GET THE 6:10 PLANE TO NEW YORK. YOU GOT RESERVATIONS. DON'T TALK TO NO ONE. NO PHONE CALLS. WE'RE STILL WATCHING YOU. DON'T BE NO HERO.

He looked down at his daughter's frightened face. "Don't worry, sweetheart, it's going to be all right."

"They're not nice men, daddy."

"I know, sweetheart, don't worry. You go back and tell them I'll . . ." and impulsively, he changed course, "give them the book, and promise to send the girl out of the country. She'll never say a word." He looked over to Felicia, saw a touch of hope in her face. "That's a promise. If they send you two back."

Patty looked doubtful. "It's OK, honey," he assured her. "Go on, tell them. It's going to be all right." The girl walked off. He hated sending her back. She disappeared among the tourists.

"Thank you," said Felicia.

He just shook his head. "It's not going to work."

His daughter reappeared down the wharf, emerging from a knot of people admiring a huge Chris-Craft, and came quickly toward him.

"They said, the girl *and* the book, daddy; they said you've got two minutes."

He reacted quickly. "Run back and tell them OK. I'll start her walking. They should start you two. Go ahead." He watched her go off, disappear, this time way off at the end, behind a boat. He couldn't see if she was boarding a fifty-footer or a din- ghy.

Schroeder turned to the girl. "I'm sorry. I wish there was something else I could do. But there isn't. Their note said they wouldn't hurt you."

She looked at him in a kind of a daze. "You don't believe them, do you?" He couldn't decide if she was trying to refute him, or to grasp at some last hope. He didn't care.

"I'm sorry. Start walking. If you try to get away, I'll come after you. I'll shoot you if I have to. Start walking." The hand on her arm moved her forward. She took a few steps, turned around and looked at him. Her face was deathly white. He had an impulse to say something like, and may God have mercy on your soul.

Instead, his lips formed the words: Get going. He put his right hand in his pocket, where the gun was. She turned and walked forward.

Again, the question: What else could I do?

Then he asked himself, what's to stop her from jumping off the side of the dock, or onto a boat? Or screaming for help? Or running right back at him. Did she really think he'd shoot her? He knew he wouldn't. But he would grab her and drag her out on that dock. Yes, but she could scream and fight, and there were lots of people around.

Schroeder knew she wouldn't do anything. He'd seen it in her voice, the set of her shoulders, the look in her eyes. Her one flare-up of resistance had gotten her to Nantucket. When that failed, she had nothing more to give; she'd been broken.

Then, at the far end of the dock, the sight of his kids, both of them, coming toward him, slowly, took his attention away from her. Again, he could see the slow walk was the result of instructions from the two men. As they grew closer, he could see they were holding hands. His own dear children. There was *nothing* else he could have done.

Now the hostages were approaching each other . . . and passing each other, the children headed for their father, the girl headed for . . . Schroeder wrenched his mind away from the end of that sentence. Again, he forced his mind off her and watched his children getting close. Obviously they'd been told not to run and were trying to stretch their walking strides, to make them as long and as fast as they could. He could see in Patty's hand another piece of paper.

And then they reached him; he bent down, threw an arm around each and hugged as hard as he could.

"You OK?"

"Yes, daddy." "OK, daddy."

"Am I glad to see you!"

"We're glad to see you, daddy."

"Did they hurt you?" He stood up without letting go of them, and turned them. The three of them started walking toward the car.

"No, daddy," Patty replied. "But they blindfolded us, and were awfully rough; they sort of pushed us from one place to another. They said if we made any noise or gave them any trouble or tried to get away, they'd bash our heads in."

He felt furious, impotent. That those men had manhandled his kids with no response from him was humiliating. A father is supposed to defend his children, to be big and strong and beat the hell out of anyone who harms or threatens them. In pushing Bobby and Patty around, those two men, Schroeder realized, had damaged him more than they had the children. He remembered the note. "May I see the piece of paper, sweetheart?" Patty handed it to him. He opened it.

THE PLANE IS AT 6:10. YOU GOT RESERVATIONS. DON'T STOP NOWHERE BUT YOUR HOUSE. DON'T TALK TO NO ONE. NO PHONE CALLS. WE'RE WATCHING YOU.

"What does it say, daddy?" his daughter asked.

He smiled down at her. "It says what delightful guests you were, and how they hope you'll drop by again real soon."

"No, daddy, what does it say, really?"

He was grinning, feeling lightheaded, so elated to have them back. For the moment he'd forgotten the humiliation, the violation of him by those men. And he'd forgotten that poor forlorn girl, now in their hands, turned over by him. He remembered, and stopped smiling. "It doesn't matter," he replied. "They're terrible men, and we're just going to forget about them as soon as possible."

They reached the car and he put the children up in the front seat with him. He hated to lift his arms from around their shoulders. "What else did they say to you?" he asked.

"Nothing," said Bobby. "Not until they spoke to Patty when she went to meet you."

"But we could hear the sound of their voices talking to each other sometimes," said Patty. "We couldn't hear the words, though, they weren't talking loud enough. Except once, when one of the men was talking on the radio on the big boat."

"Big boat? How do you know it was a big boat?" Schroeder asked. "You were blindfolded."

"We could feel," Bobby explained. "First they put us in the little boat. We had to step down from the dock. Then the little boat took us out to a big boat. We had to climb up to get on it. The big boat didn't go anywhere. But it rocked, so we knew we were on water. Then they put us on the little one again, and brought us back to the dock."

"That's wonderful, Bobby," Schroeder said. "You're going to be a great detective when you grow up." They were driving away from the dock, up Main Street. "But neither of you could see the name of the big boat, could you?"

Bobby just shook his head.

"All I saw was the name of the little one, with the outboard, dad," Patty replied. "It was the *Sloppy Joe*."

"You mean, like the Sloppy Joe sandwich?" Bobby asked.

"Yes, the *Sloppy Joe*," answered the girl, slightly offended that her brother should question her.

Schroeder knew that usually the dinghy belonging to a larger boat had the same name as the big one. But he said nothing about that. Instead, he asked his daughter, "How come you were able to see it if you were blindfolded?"

"Well, daddy, when we got close to the dock, we heard one of the men say to the other, 'Them blindfolds will look suspicious, maybe you better take 'em off.' And the other said to us: 'Don't try to look at us. Keep your eyes shut tight.' Then he took them off. And I kept my eyes shut tight, the way they told us . . ."

"So did I, daddy," said Bobby.

His sister looked pained at the interruption, then went on. "But when they sent me to deliver the note, I had to open my eyes so I could walk along the dock. And when I came back, as I was climbing into the little boat, there was the name. I saw it."

"Oh, good, sweetheart. You're quite a detective yourself." So, he thought, chances are the big boat is called the *Sloppy Joe*, too. That's good to know, he said to himself, although he wasn't sure what he could do with the information. They pulled up to the house, and he opened the note for another look. The 6:10 flight. He glanced at his watch, 5:05. Not a hell of a lot of time to pack and get there, but by God, they were going to be on that plane. He heard the sound of an engine on the quiet street, looked up into his rearview mirror. By God, there was the Land-Rover! Coming right at them! Then, moving fast, it went by and out of sight, Schroeder just glimpsing the darker man in the big hat and dark glasses, as the vehicle swept past.

The man was not trying to conceal the fact that he was tailing them, Schroeder realized. On the contrary, he was advertising it, to scare them. And it was working. Schroeder stared at the note again. WE'RE WATCHING YOU. And so they were.

At least, he thought, they'd omitted DON'T BE NO HERO from the third note. Were they getting cocky? No, he said to himself, *you're* getting cocky, flippant, now that your kids are safe. Then he remembered Felicia O'Brien. She wasn't safe.

"Why are you just sitting there, daddy?" said Bobby, shaking him out of his reverie.

"Just thinking about those men, sweethearts, and thanking God you're all right. Come on, let's get in the house, get grandma, pack our stuff and get off this island. We've got less than an hour to catch a plane. Come on." He started to climb out of the car, when his daughter brought him up short.

"What's going to happen to that girl, daddy? And who were those men?"

What the hell should he tell them? "Well, neither one of them is Mister Nice Guy, that's for sure, but I think she had run away, and what they want is to return her to her home. They thought I was helping her run away, which I wasn't, of course. They took you so that I'd return her." Would that it were so, he said to himself.

"She was the one who talked to us after the movie last night, wasn't she?" Bobby asked.

"Yes, she was, that's why they must have thought I was help-ing her."

"If you weren't, then how come you could get her and return her?" Patty asked.

"Well, honey, when those men said they had you, I just went out and found her, and gave her to them, because you are the two most precious things in the world to me."

"But daddy," Patty persisted, "How come they just didn't go

out and get her, the way you did? Why did they have to bring us into it?''

Oh, God, why did they? he asked silently. "I suppose they lost track of her, and having seen her with us, figured that I was hiding her." He didn't want to tell them about the meeting last night, and the drinks, and the beach.

"Were you hiding her?" his son asked.

"No, of course not."

Patty continued on the scent. "Then how come you *could* find her and they *couldn't?*"

"I guess they didn't try very hard. They just let me do their work for them because they knew how important you are to me. Now we'd better get moving." He got out of the car, went around and opened the door for them.

"Look, you two," he said as they walked toward the front door, "Not a word of this to grandma. Let's just tell her I took you to the Cobbs' to play with their daughter, and I've just picked you up. OK?"

"Why, daddy?" asked Patty.

"Because we don't want to upset her. In fact, I'd be very proud of you if we could keep this our secret, and not tell anybody, not even your mommy, because she'd be upset, too. Is it a deal?"

They looked doubtful. "It's important, OK?"

"Yes, OK, it's a deal," said his daughter. "OK, daddy," echoed the boy.

He reached for the doorknob and stopped. "And I'm going to tell grandma we've got to go back to New York right away, because of business, OK?"

"OK, daddy," said Patty, "But what's the real reason we have to go. We were going to stay till tomorrow."

"Because those men want us to leave; they're afraid I might try to help the girl. It was part of the deal to get you back."

"Would you try to help the girl?" his daughter asked.

"No," he answered. Not I, he added to himself. Not the no-hero. "Now, let's go in. Remember the deal." He put his finger to his lips. Then opened the door and they walked in. His mother was sitting and crocheting. She looked up, at first worried, then relieved to see the children.

"Grandma," he said, trying to make it sound brisk and matter-of-fact, "there's a long, dull story attached to this, with which I'm not going to bore you. But those men, believe it or not, *were* after me on business. The magazine wants me to work on something special, and I've got to get back right away, catch the 6:10 plane. I've made reservations for all of us. You can bet that after I rush back, they'll stall for weeks. But I can't lose the chance. All of which means we've got to pack and get out of here in a half hour."

His mother looked startled. "My goodness, that's unusual, to say the least. You have to be in New York tonight? And those two men were here to find you for the magazine?"

Damn, he thought, she and his daughter should both be DAs. He looked at his kids, who'd seen their daddy caught in a lie. "You two go into your rooms," he ordered. "Pile everything you brought on your beds. Everything! Socks, toothbrushes, comic books, games, everything! Go on. If we do this right, we'll have time for one of those super ice-cream sodas at the airport. Go on, move it!"

The kids hurried off. Schroeder wondered if they made ice-cream sodas at the airport. He'd worry about that later. One thing at a time.

"First of all, mom, those two men happened to be on the island, anyway, they weren't sent just for me. Second, magazine people are nuts, remember that. Besides, we'd have caught the 11:45 ferry tomorrow morning anyway, so we're not losing much except three hours on the ferry and six hours in Sunday traffic. And the magazine is paying our plane fare. So we're ahead of the game. Now run along and pack. There's an ice-cream soda in it for you, too."

But she was not to be put off so easily. "That girl. Was she here on magazine business, too?" She knew damn well what the answer to that was.

"A completely unrelated matter, mother, I assure you, one having to do with my talents as a ladies' man, not with my talents as a magazine writer." He started toward his room to end the questioning, but she wasn't having it.

"She is almost young enough to be your daughter."

Well, good, he thought, he'd rather deal with that. "That's it, mom, you've got it. She's a classmate of Patty's. She met me on Parent's Day and has a thing for me. She follows me everywhere. I keep telling her, this is crazy, can you see yourself in the same class as your stepdaughter? But she won't listen, the poor, smitten fool. And those men are really her uncles, warning me to stay away from her." He was on thin ice, but playing around anyway. What the hell, he thought, I've got to show a little bravery somewhere. His mother got up from her chair, slowly, wearily, shaking her head.

"Sam. Sam. You are a forty-year-old boy. When are you going to grow up?"

He walked over and put his arm around her. "I avoid growing up; it keeps me young. You can always tell people you've got a mere boy for a son. Now do I get a thank-you for that, or a third-degree?"

He hugged her, and not waiting for an answer, added quickly, "Get in there and get packed, or no ice-cream soda!" Then he headed for his room and began filling his suitcase.

Wow, the questioning, he thought. But of course he couldn't blame them. Some of his answers had been lies, but there was one question he had to think about: Why had those two grabbed his kids, when they could have grabbed the girl, and avoided Schroeder as middleman?

He decided that they'd lost track of her, somehow. What must have happened, he figured, was that they'd first spotted her outside the restaurant, but he'd been in the way of their move. Yes, of course! He remembered the Land-Rover, and the two men in the big hats, as they were crossing the street! And then again in front of Cap'n Tobey's!

So the two big men had followed Felicia and her protector, Fearless Sam Schroeder, to his house, where they'd picked up the car. The pair had either then lost them, or not wanted to involve Schroeder, not knowing who he was. After all, he was big enough, his hair was short enough, he'd been told often enough he looked like an FBI man. So the two big men had decided to wait for the girl in front of her rooming house. Only she hadn't returned to it. They must have grown angry and impatient, and had gone looking for her and her protector, and with the information supplied by Schroeder's mother, ended up at the beach, found Schroeder and his children—but no girl. That's when they'd grabbed the kids and tossed the Don't Be No Hero note.

He had to laugh to think about it. He'd probably shaken up those two brutes! They might have actually been worried about her new champion! Worried about the police being called. Worried about her being spirited away on this fearless stranger's jet, or yacht, or white charger. Oh, as the old joke went, did they have the wrong number! How they had misgauged the mettle of the opponent! They'd actually thought him a threat! Someone to be reckoned with! And so had poor Mary Jane Brosnan, Mary Maloney, Mary J. Bresnahan, Felicia O'Brien. She'd probably thought she'd found her white knight!

Well, he'd shown them! And her!

Had they actually been worried? He remembered the bulk of those men in the vehicle, especially the upper arm he'd seen showing out of the open driver's window, the arm of the swarthy man. Then he looked down at his own arm in the short-sleeved shirt. A respectable arm, fairly firm of bicep, moderately thick of forearm. But no match for that colossus of an arm bent double on the window of the Land-Rover. And the man in the passenger seat had seemed even bigger.

Besides, they are armed, he told himself. Then, he remembered, so was he. He had the girl's pistol in his right pants pocket. Yes, but he wasn't ready for a shoot-out. For one thing, he'd never fired a pistol. For another, he didn't even know when the safety was on and when off. For another, he was scared. He pulled the gun out of his pocket and looked at it. Then just held it and thought of something else. What in hell was he going to do with the thing?

Should he put it into his suitcase? He remembered airline security. Nantucket was just a tiny airport, but suppose they searched his baggage? And the police were called? With the swarthy man in the Land-Rover watching? He had to do something, but what?

Schroeder put the gun back into his pocket and walked into the kitchen, looked around. The garbage! Why not? He stuffed it down into the plastic garbage bag, made sure it was in the middle, then took the bag and put a twist tie around its top to close it. He carried it outside, put it into the large metal can and replaced the lid. Unless they put their garbage through metal detectors, he told himself, the gun would soon be part of landfill, or on its way out to sea—or whatever they did with their garbage on Nantucket.

Then he went back to his room and finished packing.

In twenty minutes they were loaded into the car. As Schroeder pulled away, he took a last look at the house, and wondered if he'd ever be able to walk into it again. He didn't think so. Jane had rented it for the summer; he'd counted on spending his vacation there. Now, he didn't know.

He drove a few blocks, kept checking the rearview mirror for the swarthy man with the big arms, driving the Land-Rover. And there he was! Moving slowly behind Schroeder's car, keeping them in sight. Schroeder realized that he *wanted* the dark man there, that, strangely, he was a comfort.

At the airport ticket counter, Schroeder wondered what name would be on the reservations. "My name is Schroeder," he told the clerk, "Somebody made reservations for me for the 6:10 to New York, two adults and two children, but I'm not sure if they got the name right."

The clerk looked down the list. "We have nothing for Schroeder." He kept looking, then said, "But we have two adults and two children on that flight, under the name of Mr. Sam."

"That's it," said Schroeder. "The man who made the reservations always calls me that." There was no problem, in any event; the flight was half empty. Why would anyone leave Nantucket on a Saturday evening? Especially for New York?

As he turned in the keys to the rental car, he asked himself what he'd be doing on the island tonight, anyway. Having a drink with the Cobbs? My God, the Cobbs! He'd forgotten them, forgotten Thursday night, completely. It seemed a year ago. Rocky and Stoney would be wondering where he was, what had happened to him. Without thinking, he headed for the public phones just inside the terminal entrance. Three steps from them he saw, through the plate glass windows of the terminal, the Land-Rover, parked in a no-parking zone, the dark man at the wheel. He stopped in mid-stride, then, elaborately, mimed a gesture that said, oops, and turned back. He wondered if he'd been seen and the gesture appreciated.

Then he felt a self-revulsion for attempting to communicate a pleasantry to the brute who'd grabbed his children and who now was planning—God knows what—for Felicia O'Brien. The hell with God knows what, Schroeder told himself. *You* know what.

He remembered the ice-cream soda, and went back to his mother and children and led them to the lunch counter, where the kids had two black-and-white sodas, which were hardly candidates for island-wide renown, and he and his mother had black coffee.

What Schroeder really wanted was a shot of vodka, but the bar was out of sight of the plate glass window, and might have a phone in it, and he'd been a model quarry up to now and didn't want to spoil it at the last minute. For a moment he was tempted to make the bravado gesture of lifting his cup toward the man in the vehicle outside. He decided it wouldn't be bravado, it would be ass-kissing.

They were just finishing when their flight was called. He paid the check, and the four of them walked through the terminal gate out across the tarmac to the plane. Rain was sprinkling and the wind increasing. The plane was a jet-prop Fairchild 227, which they boarded from the rear. As he walked up the steps, he thought how delighted he was to leave this weekend behind. Then he thought of the girl in the hands of those two men. Felicia O'Brien could not leave the weekend behind.

He could almost see her pale, passive face, pleading yet resigned. Before stepping into the plane he took a look at the glowering, majestic Nantucket sky, dark storm clouds building in the east. He half shrugged, not sure if it was for the benefit of the swarthy man, or in answer to the question he asked himself.

What else could I have done?

He felt relieved that he could put it in the past tense.

Chapter

MIKE WAS WORRIED ABOUT GRABBING THE KIDS, ABOUT DRIV-
ing with them in the Land-Rover, about putting them in the dinghy. When finally they were aboard the *Sloppy Joe,* blindfolded,
he relaxed. On deck with Red, waiting for their father to deliver
the girl, he asked, "What did we have to grab 'em for? It leaves
us vulnerable!"

"Jesus, Mike, *vulnerable!* Easy on the big words, it'll give me
brain fever trying to keep up with you. Listen, you've got to
have confidence in me. What's the matter, where's your fucking
confidence?"

"It's just that when you grab kids, Red, the cops go ape shit. I
never like to start any more trouble than I have to. It's easier
that way."

"Oh shit, first big words, now a fucking philosopher." Red

never missed a chance to mock. "Listen, Mikey, let me do the thinking, will you? I didn't want to grab the kids, either. But I'll tell you what I wanted to do a hell of a lot less—go back without the girl; have to tell them we had her in our hands and let her get away. Those kids are our best shot to get the dame. That is, their father is. And I told them right off to shut their eyes, and then we put the handkerchiefs around them. And don't forget we got the hats and the glasses, so I don't think they ever got a good look at our faces. And besides they're only seven or eight, or whatever. And their old man never saw us, either. Pussycat I got stashed away on the bridge so they can't see him, all they can hear is a belch once in a while from all the beer the old fart is putting away.

"And let me tell you something else, Mike. We are not going to get any trouble from the father; he's got no balls, I can size them up pretty quick. He's one of those artsy-fartsy types who sits on the beach reading the latest faggot novel. Did you see his face when you almost ran him down? Did you?"

"Naw, I was too busy tryin' to get up close with the Jeep."

"I'll tell you, Mike, I was watching his face. And you know what I saw? Terror. Pure shit-in-the pants terror. Not for his kids, either, for his own ass. And you know something else, Mike? Right then, we could have got him to do anything, to anyone, to save his own ass. That guy is no fucking hero, you can bet on it." He chuckled. "That's what I wrote on the note. Don't be no hero. It's not good English, Mike. I could get points off for it in school, see? But I want him to think we're uncouth. If he thinks we're couth, he might try to reason with us. I don't want him to reason with us. I want him to do what we tell him."

"You ain't worried about him callin' the cops?"

"Mike, look at it from his point of view. He doesn't know we're aboard a boat, let alone what boat it is. He only knows he's got to meet us at the wharf. He also knows if any cops show up, it's a good bet, we'll spot them before they can spot us. And there go his kids. So if he can deliver the girl—and he can, Mikey, I have the definite feeling he can—he's going to do it. Besides, he's from New York, you saw his license plates. That means he doesn't trust anyone, and he doesn't want to get involved in any crusades. Besides, he thinks we're watching every move he makes. He just wants his kids back. And he's no fucking hero. You watch, see if I'm not right."

"Yeah, but what about afterwards?"

"Afterwards?"

"Yeah. After we get the girl, if we get her, and he gets his kids back. What's to keep him from calling the cops then?"

"Oh, he might, there's a good chance he won't, because he's a fucking coward, but he might. But he won't until he gets back to New York, I'll tell you that. Because he's scared, and because we're going to be watching him—*you're* going to be watching him, and we're going to let him know it. So let's suppose he gets back to New York and then calls the cops. He can't identify us. He can't say what boat we're on. We might be out of here, anyway, with any luck, before dark."

"What's this about me watchin' him?"

"Yeah, I've got a few things for you to do, Mike, so you can earn your money. You're going to get in the dinghy and go ashore. First you're going to drive over to the guy's house. North Liberty. Can you find it?"

"Yeah, this time I can."

"OK, cut their telephone wires. Then come back to the dock and get on a pay phone and call the airport, and make reservations on the early evening flight back to New York, for him and the old lady and the kids."

"What airline?"

"Air India."

"Waddya mean, Air India?"

"What I mean, dumdum, is whatever fucking airline flies out of here to New York. That's what I mean. Just call the airport and find out! OK, then, next. When you've done their phone, and the plane reservations, park the Land-Rover out of sight, and keep an eye on the dock. If you spot any cops, go to the edge of the water, where you can see this boat—which means I can see you—and stretch your arms like you're yawning. Then take off. Don't try to pick up the car. And *don't* try to make it back to the boat. Got it?"

"Yeah, got it."

"If you see the guy coming with the girl, and it looks clear, bend over, like you're trying to tie your shoe. Then stay there, wait for the guy to leave with his kids. Follow him, let him catch sight of the Land-Rover a couple of times. Make sure he doesn't stop anywhere but at his house. Make sure he doesn't talk to anyone, or make any calls. Like I said before, he'll be scared shitless. He won't try anything. But just make sure. Stay till he boards the plane. Got it?"

"Got it."

"OK. Tell me everything you've got to do."

"Aw, Red."

"I want to hear it."

"Cut their phone line. Make the reservations. Signal from the dock. Then either take off if there are cops, or wait and follow them to make sure they get on the plane and don't make no calls. Red, how rough do I get if he tries to make a call?"

Red laughed. "Just start closing in with the car. Don't worry, you just make a move and that guy'll shit in his pants. I guarantee it. You got it all now?"

"Yeah."

"And Mike, keep the hat and the glasses on, so they can't see your face. With those things on, nobody could tell you from Robert Redford." Red thought that funny; he laughed again.

Mike said nothing. Finally, he asked, "Suppose no cops and no guy shows up? What do I do then?"

"You wait it out, Mike. I guarantee someone's going to show up. The guy is not going to leave his kids here. Someone will show up. Now you better get going."

The swarthy man stood quickly.

"Atta boy, Mike. I'm going to be thinking about you while I'm sitting here lapping up the owner's booze."

Climbing over the side into the dinghy, Mike said: "Hey, save some for me!"

"Don't worry, there's plenty," Red answered, and watched the other man start the outboard and head for the dock.

Even as he left, clouds were thickening and lowering. By the time he returned, around 7:30, it had grown dark, the wind had picked up and a driving rain had begun. The storm had begun to rile up the waters of the harbor.

Mike climbed aboard, looking worried. "Jeeze, it's fierce out. I was afraid that little boat wasn't goin' to make it."

But Red was exultant. When Mike said, "Everything go OK, huh!" he answered, "To a T. To a fucking T!"

The three men were in the cockpit, Mike drenched from the rain, Red with a glow on from his success and an open bottle of vodka, the old man working his way through a second six-pack of beer.

"Where is she?"

Red looked toward the cabin. Mike got up, walked to the hatchway, and stuck his head in. The girl was sitting on a bunk, propped against the bulkhead, her hands tied, the same rope leading down to her ankles, which were also tied. Her cheekbone was swollen and discolored, the left eye closed. A gag was tied around her mouth. Terror showed in the one open eye.

"What happened to her?" Mike asked. "She trip climbin' on board?" He smiled toward Red in a show of camaraderie, but his heart wasn't in it. Although only ten years older than Red, he was of the old school. You didn't punch a woman, except in passion. But then he didn't think there *was* any passion in Red.

"Yeah, she tripped over my fist, after she tried yelling once. That's all she tried, was once. How'd it go for you?"

"Perfect, everything according to plan."

"You mean, Mike, just like I said it would."

"Yeah, just like you said it would."

"Did the pansy try anything?"

"Nah, he was just like a little pussycat. Well, yeah, once at the airport, he heads for the phone on the wall, at least I think that's where he was goin'. And then he stops. And he looks out the window to where I'm sittin' in the Land-Rover. And he turns and walks away. It was perfect, I tell you."

"You don't have to tell *me*, Mikey, I told *you*. That guy's going to be looking over his shoulder for the rest of his life, waiting to see if we're going to pounce on him. He'll probably be afraid to go near a phone for a *month*."

Red let out a laugh that made the Pussycat lift his head from his beer can and look up. "I should have put that in the note," Red went on, grinning, "Don't use no fuckin' phone for no purpose whatsoever, for a *month!*" Red laughed again. "I bet he'd have done it."

Mike had never seen the redhead come so close to emotion. Then Red caught himself, and stopped, as if ashamed to show enjoyment at anything. "Anyway," he said, clinically, "You watched them board the plane, right?"

"Yup."

"And you stayed till the plane took off, right?"

"Yup."

Red nodded. "We got the bitch. And we got the book." He nodded again.

"So we're in like Flynn," said the darker man, trying to forget his antagonism to the redhead. "Now all we gotta do is get outta here."

Red looked through the glass at the weather outside. The wind was whipping up to a gale, the rain driving down at a forty-five-degree angle, the sky inky. "I don't know, Mike, I don't know. We got a fucking storm on our hands, and from what I heard on the radio it's going to get worse."

"What's the point of hangin' around here?" Mike asked.

Camaraderie did not stick with Red too long. "The point is, who's gonna be the fucking skipper, and get us to Boston in the dark, with fucking gale warnings? That's the point. Can you do it? If you can, you're a better man than I am. And I'm a pretty fair skipper. I don't know, maybe you can, after all, Columbus was an Eyetalian."

"Goddamn right he was," said the Pussycat loudly, his speech fuzzy around the edges.

"Yeah," said Red, "two goddamn Eyetalians! How about it, Pussycat? I don't hear anything from your paisan over here. You gonna get us to Boston in the middle of the night in a fucking storm? Huh?"

The old man let out a tremendous belch.

"That's as smart as anything else you said," Red replied. As he had more and more vodka, his speech grew rougher as well as more slurred, more and more stripping the veneer of a couple of semesters of college. "I'll tell you what. First I'll tell you why we shouldn't go. 'Cause it's fuckin' dangerous. 'Cause we don't know how to handle this boat well enough. 'Cause nobody's after us, and if they are, they ain't gonna be out lookin' in a fuckin' storm; they're gonna wait till morning. And in the morning, by the very first light, we are gone. And when we get where the water's real deep, we send the little bitch in there for a swim. And then we are clean. We are home free. Meanwhile we ride out the storm, safe and snug, with enough booze and food to last the night. All right, now, you tell me why we *should* risk our asses in the dark in that storm." Red looked at both of them. No answer.

"Go on," he said.

Finally Mike ventured something. "Maybe the cops are out lookin' for her."

"But they *ain't* out lookin' for her." Red smiled, then laughed. "They sent *us* to look for her. And we found her." Then he dropped the jollity. "Why should the cops be looking for her? The poor girl's father was killed, in an accident. Naturally, she's upset. So she goes away for a while. It figures. She's not a minor. Now, maybe in a few weeks, or a month, if she don't show up, somebody'll think she's missing. And maybe the cops'll sent out a missing person notice. Or even start looking. In a few weeks or months, let 'em look!" Red smiled again; he was enjoying this.

"So if you got no better reason for going now than that, just sit back and lap up the booze, and relax. I ain't steered you wrong yet, have I, Mike? Stick with me, you'll be fartin' through silk."

Mike found himself a bottle of Seagram's Seven, twisted off the cap and had a long drink. "Yeah, fartin' through silk. That's good."

For a while the three men sat on the *Sloppy Joe* in the murky, stormy evening, each drinking from his own source of alcohol, Red from a bottle of vodka, Mike with his freshly opened whiskey, and Pussycat working on his second six-pack of beer. Then, to the accompaniment of the snap and fizz of an opened beer can, Pussycat said: "Hope you got enough beer to get me through the night. I only seen six six-packs." And he threw his head back and laughed, punctuating the laugh with another huge belch.

"Remind me not to take you to the White House with me, next time I'm invited, Pussycat," said Red. And then: "I'll tell you what, if thirty-six cans of beer don't last you the night, know what we'll do? We'll recycle some of your piss; by then it'll be pure beer, anyway, the beer is pure piss to begin with, so what difference'll it make?"

The old man grunted.

"What'sa matter, Pussycat, I mean Pissycat—that's good!— don't know what to say? Oh, yeah, I get it, you don't know what recycle means, do you?"

The old man just took another gulp from his beer and said nothing.

"Well?" Red leaned forward, his eyes as red as his hair and flushed face.

"You think you're so fuckin' smart, don't you, Red?" Pussycat replied.

"Naw," answered the redhead. "Just compared to you, Pissycat."

"Well, lemme learn you somethin', wise guy."

"You gonna *learn* me something?" Red thought it was very

funny. He looked at the dark man. "Hey, Mike? Do you hear that? The old fart is gonna *learn* me something!"

The dictionary points scored by the big redhead were lost on Mike, who was more concerned about the storm building up inside the boat than the one outside.

"Yeah, I'm gonna learn you somethin'," said the old man, not realizing Red was ridiculing his use of the wrong verb. "What I'm gonna learn you is that you ain't gonna get nowhere thinking you're so fuckin' smart. You ain't gonna get *nowhere*."

"Is that so?"

"Yeah, that's so," the old man replied. "The big guys don't like you. They say you think you know everything, always tellin' everyone else what to do. I heard 'em. They think you're a wiseass Mick, and you ain't goin' *nowhere*."

It sounded authentic, it hit Red hard, and it worried Mike.

"You mean they don't like brains, huh? Well, tough shit for them. Too fuckin' bad for them if they'd rather have a fat, dumb, overaged Wop hangin' around, who can't do shit, besides drinkin' six-packs and belchin'."

Mike saw it coming, but didn't know what to do.

Red took another swig of vodka. "Tell me, old fat man, what do they keep you around for? Why do they need an overweight, overage shit like you around? A big lump of shit. I bet if I punched you in the face, I'd have to wipe my hand off with toilet paper."

Mike knew why they kept old Pussycat around. Because in past service to the leadership, he had shown himself to be stupid, lethargic, rigid, but totally fearless and indestructible. If ordered to, he would have attacked a tank, and made a few dents in its armor before it flattened him. Mike also knew that one's protection in insulting the Pussycat was that he either didn't understand it or thought it playful. Mike knew that no one, not Muhammad Ali, not the United States Marine Corps, could say what Red had just said and have the old man let it go by.

The Pussycat came half out of his beery stupor; he dropped his can of beer to the deck, leaned forward, looked at Red with eyes slitted by fat and by anger.

"You think so, huh? Well, there's one way you can find out."

"And what is that, old man?" Red was being challenged, and, looking at the old man, was not disposed to accept. Nor did he want to lose face.

"You can try punchin' me in the face. I'm sixty-t'ree, but you can try punchin' me in the face and see if you have to wipe your hand with toilet paper. Or if they have to wipe you off the deck with a mop." Mike knew he should intercede, but he was afraid—and was beginning to enjoy this.

Red nodded his head. "The time will come, old man, when I will have to deal with you . . ."

"Well, how about right now, Red?" The old man leaned forward in his chair, as if about to rise. Mike jumped to his feet. "Hey, Pussycat! Pasquale! Stop it! Come on now, cut it out! Have yourself a brew. Calm down. It's all just talk. That's all, talk."

"Pasquale? Is that your name, Pasquale?" Red saw himself off the hook and was relieved.

"Yeah, that's my name, Pasquale. What's the matter, you don' like it? You wanna say somethin', say somethin'." The Pussycat's blood was up.

"Come on, cut it out, both of youse," Mike said. "What's the point?"

"Yeah, Mike, you're right," Red said. "I got no time to waste arguing with just *anybody*. I'll just have to remember this for another time." He turned away, trying to show contempt. But he'd backed off, they all knew it. Mike also knew it would make him harder to deal with.

Red took a long drink from his bottle; relieved, Mike did the same. The old man, after glaring for a while, opened another can of beer, and sank back into his semistupor.

Silent again, the men kept drinking. The younger two tried an occasional conversational opener on each other; the old man seemed out of it, as if the confrontation, which he had won, had exhausted him. Nothing worked, until Mike tried: "You think the Sox can go all the way this year?" That got them going for an hour, as they went through the Red Sox starting lineup, position by position, then the rest of the American League, team by team.

Then baseball was exhausted; the redhead looked at his watch: 10:45. He stood up, looked around, saw a clock, and examining it, found it had an alarm, which he set for five.

"We gotta get an early start in the morning," he told Mike. "So we can take care of her and get back to Boston."

"What'sa matter, you worried about somethin'?" asked Mike.

"Naw, I just want to get the work done."

"Speaking of work," said the darker man, turning professional, "what are you gonna use as a weight?"

"I don't know; we'll find something. I know . . ." Red smiled. "Maybe we'll use *him* as a weight." He pointed to the slumping form of the old man. "Except, shit floats, doesn't it?" Red wanted to show Mike the old man hadn't scared him. But he spoke softly.

"You're not worried about the father of those two kids callin' the cops?" Mike asked again.

"Oh, no, not that faggot. He don't wanna get involved." Red took another swig from his vodka bottle. His face had a permanent flush now and his drinking was getting sloppy. "Right now he's probably having dinner in one of those fancy New York restaurants with his wife, or girl friend, you know candles and wine, and thinking how good it is to be safe, and keeping his big secret, saving it to tell her some time he's fucking her, so he can show her what a man he is, what an adventure he went through. Only he'll probably change a few things in the story, so as not to come out a coward."

"If he's screwin' some pussy, then he ain't no faggot," Mike pointed out.

Red wiped his mouth messily with his hand. "I didn't mean he was *that* kind of faggot. He's the kind that likes to read books he don't understand, and looks down on the 'lower' types like you and me. And why? To cover up the fact that he's got no balls."

"To cover it up from who?" Mike asked.

"From himself, of course. No, I don't mean he's the kind of faggot that likes other men. Oh no, that New York type gets plenty of women, the tall broads, skinny, with those cute little tits, and faces that look like they been sprayed with plastic so they'll stay shiny. And who knows, maybe their pussy's been sprayed, I don't know, I never been near that kind of woman."

Red paused. "But I sure could use a little pussy, any kind, right now. It would help make it a perfect weekend on Nantucket, just like I was a fuckin' banker, come down here with this girl friend for a quickie. Yeah, I wouldn't mind a little, right now."

Then Red's drunken eyes lit up. "Hey," he said. "Let's go see how the little bitch in there is doing. She might be lonely."

When Mike just nodded without moving, he added: "Come on! I want you in there."

If Red had any doubt as to his own intentions when he first spoke of the girl, they were gone by the time he stood over the bunk where she lay, awakened by their entrance and looking up in fear.

He pointed a thick finger at her. "You make any noise, or give me a hard time, I'll close the other eye, bitch, and knock out a few of your teeth, too. Got it?" Then he grabbed her bound ankles and pulled her out full length on the bunk.

Gagged as she was, she could not scream, but she tried to roll her body away.

"Grab her, Mike, so she can't move." Obediently, the other man held her down by the shoulders, and Red reached to the waist of her painter's pants and unzipped them. Again she wriggled, but it was easy for him to yank her pants and underpants down to her ankles. Then he untied the rope around her feet and yanked the pants off one foot. As soon as he did, she struck out with the free foot, kicking him in one of his thick biceps. With his right hand, Red reached between her legs and grabbed a handful of flesh on the inside of her right thigh, close to her crotch. His thick fingers squeezed, hard. A stifled squeal sounded through her gag.

"One more like that, and I'll rip a handful of it off." And he squeezed again for emphasis. She lay still.

"Now undo her wrists, Mike, and take the rest off, while I hold on to this tender flesh, so the little bitch doesn't make a move. Then tie the wrists again, only behind her back."

Mike did as he was told. First the T-shirt, then the bra. Then retied her hands behind her back. She was naked, except that around her neck was the thin golden chain with the crucifix, and on her feet her blue sneakers.

"Look at how pale the hair is," said Red. "And the tits. Did you ever see such pink nipples?" He let go of her thigh and put one hand on each breast, squeezing and kneading. Then he grabbed each nipple between a thumb and forefinger. "Look at how pink they are, Mike."

Mike was looking. "Yeah," he said, hoarsely.

Then Red gave a vicious squeeze to each nipple. He let go, and undid his pants and dropped them. Then he grabbed her nipples and squeezed again. This time a scream gurgled out, despite her gag. "Now, pink nipples," Red said. "I'm gonna fuck you anyplace I like. And then so is Mike. And one more sound out of you, and I'll let you feel what real pain is like."

But the gurgle had gotten through to the old man just outside the cabin. He wedged his bulk through the hatch, and slowly took in the situation. He disliked it, all the more for the sight of the crucifix hanging between the pale, pink-nippled breasts of the panicked girl.

His mouth distorted, his eyes narrowed, the Pussycat spoke to Red. "You lay a finger on her and I'll strangle you with my bare hands!" And he held his hands up as if offering them in evidence. They seemed wider than they were long, the palms almost as thick as the average man's were wide, the fingers double the thickness of most.

"You pick your pants up, you fuckin' sick bastard, and get the fuck outa here, or I'll strangle you with my bare hands. You, too!" The last was aimed at Mike, who watched Red for a response.

But Red said nothing. He picked his pants up and walked out of the cabin. Mike followed.

The old man knew full well that tomorrow they would kill the girl. That was business. The kind of sadistic brutality Red had shown, that was sick. All the worse, to a Catholic girl, with a crucifix around her neck. Gently, the Pussycat covered her with her bra and pants. He retied her hands in front of her. Then reached into his wallet, removed a small pillbox, took from it four pills. He held them between two massive, stubby, fingers.

"I'm gonna take the thing off your mouth. Don' make no noise. I'm gonna give you these sleepin' pills, so you go to sleep. Be better for ya." He took a few steps into the head and got her a cup of water. She turned her head away from the pills.

"Take 'em," he said. "Be good for ya." She took them.

The old man lay down on a bunk in the corner, like a watch-dog. Soon he fell asleep.

Outside, Red, drunk, seething, drained the vodka. There was nothing he could say. Mike dared not speak, so he drank. After a while they fell asleep, too. Felicia O'Brien fell into the deepest sleep of all.

Chapter 12

JUST INSIDE THE 227, THE PASSENGER BEHIND SCHROEDER asked the stewardess, "Are we going to be able to take off in this weather? Is it going to get any worse?"

It *was* getting stormy, the stewardess answered, but this aircraft could handle it. Schroeder, with his back turned, could hear the smile in her voice.

No storm, Schroeder wished to himself, no storm. Given bad enough weather, the boat—he'd now taken to calling it the *Sloppy Joe*, although he couldn't be sure that was its name—would stay in the harbor. Even an expert skipper might hesitate to leave the harbor with darkness coming on, and a storm. And if the boat stayed, the girl would be there all night, eligible for rescue, just an arrow's flight from shore. Only he was no William Tell. He realized that with the fading of the pain about his children's kidnapping, guilt was growing about the fate of the girl and how he might have helped her; he realized, too, that he'd better stop asking himself *that* question, because one of these times he might come up with an answer, and then where would he be?

Back in New York, he muttered, and hated himself for it.

The stewardess's faith in the 227 notwithstanding, it was a small plane as commercial airliners went, Schroeder thought as he walked down its narrow aisle. It seated only two on each side of the aisle, and Schroeder found four seats for them, one complete row across. He sat on one side with his mother, she at the window, he on the aisle; the kids, in the other two, immediately began a dogfight for the window.

"OK, knock it off," he ordered, then reached into his pocket and found a quarter. "Call it," he said.

Patty spoke first, "Heads!"

Schroeder tossed the coin, caught it, slammed it onto the back of his hand and then revealed it.

"Tails," he announced. His daughter looked sulky.

"Bobby gets the window for the first half of the flight. Then you switch and Patty gets it."

The girl perked up, the boy deflated a bit. "Now fasten those seat belts," he told them, then turned to his mother. "You, too, grandma." He heard the others' click in; he snapped his.

He always preferred the tail of the plane; somewhere he'd heard or read it was safer in a crash, and when he managed to get rear seats he felt more comfortable. This time he remained uncomfortable. He wanted that plane to get the hell out of there, to take him far from the *Sloppy Joe* and Felicia O'Brien.

He looked across at the children. "Well, it wasn't such a bad weekend, even though we had to cut it short," he said softly. "In some ways it turned out to be . . . *very interesting.*" He said the last two words in the caricatured accent of a Viennese psychoanalyst, and he put his fingers to his lips afterward, a request for silence that was hidden from his mother, because his back was to her. He was sure she was suspicious, at the least, of his stated reasons for leaving today. He knew, too, that years of cryptic or flimsy explanations from him had conditioned her to swallow her questions, if not her suspicions.

His son's face showed doubt, his daughter's said, Are you kidding? But neither spoke, both got the message about silence.

Well, he thought, that's about all I can expect. It would take a better salesman than I to sell that as a fun weekend.

As he was about to swivel his body back, out of the corner of his right eye, he caught a glimpse of something surprising: daylight, the ground outside the plane. On these small planes the baggage compartment was in the rear of the plane, directly opposite the passenger hatch, and it had been left open, so he could see the ground, wet from rain, and one man handing the suitcases up from a hand truck. Near the dolly he could see part of a fuel truck.

Nervously, he looked at his watch, 6:20, ten minutes after departure time, yet obviously they were still another ten or fifteen minutes away from takeoff. He wanted them to hurry; he didn't want to see that open compartment, the ground, the daylight. He wondered if the swarthy man was still paying him the compliment of sticking around in the Land-Rover, waiting for the takeoff. Probably. But just playing it safe, not as a compliment to Schroeder.

Suppose he wasn't watching, what then?

For God's sake, stop playing with yourself, he said silently, angrily. Every day there are situations far less demanding of your courage, and you do nothing; it's quixotic to whip yourself over this one. Yes, he replied, but the everyday ones don't involve a girl's being killed. And she is going to be killed, all the lack of options have nothing to do with that. And I turned her over to be slaughtered. And don't say, what else could I do?

All right, he told himself, let's put it another way, what are the possibilities right now?

Get to New York and call the police. His immediate response was: No, not good enough. Because they couldn't do anything in time. The swarthy man and his beefy friend could kill the girl and dump her weighted body overboard the moment anyone approached—if they hadn't done it already. That's assuming the police believed his story over the phone. He wasn't even sure of the name of the boat, after all.

But he recognized that as rationalization. What he wanted was a personal revenge. Law and order, constitutional rights, all that civilized stuff aside, those two men had humiliated *him*, terrorized *his* kids, and, emotionally, calling the police would not satisfy him. He had to act personally. Yes, but to do what? Well, step into the baggage compartment, slip down to the ground, get into the fuel truck, get a ride to town, see if the *Sloppy Joe* had sailed.

And if it had? Then at least I made some kind of move.

Not much of a move.

But something.

But suppose it hadn't sailed? Then what? Board it with a cutlass in your teeth?

Keep at it, he told himself, ridicule may save you, they'll probably be taking off in ten minutes and then it will be too late. In less than ten minutes you'll be OK.

And Felicia O'Brien? How much time does she have?

All right then, no ridicule. Climb down, get in the truck, get to town. Then what?

Worry about it then. Something. Anything, is the damned point. So you can think of yourself as a failed hero, a shabby hero, a semi-hero. But not a no-hero. After all, the kids and your mother will be on their way to New York in a few minutes. Those men don't know your last name, or where you live or work.

To his surprise, he found himself considering it.

Anyway, he assured himself, something will thwart you soon enough, probably before they're even aware of you. You'll make a move or two and the situation will be taken out of your hands, by some physical impossibility, some act or confrontation legitimately beyond your means. You'll be stopped. But you won't have stopped yourself. And you won't hurt so much.

And the girl, how much will she be hurting?

Take one step at a time. But take it. For once in your life, take it.

To his surprise he found himself *wanting* to take it. Overpoweringly.

To his greater surprise, he took it. To his astonishment, he heard himself say, aloud, "Dammit, I forgot something."

"Forgot something?" his mother repeated. "What?"

"What?" He patted his jacket. "My wallet." Then he remembered he'd taken it out to get a credit card to pay for the plane tickets. He hoped his mother wouldn't remember. Did he? Or did he hope she would, and call him on it, and abort his very first step?

No, he admonished himself, you don't want her to remember. She didn't.

Decisively, he unsnapped his seat belt, stood and reached into his pocket for his apartment keys. He handed them to his mother.

"Yes, my wallet, dammit, and I've got to go back for it."

He turned to his children. "Kids, I've left my wallet at the house and I must go back for it. Grandma will take you home."

To his mother he said, "Grandma, will you please? And make sure they have their suitcase. And then will you take mine and yours back to my apartment? And don't drink all the whiskey, or invite any men up, OK? I'll see you soon."

"How soon?" she asked.

"Oh, tonight. Or early tomorrow. I can use the house another day, or stay with the Cobbs."

"Why don't we all get off?" she asked. He stopped her abruptly. "No, please, it's easier this way." Without waiting for a rejoinder from her, he turned back to the children, leaned over and gave each a kiss. They looked startled at his sudden change of plans. "Don't give grandma any trouble," he told them. "Switch seats halfway. And I'll call you tomorrow. Love and kisses."

"Sam," his mother said as he was about to walk away, "don't get yourself in any trouble."

To himself he said, not the kind you think, mother. To her, he said: "Don't be silly, mom. I run from it. Every time."

Then he wheeled around, took the two steps to the baggage compartment and stepped in. The baggage handler looked at him, astonished. Quickly, Schroeder reached into the wallet he'd said he left behind and pulled two fives from it. One he stuffed into his pocket, the other he handed to the baggageman.

He tried a rakish smile, and then said: "There's a certain lady in the terminal I'm trying to avoid. She thinks I'm leaving, but I'm not, if you get my meaning." He spoke in a whisper, put his finger to his lips, and even tried a wink. But he didn't wait to see how the act would work. He leaned down, put a hand on each side of the open hatch, and half jumped, half lowered himself to the tarmac. The distance was greater than he thought, and as he hit, he felt a pain shoot through his bad right knee. Well, pain or no pain, step one has been taken. He half walked, half hobbled to the passenger side of the fuel truck.

Step two he'd already thought about. Using his healthy left leg for the step up, he climbed into the passenger seat of the truck and slumped down. Almost at once the driver climbed into the other side and gave Schroeder a startled look.

"What is this?" he asked. "What in hell are you doing here?" This time Schroeder was ready. He pulled the second five dollars from his pocket, and grinned.

"There's a lady friend watching the plane from the terminal. She thinks I'm leaving. I want her to think it. But I don't want to leave. Where are you headed?" Schroeder was not giving the driver the option of refusing him. The two men stared at each other. The driver was a small man in his late fifties, but Schroeder, taking in his big, leathery hands on the wheel, his thick wrists and forearms, realized he wouldn't be intimidated physically; he'd have to want to take Schroeder.

The driver's face creased in a smile. "Couldn't be your wife, could it?" Schroeder grinned and shrugged, to let him think so. "I'm driving this thing to Commercial Wharf, in town; want to come?"

Schroeder was grateful, for he not only had a ride, he had a destination. Up until that instant, he'd had no idea where he was going. This gave him a little more time to think.

"Yes, thanks, I'd appreciate it."

The driver pulled away from the plane, and Schroeder immediately slumped farther down in the seat so his head barely showed above the window. No explanation was needed: the lady-friend story had already set it up. The truck moved through an open gate, around the terminal and onto the road toward town. Schroeder sat up a little higher, looked to his right and saw the FH 227 begin taxiing for takeoff. He hadn't made it by much, another minute or so and the baggage hatch would have closed, he'd be on the plane, headed back to New York. But he wasn't.

The truck was moving slowly, neither man speaking. About a mile out, a car, then a second passed them, cars that had stayed for the takeoff, Schroeder said to himself. Then a third, and a fourth. The fourth was the Land-Rover. Schroeder began to duck again, then realized that high in the truck cab, he couldn't be seen. He watched the Land-Rover pull away, catching a glimpse of the swarthy man's big arm folded out the window, and realized, too, that the man was no longer looking for him. He thought Schroeder was on the plane to New York, and he'd tell his beefy partner that. They had cowed the no-hero busybody; he was happy to be putting miles between himself and them and the girl. They'd never have to worry about him again.

Well, fuck you, Swarthy! And you, too, beefy man, he said to himself. Schroeder now had surprise going for him, for whatever he wanted to do. But what did he want to do? What *could* he do? That was still ahead of him.

The wind and rain were picking up, the day turning far darker than 7 P.M. in late June warranted. Let's assume, Schroeder told himself, that the *Sloppy Joe* did not attempt to leave the harbor in the darkness and storm, but decided instead to wait until morning. That gave him the whole night in which to act.

And do what?

The quick, "sensible" thing—call the police—was never far from his mind, but emotionally he was not disposed to do it. That, he told himself, in the adrenaline high of his escape from the plane, was not acting. That was not swinging back in any way at those two men who had kidnapped his kids and would kill, perhaps *had* killed, Felicia O'Brien, those men who had brushed him aside as if he were no more than a harmless fly. No, he wanted to *sting* them. But how? He would need help.

The Cobbs. He thought of them, at once. They were, to begin, the only people he knew on the island. But more than that, Stoney was the most resourceful man he knew, anywhere, the best man to talk to. To get ideas. To be talked out of the whole project. No, strike that, Schroeder told himself. You *won't* be talked out of it. You'll go ahead, one step at a time, as far as you can.

Big talk, he thought; what makes you think you can do it? Well, I've taken step one, gotten off the plane. And step two, a ride to town. Now step three, going to the Cobbs.

He turned to the driver. "Listen, I'll give you another five dollars if you make a slight detour and drop me at a friend's house on Cliff Road."

"I can't, in this thing," he replied. "But if you're willing to wait a couple of minutes, when I put this away on the lot, I'll drop you in my own car, on my way home. And you don't have to give me another five dollars. One is plenty."

"Well, thanks," Schroeder said. "I *will* wait."

They said no more during the time the driver parked the oil truck and the two got into his car. Going past Straight Wharf, Schroeder strained for a glimpse of the Land-Rover and the

Sloppy Joe. The former he couldn't see; the latter he wouldn't have recognized if he had seen it, for the distance was too great to read names on the boats.

"How far out Cliff Road?" the driver asked.

"A mile, maybe less; I'll warn you when the turn is coming." A couple of minutes later, Schroeder said, "We're getting to it." Then, "Here it is. It's the second driveway to the right, but you don't have to turn off at all, I can walk from the road."

"That's all right," said the driver. "I believe in door-to-door service." His leathery face folded into a grin. He drove Schroeder onto the dirt road and then into the Cobb driveway. When they came to a stop, Schroeder again offered the second five dollars.

"Nope. One's enough, like I said. Besides I'm always glad to help a man get away from a woman. Sometimes I feel like it myself." He grinned again as Schroeder got out of the car.

"Well, thanks again." Schroeder said it standing outside the car. He slammed the passenger door.

The driver just waved and smiled, then backed his car quickly, expertly, out of the driveway. In the rain and growing darkness, Schroeder made his way toward the house. Through the screen door, he could see Rocky and Stoney standing and waiting for him. Christ, he thought, they'd make a perfect ad for Chivas Regal, or a Bermuda vacation, or a Lincoln Continental. Better, a Rolls. Serene, aristocratic, in command. Yet in a mess. Schroeder knew that, though, looking at them, he couldn't make himself believe it.

He ran along their boardwalk; Stoney, smiling, opened the door to help him get in out of the rain. How damned glad he was, he thought, that he and Rocky hadn't made love, when was it, Thursday, less than forty-eight hours ago. It seemed like a year; so much had happened since.

"Well, well, what a happy surprise," said Stoney, reaching out a big, bony hand. "We'd begun to think you were going to snub us."

Schroeder just smiled back, saying nothing. His eyes hadn't yet met Rocky's; he didn't know how much she'd said to her husband. And he had a long story of his own to tell.

Rocky stepped in to fill the gap. "I was telling Stoney I was afraid I'd said or done something to offend you Thursday night, and that's why you hadn't called." She'd made of the little speech an elaborate show of innocence, teasing Schroeder, leaving him wondering what Stoney had been told about Thursday night. Schroeder not only wondered how much of the drunken evening Rocky remembered, but how much she'd embellished, fantasized, invented—up to and including lovemaking—and used as a club against her husband.

"The only possible offense," he answered, to let her know at once which tack he'd take, "was to my liver, through the generous flow of your brandy. And the next morning my head might have charged you with a misdemeanor. That's all." How elaborately clever, he said to himself, for a man who's just been through a weekend of two sexual episodes, one kidnapping and a murder-to-be.

"Ah, yes, a wonderful hostess," Stoney said with a tight smile. He could work more irony into fewer words than anyone Schroeder knew. And the terser the answers, the more the tension, that he knew, too. The fangs are out, he said to himself. Tonight the drink might be blood, not brandy. The wrong setting for his story; he decided he'd better start telling it quickly.

"Something unbelievable has happened to me. And I want some advice on what to do about it—if anything." He looked up at Stoney as he spoke, and was reminded how tall the man was, six feet four or five, but looking even bigger because he was so lean and his shoulders so broad. He made Rocky seem diminutive, and she was five-ten. Schroeder, at six one, felt small, too.

"Whatever we can do," Rocky said. "Just name it, it's yours."

"Yes, a wonderful hostess," Stoney repeated, with a smile. He put his arm around Schroeder's shoulders and walked him into the living room.

"Would your offended parts resent your having a drink?" Rocky asked. Was she trying a double entendre again? Schroeder asked himself. At any rate, he thought, he shouldn't have a drink. His mind should be clear for what lay ahead, whatever it might be. On the other hand, he could use a little loosening. On a third hand, he hadn't eaten much lately, and a drink could knock him out.

"A brandy," he said. "A *small* one. And some cheese and crackers, or something, because I've somehow neglected to eat much since breakfast."

Stoney handled the division of labor. "I'll get Sam a brandy, dear; would you see to some food?'' In the form of a question, it was nonetheless, unmistakably, a directive.

Rocky looked at her husband with clear annoyance. ''Why, yes, of course, it's into the kitchen for the little woman, so she can whip something up while the two men get right down to serious business.''

''Thank you, dear,'' said Stoney.

''Well, now, just don't forget a splash of brandy for the little woman, you hear?''

''Dear, you've already poured yourself one. Have you forgotten?'' Rocky just walked to the bar, picked up a partially filled snifter, and had a gulp of it. Then as she headed for the kitchen, she jabbed her middle finger straight up in the air at her husband. Stoney smiled, then walked to the bar, poured modest amounts of cognac into two snifters. He lifted them both, carried them to the sofa, where the two men sat, Stoney exactly where Rocky had been two nights ago, Schroeder, just where he had sat.

''Don't mind Rocky. Let's drink to solving your problem.'' Stoney raised his glass. Both men sipped.

''This morning my children were kidnapped.''

Stoney's eyes widened. ''What happened? Where are they now?''

''They're all right now,'' Schroeder replied. ''On their way back to New York with my mother. But I've had the weirdest day of my life.''

Rocky walked into the room, holding a plate. ''Jarlsberg, ham, crackers. What have I missed?''

''I just started telling Stoney,'' Schroeder said. ''For a few hours today my children were kidnapped. They're all right now. It started Friday evening as we were leaving the movie theatre.'' Schroeder told the story, omitting the lovemaking on the beach. With his kids away from the island, and the first jolt of the brandy, he relaxed, found himself settling back, ready for another brandy or two, ready to forget his mission, his revenge. He forced himself to attention.

''So, if they haven't sailed, and if they haven't killed the poor girl, she's still in the harbor, probably aboard a boat called the *Sloppy Joe*.'' He forced himself forward. ''And I want to do something about it.''

Schroeder looked to Stoney, but the first response came from Rocky.

"Call the police." It was as if she had sniffed the potential involvement of her husband, and didn't like the smell.

Schroeder was surprised at the vehemence of his own answer. "OK, I could. Maybe I will. But let me explain something to you. I don't know how to tell you what I feel: the rage, the humiliation, the impotence, the . . . the . . . sense of violation. Yes, that's it! It's what a woman must feel about being raped, having her bodily integrity forcibly violated. Yes, I can call the police. Probably, I'll end up doing it. But I've got to try something for myself first. I don't know what, but something."

"And how about that girl, while you're figuring things out?" Rocky asked.

Schroeder resented her attempt to sidetrack him. He felt a flush of anger in his face; his head began to throb; he'd had two drinks of his brandy, but thus far, none of the food.

"Look, *if* the police believe my story—considering I have no kids around anymore, and I'm not really sure if the girl *is* aboard a boat, and if she is, where the boat is and what it's named—*if* they believe me, there's still a question of what they can do. First of all, the girl may already be dead and dumped overboard. The boat may be long out of the harbor. In which case there's no hurry to tell the police. Anything they can do now—search, for example—they can do better in the morning. If the boat she *may* be on is still in the harbor, she'll be there till morning. And that gives me some time."

"You're crazy," Rocky said. "Call the police, dammit!"

The throbbing in his head was growing, becoming a fullfledged headache, which didn't surprise him, considering the lack of food, and the alcohol and the tension. "Listen," he began, "*you're* the one who called me a coward, and . . ."

Stoney interrupted him. "If we keep egos out of this, we can figure it out better. Let's stick to reasoning. Sam, I think, is right in that, if she's on a boat, and if it is headed out to sea tonight, it will have already gone. There's still some light, but not a hell of a lot. If it's still there, it will stay till first light. Next, don't think it will be easy to get a search started for the daughter of Henry J. O'Brien, who is regarded by authorities, statewide, as some kind of crazed, paranoid Italophobic zealot. But if we do, it will be pitch black before it starts, and then chances are that the motors and the lights will alert those two men and give them lots of time to dispose of the girl. The police will want to get a warrant, because everyone is suspicious of anything connected with O'Brien. Then they'll have to locate the boat. No, it seems to me, that's not going to be much of a nighttime operation, if we can get it started at all."

Stoney had dissected the situation with admirable clarity, Schroeder thought, and come down on his side. And in doing it, he was taking Schroeder closer to action. His headache got worse. He didn't want to stop of his own accord. But being stopped by circumstances beyond his control—that was another matter. That might salve his conscience and save his ass at the same time, he told himself. He wanted to—and was afraid to. Perfectly understandable, but it made his head throb.

"What do you propose to do, Sam?" Stoney asked.

Of course he didn't know, another reason for his headache. "Something, but I'll be damned if I know what."

"Call the police!" Rocky shouted.

"Just hold on, dear. Volume is no substitute for reasoning. It seems to me the next move is to go out into the harbor, while there's still some light—there won't be for long—and see if we can locate a *Sloppy Joe*."

"We?" asked Rocky, loudly.

"I'll just run him out in the Boston whaler," Stoney answered with a finality designed to settle the question. "Sorry I can't offer you the big boat, Sam, but it's in dry dock at the moment."

The question wasn't settled for his wife. She got to her feet. "Now, wait a minute! Stoney, you are not to get involved in this. I'd say the same to Sam, but he is not my husband and the father of my daughter." She turned to Schroeder. "But I can implore you not to get yourself or my husband into a fight with a couple of trained hoods. No! No Stoney." Then she turned to her husband. "No, Stoney."

She was right, of course she was right, Schroeder knew it. For him it may have been a foolish fight, but at least his own. Yet Schroeder felt himself leaning on his tall friend. "I didn't ask him to go, Rock. I only asked his advice. Whatever I do, I want to do alone."

Stoney ignored his wife and spoke to Schroeder. "Just reconnaissance, that's all it is, my boy. And reconnaissance is better with two sets of eyes than one, and with a small boat than with none. Besides, I know the harbor and I don't believe you do. We shall not attack; we'll merely put-put around the harbor with sou'westers on, looking like a couple of lobstermen."

It was a kind of explanation to Rocky, but he would not deign to direct it at her.

"No!" she responded, vehemently. "You must not!" She looked to Schroeder for support. He found it strange that a woman who seemed to detest her husband so should fight so hard for his safety. Schroeder didn't know what to do.

"Look, Stoney," he began. "If the little woman doesn't want . . ."

"But I *do* want, Samuel." Stoney and Rocky were both staring at Schroeder, he impatiently, she angrily.

"I just remembered," he said, "that I have a headache and need aspirin. That I must go to the toilet, too, preferably the most distant toilet in the house. Then I can get out of the middle and let you two talk. I'll go to one of the upstairs bathrooms. I know where it is." Without waiting for a reply, Schroeder turned and walked off.

He had hardly made it upstairs, when Rocky hissed at her husband, "Are you crazy? Do you want to help that little boy play James Bond? And risk your lives, and possibly that girl's— if there's any left to risk? Call the police. Now!"

Stoney looked at her with what she always called his "Brahmin disdain." "When I'm ready," he replied. "Sam's analysis is correct, there's no hurry at the moment. And Sam is in crisis; if I refuse to help, he'll try it alone. I'd like to work him around to calling the police himself. With a little more talk and a few more drinks, he may get around to it. I'd prefer that. Why don't you help with the drinks, you seem to be awfully good at it. That's the way it's going to be done."

"And that's the way you're going to show yourself a friend, by getting him drunk and tricking him? What a double cross! What a friend!"

"That's the way it's going to be done," said Stoney, like a monarch who'd allowed a subject a moment's disagreement, and then cut off the discussion.

"Why, you cold, arrogant bastard!" said Rocky. On the word bastard, Schroeder came down the stairs.

"Still talking about me, eh?" Schroeder said.

"No, no, Samuel, the words were aimed at me. Mrs. Cobb tries to make vituperation serve where logic fails, as it almost always does. 'Arrogant bastard,' and 'screw you' are her favorites."

Rocky laughed and had another drink of her brandy. "Arrogant bastard, Sam, is only what Mr. Cobb's nearest and dearest would say of him. If that be vituperation, make the most of it. As for screw you, I assure you I say it to him as a threat, not a promise."

"Oh, she is so boring, Sam," Stoney said. "Let me just splash a bit more brandy into that snifter, then let's drink to reconnaissance. And then let's do it." He took Schroeder's glass and poured, not splashed, brandy into it.

"Here's to your killing yourself," said Rocky, and she raised her glass and took another mouthful.

"I don't think we'll drink to that, m'dear," said Stoney, and turned to Schroeder. "But then Rocky will drink to *anything*."

"At least it doesn't keep *me* from getting it up."

For the first time since he'd arrived, Schroeder saw Stoney wince. The three of them had remained standing since he'd come downstairs, and now Schroeder watched the tall man's body tense.

What the hell had he gotten into? Schroeder asked himself. Then put down the snifter he'd just picked up. "Well, I've got to be going," he announced. "I came for a little help, and seem to have arrived in time for the bloodbath. Thanks. Be seeing you." He started for the door, but before he could take two steps, Stoney spoke:

"Sam, we're going together, and our first step should be to grab some foul weather gear from the shed. Then we'll jump into the station wagon and head for the dock." He turned and looked at his wife. "Don't want to disappoint you, but we'll be all right."

"Well," she answered, "a girl can always hope." But her voice sounded softer. "If you stuck with women your own age, instead of picking up twenty-year-olds on the street, none of this would have happened. Be careful, both of you. I think you're nuts."

She looked at her husband and her eyes said, don't forget the deal.

After they'd picked up the parkas and were driving toward the dock, Schroeder said, "It seems you two are living a rather volatile emotional life. From love to hate and back in the twinkling of an eye."

"Don't know about the love part," Stoney replied, "but it is volatile, you're right about that." He looked straight ahead, watching the road; Schroeder looked at him and saw crow's-feet at the eyes, a dusting of gray throughout the hair, a touch of skin sagging below the jawline. The lean, powerful young man Schroeder knew was looking middle-aged. Schroeder felt sad, for the look of it and for the tension and bitterness coming with it. You were supposed to grow old gracefully, tranquilly. Schroeder felt sad for himself, too, because the same things were happening to him, age without grace, without tranquility.

"I must say, though," Stoney went on, "we both overdo it, overdramatize it, overpolemicize it. Play the *Sturm und Drang* for all they're worth."

"Why?" Schroeder asked. "It's so destructive."

"Granted, but it makes sparks fly. And we are both bored and disappointed. With each other, with ourselves. As I'm sure you gathered from what was said a few moments ago, as well as from what Rocky may have told you Thursday night, there is almost nothing we enjoy together, except the destruction."

The mention of Thursday night put Schroeder on his guard. He shrugged noncommittally. His friend got a glimpse of it, and smiled. "Not at all trying to break the silence your gallantry may have imposed on you, old man, but I know it takes only three minutes and three drinks for Rocky to spill out a long list of sexual maladjustments, and peccadilloes, real and imagined.

Stoney often disconcerted Schroeder because he stopped when Schroeder expected more.

"What's the answer?" he asked.

Stoney shrugged. "A statute of limitations on marriage, perhaps."

They reached the dock nearest the Boston whaler's mooring. Schroeder tucked his borrowed binoculars under his borrowed parka before getting out, for the wind was now fierce and it was driving the heavy rain.

Easily, Stoney started the outboard; he was as adept at machinery as Schroeder was clumsy. Engines always started for W. Stonington Cobb.

The harbor waters were choppy but there was no swell. "Quite a harbor," said Stoney as he moved them away from the dock. "For small boats, one of the best in the world, the making of Nantucket—until the whalers got too big to cross the bar. Then the island was left to upper-middle-class vacationers and restorationists."

"You make it sound like a fate worse than death," said Schroeder.

"Not at all," his friend answered. "To be left to *lower*-middle-class vacationers, *without* restorationists—*that's* a fate worse than death."

Slowly, without making it seem too deliberate, Stoney moved his boat around the harbor. Many of the vessels he knew; whenever there was a strange one, he got in closer to it. After a few minutes of searching he asked: "What are you going to do if you spot her, Sam?"

For the first time Schroeder came up against the fact that he didn't know what he'd do, didn't have the vaguest plan, that he never really expected to find the boat still there. If the boat was not there, he could call the police, and end the affair honorably. But how about the girl? Wouldn't it be better for her if the boat *was* still there? He realized he was more interested in saving his honor than her life.

Once again, he found himself waffling, and knew that in his answer to Stoney he had to commit himself, aloud, to some action. "I'd like to disable the boat in some way. And get her off."

"Got any idea of how to do it?" Stoney asked. Schroeder could see his binoculars were concentrated on something.

"Nope. Not yet."

"Well, you may as well start thinking, because you've now got a boat to do it to. She's ahead, at eleven o'clock, about seventy-five yards off."

Schroeder felt his stomach drop violently. He lifted his binoculars, and in the dying light could just make out on the transom of the boat: *Sloppy Joe,* Nantucket, Mass.

"What kind of a boat is she?" he asked. Handling the tiller easily with one hand, Stoney stared through his glasses. "Cruiser, perhaps twenty-seven, twenty-eight feet, fairly new, powerful, expensive. Big engine."

"Quite an investment, just to go after poor little Felicia O'Brien," Schroeder said.

"Local boat," said Stoney. "Probably chartered. Usually people charter her for tuna or shark."

"This time the sharks chartered her, to go after people. Doesn't look like they're planning to go anywhere, does it?" He knew as he spoke that he was hoping they were.

"I doubt it," Stoney replied. "Even the best of skippers would stay put tonight." He'd put the whaler in a wide arc around the *Sloppy Joe.* "Their anchor's out; they're probably going to wait for morning's first light, which gives us about eight hours to come up with an idea."

Schroeder heard the "we" and was comforted, and ashamed of it. "Of course, we don't even know she's still aboard," he said, and knew he was maneuvering, and was ashamed for that, too.

"It doesn't make any sense that she be elsewhere," answered his friend. "She's hidden, guarded, can't be heard, can't run, can be transported easily. The only difficulty with that location is you. And from what you say, they think they have you taken care of, back in New York, scared for your kids"—Schroeder thought that tactful of him—"clearly handleable, properly threatened. And as far as they know, you don't know the name of their vessel. They also know the police need a warrant to board, and couldn't approach without being spotted, which would give them time to dispose of the girl. In short, I think they feel safe."

"And we've . . . I've . . . got eight hours. And no ideas," Schroeder said, giving his friend an opening.

"First thing we should do," said Stoney, "is be able to find her again if we want to." Again Schroeder found comfort in the "we." "We can line her up on the buoy and the Brant Point Light." He maneuvered, and sighted. "All right, now I suggest we go back to the house and talk it over. See what ideas we can come up with. All right?"

Diplomatically, he waited for an answer, though he knew Schroeder would agree. "Fine," Schroeder said.

Stoney headed back to his mooring, Schroeder feeling like a novice with a master, dumb, docile. What else could I have said? he asked himself, and hated the formulation of the question. He was still being passive, letting circumstances run him, not taking charge. Angry, trying to rebut his own passivity, he said: "Boy, I sure would appreciate help with ideas and plans, because I'm a babe when it comes to boats and engines. But the execution is all mine. You're not to go near it—orders from me. The risk is all mine—orders from me. And if that won't do, orders from Rocky. Understood?"

"Understood," Stoney answered. "I go no further than planning and perhaps a bit of ferrying, as I've just done. The rest is yours."

Was Schroeder disappointed? No, dammit, no, he told himself. He would do it. Alone. If it were possible.

They were back at the dock; Stoney tied the whaler up. The wind and rain had now built to a storm. The men ran for the station wagon, climbed in, and started back to the Cobb house.

"It's got to be something we can get to from the outside," Schroeder said. "Something that would keep the boat from functioning. The only thing I can think of is the propeller."

"That's what I was thinking about, Samuel. The prop does seem the most likely possibility. The question is, what can you do to it in the middle of the night, when it isn't in motion, that will disable it in the morning when they start it? Right now, I don't know." He paused. "Hell, we've got some time to think about it."

They finished the drive in silence, and, dripping wet, walked into the living room, where Rocky sat, sipping brandy. "Home are the heroes," she announced.

"Yup, we made it," Stoney said. "Sorry to disappoint you."

"Well, then, why did you?" she countered.

Schroeder thought they'd actually seemed glad to see each other, but then the sparring resumed. "It's like we'd never left, Rock!" he said. "Look, could you two take the gloves off and concentrate on *my* problem? All I want to do is pick Stoney's brain and maybe get a ride. The danger is all mine, we agreed to that. OK?"

Rocky looked to her husband to remind him, again, with her eyes, about his promise. Then she lifted her glass. "I'll drink to that. In fact, why don't we all? Your glasses are just as you left them; I've not altered a thing, it's all stayed exactly as it was, a tribute to one of my dearest friends. And to my dearest husband—so far." Before they could get near their glasses, however, she stood, grabbed the brandy bottle, and refilled all three.

Schroeder wasn't interested in a drink; he sat on the sofa and turned to Stoney, who'd sat down next to him. "All right, then, how do I do it? Obviously, I can't wait for them to start her up before I try something. I've got to do whatever it is I do to the propeller in advance, that will put it out of commission when they start her. But what?"

Now Schroeder knew there was a *Sloppy Joe,* and she was still in the harbor. He could not be sure the girl was aboard or alive, but he now had an object, a bulky white cruiser, to direct his attentions to. And he didn't want the Cobbs to start sparring again; he needed Stoney's attention.

Rocky had her own game plan, and that was to get Schroeder

drunk and thinking about other things. She thought her husband was after the same thing, but she didn't trust him, and was ready to play alone if she had to.

"Something that will foul the prop," said Stoney, looking off to the far wall. "But what?"

"By the way," Schroeder asked, "Is it properly called propeller, or screw?"

"Doesn't matter. On a boat this size, usually a prop, propeller."

Rocky saw her chance. "Too bad!" she said. "Mr. Cobb knows much more about fouling a screw than he does about fouling a propeller! He's an expert at it."

Ignoring his wife, Stoney stood and said to Schroeder, "Let's go out to the tool shed, where we can concentrate on this. Maybe some of the materials will give us ideas."

Schroeder started to get up; Rocky jumped up. "Now wait a minute," she shouted. She was beginning not to trust her husband's promise. "*You* go," she said to Stoney. Then she linked her arm with Schroeder's. "*You* go and concentrate on the fouling of the screw. Sam and I will stay here and talk about *not* fouling the screw."

Schroeder disengaged his arm and took her hand with his. "Rock, what I'm trying to do is hard enough. Just help me get through this—or let Stoney help me, in a noncombatant way— and then we can sit around and talk, and empty your brandy supply, and I promise I'll hold your shirts, or your whips, or count for knockdowns, or whatever you want. Please, Rock!"

She gave him a look that was either resigned or disgusted, he wasn't sure which, and then said: "Yes. All right. Go on. At a whipping, three's a crowd, anyway, unless you have an orgy in mind, but we can talk about that later." She didn't speak to, or look at, her husband, just turned, grabbed her glass in one hand, the brandy bottle in the other, and stomped out of the room.

The two men put their parkas on again, Stoney snapped on the outside lights and they made a dash through the storm for the shed.

It was a large outbuilding, and an orderly one, well stocked and well organized. Efficient looking, as Schroeder might expect of Stoney. Tools hung, neatly aligned, from hooks in pegboard; boxes and jars of nails, screws, nuts, bolts, brads, tacks, eyes, hooks, washers, stood in rows on the shelves. On large hooks on one wall hung lengths of rope and chain; cans of oil, gasoline, kerosene, stood on the floor. On two sawhorses near a large worktable sat an outboard motor. Stoney walked to it, fingered the blades of the prop, started looking around.

"Foul the prop," he kept saying, over and over. "How in hell do we foul the prop?" He turned to Schroeder with startling vehemence. "Let's just think this out! You've got to approach her in the water, in the dark, do whatever you do under water. Any apparatus must be light enough for you to swim with, because we can't pull right up in our boat. And you won't know if you've succeeded until they start the engine when it gets light. Now how in hell do we do it?" He'd quickly looked away from Schroeder as he was talking, and let his eyes roam the shed again, and as he finished he strode quickly away from the motor to a length of chain hanging on the wall.

"Yes!" he said. "Of course! Of course! I've actually heard of its being done." This was about as excited as Stoney ever got, Schroeder thought. And even then he was careful not to fuse his participles.

"Tell me," Schroeder said.

"The chain," said Stoney. "Take a couple of turns around the blades; and the shaft. Fasten the chain. How? Let's see. With a padlock. Wouldn't even have to lock it, just slip it through both ends."

"Won't it snap the chain?" Schroeder asked.

"No, no," Stoney answered. "Not this chain. There's a chance it could snap a pin, but what would be more likely is that the engine would merely stall."

"What would happen then?"

"What would you do if your automobile engine stalled when you started it?" Stoney asked, rhetorically. "You'd start it again. And if it stalled again, you'd try a third time. And then a fourth, and a fifth. Eventually you'd either play with the engine yourself, if you knew something about it, which in this case would not work, or you'd go for help. The chances that anyone, even the most expert of mechanics, would guess that the cause might be a chain wrapped around the prop is so small, it's infinitesimal."

Stoney nodded. "Yes, I think it will work. Sooner or later they'll have to go for help ashore." He paused. "That will be the time for your next move." He looked to Schroeder, who said nothing.

"Have you thought what your next move will be, Sam?"

No, Schroeder hadn't, he admitted to himself, because, honestly, he'd never expected the project to get this far. But now, it not only had, he got the first glimmering that it might work. "What I'd like to do," he said, "is get the girl off that boat. Swim back to it as soon as they go ashore, free the girl, bring her back to the whaler . . ." Schroeder was excited now, he could see it happening. Then he brought himself up short.

"Wait, Stoney, I'm sorry. I didn't mean to keep you and your boat involved in this."

But Stoney was getting excited too; it meant adventure, it meant defiance of his wife. "My boat and I are at your service, Samuel. I'm even tempted to be a member of the boarding party." His promise to Rocky to sidetrack Schroeder and then call the police was still in the back of his mind—getting farther and farther back all the time.

Once again, Schroeder felt the temptation to throw the load onto Stoney's shoulders. He forced the answer out of himself. "No, no. Thanks, but no. This one's mine. I'm the one they pushed around. I'm the one whose kids they grabbed. I'm the one who turned the girl over to them. This one's mine."

"Suppose they just leave the boat, take the girl ashore, and head for the airport or the ferry?" Stoney asked.

"*Then* I might call the cops; I'd lose my shot at personal retaliation." That was a real possibility, Schroeder thought; the thought served as a balm; and he was angry for feeling soothed by it. "But it would be easier to keep the girl out of sight, and have one try at fixing the boat first, wouldn't it?"

Stoney nodded. Then offered another possibility. "Suppose only *one* of them goes ashore, and the other stays with the girl?" He waited.

"That occurred to me," Schroeder replied. "I don't know, let's see. If you think I'm dying to take on even one of those two monsters, you're crazy. Let's wait and see. I don't know what I could do against one of them. But"—he hesitated, appalled at the bravado of what he was about to say—"this may sound stupid, but just calling the cops isn't enough. I'd like to land some kind of punch they could feel, even if they didn't know who threw it or why. Do them some harm. Inflict some pain on them. Does that sound juvenile? I can't help it. Calling the cops doesn't do it for me. Yeah, if I can disable their boat, slow them down, that'll be something. More than I usually do. We'll just wait and see."

Stoney nodded. "All right, then, we attack the problem of getting you and the chain to the *Sloppy Joe*. I guess you sling it over your shoulder. Hold it together with the lock, but don't snap the lock . . ." Stoney hefted the chain he'd taken off the wall. It was about seven feet long, each link perhaps three-quarters of an inch wide. "I'd say it weighs about ten pounds. Could you swim, let's say fifty yards, with it?"

Schroeder reached for the chain, took it. "Don't know," he said. "I've never tried swimming with a chain." Suddenly he could feel the coldness of the water, the darkness, the weight of the chain, the nearness of the *Sloppy Joe* with the two big men on it. The physical reality of it scared him. He tried for insouciance. "Well, it'll sure keep me low in the water."

Stoney smiled, as if he understood what Schroeder was trying. "You don't want to be so low you can't breathe, old boy."

"Oh, are you supposed to breathe when you swim?" responded Schroeder. "I've got to try that."

"What's that?" Stoney asked. "Breathing? Or swimming?"

Schroeder dropped the joking. "On this occasion I'm going to have trouble with both. But I do think I can make my way with that around me. How long a swim do you think, fifty yards?"

"About, maybe sixty or seventy. We can't get too close, you know."

"Well, don't worry, you're talking to a former Red Cross senior lifesaver—that was twenty-five years ago. Now a four-times-a-week jogger, some weeks as much as twenty miles. Of course none of it on water."

"How can you tell if you don't try?" said Stoney, with a grin. "All right, then, I won't worry for a moment. You'll swim over, fasten the chain, and swim back. We'll wait for light. They'll attempt to start the engine, which will most likely stall. They'll try several times, stall each time, go ashore for help. You'll swim over again, rescue the girl, and we'll hightail it out of there. Is that the plan?"

"That's the plan," Schroeder answered. "And you make it sound so easy, I'm almost tempted to accept a handicap just to keep it interesting. Except that, come to think of it, I already have one."

"And what is that?"

"Cowardice, Stoney. Cowardice."

"Now, now Samuel, why dramatize yourself that way? Perhaps you are not more heroic than the average; nor are you any less."

"And how do you know that, Stoney?" Schroeder replied. "Who is this average man? Have you ever met him? Have you ever been inside his brains and guts to experience the shaking and cowering when his courage is tested? Do you know which of us shakes harder?"

"Do you?"

"No," said Schroeder, "But I *do* know *my* fear and trembling, *my* inability to stay cool, *my* unwillingness to take risks. If the average man is as chicken, as I—he, and the world, are in a lot of trouble."

Stoney shook his head. "I don't know if you are complimenting me or insulting me by forgetting that I may have some quiverings of my own. Not *may*. *Have* had. The trick is not to be free of them. That's abnormality. The trick is to have them and function with them. To feel the pressure and still be graceful. If someone feels no fear, his bravery isn't worth a damn, because he doesn't know any better. It's being scared half to death—and carrying on—that makes one a brave man."

"Let me tell you," said Schroeder, "I meet some of those requirements. Being scared half to death, or two-thirds or on up, is easy. Carrying on is another matter. But we shall see, we shall see. Let's not even dwell on it; let's just go ahead and make plans. Let's talk about the timing."

"Let's see. The sun should rise between 5:15 and 5:30, and they may be getting up even earlier to get ready. To be absolutely safe you should finish the job and be back in the boat before 4:30. Allowing you, let's say, five minutes to swim each way, another five or ten to fix the chain, you should hit the water about four; we should leave the house here before 3:30 to play it safe."

Schroeder looked at his watch; it was a little after nine. "Jesus, what are we going to do with six hours?" he asked.

"Eat something," Stoney replied, "but not too much. Have a drink, but not too many. Nap if you want, or just sit around and talk. Stay loose."

Schroeder nodded. "Stay loose, yeah." His mouth and jaw were so tight with fear, he could barely get the words out. But he would do it. He *would* do it.

Chapter

13

"LET'S SEE, NOW," STONEY SAID. "WHAT ELSE MIGHT YOU possibly need? On the first swim or the second."

The reminder that he'd have to do it twice made the rainy evening suddenly chillier for Schroeder. Each comforting bit of assistance by his friend brought him closer to the moment when he'd have no more help, when he'd be all alone. He tried to forget the shiver of fear, tried to think coolly, efficiently, like Stoney.

"On the first," he said, "I'll need the chain and a lock. Right?"

"Right. You'll put the chain around the prop, and then swim back here to wait."

Wait to see if it works, Schroeder said to himself. If it doesn't, or if the men put the girl in the dinghy with them, then the adventure is all over. And, again, he found a part of him wishing it wouldn't work. He rushed to subdue it; the out was too easy.

The chain might work. The two men might go ashore. Then there would be a second swim.

Perhaps only one man would go ashore. Then what?

"What are you thinking about, Samuel?" Stoney's voice, breaking in almost omnisciently, shook Schroeder.

"What I've bitten off for myself," he replied. "How far I can carry the chain of events I've set up. Or whether the chain will drag me to the bottom with it."

"A mistake," Stoney said. "Plan it all, yes. But then do it just one step at a time. Like climbing a mountain, or, for you, like running a long distance. Think about going from here to that next point. When you get there, think about the point after that. A lot of the long-range fears and problems will solve themselves, or disappear, or seem much more soluble up close. One step at a time, Sam. The next thing to concentrate on is what, if any, additional equipment we'll need. We've got the rain gear; we've got a tarp in the boat to cover ourselves with. On the first swim, you'll need only the chain and the lock. Then you'll need towels, blankets. I'll get them later."

Schroeder just stood there, pained at not having anything to contribute, just able to keep up with his friend, never able to get ahead and offer any ideas.

"Now, let's say you're ready for the second swim," Stoney continued. "Your purpose then is to free the girl. If both men leave her, she'll be bound, of course. A knife, to cut her loose." Stoney stood and opened one of the drawers in his worktable. He pulled out an old, formidable knife that looked as if it had come from a kitchen some years back. Its blade was only four or five inches long but wide, and serrated—on both edges, Schroeder could see.

Stoney rummaged through that drawer, then another. "This is about all I've got around here," he said, holding the old kitchen knife. "It'll do. The thing to watch out for, though, is that it has two edges. That's why we took it out of the kitchen; while you were slicing cheese, or something with one side of the knife, you were slicing your hand with the other."

He stood still for another moment or two, then announced, "I think that's it. Can you think of anything else, Sam?" He asked it more as a courtesy than for information, and he didn't wait long for an answer. He picked up two lengths of chain, an old padlock, and the knife. "Let's dump these in the wagon, and go back to the house. And," he said, "think only of the next step. Which is something to eat, and perhaps another drink to keep you loose."

They went out into the rain, Stoney dashing ahead to leave the chains, lock, and knife in his station wagon, and walked back into the house together. Rocky was sitting on the living room sofa, brandy in hand. She looked angry and slightly drunk. When her husband said, "Would you make Sam and me something to eat, besides the crackers and cheese?" She snapped back, "No."

Stoney looked startled, then annoyed. "No?" he repeated. His eyes tried to signal her: Remember our deal? But she'd decided she couldn't trust him; she was hedging her bet. She wanted to work on Sam herself.

"Yes, that's what I said, no! You two want to go off and risk your necks on full stomachs, fill them for yourselves. Don't ask me for the hearty meal; let the condemned men make their own."

Her husband's look turned to contempt, but he said nothing.

"Besides," she added, "I want to talk to Sam. I'm a better conversationalist than I am a cook."

"It would be hard *not* to be," he said, icily. "I'll get us a couple of sandwiches, Sam. I'll also get that other stuff we need and put it into the wagon. Be right back. It will probably be ham and swiss, or something like that. And coffee. Will that do?"

"That'll be fine," Schroeder answered, trying for just enough enthusiasm to please Stoney without offending his wife. "Can I help?"

"No, thank you. Just stay where you are, and sample my wife's conversation. And then try to imagine what her cooking would be like." Stoney was going out of his way to attack Rocky, Schroeder thought, which was not like him. But then Schroeder had other things on his mind, one of them being that a one-on-one confrontation with her was just what he did not want at the moment. But Stoney was gone and he had no choice.

At least he didn't have to think of what to say first; Rocky took care of that.

"You son of a bitch,?" she hissed. "You *son of a bitch!*"

"That's just what my ex-wife said to me Thursday morning, Rocky. What's *your* reason?"

"Don't be clever! And don't play the innocent, you yellow, disingenuous bastard! Too scared to screw Mrs. Cobb on Thursday night, so you try to screw *Mr.* Cobb on Saturday night! You son of a bitch! Tired of being a coward? Then straighten out your screwed-up life. Find yourself a new job. Stop this passive manipulation of women. Stop copping out. Take some blame. Take some responsibility. Grow up. That's how to be a hero! Not by playing cops and robbers. And then letting my husband play it for you!"

"He's not going to do it for me," was all Schroeder could manage in reply.

"No, but he's going to be in a boat nearby. Suppose those men spot him? Suppose they come after him? Or suppose they come after you, or grab you? Or start shooting? Do you think Stoney's going to turn and run, and leave you? If you want to play the hero, make it a solo, damn you!" Not wanting her husband to hear, she said it all in a sibilant whisper.

"How about the girl?" Schroeder asked. "Is she the product of my yellow, disordered psyche?"

"For all I know she may be, but if she isn't, call the police. For God's sake, don't take on two hoods. You're not the type."

Partly hurt, partly trying to be flippant, he replied: "What do you mean, not the type? I'll have you know I played high school football."

"High school?" Her sibilance grew more ferocious. "High school? Not even college? And those two men are professionals!"

Stoney had walked in with a tray of food. "Is she disparaging your high school football, Samuel? Don't mind. She does the same for my crew. And I rowed for *Harvard.* She doesn't understand."

"What is this?" Rocky shouted. "A fraternity meeting? Are you two children playing James Bond? This is no joke! I should have . . ." She stopped short. She should have called the police while the two men were out. She was less and less sure of the deal with Stoney. But she could always call just as soon as these two infants left . . .

"Should have what?" Stoney asked.

"Should have . . . married an *adult,*" she replied. "Not a child who happened to be ten years older than I."

Schroeder was furious, felt he was being picked over by her, and didn't want to be left out of this quarrel. "That's the point,

Rocky," he said. "From what you've been saying to your husband, I thought I might actually be doing you favor if I . . ."

"Oh, you're even more childish than my husband. Didn't you ever hear of love-hate?"

"Oh, so that's what it is?" Stoney said. "And when do I get to see the love part?"

With an underhand motion, she shoved the contents of her snifter—about an ounce of cognac—at him, catching him in the face and chest.

Elegantly—Schroeder admired just *how* elegantly—Stoney picked up a paper cocktail napkin from the coffee table and wiped his face.

"I suppose you'll be needing a refill, dear," Stoney said, and stood and took all three of their snifters to be filled. Then he turned and walked back.

"With each passing moment," she said, "I am growing less and less anxious to keep you two fools from risking your lives. As things are now going, I expect that any minute I'll be opening the door and pushing both you heroes out, and hope that Stoney's life insurance is fully paid up."

"Ah, but how about the man you love-hate?" Stoney said.

She suddenly saw a new way to upset their plans. She feigned bewilderment. "I know about the man I *hate* . . . but the man I love? Oh! You mean . . ." and her eyes widened and turned to Schroeder. "You don't mean Sam, do you? You heard about the other night? No, no, no. We didn't love each other. We came close, but no cigar. Or is that too phallic? No, the other night we were just fooling . . . around."

Schroeder saw Stoney looking at him, felt his face getting red.

"It's all right, Samuel, my boy," Stoney said. "Just the normal dose of cruelty. Par for the course. No longer a surprise." But Schroeder could see his friend's face was tight as he said it.

"All right, then," Stoney went on, "Why don't we talk about it? We have the time. If where we're going is as dangerous as Mrs. Cobb thinks—or is it just wish fulfillment?—then we'd better take the time. After all, if I don't come back, it will be a while before Mrs. Cobb can build a structure—marriage, home, family, trust—that will make the tearing down any fun, that will give any meaning to infidelity. Why *don't* we talk about it?" He raised his glass and took a drink.

Schroeder felt defensive, angry, embarrassed; he spoke

straight at Stoney. "All right, let's talk about it. For me it will be a fast conversation. We both got drunk. Like we're all getting right now. We did a lot of talking, mine dumb and defensive, Rocky's angry and, I'm sure, hyperbolic. We acted a little silly. We did *not* make love." He was mortified to be put on the spot, to have to explain, as if he were a schoolchild. Worse, he was ashamed of his shading, his semi-evasion.

"Speak for yourself, Sam," said Rocky. "For me, no hyperbole. None whatever. Surely you can see that as you listen to the pompous, judgmental Mr. Cobb! Already he has slipped on the judicial robes and stepped up onto the high bench. Or better still, the priestly cassock for the confessional booth—which, for a part-time Congregationalist, takes a bit of clerical climbing.

"He says, let's talk about it, but what he means is, *you* talk about it, and *I'll* judge; you plead, I'll render the verdict; you propose, I'll dispose. And he looks at you, Sam, and like a chastened boy, you start confessing. Next, he'll turn to me. Ah, but there he encounters someone who's not afraid to pull away the judicial robes to uncover the voyeur underneath, bulging pants and all. No, no, I respectfully decline to step into the dock, your honor." She aimed a mock bow at her husband as she said it. Then she took in both men. "I'll choose my own subject, and it *won't* be Thursday evening."

Rocky now saw the real possibility of disrupting their adventure, of getting them so angry at her, at each other, by using Thursday night—that they might abandon their scheme.

"No, we'll just let Mr. Cobb's constipated mind strain at the events of Thursday night. That is not our text for today. We'll start where *I* want to, which is back about a year or so, when, after an increasingly tense, boring, and uncommunicative marriage, Mr. Cobb suddenly burst out, like a pus pimple come to a head, and I found myself covered with the ooze he'd stored up in thirty-nine years of puritanical repression."

Her husband's mouth tightened. "Charming," he said. "Spoken with the restraint and delicacy I've come to expect from you."

She continued to talk to Schroeder. "My husband thinks the mention of pus and pimples excessive. Not a bit of it. Unpleasant, yes; yet understated, if anything. Actually, other excretions would be more apt, but being something of a gentlewoman, although, to be sure, deprived of my husband's genu-wine Mayflower pedigree, I'll hold back. So, SamSam, anything you hear from now on will more likely err on the side of euphemism than hyperbole. Thanks to my delicacy."

"Rochelle Cobb's delicacy," said Stoney, "is the best-kept secret in the greater Boston area. In fact, this is the first I've heard of it." He was forcing restraint upon himself; increasingly, tension was superimposing itself on the composure of his face. Rocky saw it, and felt that if she could break through, she might destroy the entente between these two men, and abort their adventure. Now, if ever, she needed heavy artillery. She decided, and wheeled out the Big Bertha in her arsenal. "Let me see, now," she said, putting on a mock judiciousness. "Hmm . . ." she paused. "No." She paused again. "That is *not* the best-kept secret in the greater Boston area. No. It is not. The best-kept secret in the greater Boston area, and that should be enlarged to take in Nantucket, has been kept by *me*. And, since for my troubles I'm now accused of being some kind of . . . I don't know what . . . some kind of common slob, I'm not going to keep that beautifully, immaculately kept secret any longer."

She stood up, just a bit tentatively and went for another splash of brandy. "Anyone else?" Both men shook their heads. She walked back to the sofa, carefully, and sat down again. "I'd been keeping the secret," she went on, "so as not to shatter the illusion of my husband's sexual prowess. This illusion, as far as I've been able to tell, has been mostly confined to *his* head. But that is the most important place for it—for Mr. Cobb, at any rate—and I've tried to be a good, supportive wife, so . . ."

Rocky paused to sip her brandy, and Schroeder took the chance to jump in. "Don't you want to keep on being supportive, Rocky, and not . . ."

"No, I do not want to keep on!" she shouted. "I've had to sit by and watch while the two boys plan a great adventure. The least the two boys can do is listen. Or are they afraid? Tell me, Mr. Cobb, are you afraid? Are your sexual illusions feeling fragile?"

She was daring him, goading him. And it worked. He knew she was doing it, but it worked anyway, because he was in a box, he had to let her go on. He smiled, stiffly, and said, "I'm afraid only that I'll be embarrassed for you when you've finished."

She smiled back at him, and said, "We'll see."

She was trying to make it look easy, but it was not easy. The smile stayed on her face; she took a deep breath to firm up her courage. She must stop these two demented boy scouts, she reminded herself. She plunged forward.

"Remember, Sam, how we discussed what lousy lovers most men are, how smug, how insensitive, how vain, how touchy when one dares to suggest there's room for improvement?"

"Talk about leading questions!" said Stoney with a tight smile.

Schroeder laughed. "I remember your saying some or all of those things," he said. "I don't remember agreeing."

"Yes, yes," she replied impatiently. "Understood. Solid front, boys. Anyway, I'll go on. Remember my saying how far better masturbation was for pure satisfaction? With you, of course, not agreeing to that either?"

"Yes," Schroeder answered, smiling. "Yes, to that, with no reservations."

"All right," she went on. "I did not give you the one exception."

"Don't tell me," her husband said, "there is a man somewhere who can please the insatiable sex goddess!"

Rocky looked at her husband for a few moments, saying nothing. Almost in slow motion she picked up her glass, sipped, put it down. Only then did she turn on a half-smile, all the while her eyes meeting Stoney's.

"Enough, Mona Lisa," Stoney said. "Henry James notwithstanding, subtlety's not your style. On with the melodrama." He was trying to sound indifferent, Schroeder thought, and almost succeeding.

Rocky let the half-smile widen, and waited, and waited, before saying, "I'll tell it when I want, the way I want." Only then did her eyes leave her husband's and go to Schroeder. Then her face brightened.

"As I was saying, there was one exception." She paused, because she wanted to get maximum discomfort from her husband, and because she was not finding it easy to tell the story.

"Do you know Babs and Jim Caulfield? He's a partner in Stoney's firm. She's another happy housewife."

Stoney's face showed nothing. Schroeder was startled and had no reason to conceal it. "Jim Caulfield, that Ivy League lawyer-type who still wears button-down shirts? My God, appearances *are* deceiving."

She paused, then shook her head. "No. Not *Jim* Caulfield. *Babs* Caulfield."

Still, Stoney showed no reaction. Schroeder's eyes widened. Rocky had an instant of wishing she hadn't begun. But now it was too late.

"First time for me," she said. "Not for her. Apparently she's dabbled before. And you're right about Jim Caulfield. With a husband like that, a girl couldn't be blamed for dabbling in anything. Of course, he's one of Mr. Cobb's best friends." Then she said nothing, looked from one to the other. Nobody spoke.

"The Great Stone Face remains silent," she said. "And the daring diplomat tiptoes along his tightrope, making sure he does not come down on either side. Neither speaks. So I shall go on. It happened, let's see, the last weekend in May. Right here, out on that back deck, out there." She looked over her shoulder toward the glass doors. The turn pressed her blue work shirt—the same one she wore the other night, Schroeder thought—against her breasts; he could see the nipples, and he thought of Thursday night. That was years ago. Before the kidnapping. God, Schroeder thought, if only I could roll the weekend back, undo that night! And everything afterward! He barely heard her next sentence, then forced himself to concentrate, to forget what was waiting for him.

"We'd invited the Caulfields for the weekend. Naturally, the two he-men took that as meaning they should spend all of Saturday and all of Sunday together fishing. In fact, it's only been these past two weekends that Stoney's big boat has been out of whack that I get to see him at all. Which is something of a mixed blessing, but that's off the track. So the two he-men would leave about six in the morning, and get back here about six in the evening, beet-red, soused, exhausted, keep on drinking, and fall asleep at 9:30. A real second honeymoon—for Stoney and Jim. Well, since they had paired off, that left Babs and me.

"Saturday morning is warm and sunny and brilliant, the men are long gone and Babs and I are doing what good wives are supposed to, sitting on the back deck, reading *Cosmopolitan* and *House & Garden* and eating bonbons. And sunbathing. The day is ideal for sunbathing, and since the deck is in the back of the house, and there are no other houses in sight, it is also ideal for sunbathing in the nude. We put towels down, and demurely slipping off our robes, lie on our tummies, side by side, the sun caressing us, deliciously, not with the blistering heat of July, but the delicate, teasing warmth of spring. Forgive me for being lyrical, but that's the way it was, the way it felt.

"Now, I should add that the sun has always been an aphrodisiac to me. When it hits my body I turn on, and so I am lying there, getting warm, in more ways than one. After about ten minutes, Babs says to me, casually, 'I don't think you're ready for all this sun. You're too fair-skinned, and your back is getting red. Would you like me to put some of this lotion on you?'

"Actually, I'm not all that fair-skinned, but I say yes, please, and she begins spreading the liquid on my back and shoulders. No sooner do I feel her hands on me, than I get two sensations. One is that she is performing more than the simple service offered. The other is, how good it feels. Then she says, 'How beautiful your skin is!' and I know I'm right, and I know I should stop it, but frankly I don't want to. It feels so good, and so daring. So illicit—right out of John O'Hara.

"Soon my shoulders and upper back are done, and she's working her way down to my waist, and it's beginning to feel indescribably delicious. She makes a few exploring motions below the waist, but stops, and asks, 'Shall I do your legs?' she asks.

"I guess they need it, I say, so she begins on my lower thighs, just above the knee, and works up. To the big part of the thigh, right up to the fold where the buttocks meet the legs. And I am getting moist, no, juicy, and want to spread my legs. If I do, I tell myself, I'm lost. I do. And I'm breathing so heavily, not only can Babs hear me, it's a fair guess the men can hear me out on the high seas, or wherever the hell they are.

"Well, first Babs, noticing my legs slightly spread, lets a hand slide down between them, then out again. 'Is that enough?' she asks, 'Or shall I finish?' She lets it sound slightly ambiguous, and so do I. May as well, I say. I suppose it sounded more like a gasp, because I was ready to pop off any second. I turn around to look at her, her face is flushed, she's smiling, her nipples are standing out, throwing little shadows on her boobs. 'Will you do me?' she asks. I look away quickly, because if our eyes meet too long I'll have to stop. But I say, yes. I gasp it, actually. I don't want to stop. She pours lotion on my buttocks . . . and rubs. Circles. Widening. All over. The creases below. The crease in the middle. And then she just slips a hand down. Two fingers, beautifully lubricated fingers, into me. And out, and in. Touching my clitoris. Rubbing. Knowing just how to do it. And in a couple of seconds, I'm up to the top of Everest, and over. The deepest, widest, highest orgasm ever. So delicious, so acute, it almost hurts with pleasure. And I just lie there and sigh.

"Then Babs lies down. But not on her stomach. On her back. By this time, my pulse beat has gone down a little, and I begin saying to myself I'm doing something naughty. Naughty, hell, a quote, deviant act, unquote. But a deal is a deal, and I plunge ahead, so as not to give myself time to think the better of it. I rub the oil on her breasts, a little roughly in my determination and inexperience. 'Easy,' she says, 'easy.' I realize I don't feel all that ashamed. I rather enjoy it. Her nipples are hard, standing out. Her belly is hard. She's twenty-six years old and has a hell of a body. Then between her legs. She just spreads them, wide apart, lifts her knees in the air. Of course I know just how to do it, too, and I'm curious, I must admit, at how her parts feel different from mine. Tighter, because she hasn't had any children. So I do unto her, just as I would have done unto me. Just as I *have* had done unto me. She's twisting and groaning, which I rather enjoy.

"You know, gentlemen,"—and with that Rocky took another drink—"it's a great feeling to lie back and be done to, to relax and enjoy the attention and the building to a climax, which you know is arriving, and which you don't have to rush, and which won't be aborted because your partner comes, and then loses interest.

"Well, then, Babs has her orgasm, and I'm with her all the way. Then we both turn over onto our stomachs and lie there like contented little pussycats, saying nothing. For my part, I don't know what to say. I think I should feel guilty, I know I will later, but for the moment I can't work up anything but tranquility, and deep breathing; euphoria. Plus a little titillation at the naughty, illicit thing I've done.

"After a few minutes, Babs, without looking at me, says, 'Have you ever done it with a woman before?' I say, no, I haven't. I wait and hope she'll say it's her first time too, because that would make it a game, rather than a quote, perversion, unquote. Instead she asks, 'Did you like it?' By now it is difficult for me to admit it, but I finally say, yes, and then ask her, 'Have you ever . . . done it before . . . with a woman?'

" 'Oh yes,' she says, very matter-of-factly. 'On and off since college.' Then she says, and I can remember her exact words so well—but then of course it's only been four weeks—she says, 'I've tried men, I've tried women, and I've tried myself, and of the three, men rank third, probably 'cause that's all I've tried. I have a suspicion if I tried dogs, I might move men down to fourth.'

"So I say to myself, she's a dike, and what does that make me, and the guilt that I knew would come, suddenly sweeps over me. And just at that moment, the wrong moment, she asks, 'Want to do it again?' I jump up, and say, no, no, no. And she, the nervy creature, says, 'Then do you want to try it, licking, this time?' Oh no! I say, being, I'm afraid, not very suave about it, and I run into the house. As they say, you can take the girl out of the convent school, etcetera. And the strait laces in me start tightening and I tell myself I'm on the way to becoming a queer, an outcast. A *dike*. And how much I liked the experience, which I *should not have*. But I did.''

Rocky stood up and went to fill her glass. She looked at both men, both shook their heads at the outstretched bottle. Schroeder didn't know how she could stand on her feet after drinking so much.

"That night,'' she continued, after sitting down on the sofa again, "I really went after Stoney in bed. I couldn't let myself think another woman could turn me on that way, so much more than my own husband. But my desperation was no match for his fatigue and sunburn and alcohol. What happened wasn't even worth calling an In-Out. It was more like an On-Off, and then a quick snore. I lay there afterward thinking of the emptiness of that quote, quickie, unquote, compared with the depth, the duration, the utter juiciness of that afternoon in the sun. I started fantasizing about her fingers in me, then her tongue. And right there, next to him, in bed, I licked my fingers and gave myself an orgasm, thinking all the time of her tongue in me. I'd never done it to myself before with him right next to me; I'd never done it before fantasizing about a woman.''

Rocky leaned forward. "I've never done it again with a woman. I guess my upbringing won out. But I can tell you, every fantasy I've had since then, to bring myself to orgasm, has been of her, her fingers, her tongue, my lying out in the sun, her sliding in and out. I don't know if I could have an orgasm these days without it.''

The men waited to see if there was more, but Rocky sat back. She was finished.

Throughout the telling, Stoney had kept his face a mask. When it was over, he said merely: "Oh, that old story. How disappointing! I'd expected a real secret. Everyone in Boston knows that one.''

Rocky watched him carefully, hoping for more, yet knowing how good he was at hiding his reactions. "Weak," she said. "Very weak. Come, come now.''

"Oh, yes," Stoney said. "The story is widely known, as is the preference of the lady in question for heterosexual sex, when properly administered.''

Rocky smiled. "Nice try, but a failure, unfortunately, and made so by the machismo boasting Mr. Cobb felt it necessary to add. The lady in question just put on the standard act, the same one we all use to get you men off our backs. Oops, Sam, there's a little wordplay possible right there, eh? I should say, off our fronts, or wherever you happen to be perched.''

"Oh, dear," said Stoney. "What I thought was merely childish experimentation, you make sound like committed lesbianism.''

"You see, SamSam," she replied to Stoney, without looking at or talking to him, "how boring chitchat can be with Mr. Cobb? Once I expected the clean, surgical thrust of the keen rapier. Now I get little more from him than the random hacking and chopping of the rusty cleaver. Time dulls more than one sword, doesn't it, Sam? If you know what I mean.''

Schroeder had been taking occasional sips of his brandy, and was feeling looser; he reminded himself to be careful. He was appalled at the bloodbath, wanted to step in, yet didn't want to antagonize either of them.

"I know this," he replied. "For a woman who never bothered with, or showed any affinity for, sharp words, you've honed a mighty keen blade yourself. I'm glad you're not flashing it around the offices of *Scope,* or I might find myself foiled by a swordsperson I never anticipated.''

She wouldn't let him sidestep. "No, no, no, Sam, no good. Just a cheap pun; it won't do. And do you know why? Because it's mere showing off, not in the service of any cause. And when you're a mere show-off, you have to be more than tricky. You have to be dazzling."

Schroeder was stung. "And what is your cause, Rocky?" he asked.

Stopping my husband from helping you in your idiocy, she wanted to say. What she said was: "Expressing my resentment of my husband by giving him the needle whenever I can."

"Unfortunately, my dear," Stoney replied, "you are ill equipped for the cause. Your needle is not nearly sharp enough, your aim not nearly precise enough."

"Oh bullshit," she said. "Mr. Cobb's idea of precision, Sam, is, like most lawyers', to lay down a verbal smoke screen that is both blinding and sleep-inducing, so that they can then tiptoe around robbing widows and orphans. Lean prose and vivid imagery just will not do for that purpose. But lawyers have learned to master the soporific—which is why so many lay persons fall asleep while lawyers are at work—and at play. And why some lawyers are so lousy at *lay* work—if you know what I mean."

"Yes, we got an inkling," said Stoney. "It was like getting hit by a runaway garbage truck. You know, dear, when one has a mind like a garbage truck, one should never try to maneuver it into tight places."

Just a bit too high to be embarrassed, but still slightly uncomfortable, Schroeder watched as he would a tennis match, swiveling his head from the sofa, when Rocky swatted the ball, to the easy chair, when Stoney hit it back. Unlike most spectators, he had chances to swing at the ball himself; he knew he shouldn't, for fear of scoring a point for one side and angering the other. What he didn't know was how much of this was for sport and how much for blood. The antagonism seemed real, yet he could see that Rocky loved to perform for outsiders, and Stoney, surprisingly, didn't mind. He conjectured that, without an audience, their delight in riposting might be dulled, their imagery stripped away and the combat shorter, duller, and probably less bloody. It would be mayhem without the artistry.

"You know, SamSam," Rocky said, "Lawyers are more arrogant about less learning than any other occupational group I know. Their breadth of knowledge compares with that of the plumber. And their specialty, I might add, is far less useful. What the plumber lacks is the hubris of the lawyer. The plumber does not believe that because he can fix your toilet, he is a foreign affairs specialist, an esthete, or a social philosopher. A lawyer, on the other hand, who spends his days screwing adversaries, clients, and your odd widow and orphan, thinks that this qualifies him in areas where his knowledge, if not his humility, matches that of the plumber."

Stoney had been responding briefly, but as she hoped, she was getting to him, and he began to open up. "This is an old act, Samuel, my friend," he said, "and I'm sorry you have to sit through such a stale performance of it. I can explain it. Part of her animosity toward lawyers comes from my being one. Another part is more nearly universal. The truth is, persons with weak minds always resent lawyers, for the simple reason that lawyers are taught to reason, to test ideas, surmises, theories, and to find some stronger, more valid than others—in short, to discriminate. And weak minds are threatened by anyone who can spot the drivel flowing from their brains, and call it what it is.

"Certain disciplines, Samuel—I suppose *un*disciplines would be a better name for them—encourage the drivel by calling it rhetoric and imagery. Deprived of any testing apparatus, they allow obfuscation to pass for profundity, crudeness for strength, confusion for complexity, and on and on. Worst of all, they allow shouting to pass for reasoning, so their tests are sham tests, lumps of soft substance fired from a long way off, with nothing settled, nothing proven."

"Just tell me, Sam," Rocky said, "why is it that we in the Lit game don't set up a Supreme Court to render final verdicts on whether Hemingway is a major writer or a blowhard, whether Fitzgerald is *the* American novelist between the wars, whether James is great or merely the greatest American? Wouldn't that be dandy? Then the lawyers could file it all away into the Lysoled compartments of their stainless-steel minds. James could be a final verdict, lying there next to Marbury versus Madison, and when needed, could be wheeled out, all neat and cold and dead, like a stiff in a morgue. No disorder, no complications, just wheel out the stiff you need. One stiff wheeling out another."

"As usual, Mrs. Cobb has missed the point," Stoney said. "Fuzzy minds gravitate to fuzzy disciplines, which is fine. No one gets hurt and nothing is settled. The danger comes when a fuzzy takes on a non-fuzzy on issues, where, heaven forbid, there are a right and a wrong, where one man's or one woman's opinion is *not* as good as the next. Then there's chaos." The lawyer's usual tactic was to respond to his wife's long arguments with short, pithy ones. A few moments ago he'd gone on at length, which he thought a tactical mistake. And he made a point of returning to short, sharp thrusts.

"What he means," Rocky answered, "is that one *woman's* opinion is not as good as the next *man's*. You see, SamSam, the truth is that my husband doesn't so much despise *me*, as he despises *all* women. He wants us beneath him in status as well as in sex. In fact, more. For in one woman's fuzzy opinion, Stoney really sees himself as some kind of aristocratic Greek fag who rolls on and off women to procreate, but reserves his passion for other men. After all, why not? He prefers to do everything else with other men! He abhors serious discussion with women. And serious golf, tennis, and sailing. He considers women second-rate lawyers, hired to appease the damnable affirmative action freaks, to wit, dikes, niggers, Jews, and other *untermenschen*. Women are lousy drivers, inefficient housekeepers, and scatterbrained dinner partners. He'd probably call them rotten dancers—if he knew how to dance. That leaves only fucking—as opposed to making love. And fucking he does with contempt. Aside from begetting beautiful children, for which one needs a woman, and one of the proper stock, why shouldn't W. Stonington Cobb make love to men? Why not, Stoney? Have you? Ever? Just once?"

She turned to Schroeder, her hand cupped to her ear. "Listen SamSam, listen hard. Do you hear an answer? I don't. I'm glad you're here to confirm that, Sam. I'm also glad you're here because he once tried to answer in sign language, but I couldn't tell whether his hands squeezing my throat meant yes or no. That's right, he tried to choke me."

Stoney laughed. "The woman is great on quantity, isn't she, if somewhat short on ratiocination. First, for the twenty-fifth time, I have never engaged in a homosexual act, nor have I ever been tempted to. Second, I did not try to choke you; had I tried, I would have succeeded. I merely tried a protest beyond words against your five-and-dime psychoanalysis. Third, to choose at random one mistake from that jungle of errors, Jews as a group are not in favor of affirmative action."

Rocky looked at her husband; she seemed to be waiting for more.

"Too brief for you?" he asked. "I never *could* match you for quantity."

"No," she answered. "You just missed the main point. Which is, that you hate women."

"I have answered that question even more often than the one about homosexuality," he said, "and though I'm sure you'll be asking each dozens of times again, I don't intend to answer either again."

"Oh, we'll see, we'll see," Rocky said, standing, picking up the bottle of cognac, and walking to fill their glasses. "Here, we need some more. It's only eleven and we have miles to go before you swim." She looked at Schroeder. Then turned to her husband. "And before you sink." She stared at the bottle, which she had emptied. "Well, well, let's take care of that." She walked to the cabinet beneath the bar, took out another bottle of cognac, and, with an easy stroke of the bar knife and an expert twist, opened it.

"Not that the poor chap doesn't have my sympathy," she said to Schroeder as if she'd never stopped talking. "Mr. Cobb is a Miniver Cheevy *vis à vis* women; his attitude is a hundred years older than he is. Born into a world where women knew their place. Finds it all changing on him, and cannot handle it. Thinks drinking and fucking are all there are to handling women, when all they do—the drinking and fucking, that is, not the women—is make him sloppy and impotent. The superb legal mind, which only last week, for example, scored a splendid triumph over a twenty-five-year-old, just out of law school, who was trying to protect a group of old blacks from having their humble houses being torn down around them—this Oliver Wendell Holmes has not been able to grasp the missing ingredient in his dealings with women, namely, that he should treat them as equals. Well, maybe not equals, I mustn't ask too much, but at least as sentient fellow creatures operating on the same plane as he. The times, they have a-changed, and W. Stonington Cobb doesn't know it. Why, you're at the interface, big fella, the changing of the guard, and the times, and you're not able to comprehend it, to move with it! It's a shame, you should have lived in an easier time."

A fierce gust of wind set the rain drumming on the window,

and Schroeder looked out anxiously, momentarily distracted from the savagery.

"Don't worry," Stoney said to him, "The boat will start, and it will all be a cleansing experience, after an evening of being pelted with charges that have the consistency, and the value of"—he could not bring himself to say it, and he settled for—"*merde*."

"Oh, speak for yourself, counselor," his wife said. "SamSam hasn't been charged with anything, and he may not agree with your estimate of their consistency or, your favorite word, *probity*."

She turned to Schroeder. "What *do* you think of all this?"

"I'm amazed at how much damage you're willing to do to each other; that things have reached the point where you *want* to; amazed that you're still together, that either of you has any blood left to shed." He paused, saw her still staring at him, and added, "But it sure has taken my mind off my problems."

Rocky waited a moment, then asked, "And that's it, Sam? That's all? You get a ten-page, handwritten, tear-stained howl, penned in a red fluid that looks suspiciously like blood, and you answer with a one-sentence form letter that says, something like, 'I share your concern.' Who the fuck are you, anyway, our friend or a public official? Goddammit, you answered me the way Nixon answered anti-Vietnam War letters." She jumped up, and went for the bottle again, began refilling the glasses. "Maybe you need another drink! Maybe we all do."

Schroeder felt put down and angry. "What do you want me to say?" he asked. "You want me to render a verdict: Guilty, innocent? Potent, impotent? Faithful, unfaithful? Adequate, inadequate? Want me to play Solomon, hold the marriage up in my left hand and the machete in my right, and say, I'll cut this marriage down the middle and give you each half, and wait to see who first cries, hold, enough?"

"Whoa," said Stoney, amused to see how quickly Schroeder got hot at his wife's goading. "One must not mix literary allusions—the Old Testament and *Macbeth* in the same breath. Milady has that on her endless list of no-no's."

"One learns to ignore the little cul-de-sacs down which learned counsel tries to lead us," Rocky said. "One learns to stick to the point, which is, no, I don't expect you to be a Solomon, any more than I expected you to be a Nixon. I just hoped you might take your courage in hand and say something to show you were connecting, involved, caring, about the anguish being displayed by your close friends, instead of being so diplomatic, so . . . *evenhanded.* I've watched you sitting there during all this, pissing in your pants with fright because you're on the verge of some foolhardy, quixotic scheme designed to redeem your manhood, erase the yellow stain, tear up the white feather. Don't tell me it's to save a girl. If it were, you would have called the cops long ago, and I don't want to get off the track arguing that! I've been sitting here wishing you would show a sign of guts where it'll do us and you some good, in the kind of situation you've been chickening out of all your life, rather than planning a flashy middle-of-the-night swim with a knife in your teeth and the whole Tarzan bit. Even if you do it, what will it prove? That the next time there's a maiden in distress, you'll be ready, knife in teeth? But that ain't your problem, friend. Your problem is your job, your kids, Jane, Marty, the people around you. In short, the kind of test I put to you in a small way when I asked for a reaction, and I got a form letter. Well, you flunked that test, Sam."

"Now, look m'dear," Stoney began. "Samuel has not yet developed the scar tissue to withstand your flagellation; do you think it fair . . ."

"Shut up!" Schroeder barked, surprising himself. "I don't need your help." He looked at Rocky. "While I can see you *both* enjoy the whipping, Rocky, *you're* always the one on the attack, the one always escalating the battle, introducing the new material, while Stoney does the parrying and the counterattacking. Oh, yeah, he's a vicious counterpuncher, and he does a lot of damage. But he's not the attacker. And he's always heading away from the intimate to the abstract, while you're always getting as personal and as damaging as you can. It's as if he's got in the back of his mind the repair of the break, and you've got in the back of yours, the widening of it. And as for me sitting here and pissing in my pants, yeah, I'm scared, and for once I think I'm entitled to be, and yeah, there's a little corner in the back of my mind in which I'm hoping to be let out of this situation, by a *deus ex machina,* or some damned thing. But I'll tell you something: my pants are dry, which means I'm in control of me. And I'm going to go ahead with this, scared though I may be. And I'll tell you something else. Neither one of you has been Christlike in this—I guess 'gladiatorial combat' is the best thing to call it—and I'm not about to render any verdict of guilty or not, but if I've accused you of being the provoker, the attacker, the escalater, you've just proved me right by the way you went after me. You can call me scared, yes, hell, *I* just called me scared. But you didn't do that. *You* said I was pissing in my pants, which is an effective way to do it when you want to humiliate someone. It denotes someone who can't control his orifices, who becomes a child under pressure. Why did you do it that way? I didn't hear Stoney doing it. Are you bitter and angry? So is he. But toward whom? He said you were that way toward *all* men; you said nonsense to that. Then why go after me that way? I may be Stoney's friend, but I've become yours, too. And a good one, I thought. I've admired you, been supportive, have never put you down, not in concert with Stoney, not even in concert with *you*, and believe me, when someone is being self-deprecating, it's easy to join in."

He paused for a drink; this was alcoholic courage speaking in him, but he didn't care. He needed all he could get. He went on.

"Now, you've been dying for me to say something really personal and caring about your marriage. So here it is: Break up the damned thing while there's still something of you left. Otherwise you ain't gonna be nothin' but two pools of blood on the living room floor." Joltingly, his own double negative reminded him of the note: Don't Be No Hero.

Rocky looked at her husband; he didn't seem upset by what Schroeder had just said. Which meant that so far she hadn't done it, she hadn't been able to cave the roof in on their plan. The women's lib speech hadn't done it, the lesbian speech hadn't done it, turning on Sam hadn't done it. She had one more left. She picked up the brandy bottle, which now was at her right hand, filled her glass and then filled the men's, without asking.

She looked at Schroeder. "You know why I don't take anything you've said too seriously? Why I'd expect you to come out on my husband's side? Because I'm not giving you the ride out into the harbor, and all the other help. And he is. I think if I were, you'd come over to *my* side. That's what I think of your guts. I bet you *did* piss in your pants. After all, that's what happened to you Thursday night, isn't it? Scared enough to piss in your pants. Or else you would have had them off, wouldn't you?

Right on that sofa! and I was there, and saw it all, and now you hate me for it!''

She got up, a bit unsteadily, never letting go of her glass. ''I'll tell you what, boys, I'm going to bed. Why don't the two of you stay here and play with each other, instead of going out *there* and playing with each other. It's really the same thing, you know.''

She walked toward the stairs, with the stiff dignity of someone who is drunk and trying not to show it. At the stairs she turned and pointed a finger at her husband. ''*You* made me a promise.'' Then holding tight to the banister with her left hand and tight to her drink with the right, she climbed the stairs.

Stoney had not renounced the promise; vaguely, he still intended to talk Schroeder out of any danger, but he was not sure when. And then call the police, but he was not sure when. The vagueness grew as the memory of the promise receded, for he was becoming more and more engrossed in this adventure. And he knew that while some of his wife's diatribe had come from sheer anger and lust for battle, another part was an attempt to break up their rescue plan. He knew, also, she wanted him to go after Schroeder about the Thursday night on the sofa. And so he held back. It wasn't easy, but he held back.

Schroeder sat there waiting for his friend to ask, what about Thursday night? When it did not come, he asked the first question: ''What was the promise?''

''Promise? What promise?'' said Stoney.

Schroeder was amazed at how fuzzy his friend's words sounded; he wondered if his sounded as bad. He looked at his watch: 1:30. About two hours before they were to start; both could easily doze off and sleep through the whole damned thing. What an easy way out, he thought. And how Rocky would love it! That was enough to snap him awake. He jumped to his feet.

''Come on, let's make some coffee.''

''Good idea,'' Stoney said. ''Go right ahead. Make it Irish. There's a bottle of Paddy's in the cabinet.'' He put his head back on the easy chair.

''Oh, no!'' Schroeder yelled. ''Stay awake! Get in here! No sleeping on the job.'' He strode toward the lawyer, grabbed his shoulders and half helped him, half dragged him to his feet. ''Come on! I don't know where the coffee is, or the perc, or anything.''

"Not perc," the lawyer answered groggily. "Drip."

"That's no way to talk to a friend," said Schroeder. "But I'll overlook it."

"No, no, it's a one-cup drip coffeemaker."

"Yes, yes, I got it, it was only a joke." Schroeder thought that what was funnier than his joke—almost anything was, actually—was that Stoney, drunk and drowsy, would still insist on the distinction in coffeemakers. Precise to the last brandy.

The lawyer picked through the cabinets for a can of coffee, the one-cup filter, and two cups. He took the kettle from the stove, half filled it, put it back on the stove, and lit a burner. He was showing the effects of the alcohol more plainly than Schroeder had ever seen him do before, yet as he moved, Schroeder could also see him recovering from the drowsiness that had been coming over him in the chair.

Stoney wore shorts and an old Oxford button-down shirt, its sleeves rolled up. Schroeder watched the muscles flex in his long sinewy arms, saw the strong neck, surprisingly thick for such a rangy man, and said to himself, I'm glad he's on my side. Then, noticing the button-down collar for the first time, he remembered the disparaging reference he'd made to Jim Caulfield and his button-down shirts. He laughed to himself, then said, "Listen, I'm sorry—about the shirt."

"About the shirt?" Stoney repeated, still a little groggy.

"You know, the put-down of Jim Caulfield. I said he still wore button-down shirts. I hadn't noticed yours."

"Oh, I thought perhaps you were sorry about Thursday night."

"I'm not quite sure what you think I have to be sorry about," said Schroeder, and knew he sounded cagy even as he said it.

"*I* don't know," Stoney replied. "I wasn't there. What *do* you have to be sorry about? You might say something about what happened, how it happened, and why. How and why it happened that my best friend and my wife were on the sofa, and what they did there."

Suddenly, he was standing close to Schroeder, towering over him; Stoney was drunker than Schroeder had thought, and big and fierce.

"There's no way I can win this, Stoney."

"You might give it a try, old friend. Certainly, one way to win is to say nothing happened."

"Would you believe me?"

"If you say it, I'll believe it."

"I can't say nothing happened. I can say the most important part, no, that's not the way to put it, the worst part—that may not be any better, but I'll leave it—*that* part of it never happened."

"Which part is that, Samuel?"

"We never made love."

"Never *made love?* You mean you didn't *fuck?* Well, that's something. Go ahead."

"Your water's boiling."

"Then I'll put in some antifreeze." And Stoney had another swallow from the snifter he had brought in with him.

"I meant your coffee water."

"I know you did." Stoney turned off the light under the kettle; he poured some water through the filter, making one cup, handing it to Schroeder, then repeating the process for himself. But he filled neither cup, and then emptied the brandy from his glass, half into his cup, half into Schroeder's. "There," he said. "It will warm you and keep you from boiling over at the same time." He walked back into the living room, Schroeder following. Both men resumed their seats, host in the easy chair, guest on the sofa; both men sipped their cups. Stoney looked at Schroeder and waited.

"The fact is, Stoney, we were bombed, bitter, and bragging." That's it, he said to himself, alliteration, even under stress. Marvelous. "We were trying to outdo each other in bravado, in showing we didn't give a damn about anything. But I guarantee, we would never have gone any farther than we did. Nothing more *could* have happened; neither of us was interested in . . . making love. It was all a silly, drunken game, in its way as pointless and destructive as the game you two played this evening to a packed house of one."

Stoney gave his friend a cool, annoyed look. "But what right, or need, have you two to play a destructive game? For us the dance of death—you see, despite what she says, I am not anti-literary—is an obligatory step. We have years of detestation to rehearse with. Why you two?"

"My first impulse," Schroeder answered, "would be to ask you why anyone needs a 'right' to be destructive. Or long rehearsals, or years of detestation. Didn't you ever hear of detestation at first sight? But the 'right' is not the answer, and I'm not sure I know what the answer is. Maybe I resent her, and therefore you, for being married. Maybe she, and therefore you, resent me for *not* being married. But why question our right? Do you want pain exclusivity? You seem to resent anyone sharing your oppression.''

Stoney shook his head. "I resent your almost screwing my wife. And I therefore object to your trying to share my pain, when you are at the moment part of it."

"What do you want, Stoney? I told you we were drunk and rebellious and stupid, not nearly so anxious to make love as to make war—sort of the way you're getting to be right now."

"I beg your pardon?"

"I think you're trying to pick a fight, Stoney, and it's not like you. Why? What happened Thursday was dumb and I'm sorry for it. What else can I do or say? Promise never to do it again? My God, that's a promise easily given. Why, Stoney?"

"Jesus Christ, I guess I'm an old Puritan!" Stoney was almost raising his voice. "My best friend as much as admits to almost screwing my wife, and then asks why I'm angry, as if he'd done nothing more than ask her to waltz at the cotillion. Am I supposed to be defensive about it?"

Schroeder sipped his coffee, felt and tasted the brandy in it, and stood up unsteadily. He walked to the sliding glass doors, which protected him from the strong wind and fierce rain. If he felt shaky, he also felt loose, and a little angry. Right now the anger was aimed at Stoney, but he wanted to hoard it, to redirect it when the time came. He looked at his watch. An hour to go.

"It occurred to me," he told his friend, "that you were building this up to get out of ferrying me to the *Sloppy Joe* in an hour from now."

"And it occurred to me," Stoney shot back, "that you were provoking me so I wouldn't take you."

Schroeder's anger grew. "You know, I've reminded *you* often enough of my cowardice. You and your wife don't have to remind *me* of it . . . rub my nose in it, would be a better way to put it. Why? Are you so fucking brave, the two of you?" Schroeder felt drunk, and was not trying to hold back. "You know, I may have hit it before. I think the two of you resent the fact that I'm no longer doing your dance of death. That I'm no

239

longer gouging flesh from a wife's body, and she from mine. Christ, you call me your best friend! You should be happy for me, just as I'm sad for you."

"So that explains Thursday night," Stoney said. "Of course! Sex therapy! Making her whole again! Now I understand. The only question remaining is which one of you decided at the last moment she didn't need the full treatment? You? Or she?"

"The pun is not bad, the rest of it is full of shit!"

"On the contrary, Samuel"—the lawyer paused to stretch an arm out for the brandy bottle. He poured some into his cup and into Schroeder's; each cup now contained more brandy than coffee—"it's the most plausible explanation. After all, feeling superior to us, as you apparently do because you turned tail on your marriage and got out instead of sticking it out . . ."

"*Got* out? Instead of *sticking* it out? You sound like a marriage manual—for cretins!" Schroeder shouted the words. "Would you have told a prisoner at Auschwitz to *get* out? Or *stick* it out? Is the S-M scene I was treated to a little while ago your idea of bravery? Well, it's my idea of Auschwitz!"

"Then how is it you were so anxious to climb the barbed wire and jump on one of the prisoners Thursday night?"

"Maybe for the same dumb reason you're willing to jump on half the available women in Boston."

"*They* are not the wife of my best friend," Stoney shouted. "Nor have I ever driven over to my best friend's house, when I knew his wife was there and he was not, to set up a seduction!"

Schroeder got to his feet, furious. "Oh, is that to say I'm never permitted to be in your wife's company without a third person present? Is that it?"

"When you learn to behave!"

Stoney stood, too, taking up the small space between the easy chair, the sofa and the coffee table, and almost nose-to-nose with Schroeder.

"And you're going to teach me, huh?" Schroeder didn't want to retreat an inch.

"Someone ought to."

"The man who dropped his pants for half the women in Boston? Married women? Wives of his friends? Is *he* going to teach me?"

"I'm not talking about other people; I'm talking about us. You tried to screw my wife."

"Look, I did *not* try to screw your wife. I tried *not* to screw her. And I succeeded." Schroeder hadn't wanted to suggest he was the seduced party, but it came out.

"That's it," Stoney replied, sardonically. "I was wondering how long it would take you to retreat, to hoist the yellow flag. Yes, of course, blame it all on Rocky. Damn it, she's right. And you're right—you *are* a little coward!" As he said it, Stoney put a big hand on Schroeder's head, as if admonishing a child. Schroeder tried to shake it off, but it tightened, and Schroeder responded with a right jab to the belly. He threw it as hard as he could, aimed at the solar plexus, to knock the wind out of the bigger man. But because Stoney was so tall, and because he turned slightly as the fist was coming at him, Schroeder hit him low and to the side. The punch hurt Stoney, but did not double him over, and with a hand on Schroeder's head, and the other on his chest, he half pushed, half flung his friend to the sofa.

"Ah ha, Stonecock!" came his wife's voice from behind them. "What do you do next, kiss him or strip him? I'll bet you're turned on, though. Here, let me feel." And she ran forward and reached a hand toward her husband's crotch.

Stoney seized her by the upper arms and threw her onto the sofa, on top of Schroeder.

"I'll be out in the station wagon," he said, standing over them. "You've got your choice, stud. You can either stay here and 'try not to screw' my wife. Or you can come out with me to the goddamned boat!" And he grabbed the half empty brandy bottle.

"Hey!" Rocky yelled, "You made a promise."

"So did you, five years ago. A lot of them," He was quieter.

"You're going too far!" she said.

"I'll go as far as I like!" Stoney answered, and then turned and stomped out of the house.

Chapter 14

Schroeder was trying to get to his feet when Rocky landed on him, knocking him back onto the sofa. For a few moments he tried to lift her off, but they'd both had too much brandy, and she was too heavy.

"Get up, dammit!" he shouted, partly in anger at her and her husband, partly because she was a heavy, painful load.

She didn't get up; instead she rolled over on top of him, flattening him into a supine position on the sofa, she on her stomach, her eyes looking into his.

"You see how hateful he can be, Sam? Come on, let's take him up on it. Let's make love, not war, as you said."

"You were listening!"

"Of course. Well, I couldn't hear every word, but I did hear you hold out to the very end, and I did hear you finally say that I tried to seduce you."

"I didn't say that, I never said it." Her weight made it hard for him to talk, but his drive to defend himself was so strong, he forgot for the moment that he should be trying to get her off him so he could go after Stoney.

"Well, you implied it, and it is certainly true enough. I was not only a seductress, I was an unsuccessful one. Don't you think I should at least have the chance to correct that part of it?" She lay on him heavily, he could feel the softness of her breasts on his chest, the solid weight of her abdomen and thighs on him.

"I held out as long as I could, Rocky, and even then you'd hardly call what I said an accusation."

"Oh, yes it was, and since I was accused, I think I should have the fun of it, too."

"Now? Are you crazy? Your husband's waiting for me. There's a girl out there in the harbor, maybe. And I know why you're doing this. And it all makes resistance inevitable. More than inevitable, easy. And if it weren't easy, I'd hold out because you're the wife of my best friend. Get off."

"Like you held out Thursday night?"

"We didn't make love, did we? Now get off!"

She didn't budge. "No, we didn't make love. But only through bad luck."

"Oh, no! No way we would have fucked! Now get the fuck off!"

She didn't budge. "I wonder how you'd have done, SamSam? Any better than my husband, the man with the Stoney face and the jelly cock? What do you think? And do you want to prove it?"

"Screw you! Metaphorically speaking." As he said it, Schroeder rolled his body toward the front of the sofa, dumping Rocky into the small space between the sofa and the coffee table; she caromed off the table before hitting the floor, hard.

Shakily, Schroeder got to his feet and looked down at her; she was on her back, looking up at him but not moving.

"Are you all right? Come on, let me help you up." He bent over, reached a hand down to hers. She grabbed it, but instead of trying to stand, she yanked it as hard as she could. Tired, woozy, caught off balance, he fell forward, not quite fitting into the narrow space where she was lying. His right shoulder crashed into the table; its point grazed his forehead an inch and a half above the eye. The skin of the forehead was barely opened; there he was lucky. But his shoulder hit hard. When he used his arms to help get back on his feet, he felt a sharp pain just below the collarbone. He managed to stand, put a hand to his cheek. Nothing bad there, just a bit of blood. The pain was in the arm and shoulder as he moved them, and it drove him to anger.

He'd landed on her hard, but didn't care. She still hadn't risen, but he didn't care. He shouted at her.

"Henry James, my ass, you bitch! You're majoring in the Marquis de Sade! No wonder Stoney wants to go out there. After you, it'll seem like the Elysian Fields. Stoney's no hero for going with me. He's a hero for sticking with you!" He turned and headed for the door, picked up the slicker on the floor, and put it on.

"Sam!" she yelled.

"What?" He paused at the door but didn't turn around.

"I hope you both get killed!"

"I hope to disappoint you."

"I'm not kidding!"

"Neither am I. But I'll tell you this," and this time he turned. "If I had to come back to *you*, I might well oblige you."

He opened the door, left, slammed it behind him. On the walkway he felt himself lurching, grabbed the railing with his right hand for support and felt the pain in that shoulder so sharply that he let go. He reached the right hand, this time carefully, to his forehead. No new blood. Good, he wouldn't have to stop, he told himself. He wanted continuous movement from now on, no pauses for reflection, for fear he might not resume the movement. It took him a few strides to realize the wind and rain had not let up. The porch bulb seemed a small oasis of light in a black wasteland.

As he walked toward the faint glint of the station wagon, he realized his shoulder pained him badly even with the arm at his side. Now I've got an excuse not to go, he told himself. No, not an excuse, a reason, a legitimate reason. But there the word "excuse" was, it had been said, he couldn't strike it from the record. And that tainted it for him. He had to go. It frightened him; so did the weather, the darkness, the nearness of the events. He wasn't quite ready for the step off the walkway, and his foot hit the uneven ground, jolting the stiff right knee. He limped to the station wagon where Stoney sat in darkness. Automatically, his right hand went for the passenger door. The pain stopped it, and he used his left, with an awkward backhand motion, to open the door. He slid into the passenger seat alongside his friend. Stoney would not be able to see the cut on his forehead, or feel the pain in his shoulder, and Schroeder knew any mention of them would be a move to get his friend to stop him. He kept silent.

"Opted for revenge over sex, eh?"

"Oh, for Christ's sake, Stoney, cut it out. I'm not your wife. I need your help . . . not that she doesn't. Get me through this, you can flay me to ribbons later, at our leisure. I'll buy the whips and brandy."

Stoney spoke as if he hadn't heard him. "Or did you manage a quick one first? Not revenge *over* sex, but revenge *after* sex, like brandy after dinner."

This time Schroeder ignored what he'd just heard. "You never answered before when I asked what the promise was that you two spoke of. And what in hell did it mean when she said, 'Don't forget,' and you said 'I'm not forgetting'?"

The lawyer, still looking straight ahead, smiled coldly, almost derisively. "You know damned well what it meant."

Schroeder looked at him. "No, I don't. In fact I don't know what the hell you're talking about. That's why I asked."

"Then either I've overestimated your quickness or underestimated my alcohol content. It meant what you wanted it to mean."

"Oh, cut this cryptic shit. What are you talking about?"

"What do you think Rocky and I were talking about while you were upstairs?"

"Whether or not you should help me, I suppose."

"Ah yes, then, you're not as cold as you pretended. Go on, try again, see if you get warmer."

"What in hell is this, a game?"

"Why ask me? It's *your* game."

"I guess I have to play, don't I; I'm counting on you to . . ."

"Counting on me to take you? Or stop you? The latter, as you well know—despite your pretense—is what we were talking about."

"I do not know. And there's no pretense. What were you talking about?"

"A plot to stop your plot. Rocky felt your plan was crazy; she said we should stop you and call the police."

"What did you say?"

"I agreed you were crazy, but said the best way to stop you would be to go along, get you drunk, and talk you out of it. I didn't think it would be hard."

"You didn't? Why not?"

"Because you don't really want to go through with it, Sam. You're looking for an out; you want to be stopped." Stoney waited, but Schroeder said nothing, so he went on.

"Well, now you've got several. You're too drunk. I'm too drunk. The storm's too bad. The car won't start. I lost the keys."

"They're in the ignition, you son of a bitch. Why are you doing this to me?"

"You've been calling yourself a coward, and I'm agreeing with you."

"Dammit, Stoney, I am trying for the moment *not* to be. What are you trying to do? Why aren't you helping me? Because of Rocky and me? Why treat me like a corrupter of innocence? You know what the hell is going on." The last sentence was inflammatory. Another time Schroeder would not have said it.

"Listen," Stoney hissed. "If you're not careful, in one moment I'm going to slam the escape hatch on you. I'm going to play Sancho Panza to your Don Quixote, let you take on the windmill. Think where you'll be then."

Schroeder shouted back. "Go ahead! That's what I want! Goddammit, don't you understand that?" Momentarily at least his anger was giving him a zest for the project that nothing, not the girl, not his children, not his humiliation, had been able to give him. Stoney was giving it to him, helped by the brandy. "Let's go! What are we waiting for?"

"My promise to Rocky," Stoney said, "was that if I didn't talk you out of it, I'd call the police. As soon as she hears us leave, without my having done it, *she'll* call them."

"She sounds drunk. Out of her mind. Who in hell would believe her?"

"Perhaps no one. But there's a way you can make sure."

"How?"

"Come with me." He got out of the car, into the driving rain; Schroeder, mystified, hurried to follow. Stoney walked into the shed, his friend following, and found a wire cutter. Then a stepladder.

"What are you doing?"

"Just follow me," he said, and, carrying the tool and the ladder, walked out of the shed to the side of the house. Gently he placed the ladder against the wall. He turned to Schroeder and pointed high on the wall.

"Telephone wires." He proffered the cutter. "If you're not too drunk to climb the ladder."

Schroeder's response was to snatch the tool from his friend's hand, and slip it into the pocket of his slicker. Then, using mainly his left hand, he climbed the ladder, paused, reached into his pocket with his left hand for the cutter, and clipped the wires. Replaced the cutter in his pocket, climbed down, handed the cutter to Stoney. His friend just nodded, carried the ladder and tool back into the shed, reappeared.

"What else?" Schroeder asked.

"She could get into the other car and drive to the police."

"Where are the keys?"

"She usually leaves them in the ignition when she's parked here."

"Let's see." Schroeder's eyes had by now become used to the dark, and he could pick out objects fairly well. He could not make out terrain, though, and he stumbled several times while walking quickly to their Mercedes. The keys were there; he tossed them to Stoney.

"Second set?"

"Used to be, but she lost it."

"What else?" Schroeder asked. "Neighbors?"

"None of the nearby people has opened his house yet."

"Of course she could still walk to a house, and the police station can't be more than two miles from here."

"Nothing's foolproof," Stoney said. "But given the weather, the alcohol, and the distances now involved, I think the absence of a car and a phone may thwart her. It's hard for her to see too far ahead through the drunken haze. You may have neutralized her. Sorry to disappoint you."

Schroeder decided not to react to that. "What else?"

"Let's get in out of the rain and get going." Stoney headed for the station wagon, Schroeder right with him. When they'd both climbed in and shut their doors, Schroeder turned to Stoney. "Did you ever intend to keep your promise to Rocky, about stopping me?"

"Like me to?"

Schroeder kept cool. "No, just curious as to whether you never meant to keep it, or changed your mind in the middle."

"Changed my mind in the middle."

"Because of me and Rocky?"

"Partially. Because of the way you tried to weasel out of responsibility for it. Because of the way you're trying to weasel out of your James Bond caper."

"You'd sort of like to see me get it, wouldn't you, Stoney? Jesus, I had no idea all this hostility was there."

"Just arrived, my friend," answered the lawyer. "At the same time as the news of the caper on the sofa."

"So you must be feeling pretty good to be able to put it to her and to me at the same time."

"Yes, precisely. Throw one monkey wrench and have it jam, simultaneously, her manipulation machine and your Rube Goldberg Pseudo Super Hero Tinker Toy."

"And your ultimate goal would be to see her dead of fright, and me of bullet wounds?"

"Why don't you say both of you dead of fright? Sound too yellow? I don't really believe anyone ever dies of fright. People just threaten it, as a way out. My real goal is to show, *a,* that she doesn't give half the damn about your safety—or mine—that she does about thwarting me. And that, *b,* you will stop this Hardy Boys escapade on your own when it's clear to you no one else will stop it for you. Don't you see how much better off we'd all be if you'd had the guts either to *fuck* Rocky, or say no in a loud clear voice? But somehow you greased your way between both. You had an out. I don't want to give you one this time."

"All right, old friend," Schroeder said. "Let's start by playing right into your hands. I'm scared. Also, I'm going ahead. Sorry to ruin your picture, but that's the way it is. And I'll take what help I can get. Including yours. Especially yours. I don't care how perverted your reasons are, I'll take your help. I suppose I could question your motivation, too. Could you be using the hatred bit as a cover-up for your desire for an adventure? One you know you shouldn't get involved in? You know, we could go round and round on motives, and each of us sounds right on everything we say. But, shit, the time comes when you've got to be judged on what you do, not on the validity of your reasons for not doing it. I guess it's a kind of New Criticism of the act of bravery."

"The key word in that last sentence being *act*," said Stoney.

"You're juggling the meaning of act," Schroeder replied. "I meant it as an action, a deed. You're using it as pretense. But that's OK. The act you put on doesn't matter, as long as you perform the act. And I'm going to. Call it what you want. But would you start the car and get going? And can we stick to what we're trying to do, and cut each other up later—or never?"

Still looking straight ahead, Stoney nodded. Then he smiled and stuck out his hand. Schroeder reached across with his right. Pain shot through the shoulder, got worse when Stoney's huge hand squeezed his. Schroeder said nothing, just tried to squeeze back as hard as he could. Then Stoney started the engine and they drove out of the driveway, the headlights making little impression on the wet, murky night.

"We can only get to within sixty or seventy yards of the *Sloppy Joe*, right? Then I get out and walk."

Stoney grinned. "I suggest you swim, not walk. Which is not to doubt your divinity. It's rather that you'll be less visible *in* the water than *on* it."

"Bad jokes are the one area in which I need no help. Will I be able to swim with the chain?"

"I hope so; it will take more work, more energy, harder stroking, but you should be able to do it."

"And if I can't?"

"I've got a Styrofoam kickboard. First you try to swim; if the chain is too heavy, either come back with it, or jettison it. I've got a spare chain. But don't dump the lock! I've only brought one of those. I'll give you the second chain, wrapped around the kickboard."

"Why not just start with the kickboard?"

"Because it's more noticeable. Because it may float away, and be traced to a five-year-old aquatic ace on Cliff Road. It's cleaner all around without it."

Schroeder shook his head. "Why is it you always think of the details and I never do? Christ I'm glad you're here, Stoney!"

"That's what a friend is for. His brain, his boat, his chains, his kickboard"—Stoney saw it coming—"his wife."

Schroeder turned to his friend. "I'm sorry that happened. Truly. I wish I could expunge it from history." Stoney took a quick glance over and for the first time saw the dried blood on his friend's forehead.

"What happened to you?"

"The moment you left the house to go to the station wagon, I jumped on your wife, attempted to rape her, and she fought for her honor."

"If ever there was a case of locking the barn door after the horse had been stolen . . . and stolen . . . and stolen. . . . What did happen?"

"Oh, hell, she wouldn't get up off me, after you tossed her there, and I finally managed to push her off. Then I tried to help her up, and instead she pulled me down on top of her."

"The woman is a brute," Stoney replied. "She must weigh a hundred and fifty pounds. In a baggy shirt, she could make the Harvard crew. If she hasn't already."

Schroeder shook his head. "I told you the bad jokes are mine; you're needed for the expertise, please."

"Yes, of course. It's just that in my situation, jokes help, even bad ones. Even mine. You wrap the chain around the prop, put the lock on it to fasten it; you need not even lock it."

"Will they be able to hear it through the hull?"

"I imagine if you made a point of thumping, they might. But it's fairly choppy, and there's enough storm noise, and there's their anchor chain, groaning and thumping too. If you're careful, there's no reason they should."

"Thanks for being here, Stoney . . ."

"Not yet. You haven't done it yet."

"No. I haven't." And, again, the fear jolted its way through the twin anesthetics: the brandy and the Cobb household circus. Go away, Schroeder said. But the feeling wouldn't.

Stoney parked the car near the dock, and turned to reach for the equipment. He first handed Schroeder blankets, towels, and the brandy bottle. He held the two chains, lock, kickboard, and knife. "OK," he said, "I think we've got it all."

They walked through the blustery night to Stoney's Boston whaler. The wind was high, ruffling the waters of the harbor, the rain driven at a forty-five-degree angle, but not as heavy as it had been. Stoney was a stride ahead, his tall, broad-shouldered form moving quickly toward the whaler. He jumped nimbly into the boat, Schroeder followed awkwardly, careful of the knee, careful of the shoulder. My God, he asked himself, how am I going to function? Never mind, was the answer. You've got to. Stoney started the outboard.

"Untie us, would you Sam?"

Schroeder fumbled at the line, his fingers weak and shaky. He was not going to be able to undo it. He had to. It took him a while, but he did.

"You know, I was barely able to untie that line, Stoney," he said.

"It's wet; that always makes it harder." Stoney had been waiting, patiently; Schroeder had the feeling his friend had given him the small task to loosen him up.

They moved out of their berth, past the rows of yachts and fishing boats in their slips, toward the *Sloppy Joe*, Stoney using the lightbuoy and the lighthouse as his landmarks. Schroeder, seated amidships, thought of Felicia O'Brien. Was she in terror? Beaten up? Still alive? He looked around, could make nothing out, couldn't distinguish one set of lights from another. He shuddered to think of attempting this by himself.

"There she is. At nine o'clock."

Schroeder looked to his left, saw a couple of lights bobbing in the water. "How close are we?" he asked.

"Perhaps seventy yards," Stoney answered. "We don't want to get any closer." He cut the engine and dropped anchor.

"Say," Schroeder said nervously. "How am I going to find my way back?"

"Good point," said Stoney. "Let's see . . . the lantern. As soon as you start, I'll blink it on and off regularly. It won't look suspicious, it'll be too regular. Yet there'll be nothing anywhere around like it."

"Will I be able to find it starting back?" Schroeder felt like a child, trustingly throwing all problems into his father's lap and waiting for solutions.

"If you can't, swim toward the lighthouse. You can't miss its light. Then before long you'll be able to pick up this light."

"OK," Schroeder said.

"All right."

Both men were silent. Schroeder had to get started. The convenient opiates, the brandy and the battling Cobbs, were receding. So was the resolve, the cross-examination. All of it. He sat there.

"I don't think you should let too much more time go," Stoney said.

Schroeder started to unbutton his shirt; he felt chilly. He worked faster, revving up to furious motion, to keep the impetus going. His shirt was off, his jeans, his sneakers.

"OK, the chain."

Stoney started to put it over his right shoulder. "No, the left," Schroeder said.

"What's the matter?"

"The shoulder's sore."

"Rocky?"

"Yeah."

"Women of that size can be dangerous, can't they?"

"That size, and disposition, but this is no time to begin that again."

"No. Have a swig of brandy."

"Yeah." Schroeder took the bottle and gulped down some of the liquid. "What time is it?"

Stoney looked at the luminescent dial of his watch. "It's ten to four." He *would* have a dial you could see in the dark, Schroeder thought. Schroeder didn't. And Stoney's was probably waterproof, too, which reminded him that his wasn't. He reached to his wrist to take it off, fumbled, finally managed it, handed it to his friend.

"Here, hold this." Schroeder smiled nervously. "If anything happens to me . . . I can't think of a funny line."

"Nothing's going to happen to you," said his friend.

"Oh."

"You'd better get started."

"Yeah, I'd better."

"Chain feel all right?"

"Yeah."

Stoney took the lock, slipped it through two of the links to hold it in place. "Don't forget," he said, "If you've got to jettison the chain, hold onto the lock."

"OK."

"Good luck."

"Thanks." Schroeder got up into a crouching position, put both hands on the port gunwhale and jumped over the side; at once he let go with his right hand to avoid strain on that shoulder, but he held with his left. The water was cold, much worse than it had been last night, when he was in it with her. That was hardly more than twenty-four hours ago, he thought. My God, what a twenty-four hours it had been! At least the wind and the rain had eased off.

Stoney put a big hand over his. "Stay loose," he said. "You'll be all right. I'll start flashing the lantern a minute or so after you get started, but remember, we're sitting here between that boat and the lighthouse, so if you go for the big light, you'll pick this one up. And if you can't handle the chain come back and use the kickboard."

"OK. Thanks. See you."

Schroeder let go and started swimming, breast stroke, with every stroke drawing a howl of protest from that shoulder. The chain was heavy, he was having trouble keeping his head above water. He let himself submerge slightly for a few strokes, to bob up for a breath when he needed it. Three pulls, bob, and a breath. Barely clearing the water to suck in air. Then two pulls, pained, tired, a bob, and a breath, just managing a little air before going under. One pull, exhausted, bob, a gulp for air, this time with a little water.

He wasn't going to make it. He reminded himself what a strong swimmer he was. But the chain was too heavy, he was too tired, too cold, in too much pain. He had to turn back. He twisted around, low in the water, managing another gulp of air and water as he did. He looked for the light, saw nothing. Maybe Stoney hadn't started blinking it yet. Maybe he had turned more than a hundred eighty degrees. Or less, and was staring off in the wrong direction!

And now he could not get his face above water, dragged down by the weight of the chain. Desperately he reached for the lock, fumbled, found it. For a panicky instant, he couldn't get it off. Then it came. Holding it in his left hand, he used his right, enduring the pain of that shoulder, to slip the chain off and let it drop to the bottom. The weight gone, he bobbed to the surface easily and started looking around.

There was Stoney's light, low on the water, blinking. He swam for it, clutching the lock. He'd gone only a few yards from the boat, which was bad. But he'd suffered a crisis and come through it, which was good. With a touch of panic, true, but it was the first crisis, and he'd handled it, come through the panic, and handled it. He felt a little better.

He was amazed at how slowly he was moving, how long it took to cover the few yards back to the boat. Exhausted, he reached his left hand up, dropped the lock into the whaler, and used the same hand to grab the gunwhale.

Stoney had been sitting on flotation cushions on the bottom of the boat. "What happened? Too heavy?"

"Yeah," he gasped. "Too damned heavy."

"I've got the other ready," Stoney said. The second chain was wrapped securely around the kickboard; he took the lock and put it through.

"Do you want to come aboard and rest, or start right out?"

"Start right out," Schroeder said.

"All right," Stoney replied. "Here's the chain. I've attached a loop of line to it; you can put that over your shoulder and tow it. It will still tend to sink, but there's more buoyancy this time." He put the kickboard and chain over the side and handed Schroeder the loop. Schroeder held on for a moment longer.

"I guess you'd better get going," his friend said, "or you'll find yourself swimming into the sunrise."

"Yeah. OK." Schroeder let go of the boat, slipped his left hand and arm through the loop, and resumed his breast stroke. This time it was easier; the weight of the chain no longer there, in its place a drag on each stroke, but far easier to handle than the downward thrust of the chain around his shoulder. The right shoulder felt a little better, too, a little looser, and he kept his arm pulls short, making tight little circles.

Up ahead he could see the lights of the *Sloppy Joe;* from the water they seemed a long way off. He moved slowly, very slowly; the kickboard awash, taking the weight off his back, and slowing him down so that he barely made headway. Or maybe, he thought, it was that he wasn't anxious to get there.

He tried to get a rhythm going; he hadn't done much swimming lately and his arms began to feel heavy almost at once. The big boat was never more than seventy yards away, fewer now, yet it didn't seem to be getting closer. He concentrated on the rhythm. Yes, the lights were drawing nearer, he thought so, anyway. Top competitive swimmers could do fifty yards in what? Twenty-three seconds? Maybe less. But that was freestyle. OK, then, add five for breast stroke. So they could swim the seventy yards in perhaps forty seconds or so. The idea of it made him smile; it was taking him hours, at least it felt like hours. But then they don't have to drag a chain and kickboard! Suddenly he conjured up a silly picture of Mark Spitz racing through the water with a line over his shoulder, pulling a chain and kickboard.

He smiled again. It was amusing. He felt better as he got

closer, and now he was only twenty yards from the *Sloppy Joe*.

Still he could see nothing but the lights.

Then ten yards. And the outline of a shape.

Then five.

Then he was there.

Carefully, he put out a hand to grab the ladder attached to the transom. Don't rock the boat, he said to himself. He took a few deep breaths, then slipped the rope loop off his shoulder and held it. How do I do this? he asked himself, for he knew that if the rope slipped from his grasp, the chain—the second and last chain—would be gone. How do I do this? No, he corrected himself, how would Stoney do it? That helped the answer come.

Undo one end of the loop, tie it to the ladder, leave the other end of the line attached to the chain. Loop the end of the chain around the propeller, and only then untie the line from the chain. Yes, Stoney had solved another one.

He remembered the lock. What should he do with that? He took it off the chain, hooked it to a corner of a ladder rung. Then he tied one end of the line to the ladder, unwrapped the chain from the kickboard.

Delicately, he let the chain go; it sank in the water, held by the line.

Now he had the kickboard to dispose of. What do I do with this one, Stoney? he asked himself. Let it go? Suppose it's spotted? Suppose it has the name Pamela Cobb on it? No, don't let it go. He wedged it between the boat and the ladder, telling himself he must remember to take it back to the whaler with him.

OK, he thought, now I go and do it. He took a deep breath, put a hand on the line, submerged, ran the hand down the line to the beginning of the chain. With his left hand he groped for the prop, found it, at the same time letting the right slide along the chain. When he started lifting the chain toward the prop, his shoulder said, stop.

Sorry, he thought, this time I can't listen. The order became a scream of pain, but he had to start the end of that chain around the prop. He got it up to the shaft, took a turn. Careful, he warned himself, no loud thumps. Then another turn, then wrapped it around one blade.

Then his lungs ordered him to get a breath, so he let go and surfaced, grabbed the ladder, gently, and took three, four, five, six, deep, panting breaths. His heart was thudding, he figured its beat must be way over a hundred twenty, partly out of exertion, partly out of fear.

He sucked in air and went under, this time briefly, to take the chain around another blade. Now he was sure it was secure, and he needed the slack, so he surfaced, untied the line holding it to the ladder. Again, he paused for a half dozen deep breaths, and submerged. Again, he grasped the chain, wrapped it around the third blade, then around the shaft again, and back to the blades, his breaths lasting him fewer seconds each time.

He surfaced, gasping, but beginning to feel good. He was functioning. He was doing it! Sucked in a deep breath, went under again, took the chain around the blades again, at a different angle, until there was not much left; he wrapped the remainder around the shaft, surfaced to get the lock.

A few more breaths, then under with the lock. He found the end of the chain, put the lock through, then through a link near the beginning. He snapped it shut. Stoney had said he didn't have to, but he didn't see any reason not to. Besides, it was a touch of impudence, and Schroeder was feeling good, cheeky.

He pushed himself clear of the boat and surfaced. He'd done it, by God, he'd done it! Exultantly, he began the swim back to Stoney.

First he spotted the lighthouse, and started toward it, hurting, but feeling like Mark Spitz, with a little Johnny Weismuller thrown in. Now he could see the blinking light from the whaler, and felt even better. For the moment he wasn't worrying about the next step. He allowed himself the possibility there wouldn't be a next step. The chain might fail; they might take the girl ashore; only one of them might leave. Legitimately, no next step. Then he thought of Felicia. No, he couldn't wish her no next step. That was shameful, he told himself, but the feeling was weak; he was still exulting from this triumph along the way.

Moving quickly, he reached the whaler, grabbed the gunwhale. Stoney flicked off the lantern and said, "Well?"

"Well, we're in business. The chain's on. Help me aboard, but watch the right shoulder."

"Terrific!" his friend said, and reached out a hand, which he grabbed with his left. No, that wouldn't work. "Let go," he told Stoney. "I'll start climbing, you help me roll in."

He pushed himself up on the gunwhale, pain shrieking through the shoulder, got a leg over the side, and Stoney helped him into the boat.

"Nice going," said Stoney. Then a pause. Then: "What did you do with the line? And the kickboard?"

"Shit," said Shroeder. *"Shit!"*

"Did you leave them floating free?"

"No, dammit! They're both still attached to the boat. Could they get us into trouble?" He was letting Stoney do the thinking again.

"If they're spotted, they'd certainly make your friends suspicious."

"Then I've got to go back."

"Why don't you let me do this one?"

For an instant Schroeder hesitated, and his friend started to unzip his slicker.

"No!" Hating himself for considering it, Schroeder said the word with a fury that startled Stoney. "This is my project, buddy. And I'm doing it all. Except for the transportation and the brainwork." Partly the last was a quip. But what Schroeder wanted to underline was that the *doing* was to be all his. Without waiting for an answer, he grabbed the gunwhale and jumped over the side. In the water, he looked up at Stoney. "Keep the light blinking."

"Of course. And don't waste time. It's nearly 4:30. If they're planning to leave by first light, they'll be stirring soon."

Schroeder started out, wishing his friend hadn't said that, for he now thought he saw a faint glow of light in the east. He tried to swim harder, but the pain in his shoulder wouldn't let him.

And he fantasized. Suppose he had awakened them? Would they be looking around? Would he swim up into the sudden glare of a searchlight, and a pointed gun? Suppose, most mysterious of all, he arrived and found the kickboard and rope missing? Don't be ridiculous, stop scaring yourself, he scolded.

The kickboard and the rope were there when he swam up; everything was quiet, yet he was holding his breath, waiting for the light, for the gun. Neither appeared; Schroeder untied the rope dangling from the ladder, put one end around the waist of the kickboard, fumbled his way through a slipknot—how much faster and better Stoney would do this, he thought—pulled it tight. Then he made a small loop at the other end and slipped his left arm through it. He turned and began swimming back, this time spotting the light at once, and he realized the weather had calmed, the wind and the rain down, the chop almost gone. He reached the whaler, handed the line and kickboard up to Stoney, and made the mistake of trying to climb into the boat too quickly. Pain streaking through the arm and shoulder slowed him, and again he needed help from Stoney as he rolled, slid, scraped, bumped into the boat.

For a moment he sat there, tired, wet, cold, bruised, in pain, victorious. For now, anyway.

"Dry yourself," his friend said. "Put your shirt on. Have a shot of brandy. All we can do now is wait."

His adrenaline dropping, Schroeder felt the pain rising; he did most of the drying with the towel in his left arm; he barely managed the shirt over his right arm. As he sat there he kept rotating the arm and shoulder gently, to keep them warm; he knew when the tissues got cold, they'd grow closer and closer to being useless. And it looked more and more as if he'd have to use them again.

"What time is it?" he asked.

"Just about 4:30. We don't have too long to wait. You must be cold."

"Yeah, a little."

"Have some more brandy."

Schroeder took the bottle, pulled the cork and took a short swig. It felt hot, almost rasping, going down. My God, he said to himself, the brandy I—we—have swallowed in the past half day!

"Better?"

"Yeah, a little warmer."

"Too bad the big boat's out of commission; you'd be a lot more comfortable aboard it."

"This is OK. What's wrong with it?"

"Broken gas line."

"Doesn't sound too hard to fix."

"No, it isn't, but you've got to have the bilge pumped out, and while that's being done I thought I'd have the whole thing overhauled."

"Why do you have to pump out the bilge?"

"Because the gas line is a gravity feed, and when it's broken the gas leaks into the bilge, and forms fumes. And one fine morning you can start your engine and blow yourself and your boat to kingdom come."

"Really? Just from a leak in the gas line?"

"Really. Happened last summer to a big fishing boat on the Cape. Blew the captain and his mate to pieces."

"Wow! Dangerous."

"Oh, yes. Of course, you might start your engine and have nothing happen."

"What are the odds?"

"Perhaps fifty-fifty she'll blow; perhaps better."

"From a broken gas line?"

"Yes, indeed."

"The gas line is that thin metal line that goes into the fuel pump, right?"

"Yes, it is. I've never heard you so interested in mechanical problems before."

"Just curious." Schroeder shut up, reached for the brandy bottle, had another swig.

After a while, he asked Stoney, "If you were the mechanic they came to when their boat didn't start, what would you tell them?"

Stoney thought for a moment. "Well, unless I was really gung-ho, and desperately anxious to go out and look at their boat, I'd tell them the engine was cold, and that they'd probably flooded their carburetor, and they should give it a few minutes and try it again. That assumes of course I knew nothing about the chain."

"So they might very well return from shore, and try to start it up again." Then Schroeder changed the subject. "You know, Stoney, a frightening thought occurred to me. Supposing I swim to the *Sloppy Joe*, get Felicia O'Brien away. What in hell am I going to do with her?"

"In some societies," Stoney answered, "if you save a person's life, you are thereafter responsible for him, or her. Why don't you marry her and live happily ever after? It would make a great story."

"Yeah, especially the part where we spend the rest of our lives hiding from the avenging Mob. No thanks. She's too young for me; and she's not my type. I prefer the type who doesn't get your kids snatched, who doesn't leave you cold and wet and scared and aching in a small boat in the middle of the night. Her type I want to unload as soon as I can. The only question is, to whom. There's got to be at least one honest cop or prosecutor I can turn her over to."

"Of course," Stoney answered.

"All right, then, it's settled," Schroeder said with a smile.

"You take her back to Boston with you and find one." With a smile, but half hoping.

Stoney seemed surprised, then said, "All right. I shall."

Schroeder shook his head. "That's wonderful, Stoney, but why, for God's sake? I wouldn't do it for you."

"Oh, nonsense," the lawyer replied. "You're risking your neck for a young woman you don't even know. I'm not risking very much at all, and you're my closest friend."

"As my closest friend, you do me too much credit, Stoney. I'd like my motive to be as selfless as you make it sound, but the truth is I'm furious because they've raised the question of my bravery, I suppose I should say of my cowardice. They've trod upon my escutcheon, treated me as if I had no balls—and in front of my kids. Another part of the truth is, I'm not sure I *have* balls. If I were, I might—*might,* mind you—have said to myself, well *I* know I've got them, *I'm* not worried, I'm not insecure, and I'll be damned if I'll risk my neck to prove it to *them*.

"No, no, it's Sam Schroeder I've got to show, that's why I picked this dumbass battlefield, on which I'm stumbling around scared to death, hoping each step will be the last. Yet damned determined not to shrink from a step, once it's there to be taken."

"And as your closest friend I tell you you may be too hard on yourself. I don't know that it's dumbass, Sam. It's surely not the safest battlefield, but no battlefield ever is safe, by definition. You don't test anything unless there's a risk, a danger. And sometimes you do your best fighting at the wrong time in the wrong place for the wrong reason. After all, that New York general—he would be from New York, wouldn't he?—precipitated the battle of Gettysburg by his dumbass aggressiveness—at a time and place the Union command didn't want to begin it. And yet it turned out pretty well for the North." Stoney laughed. "It would be one of you pushy New Yorkers, wouldn't it? What was his name, Sickles, wasn't it? Dan Sickles."

"Yes, Stoney, Sickles, but come on. The Union army was lined up and ready to fight. If it hadn't begun right where and when it did, it would have begun a couple of hours, maybe a day, later, maybe a couple of hundred yards away. I, on the other hand, am in no way, at no time, in no place ready to joust with a couple of professional killers. My troops are not lined up. In fact I have none."

"Are you a pacifist?"

"No, just a coward."

"Well, for a coward, with no troops, you seem to be doing all right. You've got your plan and your equipment, and you've pulled off the first maneuver. And you've got a damned good shot at pulling off the whole thing. I hate to alarm you with that possibility, but you have."

"Because of you, Stoney. You've supplied the plan, the equipment, the boat, and a good deal of whatever backbone I've been able to muster thus far."

"Hell, no, you're supplying your own backbone. As for the rest, all right, I've helped; perhaps I'm your army."

"And I don't know where I'd be without you."

"Perhaps back in New York, safe, dry, asleep in bed, and a damned sight better off than where you are at the moment."

"You think I should blame you, eh?" Schroeder smiled. "No, what I should say is, if ever I can repay you, help you in the kind of spot where you're helping me, just shout, whistle, snap your fingers, whatever you want to do. I don't honestly know if I could deliver on a promise like that, but at any rate, I'm making it. Just name it."

There was an unusual pause, and then in a voice Stoney tried, and failed, to make light, he said, "Let's see. You might try keeping your hands off my wife."

"Ah, Stoney. Yes. Granted. You don't understand what happened. I wish I could . . ."

"Yes, yes, I understand. Do you think it's the first? My God, there have been enough others to man Pickett's charge, as long as we're on the battle of Gettysburg. Only their penetration has been a lot more successful than Pickett's. She's been running a regular Fuck of the Week Club for the past year. And some weeks I think she's awarded special bonuses, that is, if one could call my wife's sexual favors either special or a bonus."

"Then why does Thursday night bother you so?"

"Because she is mine, dammit, and she is not supposed to do that."

"Yours? She says you're a male chauvinist pig, and the noises you just made sound suspiciously like oink, oink."

"Oh, for God's sake, Sam." Stoney's voice sounded annoyed and peremptory, as if admonishing a junior lawyer in his firm. "Just because you *write* catchy claptrap, in disappearing ink, for that rag, doesn't mean you should think it, too. Suddenly, in, let's give it half a century, which in the history of the species is the mere blink of an eye, a handful of lady politicians want to legislate away what millions of years have bred into the blood, the bones, the genes of the human animal. When a Lionel Tiger and an Edgar Berman write about it, they are pilloried, one labeled a reactionary and the other a joker. For Christ's sake, Sam, you can teach a dog to stand on its hind legs and put tights on it, but does that make it Baryshnikov?

"Man has always been the hunter, the fighter, the aggressor, the sexual penetrator; woman has always been the mother, keeper of the hearth, the yielder, the penetrated. For uncounted generations, nature and nurture have advanced, sharpened, developed that specialization, that difference. That glorious difference!

"Remember Katherine in *Taming of the Shrew?* 'Why are our bodies soft and weak and smooth, unapt to toil and trouble in the world, but that our thoughts, conditions and our hearts should well agree with our external parts?' And of course Kate is right; it's painfully, beautifully clear to any eyes unhampered by the blinkers of feminist chic. Man and woman are a splendid, miraculous, complementary set, designed to fit together perfectly, one convex where the other is concave, and vice versa.

"Then, suddenly, it becomes politically necessary to deny the evidence of one's eyes and mind, and to yell 'oink,' and 'reactionary,' at anyone like Dr. Tiger, or Dr. Berman, who has the temerity, and the lack of chic, to remind us of that miraculous, glorious, inevitable difference. It becomes politically necessary to look at a penis and a vagina and maintain we cannot see the difference. Which is destructive not only to holders of both sets of equipment, but to rational dialogue. And it is no accident that the ultimate argument is an animal noise, the cry of oink, oink, which means that thinking has been drowned beneath the slop."

"Sounds like you've taken the long way round to saying you believe in a double standard," Schroeder replied. "Admit it."

"No, I don't admit it, Sam. I proclaim it. It's what I've been talking about. Of course, there's a double standard, a whole set of them, praise be! To proclaim, flatly, a single standard is to ask both a basso and a soprano to hit a high C, to ask a one-hundred-thirty-pound marathoner and a two-hundred-sixty-pound shotputter to run twenty miles a day and press three hundred pounds. What's fine for one may be deadly for another, and without the distortion of those chic spectacles, that's plain to see. In all sorts of important areas, being a man involves different burdens, rights, functions, from being a woman. In short, a massive set of double standards. Now some of these are functionless and therefore unfair. And I proclaim that, too. Others are cultural and will take countless generations to change. Still others are intrinsic and will never change. The problem lies with those who are too stupid or too politicized to tell one from the other.

"I remember, as a schoolchild, hearing a female classmate saying to a male classmate, 'I can do anything you can do.' And the boy answering, 'All right, let's see you pee standing up.' There are women today, my wife among them, who think the solution to that discrepancy lies in passing a law giving women the Constitutional right to pee standing up. Well, dammit all, they don't have the *equipment* to pee standing up, they don't have the *brains* to squat, so they make a mess all over everything."

Schroeder smiled in the dark. "Sounds like the long way 'round to the position that husbands can screw around and wives can't."

"Not exactly, Sam. But not far off. What I believe is that screwing around *never* helps a marriage, *always* presents a danger to it. But as between the husband and wife, there is absolutely no question which is more destructive. The woman, as hearth keeper, mother, rearer of the young, is the fixed central element of the home. The man, as fighter, protector, provider, is out, is mobile, and his fidelity has nowhere the importance that the woman's does. Across many generations and many societies, the pattern of relationships has recognized that difference. Now, it may be, in the long, long run, that will change. But when you change it by fiat, you change it at your peril, even with the imprimatur of Erica Jong stamped upon it."

Then Stoney's face took on the rueful vulnerability of a small boy's. "Besides," he said, "she screwed around first."

Schroeder was struck by the look on his face as he said it. And immediately was struck by the realization that he could see the face. He glanced up, and in the east there was light in the sky. Suddenly, Stoney's polemic on women's lib was forgotten. All of Schroeder's attention was now fastened on the twenty-eight-footer anchored seventy yards away.

Chapter

15

THE RAIN WAS OVER, THE WIND STILL GUSTING, VISIBILITY good, the day glowering and majestic, when Red came on deck. But he was not admiring the day. He wanted to be sure they had enough light, and seeing that they did, he went below again at once, started the engine, let it idle, turned on the electric winch to haul up the anchor, and then put the engine in gear.

It stalled.

Once more, he started the engine, put it in gear.

Once more, it stalled.

A third time he tried.

A third time it stalled.

"Shit!" he said aloud. Mike looked up. Both men had spent the night in chairs, drunk and sleeping fitfully. "Whatsa matter?" he asked.

"The fucking thing keeps stalling," answered Red. He tried a fourth time; again it stalled.

"Maybe it's not warmed up," Mike offered.

"I warmed it up, I let it run," Red answered, testy at being questioned. He tried again. The engine stalled again.

"Maybe you're floodin' 'er," Mike suggested.

"Well, here then, goddammit, don't just sit there, you try." After old Pussycat had faced him down last night, Red was sore about looking bad.

Mike turned on the engine, put it in gear. It stalled.

"Why don't you go out and look, see if you can see anything?" Red said.

Mike hesitated. "I don't know nothin' . . ."

"Go ahead," Red ordered.

Mike went on deck, lifted the hatch cover. "Try to start her." Red did, with the same results. "I don't see nothin' " Mike said. He replaced the hatch cover and squeezed back into the cabin.

Red gave it another try; it stalled.

"Well, shit! Now what the fuck do we do?"

"Find someone to fix 'er?" Mike suggested. He was trying not to arouse Red, who got angrier, quicker, for less reason than anyone he knew.

"How come you don't know how to fix an engine, Mike?"

"'Cause I never learned. How 'bout you?" Mike had learned a new trick for handling Red.

This time the big redhead just ignored the counter-question. "I don't suppose the Pussycat knows anything," he said.

"Want me to ask him?" said Mike.

"Nah," answered Red. "He's not going to know." Red didn't think the old man would, and certainly didn't want to risk the chance he might.

"I guess somebody's got to go ashore, and find a mechanic, Mike. Want to do it?"

Mike looked dubious. "What'll I tell 'em?"

"What do you mean, what'll I tell 'em, goddammit!" His face was turning as red as his hair. "Tell 'em, the fucking . . . oh, shit, never mind, I'll do it. Just stay here."

Red started out of the cabin, then turned back. "One more time," he said. He started the engine, let it idle, then muttered, "Come on, you mother . . ." and put it in gear. It stalled.

He stomped out of the cabin, grabbed hold of the dinghy's line, pulled it to the ladder, and climbed in. Then he thought of something. So far, they'd made a few mistakes. But he could find a way to lay them on those two dummies. What he didn't want, though, was the two of them talking behind his back, deciding he was to blame, getting a story together about how Red had screwed up. And what he especially didn't want, although Red wouldn't admit this to himself, was the two of them gloating behind his back about how the old fart had made him look bad. Uh uh, he couldn't let that happen. And there was a simple way to stop it. Take Mike with him, leave old Pussycat to guard the girl.

He'd already started the outboard—at least that fucking thing worked, he said to himself—and he shut it off. "Hey Mike," he said, just loud enough for the man inside to hear. "Hey Mike!"

The swarthy man appeared at the hatchway. "Yeah?"

"Come on, I want you with me. I might need your help." Mike looked dumbfounded, then started forward. "But first tell the old man to keep an eye on the girl. And to keep that cabin door closed!" Suddenly he could see them coming back with a mechanic, who'd catch a glimpse of the girl, tied up, with almost no clothes on. Better be careful, he thought.

"Mike," he shouted. The man turned back. "Make sure to have that door closed. Got it?"

"Yeah, got it."

Mike made his way into the tiny cabin, saw the girl and Pussycat both motionless. He shook the old man by the shoulder.

"Wah? Wah?" was all Pussycat could manage.

"Hey, Pussy, we're goin' ashore. Keep an eye on the girl, and keep . . ." But he could see that the old man was in a beery stupor and he stopped in mid-sentence, turned, went up on deck, and climbed into the dinghy.

"All set?" asked Red.

"Yeah, all set," he replied.

For Schroeder, watching the one man, then the second, get into the dinghy was like watching a mystery drama without being sure which ending he was rooting for. He hadn't felt such acute physical suspense since . . . he tried to remember . . . since his first start as a high school football player. As they lined up for the kickoff, his knees were so weak, and his heart beat so fast, he feared he'd never be able to run forward. But he did, and threw himself at a blocker, and the contact dispelled the tension.

Now, he hoped, physical action would have the same effect, and when the two men got into the boat and rode toward the dock he realized he'd be going ahead. It was the first look at them he'd gotten without their hats and glasses, and they were even more frightening that way, especially when he realized how big and thick both men were.

"Looks like you've got your chance, Samuel," his friend whispered. "They are playing this thing as if you'd written the script for them. Are you all right? How do you feel?"

"Terrific. Capable. Serene. Masterful. Trying to control my bowels. I'm suddenly understanding where the expression, keep a tight asshole, comes from. Did you get a look at those two guys?"

"Yes, I did," Stoney replied. "Looks like someone borrowed two tackles from the Boston Patriots."

"Only bigger," Schroeder said.

"You'll be there and gone by the time they're back. But you'd better get going. All you need is the knife this time."

"Yeah." Schroeder got into a low crouch, jumped over the side, held on with his left hand. "OK, hand me the knife."

Stoney handed it to him. "Careful," he said. "It's double-edged and serrated."

"Hell," Schroeder said. "I don't know how to carry it. I *am* going to have to swim with it in my teeth." Carefully, he gripped the blade with his teeth. The edge was right at his lips. No good. He took it out, clenched his teeth on the handle. That would have to do.

"Good luck," said his friend. "You'll be OK. Try to keep an eye on me, and I'll try to signal you if there's anything coming."

Schroeder nodded, then removed the knife from his mouth again, for he remembered a question.

"You said the gas line was that thin metal line that comes out of the fuel pump, right?"

"Yes, right," replied Stoney. "But . . ."

He never finished the question, for Schroeder had already turned and begun swimming toward the *Sloppy Joe*.

Schroeder knew that daylight increased the danger, but he preferred it, it seemed less forbidding and mysterious than the dark. The pain in his shoulder was, if anything, worse. Sitting around had let the tissues grow cold and stiff. Then he discovered a new ache. His jaw muscles began to cramp from the strain of holding the knife, and the drag of the water on it increased the strain. Within ten yards he had to take the knife out of his mouth to give his jaw muscles a rest. He tried swimming with it in his left hand, but he couldn't get anywhere.

After a few more strokes, he put the knife back in his mouth. He was weary, aching, thoroughly vulnerable. He couldn't fight off his grandmother, let alone those two hoods, should they decide to return ahead of schedule. Schedule? Whose schedule? Mine, Schroeder said to himself, and they may not want to keep to it. His best protection was to keep the *Sloppy Joe* between him and their dinghy. As long as he couldn't see them they couldn't see him, he told himself.

He was getting close now, perhaps thirty yards away. He stopped, took the knife in his hand, clenched and unclenched his jaws a couple of times, put the knife back in his teeth, continued swimming. He suddenly realized he'd managed every step up until now, and was damned close to getting her away. Damned close! A streak of elation found its way through his fear.

Then he was there. He grabbed the ladder at the stern and pulled himself up until he could look over the transom. Nothing. He tried to raise himself high enough to get a look at the dinghy with the two men; he couldn't see it. Carefully, he pulled himself up and onto the deck. Still no sign of life. He stayed low, to avoid being spotted from shore. He saw the engine hatch; quickly he moved to it, lifted it. He found the fuel pump and the gas line. Using his knife as a lever, he pried the line loose and forced it down as far as he could to speed up the flow of gas into the bilge. He replaced the hatch, then headed for the cabin. He slid open the door, and saw her, tied up on the bunk, apparently naked, although her bra and pants had been put over her. He couldn't see whether she was asleep, unconscious, or dead, but she did not stir when he entered.

Starting toward her, he kicked a couple of empty beer cans which rolled with a clatter. He looked down; there were many empties. Whose? Then he heard or sensed something at his right rear, and he whirled around.

There was a third man!

Goddammit, why didn't I see him? Schroeder asked himself in

a flash. Because, he realized, the man had been lying asleep on a bunk to the left of the hatch and slightly behind it, and Schroeder, never dreaming of the possibility of a third man, riveted his attention on the girl. The sound of the beer cans had roused the man, and now his feet were on the ground and he was rising from the bunk.

In that squat position he looked like a cross between a Sumo wrestler and the old gorilla in the Central Park Zoo. He had a neck as thick as his head, it seemed to go from the tops of his shoulders to his ears in a straight line. Beneath his sleeveless undershirt, huge, flabby, hairy breasts stood out; a massive gut strained the shirt at the waist. A pair of old trousers, worn low, were lost to sight somewhere beneath the belly. His arms were thick with muscle and meat, the rounded bulk of the shoulders thickened by a set of heavy trapezius muscles. Much of his plentiful body hair was white. What was left of the hair on his head was gray; his face was puffy with fat, his eyes slits, his nose stubby, wide, and misshapen, like a fighter's.

He was not young, or tall; he must have weighed two hundred and thirty pounds, Schroeder thought. He looked like a hit man emeritus, given the sinecure of watching a bound, unconscious girl while younger men did the main job.

He seemed only half awake, groggy, moving slowly, but then he had only two short steps to take to reach Schroeder. His right arm, almost as thick as it was long, arrived first, the broad, stubby fingers and massive palm jamming into Schroeder's chin and neck like a football straight-arm, propelling the taller, thinner man backward as if he'd been caught on the crest of a wave, ramming him into the girl's bunk and the bulkhead above it.

For an instant Schroeder was paralyzed. Then he reached his good hand, the left, up to grab the old man's wrist. Against his power and momentum, Schroeder's move had the effect it would against an ocean wave. The old man brought his other hand up to Schroeder's throat and began squeezing; Schroeder's left hand was ineffectual, almost unfelt.

The right hand, incapacitated by the injured shoulder, was at his side. In it, he held the knife.

Although he'd begun to turn when he heard the other man, Schroeder had not gotten more than halfway around, his left shoulder toward the man, his right arm hidden by his body. The right hand was at his side holding the knife lightly, because even to squeeze it sent pain shooting through the shoulder.

The old man's powerful fingers tightened on Schroeder's throat; when he tried to take a breath, it was a choking gasp. He didn't have too many moments of consciousness left; he knew it.

Yet he could not bring himself to raise the knife to that protruding gut less than a foot away. Ten inches, perhaps less, would take the knife through skin. For what seemed a choking, agonized eternity, but was only an instant, he could not lift it.

Even feeling blackness coming on him, Schroeder thought of the civilized thing. A warning. He tried to shout, "Let go! I'll stab you!" What came out was an inarticulate scream.

Then he punched the knife into that massive belly.

It went in to the right of the navel, just above the low-slung pants top. At his end of the knife, Schroeder felt white-hot pain burn through his shoulder and set his entire side aflame. At the other end, it was like putting a knife through a melon: resistance at the rind, then an easy slipping through the inside.

And through it, Schroeder looked straight at his opponent's face. At first it had been fierce and angry, a beast defending its turf. Then strained, wrinkled, eyes slitted with effort, an old man over-trying as he did a young man's work. Then gloating, as he realized this invader was no threat. Then the surprise that came with the knife, eyes popping wide, immediate awareness that it was all over for him.

Still the fingers on Schroeder's throat did not seem to relax, and it seemed that only the pain in his shoulder kept him conscious. He knew he must keep the pressure on that knife, and on that shoulder, longer than the old man could hold the pressure on his throat. As much as an agonized reaction to the pain as anything else, Schroeder kept pushing the knife. He could feel it moving up, as he saw the old man's eyes grow wider.

Yes, of course, He remembered. It was a double-edged knife.

Still the fingers would not let go; choking, Schroeder pressed harder. And then he felt the fingers ease. The old man reached both hands down toward the knife, clutching, tearing at it, growing more frantic, but weakening, because Schroeder, despite the pain, kept holding the knife while the man's weight did the work for him; the more he sagged, the more the knife worked its way upward, its serrated edge opening a deep, frightful gash in the old man's belly.

When Schroeder felt the warm wetness of blood on his hand,

he looked down, saw the red spreading over everything, knife, hand, the man's shirt, his grayish-brown pants, which now began to take on a new brightness. Without thinking, Schroeder reached his left hand to the knife to help hold it; the old man kept sliding down on the knife, the cut getting bigger, the blood flowing faster.

Then the old man gave up trying to seize the knife, and pressed his two bloody hands to the spot where it was in his body. Schroeder watched the blood ooze between the man's fingers; in that moment the man's feet slipped out from under him, and his weight, now sending him backward as well as downward, freed him of the blade. More and more the man sagged, his hands clutching the huge cut, the blood pumping out between his fingers, his eyes, and Schroeder's, fixed on the wound and the blood.

But he did not fall to the ground. He seemed suddenly to have forgotten Schroeder, as his hand reached out for support, and his attention took on a new goal: to get out of the cabin. Grabbing the berth, he managed to half straighten, and began staggering toward the hatch. Schroeder watched him, paralyzed. How could the man move, with all that blood pouring out, over his hands, his body, down his legs, over the floor? So much blood! Yet he kept moving.

Schroeder knew he must stop him; on deck, the old man might scream, wave, and no matter who responded, Schroeder would be in trouble. If the two big men saw him, Schroeder was a dead man. If anyone else came, there he would be, bloody knife in hand, two bodies—dying? dead?—near him.

He had to stop the man. But nothing could make him move, could get him close to that bloody hulk, which had reached the hatchway, was trying to open it, trying to get up the two steps, trying not to topple over. He actually had the hatch partway open, and was trying to wedge his bulk through. Schroeder *had* to stop him. How? With the knife? Never. Never, never, never again would he use a knife on human flesh. Once was a lifetime's supply; it would last him forever. In his dreams each night of his life he would stick the knife in, and it would pop through, as if the old man were a melon, a red-juiced melon.

But he had to stop him. And with the old man halfway out the hatch, Schroeder forced himself to move forward. Nauseated, he reached out his left hand, grabbed the rear of the old man's pants at the waist and pulled. The man didn't budge; he was bent over, trying to make his way out; Schroeder's tug seemed to make no difference.

Schroeder braced himself with a foot against the bottom step, pulled harder, and backward came the old man, like the stump of a dead oak, toppling, with no struggle, no resistance. Schroeder shrank back as the massive body hit the deck on its back, the shirt, pants, shoes sopping with blood. It was too much for Schroeder; this was beyond his control. Racing up the steps slippery with blood, he just made it onto the deck, leaned over the side and heaved the food and brandy he'd ingested in the last few hours.

Woozy, dazed, tasting acid, he tried to force himself to go below. His impulse was to dive overboard, to get the hell away. But he had to go back; the girl was there, possibly alive, although he'd seen no movement from her. Gritting his teeth he went below, through the hatch, down the steps, trying to ignore the blood, which was impossible because it covered steps and cabin deck, trying to ignore the old man, which was impossible, because his body took up most of the deck space. Clenching his jaws harder, Schroeder stepped over the body to get to the girl. He looked down at her, carefully, for the first time; she hadn't moved, but her face had color. She was not dead, at least she didn't seem so, but then he was far from expert.

"Felicia?" He said it softly. Why, he didn't know. Afraid of waking the old man? He reached out and touched her face, which was warm. Yet she didn't respond.

Suddenly, he was seized with a panicky need to be out of there. Supposing the men were told quickly they couldn't be helped, and had started right back toward the *Sloppy Joe?* Supposing they were getting close at this moment? He almost turned to go above deck again, fought the urge, turned back to the girl.

"Felicia! Wake up!" This time he said it sharply, and slapped her face. Her head moved to the side, her lips parted but she did not speak, her eyelids fluttered but did not open. She's alive, by God, he thought. Yet, she did not stir.

Dammit, he said to himself, the plan depends on her swimming back to the whaler, and now she can't move. She must be drugged. What in hell do I do? Yell to Stoney for help? In the quiet of the morning, he'd be heard across the harbor. Yeah, but what should he do?

Get her in the water, swim her back. Swim her back? Sure, he knew his lifesaving carries. He pictured it, and realized he'd have to use his right arm for something, either to hold her, or to swim. And it would do for neither; the arm was limp at his side, shoulder constantly, excruciatingly, painful the moment he thought about it. No, the carry was no good. What then? Stoncy, where are you? Not here. He was on his own; he must think! He looked at her tied wrists.

Let's see. Put her tied hands over your head, let her ride on your back as you swim. Yes. Yes, it could work. He sat the girl up; the bra and pants with which the old man had covered her, slipped off; she was naked. He saw the ugly welts on her breasts where Red had kneaded and pinched her. Holding her in a sitting position, he lifted her bound wrists in the air, then sat down on her lap and dropped her hands over his head. Bent over, he slowly got to his feet, lifting her on his back.

Schroeder started for the steps and the hatch, holding the girl's bound wrists in his left hand, knife in the right. Carefully he stepped on the bloodied deck, and over the bloody body; if he ever slipped and fell, he thought, that would be the end of him, he'd never get up again. Softly, the girl groaned, once, then a second time.

"It's all right," he said, soothingly. "It's all right." He could feel her soft breasts on his bare back, her abdomen, pubic hairs, thighs, on his lower back and buttocks. His foot was on the lower step when, on the bunk the old man had been using, he spotted the small leather notebook. My God, he thought, could that be? Would they not have destroyed it by now? Obviously not, he decided. Maybe their boss wanted proof they'd gotten it. He reached over, picked it up, then asked himself how to carry it. Only one way was available to him. He thrust the notebook into the front of his jockey shorts, and walked up the steps, out onto the deck.

Move quickly, he told himself, You're visible, vulnerable. As he made his way to the ladder at the transom, he took a look at the engine hatch. How much gasoline had leaked into the bilge? Enough? And would the two men try to start the big boat again?

Girl on his back, Schroeder laboriously got over the transom, onto the steps of the ladder, dropped the knife into the water, and let himself and Felicia drop in.

Red and Mike strode into the ship's store at the dock, startling the man behind the counter, who opened early but never really expected much business before six.

"Good morning!" he said. "What can I do for you?"

Red had neither the time nor the temperament for amenities. "Our goddam engine keeps stalling out on us. Got a mechanic?"

The man shook his head. "Not at this hour, not on a Sunday morning. I'm crazy to be open at all. What seems to be the trouble?"

"I told you," said Red, impatiently. "She starts and stalls, she starts and stalls."

"Sounds to me like she's just a little wet, from all the rain."

"Think so? What should we do?"

"I'd let her sit for a couple of minutes, try her again. You'll get her going, probably."

"Look, why don't you just get us a mechanic?" Red said.

The storekeeper shook his head. "If I call someone at this time on a Sunday morning, just 'cause your points are a little wet, and that's all it sounds like to me, he's never going to work for me again." The man hesitated. "Tell you what," he said. "There doesn't seem to be much business around anyway, I'll take a ride out there with you, and see if I can start 'er up."

"Yeah, OK," said Red. Then he thought of the girl below deck. Suppose she heard a strange voice and screamed? He didn't have to take a chance like that for a wet engine, if that's all it was. No.

The man had started out from behind the counter. "No, wait," said Red. "We'll go back and give it another try. It's probably just wet, like you say. If we can't get it, we'll come back for you."

"All right," said the man, pleased not to have to go. "I'm sure you'll be all right. Come back if you need me."

"Yeah, thanks," said Red perfunctorily, and turned away. "Come on," he ordered Mike. The two hurried out of the store.

"Why didn't you want to take the guy?" Mike asked.

"It's taking a chance. He might spot the girl. She might hear him, and scream. Maybe we can start 'er on our own; anyway, it'll only take a couple of minutes to try. I can always come back. Hurry up."

The two climbed into the dinghy and headed back for the *Sloppy Joe*. The sun was rising on a clear, gusty day. Both men were thinking how they'd almost let the girl slip through their fingers yesterday. Neither wanted to say it, Mike because he knew how irritable Red was, Red because he didn't want to put into words what they both knew, that they'd messed up. But, Red told himself, they'd come out of it all right. They'd screwed up, and gotten away with it, almost.

Except for two problems: the New York guy and the boat that wouldn't start. The New York guy they'd taken care of. Even if he'd had the balls to call the cops from New York, which Red doubted, the cops didn't know where to look. The minute they started searching Red would spot them. But Red also knew, if the cops should come cruising up in the next couple of minutes, there could be trouble. Because he and Mike were not yet back to their boat. Because they might have difficulty dumping the girl into the harbor. Which brought Red to the second problem. The boat. The sooner they got it started and got out of the harbor, and disposed of the girl, the sooner two problems would be reduced to none. And that was the best number to have.

"That goddamned boat better start!" said Red as they pulled up to the *Sloppy Joe*. He was not sure why he decided to look below before trying to start the engine. Maybe a jitteriness about the old man, Pussycat.

Pussycat, lying in his own blood, was the first thing he saw. The empty bunk where the girl had been lying was the next.

He turned and yelled to Mike: "Holy Christ! The old man's dead! The girl's gone!

"What?" yelled Mike, and took a look for himself. "Jesus!" But the big redhead was already on deck and looking around, cursing as he did. "Shit! Goddamn that old fuck! A lousy little cunt! Tied up! And she gets away! Shit!"

Then Red spotted the two heads bobbing in the water, moving slowly, not much more than fifty yards away, near a small boat. "That's them! Swimming!" he shouted. He pulled out his pistol, yelling to Mike as he did: "Start the engine! That fuckin' thing better work!"

Red fired a shot, but the rocking of the *Sloppy Joe* and his underestimation of the distance sent it short and to the right. He tried a second. Straighter, but still short.

Meanwhile, Mike ran to the bridge, turned the key and pressed the starter.

When Schroeder and the girl hit the water and went under, he had a moment of acute panic. If he couldn't swim the distance between the boats with a chain that weighed perhaps fifteen pounds, how was he going to make it with a one-hundred-and-twenty-pound girl? As he struggled to rise to the surface, he tried to assure himself: Specific gravity made all the difference; she'd practically float by herself. Her density was far less than the chain's; she was almost chubby, and therefore buoyant. Schroeder swam himself to the surface, doing a fierce breast stroke despite the pain in his shoulder.

He fought to get his mouth above water for a breath, managed a couple of strokes, then another breath, laboring, heart pumping, right hand barely finning in the water as the shoulder demanded a respite. On one of his gasping breaths, he got a glimpse of the Boston whaler; it seemed a half mile away; with each breath, he seemed a little lower in the water, it seemed a little harder to surface.

Then he had a new problem; the shock of the water began to revive Felicia, she began to twist and thrash.

"Stop it!" he tried to yell on his next breath, but it cost him air. He had to go for another breath on the next stroke, and this time he heard her groaning, felt her thrashing harder, her arms tightening on his head, neck, and shoulders. He realized that the more she struggled, the more vertical her body became in the water and, therefore, the less buoyant.

On the next breath he tried yelling, "Stop it! I'm helping you!" He got some of it out; he also got a mouthful of water. Needing air, he put his head down, took two desperate strokes to get up the momentum to surface, and paid for the effort in his right shoulder.

Felicia would not stop moving; this time he heard her say, "Help!" and he took a precious breath to shout, "Stop it, goddammit, or I'll drown you!" Suddenly he felt a tremendous resentment against this girl, whom he'd encountered on the wildest of chance, who'd gotten him into this unbelievable situation he didn't want any part of, who'd made him a killer. Yeah, it was a disreputable-looking ape of a man he'd killed. And in self-defense. But he'd killed him, stuck a knife in him, poured his blood all over the cabin. The old man was a bloody corpse now, cut wide open, his life ended by a mild-mannered, modestly talented milquetoast of a magazine hack. Hereafter to be known as a killer.

Sam Schroeder had killed a man. That he could never undo. And not even one of the men who'd kidnapped his kids!

His shout may have quieted Felicia, something had, for now she was not thrashing, which made it easier. Still, not easy, though, for he was exhausted, shoulder tortured, lower and lower in the water between rasping breaths, needing the air sooner and sooner. And waiting, almost with prickles on the back of his neck, for the two men in their dinghy to come after him.

Yet somehow he did seem to be closing on the whaler. Now it was barely twenty yards away, and its nearness served as adrenaline. He pulled as hard as he could, which was not very hard with the right arm; he gave to his frog kick all the power in his legs.

And now he was ten yards away, and on his next breath he could see, just above the gunwhale of the whaler, an arm, Stoney's arm, waving him on. Why? he wondered. Stoney must see something; he tried to pick up more to his stroke, but he was already giving it all he had.

And now three strokes away. Almost there! Almost finished! And he'd done it! Well, practically. Three strokes. Now two.

Then he heard the crack, and something told him it was not an engine backfiring, but the sound of a gunshot—aimed at him. Stoney reached out a long arm. Schroeder stretched for it and missed, going under as he lost the stroke. His head was barely above water again when he heard the second shot. And then he made contact with Stoney's hand.

"They're shooting!" his friend said. "Let's get you aboard and let's us get the hell out. Come on!"

Stoney grabbed the girl by the hair and lifted her so Schroeder could slip out from under her arms. "Ow!" she yelled, as if still half asleep. Then Stoney put a hand under each arm to haul her aboard. Schroeder grabbed the gunwhale with his left hand, put his right into her crotch and pushed up, to help Stoney. Apologies for the indelicacy, he thought. He felt she'd excuse it.

They'd gotten her upper body over the gunwhale when the explosion sounded, a shattering roar in the quiet harbor.

Luckily, Schroeder was able to push the girl the rest of the way himself, because his friend was so startled he let go of her.

"What the hell!" Stoney shouted. "She blew up! She's blown apart! There's nothing left! What in hell happened?"

"Give me some help," Schroeder gasped. "Get me in first. I can't make it by myself."

"Yes, of course." Stoney was apologetic. He rolled Schroeder into the whaler. And then remembered. "The gas line! You snapped the gas line!"

"Yeah, I snapped the gas line," Schroeder said. "Don't you think we should get out of here?"

But Stoney was already starting the engine and moving them away, toward the dock, fast. Schroeder looked back toward the spot where the *Sloppy Joe* had been. He could see part of a hull, sinking fast, the surface around it covered with debris. There was no sign of life, no body. But then he was sure nothing could survive that blast. Probably, there'd not even be a body in one piece.

"They're dead, the two of them," said Stoney, as shaken up as Schroeder had ever seen him.

"No, three. One was guarding her." As he spoke, Schroeder looked at Felicia O'Brien, sitting on cushions, entirely naked, one eye open, groggy.

"Are you all right?" Schroeder reached for a blanket, and covered her with it, without unfastening the rope around her wrists.

She stared at him; at least her right eye did. The left was still shut and discolored from Red's punch.

Finally, she said: "You're Schroeder."

"Yes, I'm Schroeder."

"How did I get here?"

"I saved you."

"Oh. God. Thank you. Thank you. Where are those other men?"

"They're dead."

"All three?"

"Yes, all three."

"Three?" Stoney asked.

"Yes. One was on board, guarding her."

Stoney broke in. "No one could have lived through that explosion."

"The explosion didn't get him, Stoney. Your knife did. In the belly. He jumped me when I went below. Damn near strangled me."

"He helped me," said Felicia.

"What?"

"The old man helped me. The other two wanted to rape me, and he stopped them."

"They would have killed you before long," Schroeder answered. He knew he was right, but a jolt came with the reminder that he'd knifed a man to death.

"Samuel, you have done it," said his friend. "What you wanted to, and then some." A moment later, he had the whaler pulled into its slip.

Stoney tied up the boat, jumped onto the dock. "Come on," he said. He reached out a hand. Docilely, she stood up, and the blanket started to fall away. Schroeder wrapped it around her as securely as he could, then the two men pulled and pushed her up to the dock. She could barely stand, let alone walk. Schroeder picked her up and threw her over his shoulder. "Just relax," he said. "We can move more quickly this way."

Walking so fast that Schroeder could barely keep up with him, Stoney headed for the station wagon. They put her in the front seat.

"A third man, wow!" said Stoney.

"I guess he'd been aboard all the time. He would have killed me if I hadn't had the knife. As it was I damn near tore my right shoulder off when I shoved it into him. Did a lot worse to him, though. So much blood."

Stoney climbed into the driver's seat, Schroeder into the passenger seat, with the girl between them. When he sat down, Schroeder felt for the first time, the pressure of the notebook he'd shoved into his underpants. He started to reach for it; something made him stop. He would hold the book.

Stoney started the car, drove off.

"You saved my life," the girl said, still in a kind of haze.

"He sure as hell did," Stoney answered. "And now we're going to see to it you don't try to toss it away again. You're going back to Boston to be turned over to the authorities. *Honest* officials."

"Oh, no!"

"Oh, yes. This time I'll be with you, and we'll do what you should have done the first time. After all, next time you run away you might not be able to find a genuine hero to save your life."

"Yes, I know. But . . . ."

"You've got to do what he says, Felicia," Schroeder warned. Then he asked himself, but what do *I* do?

They drove into the driveway of the Cobb house. "We're going to get you dressed, feed you some coffee," Stoney told the girl. "Let's go." The two men half helped, half led her into the house. Stoney walked into the bedroom where Rocky was asleep. He awoke her quickly, and after she'd put on a dressing gown, led her out to meet Felicia.

"For now, Rocky, please don't ask any questions, just dress her and give her some coffee. I'll explain later."

Rocky gave her husband a disgusted look, and Schroeder said, "Please!" to reinforce her husband's instruction. After a moment, Rocky took the girl's hand and walked her away.

"Wow!" said Stoney. Schroeder had never heard him use the expression before, and now, in the past ten minutes he'd used it twice. "I don't believe all this. Things like this don't really happen."

Stoney's incredulity made Schroeder realize that he, too, was in a kind of trance, unable to absorb his own heroics.

"What do I do now, Stoney?"

"I've been thinking about that." Stoney paused. "Turn yourself in, I suppose."

Schroeder's heart sank. "I've killed three men."

"One was clearly self-defense, right?"

"Sure as hell was."

"The other two . . . well, you tried to disable the boat by breaking the fuel line. You had no way of knowing the thing would blow up."

"Will that wash?"

Stoney nodded vehemently. "Absolutely! Three hoods killed? A girl's life saved! No one will even try for an indictment. More likely, you'll get a medal. Or a movie offer."

A movie offer! It triggered something in Schroeder. Of course! But a book first! Hard-cover sale. Paperback sale. Then the movie sale. And he'd write them all! Not only that, he had the little notebook. A second time he started to take it out of his undershorts, and a second time he stopped.

No, the notebook would be his secret for a while. He realized he'd been standing around, holding a towel, wearing only undershorts. "Give me some dry stuff, Stoney, would you?"

"Of course," his friend replied. "How stupid of me!"

Stoney got him shorts, shirt, pants; he had to roll up the pants and sleeves. But the pants had a big pocket, big enough to tuck the notebook into. This notebook, this adventure, Schroeder realized, were his tickets from Mediocrity to Fame and Fortune.

One way. First class. And fame and fortune were the right words. No exaggeration at all.

Why shouldn't he make a half-million out of this story? And leave *Scope* forever?

Wearing his oversized clothes, Schroeder walked out into the living room again. Rocky, Felicia, and Stoney looked up at him. "How about these potato sacks?" he asked.

"You look like a hero in them," Stoney said quietly. "A god-damned hero!"

Schroeder nodded and half smiled. He remembered the last sentence of the kidnapping note from the killers.

Serves them right, he said to himself. That'll teach them to use a double negative.

FICTION

CRIME/ADVENTURE/SUSPENSE

☐ The Organization	David Anthony	90p
☐ Stud Game	David Anthony	95p
☐ Five Pieces of Jade	John Ball	85p
☐ Siege	Peter Cave	£1.15
☐ The Execution	Oliver Crawford	90p
☐ The Ransom Commando	James Grant	95p
☐ The Rose Medallion	James Grant	90p
☐ Barracuda	Irving A. Greenfield	95p
☐ The Halo Jump	Alistair Hamilton	£1.00
☐ The Desperate Hours	Joseph Hayes	95p
☐ A Game for the Living	Patricia Highsmith	95p
☐ The Blunderer	Patricia Highsmith	95p
☐ Those Who Walk Away	Patricia Highsmith	95p
☐ The Tremor of Forgery	Patricia Highsmith	80p
☐ The Two Faces of January	Patricia Highsmith	95p
☐ The Heir	Christopher Keane	£1.00
☐ Cranmer	Steve Knickmeyer	90p
☐ The Golden Grin	Colin Lewis	£1.00
☐ Confess, Fletch	Gregory Mcdonald	90p
☐ Fletch	Gregory Mcdonald	90p
☐ Flynn	Gregory Mcdonald	95p
☐ To Kill a Jogger	Jon Messmann	95p
☐ Pandora Man	Kerry Newcomb and Frank Schaefer	£1.25
☐ Sigmet Active	Thomas Page	£1.10
☐ The Jericho Commandment	James Patterson	£1.00
☐ Games	Bill Pronzini	85p
☐ Crash Landing	Mark Regan	95p
☐ The Mole	Dan Sherman	95p
☐ Swann	Dan Sherman	£1.00
☐ The Peking Pay-Off	Ian Stewart	90p
☐ The Seizing of Singapore	Ian Stewart	£1.00
☐ Place of the Dawn	Gordon Taylor	90p
☐ Judas Cross	Jeffrey M. Wallmann	90p
☐ Rough Deal	Walter Winward	85p
☐ The Ten-Tola Bars	Burton Wohl	90p

NAME ....

ADDRESS ....

....

Write to Hamlyn Paperbacks Cash Sales, PO Box 11, Falmouth, Cornwall TR10 9EN.

Please indicate order and enclose remittance to the value of the cover price plus:

U.K.: 30p for the first book, 15p for the second book and 12p for each additional book ordered to a maximum charge of £1.29.

B.F.P.O. & EIRE: 30p for the first book, 15p for the second book plus 12p per copy for the next 7 books, thereafter 6p per book.

OVERSEAS: 50p for the first book plus 15p per copy for each additional book.

Whilst every effort is made to keep prices low it is sometimes necessary to increase cover prices and also postage and packing rates at short notice. Hamlyn Paperbacks reserve the right to show new retail prices on covers which may differ from those previously advertised in the text or elsewhere.